WHEN I BECAME NEVER

NATHALIE GUILBEAULT

MONTREAL PUBLISHING COMPANY

ISBN: 978-1-998353-04-0

When I Became Never/Nathalie Guilbeault—1ˢᵗ edition.

Any references to historical events, real people, or real places are used fictitiously. Names, characters, and places are products of the author's imagination.

Editor: Christian Fennell
Cover art: Garo Hakimian.

Montreal Publishing Company
www.montrealpublishing.com

www.nathalieguilbeault.com

I am a beautiful girl not yet conceived; not yet born—fully.

I am a beautiful girl who will die and come back—to remind you some survive and some die.

That some seek refuge in insanity.

That is I.

That is we.

This story is for us.

Alana Doyle, your humor made my journey less frightening.
Christian Fennell, without you, the journey may never have been.

WHEN I BECAME NEVER

A Novel

"The Edge … There is no honest way to explain it because the only people who really know where it is are the ones who have gone over."

– Hunter S. Thompson

CONTENTS

BOOK ONE

I had heard the garage door open, the clunking of its chains pulling me from under the duvet, heavy and dampened by my sweat. This sound, the usual cue telling me my parents were off to their weekly bridge game, three houses down our street.

Friday night freedom, I called it, the end of my workweek at the miso plant. Just like punctuation quiets the pulse of a text, the noise silenced me, allowing me to breathe again.

My parents, Georges and Mary, had become trusting of my behaviors; my words, the way I hummed to Rachmaninoff's evening vespers when I felt alone, and yet, more alive. They kept me by their side because I had been damaged, pushed into some sort of dysfunctional mode the way some are pushed into drugs. Because, yes, one can become addicted to abnormality. I knew they believed I had landed back into some form of normalcy, and one would have thought that, yes, it's been thirteen years, she should be back. And there were days when I did feel normal, just not as normal as they thought me to be.

My mind is something I have learned to conceal, you see. It is a bastion inside which I can retreat, a place where I can fully be, where my quirks—my fantasies, and my truths, co-exist. This time, since then, I hold it, like I hold a dead leaf crinkled by the rain and the sun and the wind—fodder for new life yet to be sown, like poking my finger into blood-pricked skin. This time, here, since then, yes, I smell it. Do you know what time smells like? It smells *of mildew, black and slimy; it smells of sweat; it smells of cinnamon—it smells of feculence.*

I got up from my nap wearing black jeans and a T, but mostly, still wearing the smell of umami. And I remember the scent, another one.

Salt.

Sugar.

Fruit.

A kind of earth we all crave, in our mouths as much as in our hearts.

This savoury me.

I went to the kitchen, an avocado-colored thing they didn't care to update, opened the refrigerator door, took the beer can, snapped it open, and stared at the pasta, crusty and unappealing. Still, I grabbed the cover-less Tupperware, sat at the kitchen table, and dug in. Once done, I placed the container inside the dishwasher and made my way through the house.

Those nights, when alone, I alternated between Chet Baker and Rachmaninoff, more of it. And that night was no different, except I ached for loudness, more absolutes, treble that makes the ear shriek, bass that makes the body shake, to flood my ears. I wandered a little more, stopped on the second floor, and decided to enter my parents' bedroom, something I had never done since they had brought me back from that dead place, thirteen years before.

Why did I do that?

Because the steel bolt had been removed, something to this day I've never understood. I still wonder. What had pushed this new nonchalance onto them and made them forget about their own rules? For my protection. But they had, and that was good enough for me, and in I went.

The crocheted bedspread had wrinkled over a queen size mattress that had sunk in its center. Over it, two Diane Furstenberg wraparound dresses my mother had tried on before deciding on a simple jean A-line skirt and black jersey blouse. I knew because I had heard my father insisting on her wearing her usual good luck attire. Diane Furstenberg. I brushed the top of the cover with my hand knowing the elevated patterns—series of daisy chains, interconnected garlands—would tickle my fingertips. And I remembered my feet sinking into the carpet as I would sneak into their bed and stay there, little me, little moon they called me. Little moon. That was me.

I saw the door to the walk-in closet was unlocked, too. I saw there had been a bolt there as well, the space where it had been—a white imprint on a beige-colored door.

I entered and spotted it right away, the pile of newspapers at the end of the closet beside my mother's shoe rack. Before fanning through them, I slipped them on, slowly. Kitty heels. Ballerina flats. Slutty heights, too. Twenty-two pairs of size 9 shoes. I wear a narrow 6 ½. Mirrors furnished two of the walls, and I had been avoiding them, but even so, I strutted into the cool leather of the shoes, pretending I was on a runway somewhere inside the walls of a posh Parisian venue. Maxime's, maybe. Harry's bar. Stolly's.

I came back from my imaginary travels, quickly placing the Louboutin's in their place and sat down. It took me some time to realize what they contained. I read the articles, all the ones highlighted in fluorescent green, some translations mostly. I scrutinized the images, the pictures of people—especially … that one. I felt the inside of my brain freeze, my pulse quickening. Inside the New York Times the killer's hands were mentioned. And there, inside Nicaragua's newspapers, The Jornada and El Nuevo Diario, I read and saw more of what I thought I had never known. Agile, they had written. His hands. Artfully scalping squares of missing skin. Just then, flashes poked at my mind, imaginations, of Rachmaninoff's own large hands. They had to have been pure to create, I thought. How can you create without purity floating somewhere in your body? Had the heart been pure, too?

No no no. No heart. Only the mind. And the thought of his, what it had told him, sent a cold over my skin.

Still seated on the carpet, feeling dizzy, I started to remember.

The sea, its turquoise set against the lead of the sky.

Sheets of rain falling on my body stretched out on the sand.

The coming of storms smelling of sewage.

Promises hidden inside the goodness of the world.

And the sweat, the sweetness of my own, dripping everywhere it shouldn't have been. And I thought of her, and I thought of me, and I thought, why not me?

Deus ex Machina

These men chose their prey carefully, their words cloaked and masked and wrapped in dogmatic charm, and he was one of them—a cove of God who battled a land aching to remove the bowels of popery the way grandmothers yanked teeth out—riding high under a full sun. Father Antonio Ruiz tightened the Cordovan's string below his chin and smiled, his face reddened by the dusty winds sweeping the earth. Look, he said, pointing ahead, our grounds, more of Spain. Andalucía. A blow, short and loud, coming from the horse's nostrils, as if in agreement. The tall man squeezed his thighs against the animal's sides, and bending over its neck, pressed a finger along the vein bulging from underneath its taunt coat. The horse trotted, faster, ears straight and twitching forward, tail up, its pace now constant.

As if entering his own home, the priest walked inside the Munduyas' small house, a hovel smelling of wine that would never age, lavender that would never heal, candles that could only burn—where confusion, contrived and well fed, reigned.

And while this southern land rebelled against the Church's quests to dominate loam as much as ether—the family patriarch tried to remain faithful to it, clenching to all its veiled illusions. The man hoped, and struggled in doing so, pulled by the quelling of holy uncertainties; life's in-betweens—lethal, and always so, and it seemed to him, a victor.

Those were Romero's Munduya's battles. This man, a descendant of Moors, a proud lineage—a lifeline, long ago pushed by the rulings of ruthless monarchies to convert to Christianity in order to save themselves, becoming Moriscos.

Señora Raquel, Father Antonio said, moving toward the small kitchen table, I haven't seen you this week at confession.

Romero's wife repressed a smile. You've just been assigned to the village of Ronda, young man. For one year you've been knocking on our door—reminding us. Have we ever let you down?

Father Antonio pulled a white handkerchief from his inside coat pocket, removing dust from around his face. The Lord can never go hungry, you know that, he started. And I was worried, too, Raquel. Your last absence ... you were sick, weren't you? A fever, I recall. I came to see if all was well. He looked around, his eyes lingering. So much disease around us, you know that as well as I do. So much death.

Of course, Padre. Gracias. She paused, looking at her hands where she saw the faces of loved ones passing, lost to war's lotteries; lost to plagues—of the flesh, and of the mind. She turned to Romero and smiled. I need you, her dark eyes said. Still. We all do. She turned to the priest. The grapes have kept us very busy this time of year, more than last year's sad crop. And that is all. Join us, won't you? She pointed to the wine carafe placed in the middle of the table, and to the empty glasses, as she searched for her eldest daughter's eyes. Dolores, Amorita, por favor, pour Father Antonio a glass? All of us, in fact, if you will. The taste of our earth, she said, and she smiled, and she raised her head to him, eyes knowing. She took the man's soft hand in hers, pulling his body to the chair next to hers. Come and sit Padre. Eso.

The wooden table, long and narrow, around which everyone sat, Romero at its place of honor, observing his ten-year-old twin girls, Marisol and Luna. With cheeks rotund and plump, with faces around which thick and curly hair ruled from above like an aura, they smiled back at him, huddled inside the picos Raquel had sown for them the week before. One day, she had said to her daughters, while bent over her late mother's old sewing machine, one day I will make them with silk, the best kind of silk, and then you will know the true levity at the heart of our sevillanas.

In the soft, cool wind, the purple-colored curtains swayed, brushing against Father Antonio's shoulders. Delicately, he shooed them away, his eyes narrowing on Matías, his tone grave. I come here almost every month, yet you my son, are rarely to be seen.

Upon hearing these words, Matías felt his lanky body stiffen, his hairless face flush. He turned to the priest and tightened his lips.

You come here to teach the twins, not him, not Dolores, either, Romero said, ignorant of his son's discomfort.

Matías Munduya looked at the priest, this mouth always half-opened; always telling; of things to be done and not be done. And he knew, when this man, said to be of God, visited his family, each time, another moment came when everything that mattered was not named. We have remained dark-skinned Spaniards to you and your kind, he thought. Morenos. And that is why you teach my sisters, because you fear their skin, darker than most, darker than mine, will deny them entry to paradise. That's what you told them, that a better understanding of the Bible will make them acceptable to God. Worthy of Him. His eyes to the floor, he spoke. Papi, todo está bien.

Below the table, quieting his anger, a foot dropped onto his, her signal, maybe. Matías moved his fingers next to his sister's. So warm, he thought, so you. And looking at her pushing the now emptied carafe back to the middle of the table, he moved his fingers farther inside her hand. No one noticed, the young woman remaining silent, observant. Dolores, beautiful sister, he thought, mi alborada. My beloved dawn. He turned again to the priest. I fear God's wrath as much as anyone, but what good

11

are the texts, Father, if the Reds kill us? 1927, and Spain's monarchy will die soon. Give it two years. I can feel it. The country feels it. He paused. Then, Father, your life's work as a man of the Church will have been for what? He leaned forward, whispered, hell, more of it, will be here soon enough.

Romero raised his hand, considered his son. No more, Matías. We know about the fear. We've inhaled its fumes since the beginning of time, Matías. Our ancestors' fear has been walking in our blood for so long. Hijo, he said, por favor, no more. We all know.

Behind the twins, a window from which another gust of wind came, the fringe of the mantòn dancing and tickling their skin. The girls stilled, their arms hanging side-by-side, their hands meeting, and sifting their unease from the moment they searched for Romero. For something. Their father was still holding the priest's eyes.

This smell, Romero, the priest said, as he fanned the air, such rancid sweetness, no?

We live inside this scent, Father, Raquel said, impatience in her voice. And it doesn't leave us, either. Her head still, her eyes wandered beyond her husband. She brought a hand to the back of her neck, grabbing large portions of the curly mane that had escaped the Kanzashi pin's grip. Delicately, she collected the rogue thickets of hair in her fingers and pushing the hairpin farther toward the top of her head, secured the chignon made that morning before preparing the workers' breakfast. I know too much, she thought, of this gaze that weighs on me; on them; of the heat tingling across my shoulders because of it. I think the harvest will be a good one, she finally said, her mind absent. Better than last year's.

One's house usually smells of one's earth, I would think, Father, Romero continued. I would expect the scent of holy wine in yours, no? Just as sweet, if not more. The father of four lowered his head, and with eyes half shut, and trembling lids, he let his imagination fill voids—all the spaces he felt, wanting to fill them, too, with what he saw, what he was certain was there, on his soil—sweat starting to drip from his temples. His eyes now open, his gaze became caught between two of the floor's wooden planks as he listened to the words coming from his wife's mouth. His vacancies staying.

I will come to you, Father, of course, and Raquel stood and let her hand slide along her son's back. There were notes mingling inside her head, lyrical and staccato, their essence known to her bones; to her mind—the sound of fandangos beating between her temples, and she walked the short distance separating the table from the entrance door, changed by them. Tonight will be filled with dancing, she told them, more flamenco, for it quietly lures our feet into the present only—hopeful escapes, palatable deceptions, she thought. She stilled at the entrance, pushed the door open, and looked to the vineyard. The breeze had gone, and the cold, poked by the absence of the breeze, became quiet.

For almost two years, fourteen-year-old Dolores had witnessed these scenes unfold. The actors; the words; the tone, an immovable script—usually. Today is different, she thought, looking at her sisters. They were wriggling on their chairs, as if a long ripple was unfolding beneath their muscles. They always do, she thought, trying to dismiss her unrest—move. They rarely stopped, she thought more, scurrying through the maze-like vineyard, morning to night, draped in laughter so crisp and generous the laborers nicknamed them pequeñas diosas de la tierra—little goddesses of the earth. But this wasn't movement. No. This was agitation. Dolores mouthed to them to stop fidgeting and listen. The girls obeyed.

Inside the long silence, a space where the world around them continued, the workers sang of love and loss, off pitch and low, their voices reaching them from the fields, and as it did, a barn cat landed on the windowsill, an orange feather-like particle hanging from its mouth.

13

He keeps doing that, Luna said, as she stood. He catches all the butterflies and brings them back here. Siempre. Amused by the interlude, they watched the young girl walk to the window, and with her small hands, delicately remove the butterfly from the cat's soft bite. Gato malo. Malo malo malo. The insect was still alive and when she saw that it was, she placed it atop her hand, watching the wings slowly stroking the air. Come with me, she said, and she walked back to her chair and sat. I will take care of you.

It's time for me to go, the priest said, pushing away the emptied glass in front of him. Hasta mañana, Dolores, he said. Y recuerda que Dios es grandioso. He stood, feeling restlessness gripping his thighs, and meticulously replaced his hat on his coiffed head. Remember, Luna, that butterflies carry the beauty of struggles with them, and the certainty of new beginnings, too. Just like the Bible does.

Luna turned to her father—the moment escaped his grasp.

Raquel held the door for the tall man, her knee pointing into its broken panel, below the hem of a skirt, circular and long. Her eyes fled, not wanting to meet his, not there.

Not now.

The priest stepped over the sill and turned back. I'll be waiting, Señora Raquel. Mañana.

Squinting, she looked away, Dolores in her sights. Si Dios quiere, Padre. Mañana.

Dolores's gaze followed that of Romero's, to where the priest was, at the door, his silhouette, broad and menacing. God's spy, she thought, as she walked to where her sisters stood, her hand searching for theirs. That or it's the Devil's. Stay with me, she told them.

Standing on the porch, they watched the priest saunter to the makeshift enclosure surrounding the house. They watched as the light waved onto the weak-tea colored coat of the Lusitano, the sun dappling flank to neck. Sensing his master approaching, the sixteen-hand horse grew even larger, and stomping the ground, neighed. Once by his side, Father Antonio spoke to the animal, a jargon drenched in softness—hypnotic and lulling—and as he did, he cinched the girth strap, pulling twice on the latigo. Still talking, the man slid his hand across the horse's mane, and grabbing the black stock of bristly hairs, climbed onto the saddle.

With the weight of eyes pushing on his back, the priest left Romero Munduya's propriety knowing what he was leaving behind; what he had continued to feed—suspended specks of dust in lieu of brightness—porous ignorance.

And seated behind the girls, unseen, the cat slowly swallowed the butterfly.

The fire was not completely out, the priest opened the door to the cast oven, tossing more lumber inside the small space. Pensive, and waiting for the flames to grow taller, Antonio brought a stool next to the stove and sat, his hands hovering above the burgeoning heat. Outside, the smell of war, of collective indigence, voices about to fall from an edge, about to burst and bounce off the neighborhood's walls.

In this modest dwelling, adjacent to this modest church, a backdoor led to a yard. As he walked out, he nodded to the horse standing in the middle of it. This horse, he thought, the only thing I truly own. Folding his naked body into a large basin, oblivious to the world, he felt the water, brown and smelling of iron, wrap him with tepid warmth. He brought his knees to his chest and thought—about his ending, unavoidable. Hide and hide well, the archbishop had said, stay alive as long as you can, keep the faith alive where you can. And be happy Madrid is your friend.

He looked up, the sound of them impossible to ignore—bombers like flies appearing from below the clouds, engines never hushing, and he thought, until this carmine fed ideology sends me to my death—and it will, he knew—I will continue to live, as I know how. And no other way.

Stepping out of the basin, he stood, wet and dripping, and he walked to his horse. Water running over his body, the cold wind pulling shivers from his skin. What would I do without you? he asked, in whispers. The horse's head pushing against his and their eyes synchronized. I'll see you tomorrow, he said, as he caressed the horse's mane. Mañana. He turned toward the door, sauntered inside the house, directing his attention to the mattress facing the small wooden table. Slumping, naked, underneath the bedcover, Antonio thought more, about them, this family—the girls.

From the floor he brought a bottle of wine to his lips and closed his eyes: He would need to travel to that space where he quarreled with God. In there, Antonio stood at times, unbent and pious, but remaining—a Father burdened by a mind, ductile, slave to the baseness of an unstable core.

On the porch of the white two-storied house standing in the middle of a field, three scantily dressed women, content in their waiting, smoked their pipes. Romero stood, facing them, a foot resting on the bottom step, and listening to the music coming from the gramophone's sound horn. A gift, one of the girls had once explained, from a wealthy client.

Romero had walked the following night to where men go when wanting to grasp the nature of their own, because inside the walls of a house made of women only, something other than flesh could bloom.

Sometimes.

A shift occurred, that night, within him, the settling of truths he had not been prepared—wanted?—to see. Torments were forming inside his heart, and he wanted them unleashed. A cleansing, and penetrating her small body, he surrendered, softly speaking to her, about women, of how they understood what a man must do. To be more.

Yes, a woman always knows, she responded, a hand on his chest, and slowing his thrusting. A woman always knows. The question, she added with mischief, is how much does she really cares?

Romero paused, pushing the girl away from him, this contrived verse, like a man-made virus inside his mind, replaying: All the secrets that never are, they roam, and then they land, somewhere, don't they, in the coldness of a touch; in the absence of a gaze, inside the desertion of what had been, in its place, the skiving of a lover unable to look at you in the eye while penetrating you like a truant. When does one know, one cares? he asked, thinking of his wife.

Pregúntale a Dios, Romero, no a mí.

¿Dios?

Sí.

God is elusive to me. Not to you? And I don't know anymore, isn't He a clear illusion fed by the fascists, the monarchs, and the tyrants? And can't He be but an opaque one fueled by the commies, too, and so maybe—what am I really?—unreal to Him, just as opaque, just as unclear—an illusion still, and yet, a real one? As volatile as Him. But what if He was? Is?

What if.

The small girl kissed his lips, left her bed, and picked her clothes off the floor, dirty and damp. If God was here, my Romero, with me, looking over me and my baby, you wouldn't be.

And those waves brimming with dissonances haunted and trashed in his mind.

So slippery, this thinking where not much holds.

The man stood and dressed himself, the movements, slow, hindered by images of his family; his vines—Father Antonio's last visit.

Numbness, as sudden as unexpected, blanketed his heart, and he walked to the girl. Seated on the bed, a stained blouse, loose and unbuttoned, floating around her small shoulders and breasts, with hair carefully undone, she looked as though she was waiting for something. Someone. Her next client, he thought. Of course. He looked at her face, this fading of a youth, and for the first time, he thought of his daughters.

See you next week, Romero.

With tears in his eyes, he picked his hat from the coat hook, and not turning to the voice, vowed to never come back.

The morning's shadow lay on half his body, the half she wasn't looking at. She smiled. Your face was barely leathered and carved by the sun when I married you, she thought, you, a man twenty years older than me. And yet her own features, the mapping of harshness, her life, her down turned mouth framed by lines never having been carved by laughter. Romero's face had almost remained, and over time, only his cheeks, wine-puffed flesh that gave his angular shape a soft roundness, and his curly hair, now white and sparse, betrayed the truth of his age. Approaching his sixtieth birthday, the man, his stature, was as imposing as a young bull's shadow.

Romero, Raquel whispered, as she placed a thin lock of hair behind his ear, do you remember the day before we married, the question you asked me? It still lives with me, you know. Raquel closed her eyes. If I give you a moment no longer belonging to this time, our time, you asked, will I be able to care still for us? And not waiting for his answer, she said, it's time to go. Listo.

She threw her legs to the floor, walked to the closet, and picking up the day's attire—a flower patterned dress, she looked once more at Romero, his back still to the mattress, his torso a constant seesaw. ¿Me pregunto, mi Romero, si le pidiera lo mismo, me dirìas que sí? If I asked you the same thing, would you say, yes? That you still care for what once was, and still could be? With us?

Again, Amor, por favor.

Reddish dust surrounded her as she walked the road to Ronda. And cacti so many, dispersed, too. The devil, she smiled. That is what you all are. Above her, the sky, a brighter blue, the sight of it almost blinding her. And all around, the mountains burned a little less. Raquel lifted her head, her loose black hair swept by the morning winds, and smiled—the summer not lost yet, at the end of its course.

On the road carving into the lowland, buggies loaded with grain, grapes, and nuts, and all the land would gift, passed her. Singing and smoking and spitting life from their mouths, the men drove, young and old, sometimes nodding at her, sometimes not. As she followed the queue of women heading like her to the city's market, Raquel scanned the surrounding hills. This land was the land she was born from, the one she would be buried in. Like all of them.

Thrust underneath her arm, a large straw bag and inside the bag, carefully folded, shawls and dresses, piled up, ones she had sown the month before. She was heading to Lucia's shop to collect the money for the previous month's sales and drop her new confections as well.

Then, the church.

The small confessional seen from the entrance pulled Raquel as it always had and she walked to it, ignoring the flock praying and weeping and asking for the impossible. To this man, waiting, dressed in black, hair slicked to the side with a mouth wet and eager.

She walked farther to the back, hoping to be unseen. She opened the door, sat on the narrow pew, and crossed herself. Why do I come? she asked herself. Why am I really here? Staring into the wall of the confessional booth—flashes of words coming from his mouth. I am God, he would say. I am always with God. Through me, so many gates. Soy Dios. A golden ticket.

His voice, filtered by the wooden mesh, soft and heavy. You came, Raquel.

Bless me, Father.

Te necesito, he said, aquí.

She drew inside herself a little more and did what she always had done when confronted with this choice that shouldn't be one, staring at her—his Heaven, her Earth—with this slow and abysmal-filled voice—thought of Romero, of all he was, and wasn't. Of the girls. Of Matías. Of malaises hovering over her family.

My heart seeks, the priest said to her, of what lies underneath your own. What leans beneath your skin, too, Raquel.

And failure, she thought, a sad certainty, staying.

He flicked the locket, the sound of metal on wood warning of more to come. Walking around the booth, scanning the church, he saw women, men, and children, eyes closed, some weeping, all surviving inside a prayer. He opened the door, reached for her, pulling her to him. Ven aca.

Her head could have fallen, her body soft, almost unwilling, but not completely. To him. Into him. God. But who is he, anyways? she asked herself. And why us? A year of him, this pressure. And her eyes, black and deep not obscuring anymore what she saw—in him. She stared. I am sorry for all of this and all that could follow, she could have almost sobbed, her hand wanting to push against his chest—a new signing of the cross, dirty, in that place reddened by man's shallowness, much like the words he thought to himself now, like a penance of their own, and only for her: How beautiful are your sandaled feet, princess. The curves of your thighs, like jewelry, the handiwork of a master. Your navel, a rounded bowl, never lacking mixed wine. Your waist, a mound of wheat surrounded by lilies. Your breasts, two fawns, the twins of a gazelle. And he repeated, these whispers, to her, the Bible's Song of Songs, and he took her hand, told her to stand, and follow him.

Her face, the skin of it darkened by the rays of many unforgiving suns, remained—still like death swimming in a swamp.

Her head held straight, she said nothing, and left.

Daybreak—inside it, the same pledge, the same promises. Around Romero's house, the rust-colored soil from which countless oases rose, the land was preparing to receive light, heat; their life. He paced the kitchen floor, barefoot, at times looking through the open windows, his eyebrows speaking of doubt, large and thick and black, a straight line no more, waving each time he examined his land—as if terrene wisdom lived inside his vines. They must have seen her, he thought, and in the middle of the floor, he paused, looking up. Where is your mother, Dolores? I didn't hear her leave, and the workers tell me they haven't seen her either this morning. He paced some more, this time halting each time he reached the other end of the room, breathing a breath that wouldn't soothe.

Seated at the top of the narrow staircase leading to the bedroom, Dolores watched her father closely. His shoulders had slumped farther down, making his already longer than normal arms appear as though they belonged to a creature from another time. No, I haven't, Papi. She wrung her hands, because they itched and felt as if a million needles moved inside of them, and as she did, she tried to quiet him, reminding him how Raquel loved the early morning.

He turned to her, angst in his eyes. And why do you think the workers would have not seen or heard her?

Papi, they almost slept through last year's barn fire. El mercado, tal vez?

He watched his daughter smile, and he thought, she is wondering, too. Vida. Dios. Amor. Beautiful Dolores, the village's prize. It's Saturday, he said, your mother knows. She knows I need her. She knows to go to mass later in the day.

The sound of light footsteps found them, Luna appearing from behind Dolores, running down the stairs to her father, her words lisping, hindered by her hare lip. I'm old enough to go, I'm almost twelve, she implored, please bring me with you. She wrapped her arms around his waist placing her head against his chest, closed her eyes—the certitude of safety weaved inside a father's strength. Nothing can touch me, she thought to herself. No one.

You girls help Matías today, he said, after kissing Luna's forehead. All of you have your chores lined-up. And one of the sows delivered last night, remember? See to it she doesn't savage her babies like the last one did. None of them survived …

Why do they eat their newborns, Papi? Luna asked, alive with sudden curiosity.

New mothers, Dolores said, rolling her eyes, the farrowing makes them nervous. *Everybody* knows that.

It's a case-by-case, Romero added. Inside every species, you have different temperaments.

Does it happen to humans, too?

Of course not, Luna, Dolores yelled.

Luna turned to her father, perplexed. First time mothers? Was Mother nervous? Matías was the first, could she have eaten him? And what about the male pigs? Do they also eat the babies? What about the second and third times?

Romero shook his head, love in his eyes.

You know what, Luna, Dolores smiled. I bet you twins were tempting. Double the portions. Double the fun.

Luna's eyes widened, and Marisol, having heard parts of the conversation, had left her bed and was standing behind Dolores. ¿Quién nos comerá?

Mother will eat you, of course, said Dolores, and she laughed. And she went to the market, too. You'll taste much better with garlic and paprika. The perfect little-girl-made stew.

Romero listened to the children's words and smiled, worry at arm's length, it seemed, a needed respite—this vision of her, Raquel. The mother. His beautiful wife. She's always been so good, he thought—to all their children. But do pillars crumble, even when molded by God, he wondered.

He stepped toward the sink, leaving his hands to rest onto the edge of its porcelain, soft and dripping of cold water. Through the window, he saw his men tending to the vines. The vines gave generously this year, he thought, so much more than the previous year. Yes, Papi, he heard, as Dolores slid her hand inside of his, let me go. I'll get her back in time for the filling of the barrels. I promise.

Yes, he said, Father Antonio on his mind. Go.

Pain is my name, and sorrow lives inside my name, too, Dolores kept thinking as she walked to town. Am I to carry it? Am I to spread it? For how long? And she thought, convinced, my name is Dolores, polluted Dolores.

She saw the bell tower, short and lean, the small doors of that small house she knew too much about. Disquiet spread inside her. She grabbed her shawl and tightly pulled its extremities to her chest, wishing these to be her mother's own, but Raquel, Dolores had just seen from afar, had entered the church, with arms which no longer seemed to belong to her.

The young woman pulled both doors, her eyes to the black and white carrelage of the ground, and she entered, scanned the few pews before her, men and children whose face were familiar, and recognizing the black and rounded backs staining the white of the pews and the white of the stucco walls.

Polka dots, little rogue specks that swayed to the rhythm of pain. The Seven Weepers of Ronda, they were called, always moving together during religious festivities, even, still, with the Reds hovering over the region, like a herd, holding hands. They had dispersed inside the small nave, unchaining from one another, yet, holding onto their grief like a new mother squeezes her new-born child. Señoras Lucía and Monica, whose young sons had died from typhoid, were the only widows who shared the same pew. The boys had been her sister's age when they died. Dolores smiled, remembering how they had played with Marisol and Luna following mass each Sunday. Her eyes continued to gently sweep across the space before her, gathering in her head señoras Jacqueline, Paulina and Ava, the middle-aged women whose large bosoms overflowed from seats, and had just parted, leaving señora Jacqueline alone at the back, not too far from the aisle.

Dolores closed her eyes and recalled their sadness.

Early January, 1927.

Two months ago.

The three boys had left, happy, alive with purpose, but gone before gone; dead before dead, cursed by Andalucía's thirst for honor, stepping into the horror of their country's belligerent belly—the other one.

Protest they had said, for God.

For Spain.

The night of their arrival in Madrid—leftist coteries, sanctuaries for the rebels, abodes where nothing but lack of reason and godless morality lived, that's where they had landed.

Relics, the awkward looking leader had said, with their gems and gold. Many of them. Priceless tapestries. What for? Who for? For us?

Fairness, generosity, is that what it is? Taking care of the poor, is that what they were doing? While our parents live in houses meant for pigs; for dogs, if we are lucky, leeches that they are, stuck in the old world, not wanting to let go of their privileges, too cowardly to truly serve the poor, enticed by wealth.

Through smoke, thick with blue, they had listened in disbelief. To the offences. The insults. The threats. What is this, one of the boys had finally asked, puzzled. *Where* are we?

Some say their true allegiance had been exposed, that they had been savagely punished for exhaling their foul-smelling incantations, others that they had been the victim of a lethal police beating, by a particular cell said to roam at night looking for meat to pound. The trio of boys, never to be seen again after that night.

Dolores opened her eyes. Just behind her, smaller silhouettes prayed—young widows, Marissa and Ana, too poor to secure a pew like the wealthy families of Ronda had, they knelt on stones cemented to the floor at the back of the church. Each of their husbands had left for the port of Málaga, to work as stevedores. They, too, had never returned, only their sand laden heads had been found, rolling along the beach.

A voice brought her back from the tales inside her head. Do you always believe what you see?

Dolores looked up, barely recognizing him, the priest wearing his cassock from which a wooden cross hung, so that now he appeared truly as a man of God, a collarino kissing the base of his neck.

May I? he asked, pointing to the pew.

She slid to her right, hesitantly, clenching the side of her dress, leaving enough space for him to sit. She kept her eyes down, her chin tucked and retreated.

The women had started to stir, re-emerging. Silent, Dolores remained, and watching the parade of calves—fat, veiny, skinny verticals of flesh passing her by.

He took her hand in his as the other women simultaneously straightened and awakened, the solitude broken by the imperative to continue; to live, with whatever was pressing against their chests, the dimness, palpable, untouched by their prayers, and broken onto their faces. He squeezed her hand. And what did you see today?

The priest waited for the women to be gone and, when satisfied no one else was in sight, turned to face her and pressed her for more.

The church's silence, deep and heavy, drilled from her feet to her throat. All those stories soaked in tragedy had tumbled inside her mind, making her forget why she was there, inside this church, on an early Saturday morning. Mother. Releasing the sides of her dress, she said, I don't know what I saw, but I will tell you, Padre, what it is I didn't see. She took another deep breath and fixated on the scruffy chin pointing at her, and then his eyes. How beautiful and disgusting his face was, she suddenly noticed, angular, dark, inquisitive. She cupped his face in her hands as a raven came without warning, resting on the back of a pew, making the priest stare. God, Father. Your god. That's the thing I didn't see. She stood, turned around, and left the pew.

When Dolores walked onto the church square, she scanned the few houses that surrounded the small church nestled at the far end of its barrio. Slowly lifting her eyes, she saw a woman, elbows to the sill of a window flanked by two wobbly shutters and looking straight at her from the second story of her building; the face long, thin, with waves of curly black hair, like hers, unruly and descending to her chest, seemed restrained, closed. She has something of the twins' light, she thought to herself, in her eyes. Yet, Dolores could tell a different age had been etched on her skin, blackish and flask, the young woman's features, death-like and bearing the traces drawn by the restiveness of hardships. They looked to one another, pausing inside each other's time. The sound of a rising pitch startled her, and she looked away from the girl, considering the dozen ravens that had gathered not far from where she stood. She smiled, almost relieved. What do you want to say to me, she thought, all of you? She shrugged her shoulders and looked back to the window. It was empty. The girl had disappeared inside her apartment. Returning her attention to the birds, she saw them fly a low flight to the base of a large tree standing by the square. From there, they looked at her, this time, soundless. I need to go, she suddenly thought, I need to go back home.

The young woman, walking away from the church's stairs, heard the priest's voice: Be sure to give my regards to your mother, Dolores. Her and your sisters.

She turned to the voice, low and suave—the heel of his foot, the only thing remaining of his presence. Swaddling herself tighter inside her shawl, her head extended toward the sky, her eyes drifty, she wondered why the hot air wasn't enough to shield her from those quivers that appeared out of nowhere, yet again. She shrugged them off—after all, all they did was stroke her skin.

Innocence momentarily returned, the house up on that hill forgotten. Matías, too. And maybe one day soon, a lesson to learn, the one the ravens, maybe, had, tried to tell her: The price to pay for what one wishes to do lives nowhere but inside one's conscience—the sole god.

She continued to walk, her legs less sturdy, awkwardness, more of it, now a companion. Coming from behind her, the sound of feet shuffling the ground, the feel of a warm kiss planted on the nape of her neck. Dolores, she heard her mother say, let's walk home, faster. We need to rehearse.

Dolores took her mother's hand, bringing it up to her lips, surprised, yet relieved. ¿Dónde estabas? Mamá? I came looking for you, and never saw you.

Amorita, Raquel said, a hand dismissing the question, you and your sisters need to finish learning the new sequence, our movements, remember? she simply replied, pulling her daughter in her arms.

Sé Mamá. I know.

And walking by her mother's side, Dolores forgot about The Seven Weepers; about her father's worried voice.

About Father Antonio.

Moorish blood that repulsed and attracted simultaneously, the men felt it, the women stared at it, too—the wildness of a youth that knows no mortality.

When Alberto Rodriguez first saw fourteen-year-old Dolores Munduya walking through the market's gravelly road with a red velvety dress that hugged her body and a white bonnet that framed her features— a stunning ensemble of primrose strokes—he knew she was his, this flower's beauty, sinuous and raw, of a perfume unknow to most and one that would not be escaping his reach.

This image of her, poking at his groin, haunting it, and forcing a patient wait. A three-months wait. And the moment came—

Alberto, will you be going tonight? Some of us are planning a reading, you know, just like two weeks ago.

He slowed down, resisting the urge to push the young poet aside. I don't know, Sandro, the convent asked me to help with an adoption of some kind tonight. I don't think I can make it. Lo siento, mi amigo. There won't be any duende coming from me tonight, I'm afraid. He paused, looked away. Mi alma se siente seca. My soul, you know, feels dry these days.

The boy stood in front of the man, his mouth and eyes wanting to say more—the entire village suspected, Alberto Rodriguez, raised at the convent among other illegitimate children, but now twenty-seven and still living within the sacred walls. The nuns had kept him close to them, in a small house located on their land. Vélez-Málaga. Yes, he helped them with the administration of the day-to-day bustle. But something else, too.

Something else.

Aquí, the boy pointed, debes mirar.

Impatient but curious, Alberto took the evening's program in his hands, sliding a sturdy finger over it, as if knowing where it should land.

Look, the boy insisted, there's this family, flamenco dancers performing from near Ronda. Look at her, Alberto … Mirar. Allá.

The finger stopped. His eyes tapered. All right, Sandro.

Alberto Rodriguez continued to walk on the dry road, humming and knowing, the time had finally come.

Málaga, Café Teatro Chinitas, a noble sanctuary for the minds and the intellect of the desperate. Within its walls, the promise of a socialist and communist paradise that drew the artistic community together, prompting poets, writers and painters alike to form cells meant to promote the Republican ideology. Amidst free thinkers and dreamers, that is where Alberto hid his political allegiance to the right, pretending to be nothing more than a simple man wanting to be acknowledged.

Señor Alberto, the waiter said, your table, right here, and closer to the stage this time, as you asked.

Gracias, Mohammed.

¿Lo de siempre, señor?

No, Mohammed, aqua.

Alberto looked at the program, then checked his watch—10:00 P.M. The readings would start soon, followed by the dancing.

It unsettled him—never having felt this way before, a wanting of something so unsure. Feeling the sweat gathering under his armpits, knowing his shirt incapable of soaking it all in, he removed his jacket and hung it on the back of the chair. Mohammed, he yelled, as he snapped his fingers. I've changed my mind. No aqua. Something real. Something made of fire.

Full of love for their country, their women, and their desire for justice—ten poets appeared; ten readings heard.

His time came, voices, loud and many, demanding. Alberto, they chanted, make us weep again, stray-jacket our burdens with truth, destroy our hearts.

He placed his drink on the table, uncertain, yet fully prepared—pulled by the flattering moment. Slowly, a smile emerged as his shoulders curved away from the back of his chair a little further. His lean body sagged, as if wanting to disappear. But the man sprung, reaching inside his shirt pocket, brandishing a crinkled notebook from which he would read a poem. My soul is back, in there, he thought. Wet. After clearing his throat, a sturdy listo was heard from his mouth, jolting the expectant listeners. As he started to read, without warning, the curtains, worn-out velours, ochre and mauve, parted, slowly revealing the sight he had come to see. Ignoring the slight, forgiving the interruption, Alberto took his seat, and waited.

Dolores appeared dressed in red, her ruffles tickling her shoulders as much as her ankles. Undulating the whole of her body, undulating with hips that spoke of time; of hurt; of betrayal—of life's disappointments, particularly that evening, the flamenco gods felt the devil steal her feet a little more, making them burn the floor with puntas and guelpes and talones so wild and fast, the crowd went mad.

With Romero's guitar calling to her, she answered and answered more with her hands and her wrists and her fingers, agile and loose, and when she flipped her head pushing her long hair into the air, she caught a glimpse of Alberto, just enough to make him not blink.

Inside his mind, words tumbled randomly, asking: Ashes, how they land, light and ready to blend, then disappear when we move them—like rumors flying inside the dispersion of sand, no? I like to chase them, but how much should I chase? And chasing that first hit—its scent; its texture; its noise, her image, on repeat? Will I need to?

He slid his hand between his legs remembering his only real talent had been sown into him the moment a German had shoved his strength into Alberto's mother, this gypsy, and he felt the warmth there now. But fire must burn memories, simply because, that is what it must do. But for how long, he wondered, will I make the fire last?

The music stopped. Romero stood, a hand pointing to Dolores. The crowd, frantic and wanting more, for their eyes; their hearts. She curtsied. Then, her body spent, sweat dribbling to the crease of her breasts, Dolores left the stage.

Alberto, his eyes searching, waited for her, until—he saw them, the couple not too far from him, exiting the café from the back door, alone in their minds, her head on Matías' shoulder, his mouth brushing against the side of her head. A moment, so discreet not even Raquel and Romero had noticed it. No one had. But I saw you, he whispered to himself, looking at the crowd. I did.

A faraway noise became louder to his hearing: The audience was applauding as Luna and Marisol took to the stage. The poet stood, everything enveloped inside the odd lightness of his complexion, within the blondeness of his hair, moving to the beat of his mother's blood, suaveness, the main lure.

They all nodded, walking by the priest, one by one, tired and hungry, Raquel the last one, hurrying her daughters dawdling behind her. Father Antonio, hands twirling inside his pockets, nodded back. Your guitar

31

sounded almost as good as when you play at home, Romero. And the girls, he continued, such gracefulness …

Romero pointed to the buckboard wagon and told Matías to get the horses ready, to help get his sisters into the wagon, that they were leaving. Feeling his presence behind him, he turned to the priest, Janus-faced and defiant. Romero, taller, inflating almost, spoke, sarcasm in his tone: Such an honor for us to see you again, here, so far from your own quarters, Father. So very far … Stepping away from the man, lightly pushing him aside, Romero took Raquel by the waist, helping her climb onto the makeshift carriage. Once everyone squeezed inside the box, nibbling on the bread Raquel had baked the day before, Romero hopped to the front, eager to flee, and whispered to himself, I am watching, know that I do. Watch you.

The whipping of the reins on the horse back's, the sound of relief freed into the night air, Romero looking ahead, and only ahead, for before him, his life—their life, a form of happiness God maybe had never intended for him to touch, he realized, was there and waiting, and he felt moistness form at the back of his eyes.

Father Antonio watched the wagon slowly roll away from the café, a cloud of dust in its wake. Around him, patrons, poets, and dancers were dispersing into the streets, talking and laughing—knowing of the dangers, not hidden, soldiers looking, a reminder—hurtled home, for curfew was about to fall, punctuating their light, again. Looking more, tugging at his jacket, he wished for a sign, a confirmation. Look at me, and if you do, I will know, and he prayed underneath his breath. Then, the words of another man: Quite the family, are they not? Oblivious to the voice, the priest's eyes remained, and when Luna turned around, kneeling, with her hands waving at him, he saw it—innocence wanting to be collected. I'm Father Antonio, he said, as he turned toward the poet. And I know who you are as well, Alberto Rodriguez. And yes, they are, he continued—quite the family.

The ride back from the Café Chinitas to their house was long and quiet, almost peaceful, the three girls pressed to one another, closer to Raquel's body, farther away yet from the night, at least, in their minds.

Romero upright, hands loosely holding the horses' reins, thought, I don't like him, and he pressed his feet more to the footrest. And I don't need him on my land. Inside my house, even less. He turned to his wife. We see enough of Father Antonio, don't we?

The response blended with the absence of her movements. Raquel's pulse remained, unflinching. No sé ... pero, she thought. And squeezing Luna's hand a little more, she spoke. We all need him, she said, without him we are nothing. Nada. He brings the scriptures to us at a time when danger is spying on us at every corner, she continued. He risks. Para nosotros.

We are all risking something, Mother, said Dolores, her voice clear. He comes too often and stays too long. I, also, would like to see less of him. No me gusta cuando viene. His breath. No me gusta el olor de su aliento. Always so foul.

The roads were clear, and the winds had turned to the east as a few drops of rain prepared to touch the ground. Romero scanned the skies, then looked back at the road, deciding to stop near a long and slender creek that snaked through a rich man's land, halfway between Málaga and Ronda. The horses need to drink, he said.

He stood from his seat, and placing a foot on the carriage's block, he looked at the girls. Something isn't right, he thought to himself, their moving tonight, contrived, unfelt.

Through the dark he saw her blue eyes had become inky, Luna's head awkwardly resting on Marisol's shoulders, and when he jumped to the ground, bringing the reins over the horses' heads, he saw a book sprout from underneath the waistband of her worn-out skirt. When Luna saw her father staring, she brought her shawl farther down, hiding the brown leather covered book. To her collar bone and up to her chin, she secured the upper part of her shawl, and then turned to her sister, Marisol, who had fallen asleep.

More saliva pooled at the corner of Romero's mouth, and as more worry settled within his mind, he summoned more of the liquid stuck at the bottom of his throat, spitting it out as he walked to the front of the buggy. This Bible, he thought, I recognize it.

Raquel observed her husband's agitation, wondering where her husband stood on God's path; of why he braided his own vines the way he did; of her; of the other women. Father Antonio has been sent by Madrid, she suddenly said. To help us remain on this land, to keep our right to pray. Sus visitas continuarán.

Dolores turned away from her mother and travelled to that moment where nothing should be forgotten. She looked at her sisters, now asleep. Don't worry, her look said, I will make it all go away. I will. I promise. Her mind would have a plan, not too far from then, because—tossing realness and gospel truth somewhere white and holy, an ignition of the heart, this moment imprinted with the sight of him, those times she had seen his body move through the heart of the vineyard, to them—at home, in the field and in the barn. She had seen the man's eyes follow the flow of her sisters' silhouettes from that tender age where young contours call some men from afar, the young ones unknowing of the river that runs through them, between their legs, of nascent changes atop the flatness of breasts from which nipples start to swell.

Father Antonio, he was there tonight, she reminded herself. She saw him, seated at the back, dressed as usual, a civilian, with a pale-yellow jacket. And as they had danced on the stage to the sound made by

Romero's tired fingers, the old guitar drenching the night with melancholic sounds, he had spied on their movements.

In a trance, she searched for her brother's hand. Did you see how this tall man was looking at me? The poet?

No, I didn't, he lied. But they all do, you know that. The money pours in when the men know you will be dancing. Por eso vamos, Dolores. That's why they go. That is why we dance.

She studied her brother's face, suddenly seeing more of the man he was becoming, a lankiness morphing into a block of strength, a face where meekness would give room to features, virile, arresting, even. He seemed to be different, she whispered. Quite, I should say.

Matías jumped from the carriage's box to verify the buggy's front wheels. It rattled more than usual since leaving Málaga. All is good, he thought, as he walked to Romero. Two of the four horses had been freed, and his father, holding two leads in the palm of his hand, softly pulled them to the side of the road where fresh water had collected. You take care of the other two.

Once done, the men climbed back up, this time with Matías at the helm. Four hours of travelling before them. Four hours of steady movements bringing them into the dawn.

Drops of rain falling onto their faces, now vertical and hard, like boundaries hitting Romero's mind, and as they did, Luna woke and began to sing, a voice limpid, carrying words meant to erase their doubts, about the future—even about now. From her basket, Raquel removed a large blanket, its wool thick and prickly, spreading it across the children's bodies'. Onto each of the girl's head, she placed a cañero, large brimmed and shielding from the rain. Eso, she said, as she sank underneath the blanket, too, closer to Marisol.

Romero whistled to his daughter's tune, letting his dubiety retreat, its momentary disappearance fueling hope of being rocked into dreams that had nothing to do with Spain, or her wars.

The clouds chased away by the winds' work, the rain no longer, and as they approached their small house up on that small hill, Romero saw the sun coming up. Matías, mire con atención y recuerde. Este momento. Pay attention, my son. For beauty, when ignored, may elect to never cross your path again.

Halfway to Ronda, Antonio stopped, jumping off his saddle. He pulled his horse to the nearby creek, where a fire, almost gone, weakness smoldering, had been lit. Antonio kneeled, the road silent, hard and wet, and cupping his hands, he sipped the water. Around him, the hills, desert cold, yet inviting, with whimpers of the sun's rays trying to rise. He thought of his night's encounter. How strange, he thought more.

His fingers dropped to the slow current of the water running into the land, and he stopped his thinking, resisting the urge to repeat the poet's words: the spelling of intentions; replete; incisive. A quid pro quo. The permanent access to a child of God in exchange for an entry into her sister. Dolores for Luna. Luna for Dolores.

He pulled the collar of his rain slicker to his ears, and remembered, the warnings, the punishment. Redemption, they had said in Madrid, for the soiling of those young city-girls. The rapes. The undoing of God's work. A redemption earned through the pursuit of keeping us all alive— Andalucía, red and raw, for you.

But I will die, he had implored, it is a war already lost, there, in southern Spain.

We have given you a church, Antonio. Cultivate it as best you can.

He lowered his back to the ground, and looking up, he thought of his mother, dead, and of his brother, dead, too, killed by the Reds, fighting for the Nationalists. I am alone in this world, he thought more, and turning to his horse, a sadness came over him. I never named you, he realized, and yet, for two years now, you have been with me. A companion who responds to me. And I know that you see me, too. Your ears become erect when you hear my name. I see the shivers wave underneath your coat when I tug at your mane. He paused. I love you as if you were my own, you know, he continued, his eyes staying on the horse. But I will never name you, for naming you will make you too real, and real here is the bearer of unbearable losses.

The stars melted with the morning light, disappearing into the sky, nude, devoid of clouds. His shoulders relaxing, his chest lifting slowly, he conjured the image of Luna, her smile, her body, a fragile rectangle from which curves had begun carving at her hips. Marisol, he had been unsuccessful in his manipulation. But Luna, touched by her gift, had been easy, to insert, body and soul, for they spoke the same language. What I am giving to you, beautiful Luna, is a chance to go deeper into your faith, in yourself. Like me.

Antonio lifted his arm, a diagonal raising from his body, and he spread his fingers, as if wanting to push the sun, wheat colored. Impatience running along his legs, he stood, removing his clothes hastily. Uncaring of the peasant men, women, and children walking the road, he stepped into the creek, water kissing his ankle, the creek shallow, and he walked farther in until knee deep, letting himself fall into its bed, rolling over, face down, and wide-eyed.

Romero's body twitched, waking him from a dream—a meadow in which he was bathing, surrounded by a yoke of dying bulls, swords planted deep in their lungs and aortas. Dizzy, he sat at the edge of his bed, bare chested, and walked down to where Raquel was waiting, seated at the kitchen table, his breakfast ready.

I have to go to the market, she said, and pointing to the bundle of shawls piled up on the sowing machine nestled in the corner. The market.

Not looking at her, he sipped his coffee. No church, today?

I'll be back shortly, she simply said.

He turned to her. She won't, he thought. She never comes back on time.

Finishing his breakfast, Romero remained silent, Luna on his mind. Once done, he got up, wished his wife well. Not too late, Raquel. I need you for the barrels.

For five hours Romero plodded through his vineyard with images of the two of them, the twins, unable to push the foul from his mind.

He directed his attention to the grapes—red fruits of debauchery, plump marbles that huddled everywhere, challenging the sturdiness of the branches and filtering a sun he couldn't feel anymore, feverishly touching them, as if engorged seeds spoke to him.

He bent to touch the soil, his hands sensing the fertility of his land. When he unfolded, Romero looked to the mounds surrounding him and felt the breeze tucking into the warmth of the day, a day as glorious as so many of them were, and the flutters he hated came—omens he wouldn't heed, pushing water to his eyes. He crumpled to his knees, hands to his face, and he cried the way a father shouldn't, the way a husband despised, unable to stop the traffic of thoughts jamming his heart.

He struggled to stand, as if drunk. I am tired, he thought. So tired. It scared him to feel these hints of mortality wrestling with his strength— his touchable grit? I need to rest, he thought, and he walked with this weakness, unknown to him, to the barn. Steadying his body, he opened the barn's two large doors, as if spreading an eagle's wings.

He stood, the sun hitting his body from behind. In the corner, Luna and Marisol sat, and he followed their gaze to Dolores' body moving, the weight of Matías pressing her to moan, and to moan more—pushing, pushing more, Romero seeing it all: Marisol sucking her thumb in a corner, watching; Luna absentmindedly playing with her upper lip, attentive.

The son heard the planks crackling and he looked, and seeing his father's silhouette, his father's neck arching, as if the man was imploring something only, he could see, Matías wanted to explain. His passion. Her passion. Yet, they had done this, and would again. Somehow. He said: I feel more when with her. I feel as though God understands me better when with her.

The father staggering back into the full light, left his children there, inside the dark of a barn that stood on his land. He walked without knowing, back to his beloved vines, and he thought to himself, obscurity follows me. It follows all of us. And I have let it.

He looked to the small house where Raquel stood, on the porch, seemingly waiting for him, dressed in the flowery dress he loved, the dress that molded her curves, the dress that flowed and moved as she did, making the space around her vibrate with life—with want and desire. But she never wears it, he reminded himself. Not for me.

She waved to him.

He looked straight at her and waved back, a man's shadow from behind hugging her own, and he thought again of the previous night's performance, of how his girls had danced, graciousness gone, and he thought of his children now inside the barn, and he kept moving toward his vines, walking away from her; from them, until something inside of him curled—a pain, acute, and he yelled, Raquel, before falling to the ground.

Nobody would have known what she would have done, had she heard him, not even herself. He called again, bubbles in his mouth hindering the reach of his voice. He lifted his head from the soil and the last thing he saw was his wife—her body flat on the porch.

Father Antonio standing over her.

The room was faded in color, bathed in the red dust the wind would sometimes carry inside the house.

Ven aca, the father ordered.

They looked at him, only Matías moving to Romero's bedside.

Why, hijo? Por que?

Matías shook his head, and picking a small rag from the water basin placed at the foot of the bed, spoke of love, of unavoidable necessities.

But God won't allow this, the father mumbled. You will be lost. Dolores will be, too.

With his finger, Matías pressed on his father's lips. I love her, a simple love, he said, as he turned to his mother, the weight of her gaze, a question.

I didn't tell her, Matías. She doesn't know.

Unable to hold his mother's stare, he turned to Dolores. Ven aca, he said.

Letting go of her mother's hand, Dolores walked to the other side of the bed, in passing taking the rag from Matías' hands. She wrung the excess liquid from it. It was pink. It smelled of death. A common one. Typhoid's dealings. The same smell escaping from Romero's pores. She sat, gently pushing the rag across Romero's forehead.

Dolores ...

Sí, Papi ...

He looked at her, tears coming. Telling tears. His voice, a filament, he tried to warn her. All our lives, Amorita, us Morenos have had to fight for the permission to breathe the same air as them. We always had something to prove, hija. You know it as well as I do. You must be better than them, to be seen, to be recognized for more than the flaws they see in us. You, now, and your brother. He turned his head toward his wife. Raquel's lids were closed, her lips seamed with a thin line of blood.

Dolores took her father's chin, turning it toward her. With innocence waving in her eyes, naivety, too, she told him not to worry, that this was God's plan. As she spoke, she looked across the bed, meeting Matías smile. There is nothing the world can do, Papi, to stop us.

Feeling death approaching, Romero fought to remain aware—this warning to give. Be prepared for the torrents that await you and Matías, he whispered, torrents that shouldn't belong to our time anymore. And beware of Antonio. His wrath. Luna …

In silence, Dolores got up from her chair and opened the curtains, hoping for her parents to see the light one last time, the faraway contours of the vineyard they had loved and cherished—bushes like skeletons soon to be reborn, for all seasons oscillate, but not their soils. Dolores came back and sat by her mother's side. I am here, she said, as she held her mother's hand.

At the end of the wooden bed stood Luna. Unsure of the scene before her, of what she should feel, she simply stared, brushing her mother's feet with an absent hand. Marisol, now seated by her dying father's side, looked at her, at her lips—their soundless movements. She saw the rosary Luna was holding, moving each bead, sliding death closer to Raquel and Romero. Marisol then heard what all of them heard, mumbled words rising from her harelipped mouth, her stance straightening, her eyes rolling onto themselves—the white of them: "And a great sign appeared in heaven, a woman clothed with the sun, with the moon under her feet, and a crown of twelve stars on her head." Revelation. I felt my lips kiss the Virgin's hand longer, she continued in her trance-like state, and I wished Papi and Mamá to be safe in the Heavens; safe from this war lost to all; safe from the coming of the Apocalypse, a world full of saints and gods and holy whips that make you walk as they demand of you. She came back to them, her eyes stilling, their whites' now unseen, their clouded pupils reflecting two corpses.

41

No vigil, no mass, just the chosen plot near the vineyard, close to the roots they wished to fuse with. Facing west, they lowered the caskets into the ground, side-by-side, the moon, horned and bright, casting light onto their faces. Father Antonio's voice floated to them, his prayer, the garden variety kind, one, that, nonetheless, reassured the living. We commit you, he said, to this resting place, and Father of Mercies, we commend our brother Romero and our sister Raquel in the sure and certain hope that together with all who have died in Christ, they will rise with you on the last day.

Matías approached the pyramid of earth edged at the grave. The first shovelful he dropped slowly, all listening to the spreading of the soil onto the lids of the wooden boxes, death's date engraved: December 15, 1927. I'll finish in the morning, he said, throwing the shovel to the side, it can wait to morning. He walked to Father Antonio, you do the same. Go home, pray from there. Ya no te necesitamos aquí. Taking Marisol and Luna by the hand, Matías walked toward the house, its door half-open, and still. Dolores, walking before him, climbed the porch, only Luna turning, looking back, and smiling.

In the village, they would remember them forever. And for one year, following Raquel's and Romero's passing, they observed, hungry fingers hovering over one another, barely touching, unfastened lips from which ungodly murmurs echoed, a heedlessness moving through their quickened blood, commoners and bourgeois alike having seen it all. This forbidden complicity. The muted indecency. A brother and a sister. The death of their parents—hell's bridge unsealed.

Sunday Mass, and Matías, his knees on the tuffet, his fingers intertwined in prayer, was staring at the small altar. It was empty. Father Antonio was standing on the church square, busy talking with the few parishioners who had come that day.

Since his parents had died, Matías' mind, unlike Dolores', had become restless. Inside it, Romero's voice, like a wheel, and from it, ominous passages coming from the old man's dying mind. Crossing himself, he stood, bowing to the large crucifix hanging above the altar. Go, he whispered to himself, turning to the doors. For maybe unloading one's conscience needs to be followed by the unloading of one's body. And so, he whispered to himself, I shall follow as others do. Perhaps, that will do it?

Seated in the brothel's waiting room, he nervously played with the rim of his hat. And here I am, he thought, doing what real men do, while fighting the thought of her.

The reception area was small, and he was alerted to this fact by the arrival of three other clients whose bodies crammed the tight space. That's when he saw it, surprised at not having heard the musical absurdity coming from its strings, the purple upright piano. Twisting on a stool, banging her sausage-like fingers on its black and white keys was Stella the Dwarf, the house's mascot, the Madam's plaything. Hello, sir, she mumbled, as she spread her legs. Like what you see? Unable to sustain the sight of the drooping pinkish lips, he let his head drop forward.

A new voice, pulling, emerged to save him from his uneasiness.

He looked up.

Sonia, she whispered, taking his hand. Follow me.

Apprehensive, he let himself be guided through the narrow corridor leading to her quarters. As he heard more of Stella's piano playing, faulty, melody-less, he felt a hush grip his cock. Whatever desire to take, or forsake, had woken him that morning was now gone. Dolores was on his mind. No one else. As the black-haired Sonia closed the door behind them, the man he could never be understood he had to win over the true—the only real desire he ever felt—the possessing of his sister, again. Slowly removing the woman's hand off his limp cock, he shook his head, no. The girl let him go, as if she, too, curiously, agreed. Not because of his limpness—she had dealt with that before—but because the boy had something she had rarely seen, if ever, in her clients. Despair. The realness of it, and something she knew nothing of.

They appeared as the warning they were, the one they had come to deliver. At the reception desk Father Antonio and Alberto Rodriguez waited, eyes steady. One could have assumed they were waiting to be serviced, like all the other men, but no, not this day.

Alberto lifted his hand and placed it on the young man's chest. Wait, he said. Don't go just yet. He turned around. Give me something to write, he asked the feathered Madam, and tell your monkey-faced sideshow to wrap it up. He shook his head. Hand steady, flattening the crinkled piece of the newspaper on his lap, Rodriguez scribbled his message and placed it inside Father Antonio's hand. Antonio, nodding, said all would be well. That he should go.

Walking through the town, his men in tow, Alberto Rodriguez thought, this night belongs to me, as she will too, soon. Walking more, he remembered what the nuns had repeated to him, often, as he lifted their habit, their divinity living between their thighs; inside their openings, that he was two things at once: an erudite, and a beast.

The young man had heard of it, but had never ventured beyond its entrance, afraid of becoming a heretic himself. There was no choice, Father Antonio having told him, go my son, the man has a proposition for you, one that will save you and your sister. I promise.

Why the cemetery?

To avoid being seen. Avoid the jealousy that walks through the ear of men and settles in their brains. The silence there is a fruitful one, and there, God is grand.

Hesitantly, the eighteen-year-old boy, message in hand, walked through the wrought iron gates, curious as much as apprehensive. For a moment, the scent of jasmine embraced him, sedating his senses. Looking up through the palm tree leaves hovering above his head, he took a deep breath and rested.

You're early, he heard. I like that.

He turned to face the man, tall and lean, amongst the tombs and spirits, appearing to him as—what? A messenger from the darkness? And he thought, what does he want from me? Why am I here? But the mind of a man steeped in youth is not the mind of a man, is it? It falls into the trap certitude often sets, where knowledge is yet to be touched and understood. Curiosity in the hands of a neophyte, that this night, would be his downfall.

Behind the gates they appeared. Men. The shadowy figures of men.

Don't mind them, they're just accessories. An insurance policy. Alberto pointed to the corner of the cemetery where three small tombstones had recently been erected. Follow me.

Dusk had crept in, and with it, a surge of an undertone with wavering shadows that grazed the side of both their heads. The sound of velvet. Waving his hands to the bats rarely seen there, Alberto said, surprising, they are more often seen more to the south?

The boy nodded, absentmindedly, his own questions of why unsettling him and circling inside of him like a rogue horse tethered to a carousel. Papi, he thought. Papi was right.

Side-by-side the men moved across the small plot of land located on the hillside, a mile or so from the city center. Occasionally interrupted by the odd tombstone that caught their feet, they walked until they reached the tiny graves. Barely raised, like mushrooms. A malediction, like the ones he had been taught to fear. Like all maledictions. He looked around, his eyes now accustomed to the night and guided by the sight of these random stones. A freshly planted grave captured his attention, the name and date engraved at the bottom startling him. Fanny Vargas. January 15, 1930. The week before. Fanny the local horse trainer. Fanny the gypsy. Fifteen-year-old Fanny. How many, he thought, how many have been buried here over the years? Thirty? Fifty?

You know what they do with the likes of you, Rodriguez asked?

The young man said nothing, his jaws tight, spastic almost. Yes, of course, he did remember. Who didn't? The English Cemetery, the home of Lutheran dogs.

You know, I'm a man of his word, as much as a man of words, Alberto said with a smile, but heresy in its absolute is non-inspiring. In fact, it indisposes many of us … Still.

This is about Dolores and me, isn't it?

There are rules—rules that cyclize our rhythm, keep us in check. Under God's law, we endure. Under Franco's rule, we must obey. And so, I will take over, for her sake and mine. And I can promise you this, Alberto continued, for it is a deal I have made with the town council and God, there shall be no more of the likes of you, here. Because here, sisters are to remain just that.

What do you mean, the young man asked, and what if I ignore it?

The beach will become your last solace, I'm afraid.

He turned and saw the men approaching, and Matías' breathing stopped. He looked at the man before him, the immediacy of the man's needing, his wanting, and nothing else. He thought of Dolores, the giver of life now morphed into a giver of death. He upheld Alberto's gaze, understanding he would see her again, standing side-by-side with her, twirling and communing, and holding hands—somewhere in hell.

Dolores is not your type, and she prefers, honest, hard-working men. Real men.

A flash of anger crossed Alberto's face.

You still live in the cloister, with them, don't you? Matías smiled, knowing he was doomed. I asked around. It seems everybody knows.

Alberto's eyes narrowed.

I've heard there are quite a few pretty ones inside the walls you are living in. I, myself, have wondered what they look like once their habit is removed. And so, it seems, we have both been fucking sisters, no? Or are they your mothers …?

The words—their impudence, sliced into Alberto, and he wiped the sweat from his forehead. Signaling his men to approach, he looked back at the boy. Hopefully, this will steer you onto God's path to redemption.

The men circled him. It was then Matías decided this ending suited him—the impenetrable guilt, untangling, and not resisting, he let himself be dragged, by the hair through the rocks, the tombstones, and the bushes, guided by the ocean's song, the glow of the men's torches.

Matías' mutilated body was buried in an upright position, inside the soil, embracing the wetness of cold sand—atonement's tentacles. Like all heretics before him, his farewell to the world was a violent one. Buried alive, his nostrils caressing the edge of the soil, he smelled his own death approaching.

Your departure will be touched by the seas' unavoidable blessings, he heard the man's voice speaking. These dogs' recognizing their own, will share the soil you rest in.

Blood filled his mouth, sand mixing with it, too, and Matias spoke, his voice to the winds, yet a loudness prevailing. You are a simpleton, Alberto Rodriguez. You ramble with arrogance, words that will lull for a time. With difficulty, he swallowed, his mouth drenched by the sands. Still, he managed to speak. I know that you create out of fear, Alberto the Orphan, out of not belonging; not being seen. But I see you, he continued, turning his attention to the men before him. I am young, was young, should I say, an hour ago, but I am getting older and wiser by the second. Death is a source of clarity.

Alberto nodded. Ahora.

There is a future waiting for you, Alberto. And soon enough it will become a touchable one. Dolores will find out. So will the world. The whole world.

Graced by the mind's power, illusions can become verities, and verities far away mirages. A defective hologram. And, as he heard the stray dogs run to him, racing against the tide, Matías' mind dictated the withdrawal from his body.

The only dignified exit left to him.

From a distance, Father Antonio watched the spectacle, hiding inside his cassock, his shield against the deeds men are capable of. He watched for the longest of time, the young man's face slowly fading as the dogs gathered around him, wanting, their lips curled, their whining constant. Until nothing was left of Matías features.

Dolores felt the early morning rays warm her cheeks, and hearing the girls giggle their way to the small kitchen area, she extended her hands, hungry for him. Matías, she mumbled, ¿dónde estás?

She rose from bed and walked down the stairs, toward the laughter coming from outside and pouring out from her sisters' mouths. So much pain had been endured, so much agony over the passing of their parents. But today, almost to the day, marked two months since their parents' burial. Standing by the bedroom window, and waiting for them, her hair propped up the way her lover loved, she felt life re-entering life.

Where is Matías? the girls asked in unison, as they ran into the house.

Dolores said nothing, recalling Matías' telling of a meeting he needed to attend the night before. A loan I must secure, he had said. Now, she tried to remember if she had felt him slip into bed or kiss her good morning.

She undid her hair, grabbed the end of her braid, long and thick, and bringing it to her chest, untied the tip. Fingers unlacing, fingers feeling, the silk of her hair, and throwing her head back, the weight of it brushing against the worn-out cotton of her nightgown, she remembered nothing.

* * *

The photographer scanned the sky, pleased to see clouds had foamed above them, mitigating the sun's brutal light. He gathered everyone on the church square, placing the twin-girls around the groom and the teenage bride. Amor, Alberto had said when proposing to her, it is important for us to shine your rebirth for all to see. To quiet the whispers, to shut their mouths. The rumors.

Dolores had hesitated. Across town and beyond, much of the religious ceremonies had been banned. Funerals, baptisms, and weddings, anything remotely religious was barely tolerated—an offence to social progress. She had heard of a wedding gone awry in the center of the city, a union where both husband and wife, once their sumptuous attires ripped off their bodies, had been dragged naked through the gravel piled streets, pulled by horses too eager for a chore. But Alberto had reassured her, we'll make it intimate, Amor, discreet, and besides, he had added almost quizzically, no one will touch me.

Let me think about it, she had said, unsure, while placing her lips on his. Give me a day, Alberto, Matías—

Alberto, undeterred by Dolores's timid defiance, had deployed the lies that would sully Matías' honor forever, securing his prize. Yes, he had told Dolores, your very own brother sold out to the right and the left, that's what they say, that he betrayed. And yes—your very own lover; your brother, had been caught spending time in the town's brothels. He did you a favor, Amor, by leaving you.

She had believed him; unaware she was killing Matías a second time.

No one will know the truth, he now thought, watching over his adopted family. And he was right. No one would ever know, for all of Spain had lost touch with reason, besotted by a yearning for power. No one cared. And, anyway, he thought more, nothing was left of Matías body. Nothing recognizable.

Bouquet of pinks and yellows in hand, her short veil twirling above their heads, the bride gazed at the tower from which the bells had stilled, silenced by their southern fear. Her hands slid along the seams of her skirt, as if looking to anchor—she held on to them, squeezed, feeling what she had threaded, created—this wedding dress. For an instant, she thought of Matías, remembering how their love would never have been blessed by this absence of symphony sounding in her ear. As she looked over to the girls and turned to place her head on Alberto's shoulder, the photographer capturing it—the resignation inside her eyes, the obsession in his.

Father Antonio had demanded, for her to obey. Looking at his bride, Alberto asked, are you still thinking of him?

I am thinking of what the future will hold for us.

Are you happy?

She avoided his gaze, a distant smile stretching on her face. I will be …

Peeking through the window of the makeshift office, a small space located at the far end of the living room, Alberto examined Dolores. Pregnant Dolores, the silhouette of his world. Against the sun's embrace, he watched her as she dawdled between the vines, inspecting with expertise, unaware. Unaware. His eyes continuing to float over her, existing because of her. He opened the drawer and took out a yarn-like, prickly ball made of well-chosen strands of hair; his mothers'; his sisters'—God-filled locks filled with memories of a distorted upbringing, of tolerated trespasses. So many of them, and making him forget the truth of what could have been. He had been abandoned, had he not? An ego forever wounded. He looked back at Dolores, shaken by the fierceness of images that came to him. She was his, and all she came with, more than what he had ever wished for.

The rupture of the bloom.

On October 15, 1930, seven months following the couple's wedding day, Julián Rodriguez prematurely swam out of Dolores' entrails, eyes wild, eyes strangely open. A curiosity, given his premature birth. As mother and child slid into one another, Dolores, unsteadied by the sight of her baby, so small, yet, so vigorous, slowly motioned to sit. Help me, she whispered, Julián in the nook of her shoulder.

As Marisol placed a pillow behind her sister's back, she, too, observed the boy she would learn to love as her own. The baby, she realized, was still attached to her sister, the cord pulsating strongly. A bursting of life. Julián returned her stare, seemingly observing the two women.

His eyes, already open, so wide, Luna exclaimed, her own just as wide. I think he's hungry, she continued, with a smile, and pointing to the boy's head moving to his mother's breast.

Alberto looked on, pulled in by the intensity of the suckling. The scissors, he ordered. It was then, a small and thin leg unfolded, and with surprising strength, it kicked the scissors out of the new father's hand, leaving the blades to land vertically, stabbing the wooden floor. The odd moment cut into the noise, silencing the sisters. Alberto, feeling humiliated, stilled his eyes on the blades. The deed has already been done, son, Alberto mumbled to himself, as he picked the bloodied metal off the floor. Let me be the divide. Let me free you, he thought, as he cut into the lifeline. Ahora eres mío también. You now belong to me.

It would take Alberto years to make sense of what he had felt that night, the familiar unknown. That day, as he had carried his newborn son to the window and stared at the light, bits of fright had run through both his legs, stopping at the tip of his fingers.

This cold called Julián.

* * *

Years of laughter, and they passed slowly, inside a house that harbored uncertainties. Then—

Mamá, something is wrong, Julián yelled.

Dolores ran to her son, and catching sight of her sisters, screamed.

The child, upon waking each day, would run from his small mattress to slide up against his aunts' petite frames. Underneath the crocheted linen of the bed covering, blue and heavy, he nestled against their chests and played with their curly black hair. Their play, a childish intimacy, and each morning, one after the other, Marisol often being the first, would softly draw on his cheeks, the tip of their fingers plump and fresh—a small square. Stability they had said, completeness and peace, the four corners of the earth and guarded by the four angels. Each time they had drawn on his face, a geometry of tenderness and love, Julián's mind opened. A gate had been carved.

That morning, he understood, painfully—they had left him. Swimming in shades of death, their bodies wrapped in blood-filled feces, the women who had cuddled and spanked and loved him were gone, leaving a hole to be filled only by Dolores.

The fifth harvest following Julián's birth, a portion of the year's crop were lost to a parasite infestation, and labor became scarce, as most of the men had left for the port's docks, preferring to work as stevedores, and joining the union. But Alberto's reputation as an abrasive and unforgiving man had become a clear deterrent as well. To compensate, Marisol and Luna were told to join the few men desperate enough to endure Alberto's ruthlessness.

Father Antonio will come to live with us as well, Alberto had said, with studied detachment. I need a set of reliable hands around to work with me, another man. Stability. And so, he'll sleep in the barn, though he will eat his meals with us. What about his church, Marisol had asked, a strand of her hair curled around a finger, who will take care of it? And he comes here almost weekly, she added, looking at Luna. The answer came, steeped in vagueness; something about a novice coming from Granada; something about Madrid having granted him a six-month hiatus. The man doesn't have the hands to work this land, Dolores had interjected, hearing her sister's concern, let alone the understanding of our vines, Alberto. He will be a nuisance. But the husband's words had won as they always did. Then, Amor, he will learn like all of you have. The decision has been made; Antonio will be here tomorrow at dawn. Dolores had dropped her head—abdication, the only viable response. Then, looking at her sisters, she mouthed all would be well.

For two months, the two sisters worked the soil, never complaining about the muscle aches and the feverishness of their skin, the faintness killing their senses.

A day came in 1935, when, under the late autumn sun, the twin girls, working side-by-side, each tending to a vine, and pruning a large branch threatening to die, collapsed.

They can rest when we close the season. That's when they can rest, Alberto had said. It's nothing, just normal fatigue.

His young wife should not have trusted his opinion for quickly thereafter, persistent coughs, violent vomiting, and high fevers, had won over their bodies. By the time Alberto agreed to seek help, the girls' lives were irrecuperable.

On a warm November day, aided by a few workers, they carried the wooden box to its resting place behind the last row of vines recently planted, near their parent's tombstones. Inside the coffin meant for one, two bodies lay. That's what they would want, Dolores thought, as she had clothed them with the white dresses they wore when attending Sunday mass.

I want to be alone with them, Dolores said, as she took her son's hand, leave us. Julián and me.

Stay as long as you want, my Dolores.

She bowed her head, letting the wind push her hair onto his face. Disappear, she wished. Just go, she said.

She barely heard his voice. Okay, Amor, he said, starting for the house, I'll be waiting inside.

Turning to her son now standing two feet behind her, she said, do as I do, Julián, and she bent to scoop the earth into her hand. See, just like this.

Julián was afraid to look at the dirt thrown on the wooden vessel, dried granules of earth gliding in every direction. He kneeled first, hesitant, then sprawled his body on the ground, crawling the few feet separating him from the grave.

Earth is earth, she thought, whether on him or them—a blessing— let him roll in it.

Once at the edge, the boy let his head drop into the void, his hands gripping the border, soft and crumbling. For a few seconds, he stared, unsure. As rehearsed with Dolores, he let the prayer slip from his mouth, reciting words he didn't fully understand.

Yes, the boy had bled from leather slashes and hand blows, tasted iron running in between his teeth, squeezing his eyes as Alberto planted his heel on his neck, surrendering to the weight of his father's poisoned words. Never, never had he cried, the blue of his eyes, like dry ice beaming from the netherworld's inner life. But this crushing pain now, unbearable because unknown, causing a sudden burst of wetness blurring his sight. He turned around, lifted his arm, seeking Dolores' hand. She approached, knelt and lay by his side, placing her white shawl over his shoulders.

Luna and Marisol will always be here, she said, her fingertips pressing the side of his head, with you. With us, Julián.

The words met inside his mind. He didn't feel anything lived in that place his mother called a memory box, his own box seemingly dark and lonely. And while the women in his life had sometimes shone a light into it, he would never understand what it was he had to look for or see. How could Marisol and Luna meet him there? Wouldn't they, too, disappear? He swallowed. Look Mamá, he said, pulling a small wooden statue from his pocket, his eyes lost to the fear born in that instant. He took his mother's hand and continued, Marisol said to kiss it, that when I would, something powerful would happen, every time I did. The tip of his fingers following the statue's features, worn and weighted with the look of the world's pain. A man, holy, gone to save the world. Squeezing his eyes, feeling them burn, the moment so new to him, his tears dropping onto the casket and mixing with the earth. He opened his eyes, I want them back, Mamá.

So much life had gone missing around her, she thought, as she caressed her boy's blondish hair, her parents, Matías, and now, Marisol and Luna. There was no need to try and fool him. We are the only true living souls remaining on this land, she whispered. And perhaps, not for too long. For she felt then, whatever parcel of humanity still swam inside her son, would soon evaporate and disappear under the chaos that would take Andalucía hostage, and then, most certainly, the little man inside the child would be dead.

1935, and nothing would ever hold.

The slow dripping of sand—everything a year 's time can afford to give—on the life of days and she felt grief live inside of her heart the way a worm tunnels inside fruits' flesh—twists and turns releasing the core, dropping it to the ground. And sorrow, too, its weight, made Dolores want to hide farther into her sisters' worlds.

It was the scent that did it, that made her travel to them, the scent of the lilies they carried in their hair and that now infused their sheets and pillows. That was the trigger, she thought, distressed, a trigger that soothed and a trigger that punctured—her present, one distilled with angst, a cutting and unforgiving angst. Afraid to let them tarnish inside her brain, she released them, wanting them to be recognized. That's why ghosts rise from the past, this place that is a remembering, a clenching to the unresolved, trapping it and holding it hostage, whether good or bad.

Each night since their deaths, sprawled on their mattress, she let the film roll, moving vignettes, projected on the wall before her, vivid images of the four of them running through the vines barefoot as the sun broke hot to the earth, three sets of tresses bouncing across the dry land, their feet dusting the ground, arms slicing the air, pushing Matías the conquistador away. The first kiss had not been stolen, she recalled, no.

That first time, forever with her, now. The past again, she thought.

She had let him, unable to deny him, oblivious to Marisol's presence in the corner, a corner they all had stayed in, legs crossed and thumb in her mouth—a spider feeding on itself oblivious to the body standing in the doorway, casting a heavy shadow.

With images soaring inside her head, Dolores, unable to hold on, let go. Coiled in her sister's sheets, her feet dangling from the mattress, toes clenching the warm air, she felt it, the urge to rise, to move. She could feel her mother's arms lifting hers, positioning them, like carrying the roundness of the earth, she had always said, extending her arms like a string, thick and taunt. Dolores felt her presence, a caress on her fingers, correcting them, just like her kicks. She remembered those nights—they seemed so out of reach, as if now they only had been imagined, her father leaving the head of the dinner table with a wink and a gualpe that sent shivers through the floors. Then, the riffs, reaching them, sending Raquel into a trance filled with slow contortions. Romero would walk onto the porch, holding his guitar up and closer to his heart, and, to the beat of her palmas, their hollow sounds inviting the children to move along her, by her side, with her, closer and closer, she would tell them to dive in, to kick it to your culo, and bring it to the ground, those feet are your connection to the earth, feel it, chicas, feel it.

One night, Dolores rolled off the bed, moving slowly, delicately, wondering why pain was so crucial to her survival, why she couldn't move through it? Clenching the small statue in her hand, she left the house and walked to their tombstones, through a soft drizzle of cold rain, breaking into the sevillanas Marisol and Luna loved to dance to, stomping her feet, kicking them as she released her arms, imagined them mirroring her movements, and creating shadowy tandems.

Alberto had looked on, the poet in him unmoved by the despair, the grief mangling inside his wife; a fodder, perfect in its elegiac truth, left unseen.

And this beautiful woman danced into her own remembrance of what love had been, however twisted, of loyalties tattooed on her heart, the names Marisol and Luna, Romero and Raquel. Matías. She should have remembered all that wasn't right. So many signs alive with incoherencies. But memory is like a troubadour—isn't it not?—weaved into the present enough to reimagine the past, suffocating its essence—because her mind's eye now, and forever, was a poetaster.

* * *

Julián, Dolores shouted, as she tried to cut his hair, sit still or I'll smack you all the way to Madrid!

He looked at his mother, the way he always did, his eyes shifty, askance. Fine, he said, Madrid is better than this place anyway.

The six-year-old boy slid from underneath her grip, dodging the scissors clip and ran up the wooden staircase to his room. Amused by the drama that would ensue each time a calculated transgression hit its mark, the boy came alive. And now, looking at the mirror hooked behind the back of his bedroom door, an impish laugh emerged from his mouth. The haircut, unfinished, gave his head an unruly lop-sidedness that hung to the right. Maybe that is where some fascist tendencies took root inside of his small mind, that evening, pushed by the red winds of February 1937— or would it be the left one?

Come here, now, Julián Rodriguez!

Dolores finally caught up to him, breathless, slowed by the secret life pushing inside her. A girl, she thought. I am certain of it. He raised his eyes to meet his mother's version of a reprimand. Tight lips about to snap, tighter eyes even, about to fracture. Still, whatever punishment they predicted for him, Julián felt it. The bond. When he dove into the whole of her, transfixed by the flowery patterns each of her dresses poured on his brain, he would get lost. It didn't take much for him to disappear into his mother—no. She was his world as much as he was hers', a kingdom in which both fused into the other. But, for as much as he loved his mother, he feared her to be weak, and he wanted none of that womanly weakness

WHEN I BECAME NEVER

to rub off on him. Women, his father kept repeating, are fragile, loving birds meant to fly low, if to fly at all.

But in truth, his mother was more than any man.

That day, caressed and embraced by the man she had grown to love and hate and despise and never believe, that day when she saw her husband leave for the convent, she understood, she was nothing—nothing others had ever thought, or ever seen.

I need to leave for Vélez-Málaga, this husband said to her, next week. Mother Margaret wrote to me ... I have poems to retrieve, it seems, poems I forgot about. One about you, in fact ... and some legal matters ... inheritance related.

Dolores nodded, sipping her coffee. About a year had passed since Luna and Marisol had died—grief's veil was slowly lifting, and while her heart remained heavy, life was overturning inside of her, one day at a time. She knew little of Alberto's past, the convent being the only constant lacing their otherwise shallow conversations. The state of the vines, Julián's addiction to opposition, and God's almightiness were recurring topics delineating what was allowed to be spoken about. The rest, spaces left untouched, vast blanks.

Just three days, he added, as he got up. Quick trip.

She bit into a fig, her tongue pushing its seeds around the inside of her mouth. Why now, she enquired softly, as she swallowed. You know as well as I do war is everywhere to be found on the roads. Queipo de Llano's men are everywhere, I overheard the workers say... you can retrieve your poems anytime, no? What is the rush?

Alberto placed his hands on her shoulders, his fingers lingering, flicking the strap of her dress, freeing it from her shoulders. How he loved her more when she needed him, how the sound of her aches filled him with purpose. There was so much of her to take in, but never enough, he thought, staring at her.

Dolores closed her eyes and arched her head a little more, her hunger stoked, meeting her husband's lips.

The men will take care of you and Julián while I'm away, he whispered, I trust them.

She looked out the open window and swayed, mirroring the clothesline's lull. Her face to the sky, she let the wind brush her cheeks with its dry cold. Matías had taught her that much, to explore and indulge her own being, for all indulgences, he said, led to one's truth. But the truth of what?

And now, there was only Alberto.

He stroked her gently, the way she had taught him on their honeymoon night, leading the enticement with a soft cadence she was known to respond to. He spoke to her of how he loved her, how she was his world, and how they would die together, bound by God's will. All will be well, he whispered.

Yes, she said, knowing.

Of the treasure chest waiting in their bedroom.

Of the hours of her sowing, away from his eyes, away from everybody's eyes.

Such colorful moments having left her mind.

Yes, Alberto. It will be.

Holding Julián by the hand, she kissed her husband goodbye, feeling tension expand inside her belly. Come, she said, and she tenderly brushed her fingers through her son's mane. She smiled, shaking her head. How can you possibly see anything through those bangs hanging in front of your blue beads?

Julián failed to return his mother's smile and fixated on her belly. Mamá, he said, oblivious to her question, look, it's moving! He placed his two small hands over the dress where petals seemed to unfold before him. She didn't fit into any of them anymore, so early to be so big, she had thought that morning. And Alberto didn't even notice. I can feel them, the boy said, I can see. What will we name them?

Them, she wondered, biting her lip. Kneeling to meet the child, so serious and grave, she kissed him, spreading his bangs to each side of his face. She ignored his question. A quick haircut then? What do you say?

She cut his hair while reviewing the day about to come. A day that had finally arrived, and she successfully had hidden all its making.

All of it.

Julián wanted to join in on her trip, confused as to why both mother and father had decided to leave him behind. But she couldn't tell him for he would have begged even more, the way a child begs when enticed by a want he will never get to satisfy. She had heard of Emilio Gomez Camacho, spoken about him to Julián, wanting to plant different cells in his brain, allowing them to grow, slowly. The show had been grand, she remembered reading. A prepubescent character: a daring thirteen-year-old man-child unafraid to parade the streets dressed in full priestly attire. In the middle of the town square, the newspaper said, he gathers crowds, summoning people to dance and sing, mounting a collective snub to Franco's regime. The phalanx he had tantalized had fallen for him.

Just like Dolores had.

You see Julián, where I'm going, costumes of all colors, funny ones, all dance together. I promise to bring you one back. A bright expression lit her face as she tapped her fingers on her bottom lip. A theatrical gesture meant to subdue—a grace note. I have an idea, Julián! A muleta and a montera with Romero Francisco's name embroidered on it? Would that do?

Julián's face became alive.

The matadors of all matadors.

The hat made only for men.

Yes, Mamá, yes.

Then it's settled, Julián. My gift to you.

And, she had whispered to herself, one special gift just for me.

Love seeks serendipity, not sameness—her mantra; and she had become well versed in contrived timeliness, wagering on her capacity to sublime and seduce Alberto. The cadence of sweet words had opened the gate, the caress of her scent on his skin, a snake-like embrace. Her, this believable lie.

Warned the week before of Alberto's trip to Veles-Málaga, Dolores, together with a few women and men, disillusioned villagers enticed by her vision, had decided to plan a trip of her own—time was making itself known. General Franco had forbidden the usual fanfare to deploy on the streets and prohibited all Carnival celebrations across Spain.

A mockery, he declared, a disgrace to the Church. But despite the regime's rules, private gatherings were secretly still organized, allowed and secured by Franco's men—Dolores had overheard the women of the village talk about a sought-after reception, hosted by a well-known socialite. One she had met.

And so, that same week, drinking mosto while seated on the church porch, her Lorelai's eyes staying on his mouth, Dolores invited him. Meet me there, she told him, placing an invitation card inside his hand, you won't regret it, I am told.

She knew Ronda's Republican forces had regrouped, prepared to defend against the Claudillo's men. Now was not the time to leave the house, the vineyard. No. But she didn't care and allowed a twisted certainty to flow inside her mind, the kind one can never escape for it was seeded by ancestors, years before, a bohemian wisdom bubbling from the core of a never-ending past.

She simply knew—a forest is always burned down by its own wood.

Thrice, they had appeared to her in a dream, plump and fleshy specters softly whirring inside her head. No longer looking wanly, dressed in the burial whites Dolores had slipped their bodies in, Luna and Marisol told of a story, a lore buried inside Dolores' nightmares.

The visits.

The barn.

Father Antonio.

Because the girls had had enough of him, his touches, his mouth, his spreading of Luna's legs, an invasion Marisol had threatened to expose. And now, Dolores knew—the tea ritual he had imported from his missions in Japan. Shared with her sisters.

Her visions, so many, and recurring before the break of each dawn, a pink mercurial haze surrounding them, her head burning, her eyes directing her to the back of the barn.

Upon waking two weeks before, she had gone to the barn, her bare feet crunching the hay, animal excrements, too. Reaching the end of the barn, she had opened the back door, as she had been told in her dream to do so, and she found it—the bottle hidden in the pair of boots the priest usually wore when assisting Alberto with the vendanges. Arsenic.

She steered her motorcycle toward Ronda, the ruffles of her improvised Columbine costume to the wind, and parsing through the afternoons Father Antonio had improvised in the wake of her parents' deaths. His doleful presence as he tried to allay the girls' grief, the way he cosseted them in a strange and priggish way. How those visits had increased after Matías' disappearance, and after Dolores being formally betrothed to Alberto.

No. This was the kiss of death for the girls—it never had been typhoid, Alberto's explanation.

Seducing Father Antonio had been easy, given the priest's penchant for pretty, young flesh. She had simply exposed some of her own, here and there, occasionally. How everything about him was trite, she remembered thinking when with him. The status he clung to pointed to his essence— an underling willing to stymy anyone's progress to push his own. Isn't that what he had tried with her mother? The regular walks through the vineyard, the improvised drinks, the evening conversations as they sat on the porch, the feigned accidental brushes of her hands with his, the church visits, and all of it was about to be settled—now, the purpose of her escapade.

How truly luminous they are, my beacons, she thought, as her eyes dug into the whitewashed houses that stared at her every day. The village of Ronda.

She continued rolling on the dry road, feeling more alive. It had been over a year since her last visit and she had missed it, the permission to leave demureness behind. Now, upon entering the gates of the town, the contrast, unavoidable, struck at her. For what is a young girl full of life and mischief to think about war and the freshness of its lacerations?

So much indigence. So much death.

She left the beat-up motorcycle standing against a low wall near the Plaza de Toros. My little matador, she thought, staring at the place where corridas were held. She stilled, her ears searching for the crowd's bellows, nothing coming. Such stillness, she thought, disappointed. Looking on, and for one long second, Julián was with her, his blue eyes dancing, hoping. A montero, Mamá, sí. Okay, she thought, I'll see you tonight, Amorito. I promise. She spun lightly unto herself, back into the moment, but not wanting to absorb the fear ridden voices, the merchant yells, the children's crying, the hurried footsteps that hit the cobblestones with vigor—buzzing motifs that spoke of survival; of despair; of war. Yet, stubborn Dolores ignored the chaos, the hungry peasants that loitered, the thieves that lurked, the Nationalists and their blue shirts and boots that stomped the ground, the stench of feces and urine that pervaded the air.

Resolutely, address in hand, she walked the narrow alleys that lead to her landing place.

The façade she came to, freshly washed, shined not from its whiteness but from the wealth one could guess was hidden inside. Guards were everywhere. Franco's. A celebration only authorized by Madrid and somehow tolerated by the barrio's habitants. A strange happening, she told herself. A happy one for me. She nodded to them, warily cupping her belly the way women do when taken by fear. How many of me are entering, she thought, her hands circling her small bump. This way, señorita, one of the men pointed, as he slipped her invitation card inside his coat pocket. Seeing the iron-gate ajar, she pushed it open and entered, determined to follow the music that stamped the air.

The house, planked on the edge of a majestic cliff, was splendid, ostentatious. For a moment, a long and blinding one, as her feet stepped onto the cold of the marbled floors, she forgot, about everyone, even Julián. My eyes, she thought, they might never see again. From floor to ceiling, drawings and paintings whose story spoke of godly love, of new eras, and of men and women whose shapeless bodies and faces lead us into this thinking that everything must move, change, to live and win and coat the viewer with reprieves. She looked to the end of the room, where from the window she saw El Tajo, the gorge dividing Ronda's heart in two.

Gloriosa Dolores, darling, la Bella de Ronda, she heard, a bejeweled hand dropping on her shoulder. How good of you to come! Entra. But where is darling Alberto? Where is he? the lady of the house yelled, as she swirled across the room.

Lady Roberta, your English accent—always so lovely to the ear, she said. Unfortunately, Alberto is not with us today. A last-minute trip. Another guest with me, she said, instead, looking around the room.

Lady Roberta of Westminster, dressed as her flamboyant self, smiled without looking at her. You know, Bella, I was just in Bayonne, she said, with the Señora, Franco's wife. And now, a carnival, here, she exclaimed, and all because of the General and this new guard of his, this … Guardia Mora. We are safe.

Are we now, Dolores thought.

Your Alberto, Dolores … Extrañaremos su poesía, Darling, sí sí sí. Such lovely, lovely words always pouring from his soul, she continued, as she pulled Dolores through the throng. We will miss him, Darling. Yes, we will. Grabbing a champagne flute from a waiter dressed as Queen Isabella and placing it into Dolores' hand, Lady Roberta kissed her new convive on the cheek and departed just as quickly as she had appeared.

Dolores watched her leave, the oddness of their bond, a mismatch fresh in her mind.

The large woman had fallen in love with Alberto's words—Café Chinitas, again—months before she and Alberto had married. Somehow a friendship born out of the love of words, transcending class. The power of duende, the spirit of vivid resonance, communal ecstasy, and its power to rise above all things material. Okay, she thought. Okay. She sipped her drink, absorbing the colors that surrounded her. A forbidden carnival, she mused sarcastically, how timely.

The hard rhythm of the flamenco guitar made its way to Dolores. She scanned the crowd, surprised to see so many dissidents playing with her that fateful day, risking lives, their own and their families'—just to be there. She looked on, wanting to see if the target had bitten the lure. Burrowed in a corner, dressed as a civilian, the man, his face masked, had shown himself for what he was: A voyeur.

A louse.

The eyes, she thought—bleary, glassy, but too alive, still. He stared back. The champagne flute he brought to his mouth, brushing its rim slowly against his lips. He lifted his index finger, commanded her to join him.

Just wait, she mouthed from across the room. Just wait.

She got up, clutching her bag, and she walked to the powder room located at the entrance, locking the door behind her. She had crafted this moment. From her kitchen window. From the bottom of her bed. When straddling Alberto. When bathing Julián.

When cleaning the tombstones.

She removed Columbine from her body, and slipped into the new one carefully, mindful of the alterations she had made. How mother would approve, she thought, as she adjusted the garter belts. She met herself one last time, the mirror returning an image she had seldom seen. The overdrawn rouge along her mouth, the generous cleavage, the shoes, the black skirt, short, revealing. The red veil. The skin of her thighs.

And that other thing, the device she had improvised from the steel used to punch the grapes down into barrels.

That day, iconoclasts of all ideologies had risen within their own factions, overtaking all of Ronda. Anarchists, socialists, communists, all had stuck it to Franco, for to celebrate was to survive war's inanities. Rebels had been bred a long time ago in Spain, stewing inside their ghosts' excrement. They were all, that day, claiming the fertile ground as their own.

She walked to him slowly, watching him watching her. How many of them had he seen already, she thought, all wanting to mock him, expose his hypocrisy. But hers was a little different, she reassured herself, as she stroked it. Father, you came. As promised.

How original, Antonio told her, staring at the metal-made phallus hanging from her middle, am I supposed to be offended or ignited?

The music had stopped. The guests prepared to take the fiesta to the streets where the true performances were to be held. Dolores stared, silent.

I told you I would be here, Dolores. Your intentions were made clear to me at your last confession.

Yes, she replied, I know. God always keeps His promises, you keep telling me. You've inspired me to do the same … She took him by the hand. Let's distil your religious mind a little further, can't we, Father?

Stepping outside the house, Dolores immediately spotted her accomplices amidst the buoyant crowd, surrounding what she had asked them to bring. She nodded twice, as planned. As planned, they approached, first quietly, then speeding to where the priest and Dolores stood, unburdened by their prop. She smiled at them, slipping away from herself again.

The priest felt his heart sinking, for he understood immediately the ending he had predicted, feared, for himself, was now being placed at his feet. An unavoidable one. I should have known better, he thought, and yet it makes sense. God will make sense of it. Of me. He looked to the sky, thought of his life; of his choices; of his time in Andalucía, lost to proclivities he had never been able to fight. Had he ever wanted to? His eyes to the almond-colored sky; pleading eyes, and he whispered through the noise to God: You, the one who knows, will meet the one that never cared. And what will You do then, of my soul?

He looked back to where he had tied his horse, a fence adjacent to Lady Roberta's home. He whistled a loud whistle, and the horse turned and neighed, straightening his ears. Antonio nodded, hoping somehow, the horse would remember him. The weight of him. His body. His strength. His voice, mostly. I've known all along, he yelled to the animal, his mouth trembling, your name—

In a trance, Dolores, pointed to her surroundings. To the chaos. Look, Antonio, she said with insistence, don't you love it? She turned to him, the winds suddenly lifting, and blowing her hair high above her head. And you thought no one would have recognized you, she screamed. That I was a safe place to hide—between my legs. You were sent by the capital, like so many others God-filled falsities, to keep Catholicism alive, to keep the government alive. You were sent here, as a punishment for your sins, the raping of younger flocks. Yet, I wonder, Father, if they know—if your uncle knows, you have lost your way, still, and again, fucking and killing your way to the bottom. She pointed to the women of her village, their husband's, too, whose children had been violated by the priest, her abettors—some pregnant with his child. I was never alone, she thought.

I think it's you, Dolores, who has lost your way, the man risked.

Have I, Antonio *Ruiz?* I saw the documents hidden inside your pillow in the barn. You are the Claudillo's nephew, famous General Franco's: Antonio Franco. How he must love to hate you, sending you, here. This protection, she laughed.

There was barely any time for the priest to reply, and feeling himself become weightless, he knew he had been lifted, that he had lost control— the smell of smoke tickled his nostrils warning him of what all priests feared.

Look Antonio, she repeated, look how the crowd is splitting itself into two, just for you to be seen. And see for yourself, you are not parting anything, are you? You will never part anything anymore. Your seas have become ours to split open. A banality I will repeat to myself as long as I breathe the same air as you.

A hand grabbing the back of her arm. Look out, one of the women yelled, and pointing to the sight of two guards rushing to them.

The Guardia Mora, she thought, catching Lady Roberta horrified stare, and turning her eyes away from hers.

A quick exchange, between complicit eyes, and in no time, her men and women carried the priest to the square where the celebrations were taking root, where everything and anything religious was being destroyed. Other members of the clergy, like him, pushed and shoved, undressed, all naked. He recognized some of them—Father Joaquin, Father Ramon, Ismael, the young altar boy, sister Angela. She saw their fear, their

69

helplessness, the pleas carved on their faces—disfiguring supplications. As the women and men of the village began undressing him, fueling the bonfire with his pants, his shirt, his vest, and his shoes, she smiled. Father Antonio's eyes gripped onto those of Dolores, but not the Dolores he had known. Only the factice person she had become.

Once the man was bare, a circle made of dozens of people formed around him, a rebellious madness taking hold. Dolores approached slowly. Chewing on a wooden crucifix, the pale brown aureole of her nipples pushing out of the habit she had redesigned, she walked to him. She took him in her hands, his flaccidness—a non-existence. Is this what you fucked my sister with? she finally let out laughing, This puny little mollusk?

Dolores, please …

Do you know why you are here, you little man? she asked, oblivious to his pleading.

Febrile, he looked around searching for an ally. Turning to her again, he understood all was lost.

I will remember this, she told herself, and seeing Franco's men making their way to them, embraced by their fear of losing their right to their quest—their due, wanting to appropriate the right to live, without the weight of men who believed in non-existing sanctities, preferring to feed the existence of men in black who spoke of white, of bright, fake lights.

They turned him around and forced him onto his hands and knees. The blue and white fire reaching, fed by wooden statues, the pews, and crosses—pushing the flames to a certain hell, far beyond the low clouds that hung over their heads. If you guess right, she whispered, as she inserted the phallus into him, cheered on by the delinquent mob, I will spare you the heat, some of it anyways, you lascivious leech. Two guesses, Father. Two names: Marisol and Luna.

Someone pierced the circle, and reaching her, placed a tin cup in her hand. Here, she said, as she forced it to his lips, have some of your tea. Bebe tu muerte, you fucking coward.

A hustle coming, of hands reaching, of orders screamed. At her.

And it was then, the sky fell to pieces.

Alberto never quite understood what had pushed him to leave that day. Yes, I could have waited, he thought, as he walked through the vineyard picking at the burnt leaves. Dolores had been right—the war— but then again, she had feigned her plea for him to stay with her, deceitfulness he never thought her capable of emulating.

He shook his head and kicked the ground. I should have protected the girls from him, he whispered to himself. This barter, a hellish deal with Satan himself.

He removed his hands from his pockets, and he kicked more of the ground until the sole of his shoe hung like a beat-up tongue. Maybe only with you, my son, now, the two of us together, it will be different.

He looked up. Drops of daylight were trickling through a set of clouds taking hold of the light. Julián, he yelled, feeling cold, get Papi his coat. The boy's head, lightly bandaged, popped from the small haystack piled by the barn. The smile empty. The eyes even more. In silence, he retrieved his father's coat.

Alberto continued through the vines, walking the small path that led to the family gravesite. How did I miss it, he asked himself, angered by his blindness. He turned to face the valleys that burrowed the soil that was now his. Whatever respite they had promised him would no longer be harvested. His young wife's capacity to defy his demands and escape to the real word, blunted all of which he believed he was made of. He thought he had tamed her, that he had tied her tongue with barbed words meant to dominate, dictated she walk his ground with her eyes to the

71

floor. He had not transformed her into his notion of what women ought to be, failed goddesses to be jailed to be loved. It was them he had left her for, to honor one last time, the convent and its special breed of docile females, the only species that quieted his itch. He had lied. There had been no poems to retrieve, only one last farewell tryst to savor, a closure he had promised his most treasured nun.

And for that, he believed, God had punished all of them.

Come with me, Julián, he yelled. Listo. Vamos a hablar con mamá. She needs to hear your voice, hijo.

He watched Julián. The gait, uneven, coming to him. Patches of dry blood on the right side of his face. Voidedeyes. Angelo, he thought, not seeing Julián anymore, my friend. Lo siento.

It was him who had recognized Dolores from afar. Seated in the confessional booth, in the middle of the road, clenching her exposed belly into which a thick slice of wrought iron had landed, Angelo Cabello, Ronda's baker, had gone to her. At her feet, bound and gagged, a naked Father Antonio, the white of his skin, what was left of it, contrasting with the other colors that had improvised themselves on his body. Beside him, his horse, staring at him approaching them. Striking the eye as one approached the priest was the metal probe left inside his rectum. From that orifice, blood filled excrement had trickled on both of his hamstrings.

A different signature, a jocular death.

Oblivious to the scene's grotesqueness, Angelo, weary, had made his way through the rumble, scanning the sky as much as the ground. All around him, everything destroyed, the bombing sparing nothing except for some animals. He had heard it all; their despair; their shock, at being left alone amidst the blood of their owners. Moans emerging for a time from all directions, aborted crescendos that spoke of imminent death. A cigarette dropping from his lips, beret barely hanging on to his head, he had pulled the rod out of her belly. Staring into her, the feeling of a blessing embracing him. Not to have survived, no, but because there was no wife or children for him to mourn. That was the only curse he had dodged, for he already had paid it forward three years before. Reprieving a sob, he had placed Dolores' body onto the back of Antonio's horse and had started for the vineyard.

This noise. What is it, he had asked himself, moving across the edge of the property. The winds' howling maybe? Then he had looked to the sky, convinced, expecting German and Italian droppings to dot the sky. But there was nothing. Only the barn, awkward, still erect, strangely still standing, untouched. Instinctively, he had walked to it. It's coming from there, he told himself, pulling the horse with him. As he had pushed the door in, the sound, guttural and whiny, had transformed into soft laments, and then melting into the silence's noise. Julián.

He left her body there, beside her boy, Antonio's horse, now his.

That's where Alberto found them the following day: Julián's bloody head nestled into Dolores' corpse, crying, one little hand on her stomach, and holding his statue.

The wind intensified. Alberto slid his coat on and walked farther, Julián by his side, stopping at the gravestone he had finished planting.

All together now, all but Matías.

He didn't know who to hate anymore, everything foggy; everything blurred by smoke filled images that invoked loss and dread—the window from which flames were spitted out, the silhouette of sister Beatriz fading into the orange rage. They all had died that day. At the convent—and here, too. He closed his eyes. War follows me, he thought. All wars follow all of us.

Papi, Mamá was pregnant with twins.

How do you know?

I just did. But she didn't. Girls, Papi. And I touched them, too. They waved at me.

You're a gypsy, my son, Alberto thought. And the clenching of his jaw, of his eyes. So much loss, he said. I am sorry Julián, for leaving you that day.

The boy looked at his father. No, you're not, he thought. Usted está mintiendo. You lie. Siempre mientes. Como yo.

Alberto knelt and placed both his hands on the earth, freshly tossed, yet so dry, and thought of Dolores. She must have known, though, about Antonio. That's why she did it. And it had to happen, too—

That day.

Nationalist air strikes.

German and Italian bombers sealing his fate and that of so many others.

The Battle of Málaga.

The Almeria massacre.

Ronda.

He straightened his body, and leaving the family grave site, Dolores' new resting place, he continued walking through the vines, black and crisp, what remained of them. Sígueme, hijo.

Red Pappus

1 939. They slid among the crowd, belongings left on the quay, cases of life squirming inside their minds.

Until.

One blast, then two … three, a ship singing—from the future, ahead, suspended bites of a palatable life. The ocean liner, a lifeline to the Spanish Republicans escaping Franco's regime and seeking asylum in Mexico.

Julián slipped his hand into his father's as the SS Sinaia finally departed, swerving, but slightly, to remind them movement can overtake the stillness of death?—for an eternity, or for mere seconds.

Papi, Julián, whispered. Papi, are you okay? ¿A dónde vamos? ¿Qué pasa con las tumbas? Mamá …

Alberto ignored him coughing into the silence, so much of it, every day, some which the mind kept in, stowed between right and wrong. Confusion had settled somewhere, at the surface, pushed up from two years of oblivion, two years of surviving the morass of a war that no one could ever win.

The soil of the vineyards long dry and dead as much of all of Spain was now, there would be no more eating rats and squirrels, seagulls. No more sleeping in the gutters. No more begging. No more.

Son, look, he pointed, Sète, its people, are saying goodbye to us.

Julián looked at them, the men, women, and children massed at the edge of a makeshift boardwalk, and he waved. Papi is all I don't want. Whatever is left of not wanting. Midpoints, he would later think—much later. Humans toy with them, confront the idea of retreating or outbraving. Some withdraw before. Some after. Some don't get to decide.

Four days into the voyage that would bring them to Mexico, Julián found his father on the main deck, sprawled. Above them, the sound of dark combers, the best kind of farewells—soft and forgiving. He kneeled slowly, seeing blood trickling from his father's nose. A few funny drops, he thought, looking at his father's face. The mouth had poured blood at some point, travelling to the neck, its flow broken by his collar bone, thick and hollow.

Jesus, the man whispered.

The boy turned around to look behind him. Nothing but humans lost in torpor, drunkenness, and vomit. A deck of horrors. No one sees me, anyway, and no one really cares anymore about death. About the end of the world. He raised his head. The ship's stern rail was not too far. He unfolded, and gripping both of his father's ankles, he pulled, a horse's strength taking hold of his young body, and he pulled harder, leaving behind traces of blood. To the edge, to the water. A dark buffer. He steadied himself and found his father's eyes, demanding. Too late for begging, he thought. Far, far too late for that. He let his father's legs drop to the wood of the deck, at the far edge, and moving to the opposite end of the body, he sat. He looked up, facing the night sky. The sea smells good, he thought, and he closed his eyes, remembering Dolores, Marisol, and Luna. Their stories never fully known, the ones he remembered. Even his own. His heart coming alive, he placed both of his feet on the shoulders of his father and made the easiest push of his life.

For two weeks, Julián stayed, a war-made orphan, seated on the deck, alone and waiting, keeping to himself, Luna's statue tucked inside his hand. For two weeks, water as his only sustenance, Julián lived inside his head, yet unaware his mind was morphing into one that would prove capable of holding a world only sensical to him.

The day finally came when the horizon' line appeared. When it did, all watched as the spirited creatures slit the water. He watched, too. Not the dolphins. No. He watched them, as he toyed with the statue nestled at the bottom of his pant pocket, the people; their faces; their eyes; their mouth; their brows. He wanted to be like them, for a moment, wishing for his nine-year-old self a world devoid of violence.

He looked ahead, detaching from the crowd, and walked to the ship's bow where he watched the coast appear from the distance, the sound of men preparing to dock settling within him. Inside, a quiet knowing of what was not to come. Of what was gone. The boy retrieved the statue from his pocket, bringing it to his lips; eyes closed, he kissed it, and opening them, he threw it out to the sea.

He followed the passengers. Families bound by blood and violence and fear. Suitcases that should have remained behind. Still, he thought, they wish, unaware, like wild animals, almost tamed, being set free. Hoping for more.

The euphoria waiting on the pier for those who had fled Spain's horrors, the pageantry, and the confusion of tears of laughter glided over his entire frame. Vera Cruz, it's soul, fodder for the depraved and the poor.

A girl, maybe five years of age, or less, moving by the shadow of her own gesture, and that of the world, placed a tortilla in his hand. He took it, took a bite and threw the rest to the ground. It has the taste of Spain, he said to her.

They laughed when she kissed his cheek.

At the end of the pier, unaccompanied children of all ages were gathered, and were directed to continue walking until they would reach the station. By the dozen, they slowly boarded the train, and for eight hours, huddled and continuing to dream of a better life than the one they had fled. To Morelia, Mexico. The orphanage. He and her among them.

* * *

Time expands for the hurried one, and every night from his mattress Julián heard it trickle inside his mind, with it, impatience pushing out with nowhere to go. The shelter was just that. A point in time, stretched out, elastic, devoid of benevolence. A place designed to humiliate the weak, even if filled with the best of intentions. Nine years before, when arriving at Morelia, they had walked into the wrong hands; they had followed a man disguised as a priest—a farmer posing as God's right-hand man. The orphanage but a lie.

Julián, you awake?

Yes, tortilla girl, I am.

From the girls' quarter across the second story of the small outbuilding, she had sneaked into the empty bed beside his. Julián turned to look at her. Sophia. He remembered the moment he had seen her disembark the ship, alone, the dress no longer white. With hair, sunny, with skin pale like the stars, and she had intrigued him—the kiss, soft. Real.

I want to leave this place. Go back home.

No, you don't. Home is gone. You are gone, Sophia.

She wept in silence.

So, yes, he continued, they forgot. About you. Me. Everyone here. It's been long enough …

She thought of her mother dead, of her father, too, dead. They will send me like the others. To the convent, she said. I can't keep up with the work here. I just can't.

He heard her soft crying. He heard the faint crinkles of the mattress as her tears rocked her body. He moved to her. The only one that would count, the only one who would know him.

When he would face the inevitable, later in life, his throat gargling, suffocated by men who had seen all of him, too much of him, he would recall that very moment. The obscurity sunned by her presence, the power of knowing all could be well, for once in his life.

He held her tightly, undemanding, caressing her hair, strands of gold that weaved between his fingers. They will not send you to the convent, Sophia. I promise you.

Another night came when Sophia managed to slip inside the still vacant bed located by his, and he chose to latch on to it, this planned moment, wanting to believe in the power inside the night's contrasts, nuances between which hope sometimes had a way of making herself known. Infiltrate distress.

You said that when I would get better, stronger, older, we would leave, Julián.

He looked at her. It was true. Little Sophia had become taller, yet malnutrition had signed itself onto her flesh. Like all of them, twenty girls and boys emaciated by earth's duties. Scarecrows sweating the corn fields. Her eyes, too, different, a rushed maturity coloring the gaze. Inside them, he now saw the story of her life, his too; of days too full; of days where school and chores conspired to steal existence's essence. The time is here, he thought. We can't go on. We will die here if we stay. And looking at her, her burgeoning curves, his mouth dry, he suspected Sophia had been christened by blood, her womanhood confirmed—the convent a real possibility. Or maybe worse.

Lifting his head from the used mattress, sweat clinging to his hair, he looked at her. Sophia, he said, ahora.

Quietly, he led her through the dormitory, a maze from which little shadows watched over them, crisp whispers of goodbyes sending them away. Buena suerte, they said, y no te dejes atrapar. Be safe, leave.

She shot into the air like a cranked-up doll ready to run. Reaching underneath her pillow, she pulled her tiny bundle out, now brown-colored. Holding her hand, rage dissipated by the bourn being by his side, Julián having finally decided it was time.

And to leave was to leave so many other worlds behind.

During their time at the farm, Tuesdays had become the staff's only night off, a night where tequila and zapateado stand-offs united guards and nuns alike on a makeshift tarima. There, on the wooden platform, leather boots struck the night to the sound of imagined battles, to the rhythms of defiance. Which meant, every Tuesday night, a string of drunken relays would guard the grounds. At midnight that night, Abraham and sister Emma would be the ones to stagger across the front yard, tapping their feet, and releasing.

A window, opening.

Sophia and Julián ran, disappearing into the yellow fields, hungry and raw-boned. He, hoping to never let go. She, convinced the moon would keep loneliness from eating her alive.

A small hill and they slowed their pace, stopping at the top. Look up, he said, at the stars Sophia, and remember this day.

The sky was clear, dotted with brilliance. She pointed to it. Which one are we, Julián? Which star?

He circled the night air with an open hand as if wanting to grab what was up there. All of them, Sophia.

And time, walking this earth, incomplete, mismatched, spare parts, and now, the sky rewriting their story. The fear inside her body was unknotting—no awareness other than that of her tiny breath mixing with his.

Do you think they'll look for us?

Julián paused. They might, but not for long. Remember the others that fled before us? Rebecca, Juanito, Rafa? Master, always so drunk, took so long to realize they had gone, and when he did, he barely bothered. And they recruit others, he thought, so easily. Quick, he continued, and taking her hand, we don't have much time. We have to find the railway tracks.

Where are we going, Julián? her voice pleading.

We need to head to Veracruz. Then Mexico. Then I don't know.

Do we have enough?

I've planned this day in my head for two years, Sophia, and he pulled her into a faster walk. I stole. From the guards. From the master's desk. A little at a time. He smiled, proud, took a jack knife from the inside of his pants. Even this.

Keeping up to his pace, she started to laugh, nervously. I did, too, Julián. I did like you said I should all these years. And you were right. Most of the sisters hide their money under their mattresses, or on themselves … And when they snore … Her smile suddenly disappearing, her eyes starting to shift the way they would when knowing a beating was coming. When she wet her bed. When she gagged on the rot of the food. When she spoke too loudly … breathed too loudly. But do we have enough?

We'll be okay, Sophia. I promise you. And they will never find us.

It's still so dark, she whispered, breathless.

Yes, I know. It's like a part of the night that moves between two shapes; two shades—dog and wolf. Don't you think so? The day is about to lift. And here, look … The tracks materialized, a set of three, snaking on the earth.

Which one do we follow?

Julián shook his head and laughed. They all lead to the same place, Sophia.

Holding her bundle tighter, she said nothing, her throat narrowed by the sudden understanding home was still out of reach.

Do we have far to go?

You mean to the station?

No, to where we are going.

Julián sighed. Like I said before, I don't know where we're going, Sophia.

How do we know it will be better?

We don't. He tilted his head to her. But we had to go. Come on, he said, faster, Sophia. And he gently squeezed her hand, gently telling her, the world had a place for them.

The sign for Morelia station appeared from the distance through the morning's first flush, tongues tied by anticipation, and they continued to walk the tracks until they reached the makeshift building. When they arrived, they joined the small crowd of men, women, and children lined up at the booth to purchase their passage. Veracruz, he said. Two.

They heard the train engineer's whistle, a quiet alarm, and when they did, they turned to each other. We're doing it, he said, just like I said we would. Sophia's face, thin and pale, illuminated, catching the new day's glow. ¡Vamos! Julián, I am ready.

The steps leading to the inside of the locomotive were set high, one foot apart, their incline steep, almost unattainable. Let me help you, and hold on to your bundle, Sophia. He lifted her sticklike frame off the ground, his hands clutching her rib cage. The train motioned, momentum driven, steel wheels against the rail track. Julián looked up, Sophia's features no longer belonging to that of a child. But it was the sound of her call, terror-stricken, her voice supplicating to hurry and jump, now. It reverberated inside his ears, and as it did Julián better synchronized his pace to the train's increasing speed and jumped, landing beside the girl. Out of breath, he took her hand, brought it to his lips. See?

You may look like a man Julián Rodriguez, but even strong men fail. You better never scare me like this again, she said, her throat shaking. What if you hadn't been able to jump?

He pulled his pants and knotted the belt's loose end. But I did, Sophia, and I will again.

Unbalanced by the rocking of the train, they walked through the narrow compartment, searching for seats. The train was full. None were available, and for eight hours, Julián stood, looking out the window, a hand holding the edge of a passenger's seat, lost in the blear of the scenery. They didn't talk, and they didn't touch what little food they had managed to sneak out from the farm's pantry. Sophia nestled at his feet onto the high floor, soiled and unkempt, one arm encircling his calf while the other clutched his ankle. At times, she raised her face to his, stern and closed, knowing there was angst simmering underneath—yet she had surrendered, and believed in him. Her bundle on her lap, she opened it, sliding her hand between its content. Inside, her mother's black handheld mirror, broken, a photo of her father, and the gift her mother had given her before passing on. Her fingers touched the beads, seeking relief from the remembering of blood spraying on the lace of a blouse. Her mother's. The sight of her mother wanting to atone, her failure to do so—the certainty of time coming for its end, a nervous fever that would poke at her lungs. Typhoid, then, Spain's pruning. This mother that had told her about the sixty-three miners who had died—Spain's worst mining accident—and of how her father, wearing the talisman her fingers were moving over, had been the only one to survive. It was given to him by his own mother, she said, your grandmother whose name you are wearing, and the ones before her, too. And now, Sophia heard her mother's voice, the retelling of the story. Every night, until her death.

Villanueva del Rio y Minos, Spain, 1609, my Sophia.

A young girl is lying in bed with her sisters, her parents' cot adjacent to theirs'. A sound has pierced through the door, a voice coming to her, lean and low. In shaded reverie she stands and places her feet to the wooden floor. Her legs move to the door, and she opens it, looking out —an obscurity like tenderness never felt before, looking back at her. The young girl doesn't know why she is moving away from her house; her village, to a large oak tree rooted far from the edge of the forest.

A strength 1,000 years in the making.

The heart of her village.

Bringing a hand to her chest, she whispers: What do you want from me—why now? The wind dies. Yet, in the distance, the tree still sways.

Her dress is catching the ground's surface. The soil is rocky and her feet, bare and leathered, are splitting, dragging her through newfound time, long and dissipated time, blood mixing with the hard, gravelly ground. She reaches the tree, and looking at it, wide and moving, she senses dawn's breath whispering to her: kneel. Now.

There is turmoil inside the soil, an unravelling of roots, a war of debris, but she doesn't know—how could she? For the earth surrounding the tree is suddenly warming her feet and seducing her spirit with a feeling unknown to her.

Words, exchanged between soil and a soul. She lifts the skirt of her dress, and her legs collapse—she doesn't feel the ground cutting into her anymore, for numbness is expanding inside of her, an accomplice to the indenture soon to be reached. Around her, beads scatter, and when she looks up, more coming: shiny, red, and pink. A voice, You and I are one, Sophia, coming from below and she listens to it. Slowly, she picks up the gem-like beads from the soil, rolling them between her fingers, and unknowing of her smile, she carefully gathers them inside the skirt of her dress. She folds her skirt, and she brings it up and she stands before the tree, lifting her head. The tree's branches seem to dance a dance of untangling, a tide in her eyes threatening to sway, too. She brings a finger to its bark—a monotone of slick yellow, and pushing a fingernail into it, marks its skin with the sign of a cross. Turning around, she walks back to the village, and as she walks back to her house, the wind now having lifted.

When she enters, she scrutinizes the curves beneath an old blanket covering their bodies. A few steps and she sits by the small kitchen table and feels the hem of her dress—her mother's old wedding gown, dirty and frayed, her fingers playing with its strands. From the hem she pulls a long thread of silk, and snapping it loose, she passes it through the quill of an eagle's feather. She threads the fifty-nine pearls together, forming a knot between each one, preventing the beads from sliding off, and she tightly ties the end of the silk thread together. She places it around her neck. More love, it promised her. Love that was meant to be passed on. Tired, she walks to the bed and slides in, beside one of her sisters.

She sleeps for two days, awakening to a new morning, the house silent, the village, too. Her legs leading her again to the door, half open and swinging. From there, she remains on her feet that have bled, knees that have split, the white dress, marooned by time, tossed by the air, alive with purpose. She looks up to the pale and cold yellow of the sky, dust twirling from the ground up, and she walks to the tree once more, and she stares, unable to look beyond the tree's posture; its beauty, for what is lurking from its core and its roots is lulling and coming from movement no one will ever be able to explain.

What happens to the little girl? she had asked, at the end of each storytelling, Sophia?

They say she died in childbirth, Niña.

Who raised the baby?

God, her mother had said. The heavens.

And what type of tree was it, Mamá?

Some say it was orange filled, others, that the fruits lived in the soil, with its roots.

Oh, she had said, amused by the thought of fruit coming from the earth.

Her mother's hands clenching the religious charm and dreaming more than living, she recalled the return on his birthday, Sophia's father walking toward them, his face black, the white of his eyes streaked, as if spiders red and stringy had erected their nest inside of them. He kept walking, she said, and looking at us he stopped and knelt. Give this to Sophia when I go, he had said, I don't deserve to live without my men. That is when he died, the next day, and why now I must give them to you.

Sophia caressed the beads leading to the crucifix she had made from straw while working in the barn, then removed her hand from her bundle. Looking again, face up, to Julián, she wondered, about the love of a father and the love of a mother. Her escape from Spain—a country's hate.

Fatigued and apprehensive, they arrived in Veracruz. Oblivious to the travelers surrounding them, Julián and Sophia waited for the next train to dock. Another train ride, this time along the Interoceanic Railway to Mexico City. There, Julián would do what Alberto Rodriguez had taught him to do when searching, unsure—wait for a sign, an omen of some sort. For you and I have special blood streaming our lodes: tzigane ichor. It tells of truths to come, Julián. These thoughts of him, like an anvil still, settling to the bottom of his feet.

They walked through the crowds that were large and moving fast. Above them dust floating, yet, humid and heavy. I feel dizzy, Sophia said. I can't breathe.

Julián looked around, and spotting an empty bench, he pointed to it. Wait for me there.

He walked to the vendor closest to them, and pulling a few pesos from his pants, placed them in the man's hand. Dos sopapillas, por favor.

Where are you going, chico? the man asked, as he placed the hot pastries in a bag.

No sé, señor.

No sé?

No sé.

The man paused, considered the young man before him. ¿Dónde están sus padres?

Julián's body became limp, his legs wobbly. No sé.

No sabes mucho, chico.

Tal vez. Pero, no es importante saberlo todo. When you think you know everything, things fall apart.

The thought of Sophia came, and he twisted his head in her direction. The thin body, folded in two, lay sideways on the bench, her head resting on her bundle, her eyes wide open.

Where will you go, then?

Julián, avoiding the man's look, placed a hand over his heart, and gently tapping on his chest, told him, aquí dentro—mi sangre. Y en él, todas las respuestas que necesito saber. All I know lives in there. A furnace dispensing blood. Direction.

Bag in hand, he walked to Sophia, told her to get up, that it was time to buy their train tickets, one last time. She slowly unfurled. Where to, Julián?

Let's find out.

Water coming down like stray bullets—Managua.

Julián, I'm so cold.

I know, he told Sophia. Me too. Around them, men, women, and children scattered to where they needed to go, Julián watching, listening to what this movement had to say to him. We need to leave the station, Sophia.

For five hours, they dragged their feet in the mud of the road, and their shoes, leathered things unseaming, exposed the tip of their toes, their clothes, dirty and thinned by overuse, clung to their bodies. The rain still falling. While at the station, Julián had set his eyes on a family, deciding to follow them. Soon, the family stopped, seeking shelter beneath the

Maquilishuat's wide umbrella, magenta-colored flowers, thick and lacing into one another. The man took sight of them. In their eyes, like his, he saw fear and resignation.

Julián held her closer to him, and continued, not wanting to follow the family of three. We don't need them, he breathed out.

They walked more, until a group of houses appeared through the rain's pummeling.

It looks like this one is empty, he said, climbing the balcony with Sophia in tow. The door was unlatched, and he pushed in with his foot. She opened her eyes a little more. Julián look, the sky is here. Lifting his eyes, he saw what she had seen, the sky over them, heavy over the pierced and rusty tin-roof. I feel sleepy, Julián, she suddenly said, and he carried her through the yard, an opening in the middle of the house, passing a mango tree, tall and large and full, carrying her to the beat-up couch. I need to get us some food. Stay here. He kissed her cheek, quieting the flutter in her eyes.

He never heard their steps, the rain buffering the sound of leaves being crushed, and of sludge being hauled. No-good men, three of them, had followed them from the station. And Julián, triumph levitating inside his mind, forgot about Spain, Alberto, the farm, even Sophia—stopping everywhere around the barrio, accepting a chicha from all who offered along the way. The moment stretched and stopped in a beat-up bar made for men like the one burgeoning inside of him.

Dark fate had tiptoed inside the house to where her twelve-year-old body, tired and achy, lay. A fist was lodged inside her throat, and fingers like a vice pressing her cheeks together, and she opened her eyes, and her lips pushed back, her tongue, too, the flicking of it stopping time. Tossed and turned, her body landed on the floor, her small belly hitting the wood's dampness. She felt their pushes until she couldn't feel them anymore, until the men's reel poured an ending into her, one after the other.

Julián walked back to the hovel, parcels of paradise pushing his limbs forward. He walked back to her, convinced the tree was watching over her, its mangoes, yellow and orange, most ready to burst. The new dawn was breaking, inked by cloudbursts floating above the village, when Julián Rodriguez staggered into the house, eyesight blurred by excess.

To his right, a wood crate where he placed the pupusas the men at the bar had given him. Para ti y tu pequeña, they had told him. Oblivious to the cords of water falling through the roof, Julián looked for the couch where he had left Sophia. I want you to know, he thought, searching, we have found a country Sophia, a home, Managua. And we will tame the waters that surround us.

Her feet, he saw first. From there, his eyes traveled the length of her thin frame. A gust of wind pushed through the open window moving her limp body closer to him. Her eyes, looking to the sky, her bundle wrapped around her neck, the beads of her rosary mixing with the blood dripping from her mouth as she swayed from the tree's lowest branch. Her body half naked. Her white skin translucent. Her green and purple veins curving like final roads taken. His newborn purpose vanishing, sinking into the earth, as if wanting to mingle with the tree's roots—a void, yawning, and fathomless. Sophia, he whispered, and he climbed the wobbly table, please look at me. Mírame. He gently unknotted the cloth from her neck, removing the rosary from between her lips, his eyes locked into the white of hers, and told her not to be afraid, that all would be well. Wait for me, he said, as he placed the rosary around his neck. Her body folded into his arms, and just as gently, he placed her blonde head, soft and heavy, into the recess of his shoulders, holding it in place, his hand trembling. He carried her to the couch and delicately set her down. He removed his shirt, staring at her face, the threat of a scream rising. He bent over Sophia, circling her eyes with his finger, feeling the traces of tears that had dried, granulous streams of them. Beneath her face, other faces mingled. Of women he had loved, of women who had loved him. He covered her body with his shirt, and he slid against hers. He looked up to the ceiling, watching the drops of rain coming to him, filtered by the punctured roof. And he thought, unlike his father, there would never be ambivalence at the heart of his allegiance. Let me be the arrow that comes from the right of mankind, he would whisper not too far from then, in this country that would become his to spit on.

An arrow aimed at the black and red of the Sandinistas' sun.

The rain had stopped, the sounds of the jungle becoming a constant again, spinning its web on life. Julián on the porch, not hearing, removed from the stridulating moving inside of them. Chin down, he stared at the beads, his thoughts cold. Closing in on him. He placed his arms around her, and rocked, the weight of him swinging on the porch. He had retrieved her dress, torn and bloodied, this dress no longer whole, no longer flowing, remembering how it had moved through their run in the fields, through the jungle, the laughter of her in night winds. He knew, as the world had come to as well, there are loves that grow, unannounced, that come without warning from an imagination so unsatisfied it will never leave or be replaced. I got them, Sophia. I found them not far from here. And I can't tell you what I heard them say, he thought. No, I won't.

He looked at his hands, saw the blood, smiled, and brushed the dirt-stiffened hair from her face and kissed it. He rocked and he rocked, and he rocked more, the rusty blades of the chair marking more of the wood. He knew the neighbors looked at him, that inside their silence lay some kind of lining, for him, in that house, in that barrio.

Steps were heard, voices, louder. They appeared, all three, rag-dressed, smelling of despair, speechless, not afraid yet of the scene they never heeded; of the future that could end their time in this land. We live here, the man said. Yes, continued the woman, that is our house.

Julián's eyes on the hand of the mother, the hand that held that of a young boy. Not anymore, no you don't. With one arm, he kept Sophia's body close to his chest, with the other, he took the rifle stolen from the men he had stabbed, and shooting the air above, wanting to empty life from its chamber, he yelled for them to leave and never come back for this house now belonged to him and would always and that if they came back, he would kill her first, then the son, then the father. They looked at him, this rage rising, and from his lungs came a yell, guttural and jarring.

He stood from the chair, Sophia in his arms, watched them run, the mother dragging the crying boy into the jungle, the father running, too, cursing no god in particular. I must put you to bed, Julián softly said. With the burden of the barrio's eyes pushing against his back, unseen eyes that would let him be, he walked into the house, to where the tree stood.

And for two days he dug her grave.

* * *

Early in the morning, and for three months, he swung on his wobbly chair, observed them flying kites high above, circling his head, hostage to the wind's thrusts. He watched the children, ten of them, run the small field adjacent to the barrio, dressed in their white and blue school uniform, tugging at their strings, eyes to the sky. Sometimes, once the winds faded, these children would gather in front of his house, before going to school, asking the same questions. ¿Por qué estás aquí? ¿Cómo te llamas? ¿Estás aquí para quedarte? ¿Cuántos años tiene? ¿Dónde están tus padres? Every morning, biting into his mango, Julián quietly listened, his eyes shifty, staring back, unable to say a word for his voice had become muted.

One day, upon waking up, no kites etched the skies—the children nowhere to be seen. For one week, at dawn, Julián rocked his chair, waiting, hoping to see them again, wondering where they had gone. On the last day of that long week she appeared, her small being moving on the white painted floors of her porch. The sun had risen from behind his house, casting an unsteady light onto the façade of her small villa. As she moved in and out of the light, Julián wondered why she was the only one left. She turned around and stopped. They stared at each other for a while, and when a hummingbird flew midway between the two houses, as if splitting time, she descended the stairs and walked across the road, stopping before him. I know you can speak. I can hear you at night, you know, singing this song, the same one, always. Her voice rose, unready yet gracious, sending a rover in his mind, a going away from one's flesh. A la nanita nana ... nanita ea, nanita ea ... mi niño tiene sueño, bendito sea ... bendito sea ... Bless this child ... She stopped singing, a soft smile on her face. So then, will you tell me your name?

His tongue untied itself, as if it had never stopped flicking. Julián. Julián Rodriguez.

Me, it's Philomena. Philomena Diez, she casually said. Some call me Mina, some call me Philo.

I will call you Philomena Diez.

You chased the family that lived here.

Yes, I did.

Why?

I don't know, Philomena Diez.

Why stop here?

It was raining. She was getting cold.

She pointed to his chest. I've never seen a pink rosary like that before ...

Julián looked away, to the edge of the jungle.

The little girl remained in front of the porch that was now his, this sixteen-year-old man rocking on an old chair, drinking from morning until night, yet able to stand straight and walk no particular line.

Where is she now? she asked.

Buried, and Julián pointed to the door.

Sadness fell on her, for a moment, but then the same smile, affable and light-filled stretched across her face. You've been here for almost four months, and I look at you all the time, you know, from my window.

I know you do, he said, looking up to her, I see you, from mine as well. I see you looking at me. And no one has said anything to me, Philomena Diez, not even since that day.

What would you have replied, Julián Rodriguez? Your mouth didn't move. And the barrio knows that. But now ... you do, talk, it seems. And now, my papi will want to talk with you.

He firmly placed his feet on the ground, stopping the rocking of his chair.

Her tiny mouth became idle, and she examined his make—washed-out blonde hair, deep-blue sea-colored eyes, a built, large and thickened by muscled flesh—and he watched her, too, a small tallness redefined, kinks of brown hair sprouting from her head, brown-colored skin suggesting of a blend, of thickness and softness that would ease.

Why does he want to talk to me?

All I know is that he wants to see if what they say about you is true.

I could lie.

Dead bodies don't lie.

Live ones can.

No one liked them around here, she continued. They stopped attending church and Mamá says it is a sin not to pray, not to give your soul to God. She raised her small hand, pointing to the hills around them. More and more they would leave and when they would come back, something in them was different. Papi says they caught the red fever. But the thing is, Julián Rodriguez, I liked Manuel, their son. Manuel was my friend. Her eyes welled up, but quickly she brushed the tears off and then pretended to fix her ribbon-made belt. Papi said they had to go. That the Sandinistas must be erased anyway, before they are born for real, before they erase him, me, and my mamá. She paused. Which side are you on, Julián Rodriguez? Around here, it matters …

It matters everywhere.

I know.

How old are you, Philomena Diez?

She lifted her chin, brought her shoulders back, eleven. Today …

You seem to know a lot for an eleven-year-old, Philomena Diez.

I could say the same of you, Julián Rodriguez. You look like a warrior.

He pulled up his trousers, buttoned the top of his vest, and tightened the white cloth tied as a handkerchief around his neck.

In fact, you seem to know more than many …

Well, Julián started, slowly descending the stairs to meet her, I'm not sure.

Her eyes opened wide, letting some of his light in. Come tonight for dinner, Julián Rodriguez. Mamá brought some fish from the market this morning and is making rondon. And it's my birthday, too. Eleven.

Yes, you told me.

She looked to the ground, at his dusty naked feet, slowly scanning his attire, and turned away, jumping over his shadow, walking to her home, there in the middle of the small borough. Once on her porch, she flipped her body around, and said for him to wash up and make sure he didn't smell too much of that gypsiness. Papi won't like it.

Julián looked around.

Inside his house everything had remained: the half-muddied floors; the wooden walls, mismatched and unsteady; the punctured old roof, threatening to fly away. He walked to the bedroom and stared at the striped mattress laying on the ground, stained and moldy. On it, Sophia's bundle, ragged and hollowed, her dress, too, crimson starched. Above the bed, an old, beveled mirror hung, its glass smoked by time's dirt. He investigated his shadowed self, dismissing his image with a hand, floppy and loose, images from Spain coming to him: Luna and Marisol's visages, mischievous and round, Dolores' body dancing through the vineyard—the last time he had seen his mother, a flowery dress wrapping her silhouette. A montero, she had said, for the only matador in my life. A sadness like a knife, and just then as he turned toward the door, from the string of gems wrapping in neck and falling on his chest, a burning cold. Words, too, breaking the silence in his head, a voice like a wind snaking through blazing forests. It told of temptation's tepid warmth, of it feeding men's inclinations, permissions—of randomness meeting voids. It all depends on you, Julián Rodriguez.

Yes, me.

More sweat pearled along his temples. Shaking his head, in a daze, he walked outside, to the metal bucket placed at the end of the porch. Once at the edge, he sat on the floor close to a broken plank, his feet dangling yet brushing the soil. He placed a hand inside the bucket, rainwater, cool and distracting, his fingers twirled. Twisting his body to it, with both hands he made a cup, bringing them to his mouth. The sip was long. An inhale. He stood, calmed his cheeks and forehead with his wet hands. He looked ahead to the house before him and smiled.

The door opened, and behind it, Philomena, dressed in a white tulle dress, wearing a white ribbon on each side of her head. I've been waiting, she said, her smile wide. Come in.

The low pitch sound of a ceiling fan caught his attention, its draft too, a soft and constant caress against his face. He walked to it, reaching the middle of the small villa. Everything around him seemed as if the abode had recently been erected, everything so new, polished and clean.

A man dressed in combat uniform stood near the kitchen door, watching him, his face sullen as much as curious. He walked to Julián, extending his hand. Bienvenido a nuestra casa, hijo. Julián froze, unable to breathe, and wanting to run out, back to his house, to the tree and its branches weighted by the mangoes. He felt a hand slide into his and Philomena pulled him to the side and wisely told him all would be okay, that all this was nothing more than a moment, overdue and now here. And you will see, Mamá's food is the best. She pointed to the dinner table. Come and sit. Everything is waiting.

The meal was held in silence, the sound of Bing Crosby's voice the only conversation, revered and ignored. Julián, feeling noxious, looked at the cake crumbled on the table, small candles half burned laying on the white of the laced tablecloth, by its side. The plates had been emptied except for his.

Julián, you are from Spain, Philomena tells me.

Yes, I am, señor, I am from Ronda.

You've been here for a few months now, the man said, toying with the neck of his fork.

Si, señor.

The man turned to his wife standing at the end of the table. Without saying a word, Liliana nodded and walked to the tall wooden cabinet leaning against the wall, near the entrance. She pulled the wrought iron handles, black and intricate, tugging at the doors. After four attempts, the humidity-gorged doors gave in, sending a muffled sound into the room. From the top shelf, she took two glasses, from the bottom one, a bottle of rum. She walked back the table. Eso, she said, as she poured them each a glass.

The man took a quick sip, then another, this time letting it slide a long burning slide into the heart of him, pointed to his daughter. Philomena says you are a boy made of man.

The girl nodded. Julián held the man's eyes.

Why did you come here?

To Managua?

Sí.

Julián studied the man in front of him. His face. Almost like Alberto, he thought. Tall and large. The white man's skin. The white man's eyes, icy—so pale. And the hair, too, a stock of it, like Alberto, but black, dark. I came here because I came here.

What happened to your parents?

My mother was killed by God. And Papi, I don't know, really. Typhoid most likely. On the boat.

God doesn't kill anyone, Lilianna said.

Julián, bending his head, said, God had the power to do the work of the Devil, too. Just like the Devil can imitate God's work. Fool all fools. You should know that.

Liliana turned to her husband. Hush, he whispered, turning back to the boy. What do you do all day, Julián Rodriguez? My wife says you disappear in the jungle, every night.

Well, not tonight, señor.

I can see that. The man dipped a long finger into his drink, twirling the liquid.

What do you do?

I hunt.

For food?

Maybe.

You killed those men, didn't you?

Julián took a small sip from his glass. I did.

Yes, the man continued. I've heard the story. The villagers here say you took them one by one, from behind, that you slit their throat.

Sophia swinging from the tree and the image settled somewhere in the front of his mind. It was easy, señor. They were all drunk. A piece of cake, he said pointing to the center of the table.

You loved her?

Yes, señor.

Hmm. Did you enjoy killing them?

Yes, señor, I did.

Yet, all this commotion strangled your own throat.

Philomena reached from under the table and placed a hand on the boy's thigh.

It came back today, Julián whispered. My voice.

I know, my son. I can hear that it did. And quite happy to hear it, too.

The father looked at his daughter and smiled, hints of melancholia falling over his face. My Philomena's mind is quite powerful, you know. A beauty in the making as well. The man sighed, and as he did, he slowly walked his fingers across the front of his shirt, finding a button threatening to undo, and tucked it back neatly into its hole. Philomena had an older brother, you know. Tito. The voice was soft, resigned.

He was my best friend, the girl said softly.

Oh …

He died two years ago, Philomena continued. He left for school and never came back.

Liliana nestled her head into her hands. A month after his disappearance, we found his body laid on the plaza, across the polizia. The head was gone. The birthmark—

He took his wife's hand. Don't cry, woman. Tito is in heaven.

Turning to Julián, the man said he reminded him of his son, something in his posture, like tone, more than vibration.

Julián listened, unfazed. I have questions for you, too, señor.

I know you do.

Julián cleared his throat. For about three months now, I've been watching the barrio's children play. Every morning, señor. What happened to them?

The man stood, and walking around the table, hand to his back, he started to whistle to the sound of Bing Crosby's music. They listened to his whistling, followed the man's steps with their eyes. After circling the table three times, he stopped before Julián. Do you know who I am? he asked.

No, señor. I do not.

My name is General Diez. He lifted both arms to the ceiling. I moved here, inside this small villa, this humble section, he said slowly. Two years ago. We had it built—this innocent looking house. I am here to help them.

You haven't answered my questions, General. Where are the children?

Liliana looked at Philomena, then at her husband. Ernesto …

General Diez pointed to a wooden case placed on the buffet behind his wife. Liliana reached from behind and placed it in front of her husband.

A gift from President Somoza, he proudly told Julián, as he lifted the cover. And in it, my son, is the only thing Cubans will ever do right. From the half full humidor, he removed a stubby cigar. He cut half a centimeter from the cigar's cap, tilting it toward his mouth inside which he pushed the cigar, slowly wetting it with his slime. For two seconds, it hung from between his teeth and as it did, from his pants front pocket, he retrieved a lighter. He clicked it open, wrapped his plump lips around the tube-like thing and lit the cigar's foot, pumping until the foot became alive.

The man sat back, eyes closed, and they all looked at him through the smoke as his plump and pursed lips twirled into the air, purple and dense.

Julián watched as the General inhaled repeated hardcore inhales—unforgiving. When the cigar threatened to become a thickness of ash, the boy removed it from the General's stubby fingers, placed it between his lips, and lightly pumped it.

The General stared, nonplussed. I recruit them, son, he said slowly. The girls, too. Once they become old enough—twelve is the magic number around here—all of them. We do it at night, when everyone is sleeping, when no one is looking.

Julián paused, pushing the smoke out of his mouth. You gave them kites so they would trust you?

The Americans. They send some to us, every month.

Their parents?

They hide in their houses, stay with the younger ones. They know not to get in the way. That they will lose. They come to understand. Sacrifices, all types of them, are necessary to make sure Nicaragua remains the motherland they need. If they want to live, they know they have to release their children.

You have sent them to camps?

Yes. Combat training, rifle shooting. Bootcamp. We get them ready, in the hills, deep into the jungle, not too far away from here. But sometime far, too. There we unweave their fear. To fight a young junta. The budding Sandinistas.

What if they don't obey?

Simple. We shoot them. The country doesn't want cowardice worming in its belly.

The General took the cigar back from Julián's fingers, flicked the ash into the ashtray. And I would like to do the same with you, Julián Rodriguez. The very same.

Shoot me?

Don't be silly, Julián. Train you.

The words echoed in Julián's head, and when it did, the sound—like a rock falling into water. They all looked, half surprised. From the ceiling a scorpion had dropped into Julián's rum filled glass. The brown critter wiggling its way out of the glass, trying to escape.

It happens all the time, Philomena said, laughing. All the time.

* * *

Yucca flowers, long and bell shaped, dangled over their heads, brushing against Philomena's tiara. Underneath the arbor, the couple faced the priest, and listened well to his words, dry and purposeful, to the passages of the Ancient and New Testament meant to secure the posterity of the land.

Upon the end of the sermon, Julián, dressed in his military attire, promised to hold her forever. Philomena Diez was dressed in a white gown made of lace, intricate and fine, and played with the eternity ring Julián had just slid along her finger. She, too, swore. To hold. To promote the word of the land, God. I will be exemplary, she thought.

They turned toward the guests, twenty rows of them, seated in the Presidential Palace's Garden. As they started to walk the flowered alley toward the entrance of the Palace's ballroom, the bride and groom nodded and smiled to the ones they knew, but mostly, to those they didn't. Once at the Palaces' door, they stopped and turned to the priest. The small man was still standing under the arbor, the large leather covered Bible split on the lectern. And God blessed them, saying, "Be fruitful and multiply and fill the waters in the seas, and let birds multiply on the earth."

To my son in-law, General Diez said, holding his glass to Philomena, my only daughter, and to my descendants. The country met this young man four years ago, and ever since then—more hope, fierce in its determination. He looked to his right and winked at his guest. Somoza ignored him, looking at Julián, smiling and laughing with him, clinking his glass to his. You are made of what we need, now, Julián. 1950 is here, and so much progress to be made. Te necesitamos más que nunca.

Thank you, Mr. President. I want to. I will succeed. Yo quiero. Tendré éxito.

Just keep doing what you're doing, son. El país necesita una mente como la suya.

Tus manos también. Hands like yours. Fearless hands.

Sí, señor.

The small crowd, made of guests eager to please, was quiet, almost distrustful. And while the women displayed their montage of what a woman should be, with cleavages wide and deep, mouths drawn with rouges and pinks, ears and necks weighted down by greed and submissiveness, the men drank steadily, and steadily withdrew.

I want some of that Bing Crosby music, Somoza suddenly yelled, pointing to the air as if searching for an orchestra, "Sunday, Monday or Always ..." Ahora.

The members of the band, all dressed in white, fidgeted on their seats, the singer standing erect, in front of his microphone.

The groom helped lift his young bride off her chair and placed his hand to the small of her back. Sensing the strain taking hold of her body, he pulled her to the middle of the dance floor, pulling her closer to him as the band started to play, soft and melody-filled, the singer's voice, velvety and convinced—a union had been made somewhere, but not there. Not then.

Are you happy, Philomena Diez? Julián whispered to her ear.

The teenage girl looked at him, saw his eyes, dark and bluer than before. She held onto his shoulders, then slid them to the back of his arms, and followed his steps.

Our song she said—sing with me.

Inside those long minutes, Philomena in his arms, Julian felt as though home had been touched, created—recreated? Their lips met the song's word just as she had wanted, but when they did, Philomena suddenly grabbed her large belly. Julian, she said. And she lowered her head, saw her blood, florescence pulsing red, staining her dress. Julián, she said, again. Oh, no.

* * *

The hovels were destroyed, terraced, their occupants displaced further away from where Philomena and Julián's home stood. The house was extended, a second floor added, and the mango tree kept, its branches continuing to push through the new terracotta-made roof.

But life was still waiting to be felt.

Every month, and for years, long stretches of them, anguished and gone, Philomena Diez was seen digging her nails into her belly like a crofter raked its soil, dry and barren, wishing it to yield. The neighbors watched and gossiped—about the daughter of General Diez, the stealer of innocence, about the mephitic inside her belly—stillbirths and non-births and bloody fjords that skulked from the opening of her thighs, chiseling old age on a face that became the truth of their lives.

Every month for fifteen years.

Finally, 1965 came, and two seeds rooted into her, and sprouting followed—twin girls, vigorous with health. By then, Julián had moved up within the ranks of the military—Capitàn to Mayor, Mayor to Colonel. The girls arrived, and he was promoted to General de Brigada. General Diez had died in combat the month before and President Somoza had chosen Julián to replace him. Continue the work, he had said, only this time I want more. Recruit more.

Recruit better.

Todos ellos—todas ellas.

Girls and boys.

A never-ending chase started, a purpose-filled hunt and with it another layer had been dug out. Julián, cold and long gone from himself, now a churlish crusader of children.

Philomena pretended not to see, occupied by the raising of her own blood, her daughters—perfections loving an overused woman, a mother now haunted by her dreams, of her own blood.

* * *

She lightly knocked on the glass, motioning the chauffeur to unroll the car window.

Come and get me in two hours, I should be done by then, Ricardo. She looked to the back of the white Cadillac. Andie's eyes were searching as they always did, her hands feeling the leather of the seat, not knowing it was black, only feeling the cold of them, their seams, small but thick. Holding the baby, the help braced herself a little more.

I should be back in time for Luis's feeding, Philomena said. Make sure the twins practice their piano. The new nanny should arrive in an hour.

Andie reached to the sound of her voice, sí señora.

The tall woman turned around and swayed her mink shawl across her shoulders, tightened her clip-on earrings, and waddled to the door of the radio station, one hand clutching her bag, the other holding her belly.

Come on in, said the young priest.

Philomena climbed the stairs, walked inside the studio and sat where told, looking around, to the lights, their color, and to the posters of Christ pinned on every wall surrounding her, at eye level, for all to see.

Before a small desk, the priest settled on the chair across from her and moving the headphones to his ears, examined her freely. This woman, he thought, as he waited for his cue. Finally.

A Christmas-filled jingle played. The old technician hunched over his console and across the glass nodded at them. He held his hand up and counted down from three, and pointing at the radio host, lip-synched, ahora.

Philomena Rodriguez, thank you for being with us this today, December 22, 1972. Thank you for accepting our invitation. One hour with you is a gift, sí, a gift you are giving the nation and its God, gracias.

She nodded, forgetting it was the radio but for a moment.

The old man knocked on the glass window and pointed to her microphone. Headphones on, she smiled, played with the curls of her dyed-blonde hair. Yes, gracias, Father Vasquez. A very special time of year indeed and such an honor to be here in beautiful Matagalpa. My beautiful and God-filled Nicaragua. Her eyes resting on the desk, she smiled.

Here at Radio Nuestra Señora de Lourdes we have been following much of your life. And we are all about life, aren't we señora?

Yes, we are—

First, our audience wants to know, señora Rodriguez, how is our dear General, we hear so much about him, his achievements …

She looked at him, beads of pearl threatening her upper lip, his face long and wily and aware, a smile so insincere, and knew he knew—the whole country did—of the truth at the core of all the rumors.

He is fine, Father, very fine, busy fighting this leftist movement that will kill me, you … our God.

And what do you think God thinks of our country, señora Rodriguez, of what it is we are doing in his name?

As Saint Augustine has said, God provides us the winds, and we make the sails, we the people, we the government. My husband, my children …

Some have said that without God, everything is permitted … Señora Rodriguez. Is God with us, on this land, in this world? You have studied philosophy, a graduate from New York University. And so, what do you make of Nicaragua, now?

I did study philosophy. She paused her eyes, lost. Regaining composure, she looked at him. I think that God is right, the only one right, the only one worth fighting for. Siempre. Impurity is not about God, is it? And all that is impure is an obstacle to the touching of His bliss, the one worth fighting for.

You think that God is on our side?

Yes, I think that God is on our side, that he understands the good fight my husband is fighting.

But how do we justify the killing of men, women, and children?

She cleared her throat. I have been taught to think about right and wrong, determine what exists and what does not. The heart of philosophy. And the existence of God has been established, Father Vasquez. You know it, don't you? And because it has, we must defend it. Him. We, Somoza, and the righteous ones, are willing to die for Him. The others, the non-believers, they are willing to die for an absence of Faith. For nothing. Think of that. Nada. And I ask you Father, you the priest, His mouth, if one lives for nothing—what is dying for nothing worth? Vivir para Dios es la verdadera existencia.

His eyes holding hers, he took a sip from his cup of water.

But you haven't invited me to talk about the war on God, have you?

He brushed a hand across his hair, brought his shoulder back, and touched the cross hanging from a rugged tine, just below his sternum. No, we haven't. You are right, señora. Julio Vasquez looked at the clock ticking above the glass window. He cleared his throat. As you know, here at Radio Nuestra Señora de Lourdes our listeners have voted you 'Woman of the Year'. For the last twenty-five years your pastoral work across the land, your dedication to the word of God, and your stance on procreation has made you a Saint yourself. As a reminder to the audience, señora Rodriguez is an avid believer in the sanctity of birthing. He looked at her. You have lost many children, sí?

Philomena squirmed, holding her belly—this default mode of praying. Sí. Estuve.

What saved you from what I can only assume were dark times?

God, of course. Prayers. That and studying, she replied.

Distraction?

No, she said. Focus. And carrying God's word, everywhere I can.

And for that, señora, the country is grateful, he said, his smile affable. You and your husband always continued, never quit, he went on.

Images came—those babies, lifeless and blue, placed in her arms, powerless and guilty of not holding, of not keeping—of her little girls, lost; of Julián and his anger; of a past that never left him; of his rage and of his affect for God; of this affect now, warped by his own doing; of all these children fathered by him, now running in the fields, in the jungle, fatherless. Yes, we have, she said in a whisper. Because we knew we had God on our side. Y todavía lo hacemos.

The priest saw her retreat, unknowing of the places she was visiting there in front him, nights and days when Julián disappeared, leaving her with her loss, and her pain.

And all those young women that had disappeared near her barrio.

She knew.

And the priest before her, knew that she did, too.

The pearls on her upper lip, round and clinging to the brown of her skin.

And your prayers, finally answered. Late in life, but here they are, the priest continued. He smiled at her, reaching for her hand, manicured and still and so cold.

109

Seven-year-old twin girls, Marisol and Luna, little Luis, barely six months old, and now, this one, due any day. A Christmas baby.

She did not smile.

A Christmas boy?

Maybe, but the General is convinced it will be a girl ... Sophia, he says ... Or Dolores ...

The old man knocked some more on the glass, signaling it was time for a song break. Ave Maria rose from Frank Sinatra's voice, and as it did, so did Philomena.

I need to use the washroom, she said.

She never returned.

She stood in front of this house, her home, a white villa now fenced with barbed wire. In its center, the same courtyard, and in the middle of the courtyard, the same large mango tree, larger now, its leaves stoked by the wind's continuance.

She climbed to the porch, walked inside, weighted by the life that was there, like her, waiting to breathe better, without any help.

The tutor left an hour ago, señora, she heard Andie say. The girls are braiding their hair up in their room and already in their nightgowns. Luis has been nursed and is already asleep. The food is on the counter, oh, and the new nanny has moved into her room.

Philomena watched Andie feel her way around the living room, watched her feet shuffle, her black cane searching for the base of the staircase. Julián?

Señor Julián has arrived and is tired from his trip. He said not to wake him.

How long ago did he get home?

About an hour or so, she lied.

An hour?

Sí. Andie steadied herself in the middle of the stairs, wondering if Philomena could see the marks on her arms, wondering if the blood on her back had stopped dripping, if her gait betrayed what had unfolded three hours before.

But Philomena knew: Andie: a gift from one of Julián's trips to Spain. An orphan, he had said, she will help us around the house. Yes, she thought, so much help needed from this half-blind girl. She looked at her, the whiteness of the young one's skin, her long reddish hair, the passage in her eyes of a color that once had seen. Really seen. Go to bed, Andie, I'll see you in the morning. You and this new help.

Philomena walked to the kitchen, removed the foil placed over her meal, and mindlessly started to eat, feeling the baby moving, fighting an absence of space. The twins, she suddenly remembered. I need to kiss them goodnight.

She left her plate on the counter, barely touched, removed her shoes and tiptoed to the top of the stairs. She peaked to the left of the landing and saw the girls had fallen asleep, huddling in Luna's bed. Las mejores chicas del mundo. Cómo os amo, mis flores. She tiptoed further to the left, across her bedroom, and opened the door to the nursery. She walked to him, releasing her hair to dangle above his breath. Luis, Amorito, sleep like the baby that you are. Te quiero tanto.

She left the small room, turned around, and saw Andie standing before her, her eyes empty, a see-through nightgown barely hanging from her shoulders, and clinging to her body. I'm tired, Andie, she said, and she slowly walked into her bedroom. She removed her clothes, and naked, she slid beside Julián, inside a space still warm. Still wet.

The ground, moving and trembling woke her. Julián, she yelled, understanding, ¡vamos! she yelled. Running from inside her bedroom, she heard the sky crushing—the implosion of the roof, the caving of cement walls, sections of the ceiling falling around them, inside the girls' bedroom—fresh debris blanketing their bodies, there on Luna's bed, the noise deafening and telling of an ending. No cries. No yells. Not even hers.

Just the wide silence of the earth moving.

And water, so much of it, pooling at her feet.

Her husband stood behind her, watching, his bloody hands hanging, bodies before him covered by the stopping of time. He stayed, oblivious to all, everything, and he stared, at the room facing them, its pink walls, the lace of the curtains, torn and ripped, at the dollhouse strangely still standing and alive with its wooden dolls.

Philomena, crumbled in pain, watched Ricardo, Luis in his arms, leading Andie and the new woman, an old hunchback, outside the house to safety. There is no time, she told Julián, the baby is coming!

Julián's eyes unglued from the girls' room, a rare sadness settling inside his heart. Almost gone, he crouched behind her half-naked body. Holding her legs, and pulling her knee toward her chest, he helped birth another of him. Simmering under his skin, this memory of another time came—what is it? Julián asked himself. A knife-like sensation. At my back.

The baby slid out, a last one, fully formed—alive, delivered as quickly as the earthquake had stopped. A boy, eyes open, and breathing.

December 23, 1972, 12:29:44 A.M.

Benjamin Rodriguez.

BOOK TWO

I opened the cab door, the perfume of pine and lavender greeting me. Air flowed in my direction from the little car outlets like jet engines that will never make me fly, stilling the sweat that had started to bead my forehead.

To the airport, I told the driver.

I sauntered through Newark's terminal B, passed security, and lingered inside the Duty-Free shops. Twelve hours to kill, I told myself, walk some more. The sound of shoes against the coldness of the airport's floors, the feel of the world's anticipation to move away from itself, for a weekend, a week, and for some, like me, for a no-return to somewhere; to anywhere, to a place you think you know, to a place you think will want you again—and keep you.

I walked into the bar, pulled by the rhythm of a song I once had heard, its words validating.

It was full.

And I looked up.

The barman smiled.

He wore a red bandana around his head and an earring hung from his left ear. The face, angular and rough, wore a two-day shadow bordering on the unkempt. But it wasn't. His eyes beamed through me—and they were not practiced eyes, the intent clear, for they were not the eyes of a man looking at a woman with the desire to fuck. No. He looked at me as if he knew— understood, that existence is just the way it is, that we cannot alter its course,

115

because we follow a fate written long before our knowing. Eyes holding me, telling me we are stronger than our past. And I wished I could have stayed, forever there, behind those Tahoe blue eyes, to the beat of perceptions that make us wonder less about where we are headed.

I managed to find a stool between two women. I let my carry-on fall to the floor, and I placed my elbow on the bar, and I took them in. Both were heavy, with bodies soft, fleshy, and neglected by an absent will to live. I felt the stare and turned to welcome it. A Caesar, please.

He turned around and removed a bottle from its nook. What's your name?

I watched him wet the rim of a highball glass with lime, then dunk it into a saucer filled the seasoned funk of celery salt. I watched him still, pouring the liquid from a studied height, known only to him. He planted the celery stick into the thickness of the drink and delivered it, placing it on the bar.

It's a secret.

Pleasure, then, beautiful stranger, I hope you enjoy this.

I licked the saltiness away, looking up at him. Thanks. But—yours?

He smiled. It was warm. Pure. I'll play your game—I won't tell you. Where are you going?

He looked as though I could have trusted him, and I'm sure I could have trusted those eyes, even if in them, a color, so ambivalent, was waving at me. Yet there was clearness. As clear as him, of that, I was sure. Because, when sanity returns in full force, you can trust yourself as well. You just hope it won't leave you.

None of your business.

Of course … Where are you not going, then? he asked, amused.

I ignored his question and pointed to the video playing on the screen hanging above the shelves where the bottles were standing.

The Hip, he said. My favorite band. My favorite song, too. He started to sing, this favorite song of his, repeating the title, the chorus—it's a good life if you don't weaken.

Yeah, I thought, and it's a damn good lie. Because without my own, I wouldn't be here. I would be dead.

Weaknesses saves, too, you know. And what about you, I asked. Where are you not going?

He stayed silent, took half a grapefruit from the small refrigerator encased below the counter. His hands. His hands. I saw them. Fixated on them. Large and uncompromised by real strength. He squeezed its juice inside a shooter glass still dripping from its wash, added vodka, and downed it. Then all over again, the same motions, the same hand squeezing—the same one-handed strength. He downed it again then wiped his mouth, leaving it half opened. I'm not going back home, he said.

I am. But I can't tell you where it is. Can't tell anyone.

He must have said something, because I saw his lips move, but I heard nothing, not the music, not his voice, not even mine. And I felt it again, this fear taking root inside my head, the paranoia wavering inside of me. I took my drink and my bag and sauntered to the end of the room and found the only spot available. I placed my drink on the table, brushed the crumbs off the leather bench and let myself fall, hugging my bag. From where I was seated, I could see him staring at me. It was dark. The air was fresh, casino-like fresh. I fixed my hair, suddenly feeling the weight of desire creep up between my legs. It had been so long.

But I was fading.

I pushed my bag farther along the bench, placed my head on it, and waited for morning to come.

When I left the bar, the next morning, the two women seated at the bar were sleeping on the fold of their arms. Another man was at the helm of the bar. Another vagrant. He was gone. This other human with no name. I don't know why but sadness rose to my throat, scratching it with a taste I understood too well—loss.

I walked to my gate just in time.

Once boarded, I placed my carry-on deep in the bin and stumbled on my seat, near the wing.

I should have known—they were waiting for me at the other end. Managua. Alerted by my parents, no doubt.

They brought me back here. This place.

A place for my kind.

I roam and I wander here now, but it's the same hell. A maze of corridors everywhere, a slew of robot-like people I can never recognize, and I ask myself, why? And I think, how redundant, these corridors of this hell, perfectly matching the alleys he has burrowed inside my own thinking.

Here dear, the nurse said, take these. It's 4:00 P.M. It's time.

I throw the two little white gems to the back of my throat, from where they will slide into my esophagus and down to my stomach, and hopefully, cross the blood-brain barrier. Soon. And when they do, I am no longer me, but think that I am.

Mad Honey

S itting underneath the mango tree's large crown, Julián sipped his second morning coffee, looking straight ahead to where Luis and Benjamin were kneeling, his fingers quietly squeezing a cigarette, observing their play.

Except for the vegetation, an abundance now manicured, and the removal of the terracotta roof following the large earthquake, the courtyard still breathed of a past known to him only. Tapping his fingers on the worn-out couch he was seated on, Julián lifted his head. Hundreds of mangoes, approaching ripeness, had turned red, threatening to soon drop. With scrutiny, he looked at them, his eyes pausing on the few that hung from the branch sprouting from the tree's lowest limb. Leaving them float beyond the carmine-colored hues, he squinted—a summon of his own making, and he thought of Sophia.

The sun was arching, still, the zenith far from its mark, and Julián could feel warmth penetrating his shoulders. A caress, willful in its intention. Drawing a long breath, he slowly returned his attention to Benjamin and Luis. Should I call for breakfast, hijos, or should we wait for Mamá to come down?

Luis lifted his head. Mamá is still sick, Papi. She told Mino and me to let her sleep, not to wait for her.

Upon hearing his son's words, Julián remained impassive. A week had passed since the last miscarriage. Another girl, gone, and more of melancholia's tentacles were settling into Philomena by the day, teasing her thoughts. Her flesh was never right, anyhow, he thought—the critical massing of sorrow pressing on the mother she still wanted to be, even at her age, will win over her sanity, of that, Julián was becoming certain. He shrugged the thought away, focusing on Benjamin only.

The thirteen-year-old boy, a hand wriggling inside a large rectangle glass jar, seemed elsewhere, absorbed by the battle being fought before him. Under Luis's puzzled gaze, the boy remained silent, his fingers hovering above the universe he had created.

How did you choose them? Luis asked, eyes like globes.

Not looking up, Benjamin said that the week before he had found two spiders, two large Wandering Spiders, wrestling near his pillow while resting in in the barn, late at night. The idea came to me then, he continued. We see so many on the road to school, and so I got this idea, you know, to regroup some of them, see which one is strongest, and caught the ones I thought would play with me.

He shook his head. Play ... with you ... these things?

Exactly that, Luis.

The boy's eyes stayed on the content of the jar. Inside, an eerie stage had been set—twenty large spiders, different species of them, had been trapped, together with dozens of small insects busy crawling the sides of the container. A few black scorpions, too, were still, frozen at the bottom of the jar, their tail curled like scythes. The scene—a curiosity made of delicate movements, as if the eight-legged creatures, out of synch, slow-motioned through a thickness of air akin to that of liquid, its resistance only guessed. Your collection, Benjamin, is like a nightmare.

Lo sé, Luis. But you have to agree, it's a spectacular one.

It's true, Julián thought, as he listened to them talking. Striped, horned, and of striking coloring and different sizes, the spiders seemed to form an improvised ballet few could not stare at. Yet, most humans knew, the softness and poise the creatures assembled was deceptive, something the eye would notice, quickly blinking at the strange choreography.

Intrigued by his youngest son's composure, the father reclined, examining Benjamin, and weighing on the boy's physicality. Of late, Benjamin had become taller, his frame as if brimming with new muscular density, his voice dropping the length of a few octaves. One year younger than Luis, light, brown-skinned Benjamin had always appeared older than his negro-looking older brother, and everything pointed to nature's course remaining. Luis, born with a bad case of asthma, appeared fragile, still, dainty almost, but for the width of his shoulders, making his silhouette almost schizophrenic looking. There is no fear in him, Julián thought, an eyebrow lifting, and fixating on Benjamin's eyes—the strength living inside a strange absence. Stranger than mine.

The clicking of metal on wood was heard, and then a soft and feminine voice calling to them. Andie appeared from the kitchen door that led to the courtyard, sandaled feet to the ground, her hair loose and wavy, and holding the silver pummel of a white cane. She smiled, knowing of his own, the smile her fingers had often traced when alone with Julián. So many nights. Señor Julián, where should we set the breakfast table this morning?

Julián paused, and playing with the tip of his beard, rusted by time and yellowed by his uncurable smoking. He cleared his throat. By the fountain, near the hedge of roses. It will do Philomena some good to catch the sun's warmth, no? The boys need her, Andie.

Okay, señor Julián. I will ask Anita to get the señora and set the table outside.

Wanting to examine them from up-close, Julián stood and walked to where his sons were now seated on the stone covered ground.

In silence, the boys were watching a large, white and hairy spider quickly manipulate the body of a smaller one. Observing it sink its mandibula into the soft belly of a dark and hairier specimen, Benjamin suddenly laughed, pointing to the liquid oozing from the crawler's abdomen—milk!

It's not, Luis, said, repulsed, it's gut, Mino. And it's disgusting ...

Standing from the ground, brushing the dirt off the back of his trousers, Julián looked at Benjamin, his stance defying. You said you wanted to know which one was strongest, Mino. Which do you think it is?

Benjamin stood as well, telling him to wait. Expectant, both Luis and Julián watched him walk the narrow pebbly road leading to the back of the barn, their curiosity poked, and they waited in silence. Within two minutes of having left, Benjamin reappeared, a loose fist to his chest, a black case tucked under his armpit, his pet pig in tow. The boy knelt, not acknowledging the glances, and carefully placing his case to the ground, he proceeded to remove the pierced lid from the top of the jar. Slowly unrolling his fingers, inside the palm of his hand—a baby bat, wriggling and struggling to move. Pinching its veiny wings together, he lowered the fledging inside the container, releasing the wings, and snapping the lid closed. Do you think I should get one of the newborn kittens instead, he asked no one in particular.

No, Mino. I don't think you should, Luis replied.

Why not? asked Julián. Kittens are as plenty as cockroaches around here.

Both boys lifted their heads, only Benjamin smiling.

Luis, Julián said flatly, go back to the barn, get us one kitten, the smallest one of the litter.

Papi ...

Ahora.

Papi.

Julián reached down the pocket of his worn-out army jacket retrieving a pack of Marlboros and a lighter. He gently tapped a cigarette out, and placing it atop his hand, between two knuckles, he struck the top of his wrist, sending the cigarette flipping high into the air, his lips, large and wet, catching it. Upholding Luis' gaze, he slowly lit his stick—a long and serious pump. As he exhaled, sending a straight line of smoke into the boy's eyes, Julián moved toward him and raised his hand. Luis coughed, and closing his eyes to protect them from the exhale, never heeded the motion—the back hand stroke was quick and hard, denting Luis's left cheek with Julián's insignia ring. A gift slipped out from a stranger's dead finger. One more chance, son …

Luis turned his head to Benjamin, immobile, and considering the unthinkable, pleaded with his brother to interfere—make the moment vanish. Benjamin's eyes remained to the ground, a hand on the piglet's snout. Shaunny, he said, such a good boy.

Okay, Luis, thought.

Bringing a hand to where blood had started to dribble, and with slow rolling tears burning the newly formed wound, he walked steadily to the barn and opening its doors, disappeared behind the wooden structure. When he returned, both hands were cupped, inside them a kitten, its coat still wet, its eyes still closed.

Whatever was left of his military decorations—in this no-man land where right-wingers had dispersed like lost ants, like he had, but still hanging onto to the possibility of combatting the leftist he hated, and now in power—they mattered, and feeling the beat of his ego, loud and victorious, he pushed some of the unruly hairs back behind his ears. Good, Amorito, he said. Now place it inside the jar.

In silence, Luis removed the lid from the jar, and avoiding looking at the fauna Benjamin had created, gingerly placed the newborn kitten beside the wriggling bat. Closing the lid, he took a step back, staring at his father.

The hunchbacked woman came out of the house, Andie in tow, carrying a tray filled with the morning's meal.

Where is Philomena, Anita?

Anita paused, distress in her eyes. Upon entering her mistress's bedroom, the old woman had come upon a scene, a mingling of grotesque and pathos, Philomena crying, her tears rolling down from her chin to her chest, mucus flowing from her nostrils, and she had brought her finger below her pelvis, inserting it inside herself, a well filled with the ghosts of the children she had lost—her memories. Knowing of Anita's presence, she had continued to twirl and to probe. Bringing the finger back to where she could see it, she had stared at the red slime, fluid thick with evidence of her flaws. When Philomena, closing her eyes, had started to lick it, Anita slowly retreated, a hand to her throat. She cannot get out of bed, señor Julián. She is still bleeding. She is still crying. And bowing to him, relieved, she set the table and returned to the kitchen.

Waving a hand to the air in dismissal, Julián turned to Benjamin. Go on, boy, let me have a word with your brother. He moved closer to his son, lowering his head to his. How did you kill it, Luis?

The boy fidgeted, and coughed, his father's breath, tobacco filled reaching his throat. He slightly turned his face away from Julián's.

The father considered the son, assessing his progeny with despondency. I see, Luis. You wanted to spare it or spare yourself when you choked it?

Luis took a step back, placing his hands inside his front pockets.

Do you think I don't know, Luis, that the thing you brought back from the barn was already dead? He narrowed his eyes on the boy's lips, chapped and flaky, the red of them almost emptied. You think you are clever, hijo, that you can outsmart me? Do you know what all this is telling me, Luis? he asked, rhetorically. That I need to do better, as of today. A stronger wind pushing through them, and he breathed with it, as if in harmony. The tone, formal—I should have started with you sooner, Luis. My mistake, hijo. Mine only. He looked over to Benjamin, now seated at the table, waiting for them to join him. No cowards will bear the Rodriguez name, he let out between his teeth. Not you and your weak lungs, certainly not your brother. He started for the table, confidence stamping his gait. Sitting beside Benjamin, he removed the linen napkin from under the fork, tucking it neatly inside his shirt. He pointed to the empty chair to his left. Come sit, now.

Luis walked slowly to the chair, head bent, obeying.

I will teach you, Julián went on, as he served himself some eggs and bread, to never make a mess, to plan well, and to plan for success. And if you do—answer to your impulses—clean them up. Well. With his fork, he stabbed a slice of mango, placing it in his mouth. He chewed slowly, letting the fruit glide inside his throat, his eyes half-closed, trance-like. The trick, Amoritos, is to follow my mantra—never get caught and choose worthy allies. You will see, he continued, as he poured himself more coffee, during my excursions, on my watch, you will learn how to be. I was ten when I became a man. Both of you are late to the party. Biting into another piece of mango, he looked to the barn, brooding. Like I said—my fault.

As if on cue, a small viper emerged from the tree's shadow, slowly undulating toward them, its tongue and eyes measuring space. Julián, fork in hand, quickly stood and walked to the reptile, bending to it, and he quickly placed the side of the fork against the serpent's neck, forcing the mouth to remain wide open. The serpent's tail began to curl in vain protest, twisting onto itself. Unphased, Julián squished its neck with his two fingers, and picking it up from the ground he walked to the glass jar, removed its lid, and dropped the reptile headfirst inside the container. Eso, he said, walking back to the table. The perfect tableau.

Benjamin, wide-eyed, stared at the snake, now coiled, its scaly cold skin against the glass wall of the jar. Let's see, now, he said, who will be the victor. Benjamin stood, and walking to the jar, sat on the ground. From the black case left beside the jar, he retrieved a small paper pad and a charcoal pen. Stretching his body, his belly flat to the ground, he stared at the scene and started to draw.

Julián looked at Luis and smiled, you failed son, and pointing to the container, he started to laugh. The newborn cat has started to move.

He grabbed the cup and sipped more of his coffee. It's your birthday, Amorito, next month. Fifteen—your magic number. He placed the cup back on its saucer, lacy and gold rimmed. To celebrate, we're going to the cabin, Luis. A perfect little adventure, a ritual.

Just for you, Luis. Then, of course, your brother, too.

And for fuck's sake, Luis, stop your crying.

Benjamin and Luis sat quietly in the back of the truck, scanning the landscape, flat and dull looking, the sun-yellowed grass against another cloudless sky. Mostly linear, the dirt road was busy with small buses and motorcycles, their fumes sketching circles of black behind them. The windows, rolled down, and Luis coughed, bringing the inside of his elbow to his mouth. I hate this, Mino, he said wiping his mouth.

Tough it out, Luis, his father said. We're almost there.

Luis stayed looking out the window, a feeling of dread travelling through him.

You'll soon see, his father continued, Tipitapa is beautiful. It's river mostly. And the house, a present from Somoza, he whispered, nostalgia in his voice.

I've only been here once, Benjamin added, but Papi is right. The river … the falls.

A wonderful time, Julián whispered.

It's your birthday, Philomena said with a smile. Tomorrow night, we celebrate.

Julián's wife placed a hand on her belly, soft and tentative, the other hand, on her husband's thigh, and looked straight ahead. It's a good thing we left the help at home, she whispered. A little more intimacy. Space, too.

We should have brought, Shaunny, Benjamin said. He doesn't like it when I'm not there.

Slowly, she turned around to face the boys, her chin resting on the edge of her seat, her hands gripping their sides. Andie and Anita are with him, Mino, he'll be fine. She steadied herself more, fighting the truck's rumblings. You are my loves, you two boys, she said. The men I've always wanted. She pivoted her body, sinking her bony back into the hot leather of her seat. What type of cake do you want me to bake, Luis, tomorrow night?

The truck swerved to the right, entering a narrow driveway bordered by large avocado and almond trees. In silence, they rolled on for three hundred meters more, the small two-storied house emerging, flanked by gigantic mango trees, and bushes of red poinsettias surrounding the colonial structure.

Julián cut the engine and removed the key from its hole. Vanilla, of course, Julián said, laughter pouring from his mouth. Luis will have his first ever vanilla cake.

The bunkbeds were located on the second level of the house, adjacent to their parent's bedroom.

I know we're here for your birthday, Benjamin said, but I'm keeping the top.

Already underneath the covers, Luis was focusing on the orange and black striped millipede crawling along the base of Benjamin's bed above him. I don't care, Mino. I really don't. He moved to his side, bringing the crinkled linen sheet above his shoulder. Why did he bring us here?

Steady rain had started to fall, interrupting the crickets' loud chirping, and hammering the roof—straight lines, like weighted strings.

It's your birthday, Luis. He told us. That's why.

No. There's something more, I can feel it. He swallowed, his brain on alert. Since the civil war has ended, since he left the National Guard, Papi's been different, Mino.

I know. Benjamin paused. Yes, it's true, he changed, but somehow, something in him remains.

Violence.

Yes.

The way he dresses, too, said Luis, has changed. Always in his kakis, disheveled, and smoking so much. And we know the civil war is over. They tossed him out. So why the costume, still?

I think he looks cool.

Really? Mamá hates it.

She hates everything.

No. Just him.

No. I think she still loves him. Is quite obsessed with him. Why else would she stay?

The rain increased, the winds battering into the closed shutters, untied and loose. Luis extended a hand to the windowsill, poking a finger in the pool of water that had accumulated, then closed the shutters' latches properly. Mino, he said, Nicaragua is not the same. It's changing, too. And in the wrong direction for us. Even Somoza died in Paraguay.

Murdered. I don't know how it is Papi is still alive. Shouldn't he be afraid. And us, too?

Afraid of what? The civil war never came close to killing him. And ever since Somoza's murder ... Benjamin looked around, we've never had so many men guarding our house in Managua.

And yet, none of them are here, said Luis. It's been four years now since Ortega's win. His Sandinista bullshit. And soon, he will be elected. The Contras, too, chased into the jungle. Four years, Mino. Luis closed his eyes. He killed for a living, then, you know. And not just for the cause. For his pleasure.

How do you know that?

I heard him talk last night over the phone when I went to see Mamá in the bedroom while she was packing. Something about more training—more jungle training. We know that's code for killing, Mino. They fought, too, something about a mission nearby. Women missionaries. Mamá became hysterical, and I heard his laugh, Mino. I know his laugh. Like when he goes mad, he thought. Do you think he will join the Sandinistas?

That's a weird question. Why would he? What's the link between those women and the Sandinistas?

I don't know ... Because he's bored? And you know what happens when he gets bored and restless. *Nothing* good ever happens.

Still, Luis. It's stretching it, no? I don't think it's true. He hates the Sandinistas ... They are fighting the old world, Luis. His world. We saw those churches along the way to here, remember? Burned down. Vandalized. And the billboards—Coke, Salem, KitKat, all destroyed. They're trying to purge the country from a hated trinity, one Papi loves: red, white, and blue, the right-wing cassocks and collarinos. Slavery from the Yankees.

I don't know ...

131

No, I really don't think it's true, Luis. He can't join them ... He hates them too much.

Maybe you are right, Mino, maybe he hates them. But we both know, in the end, he wouldn't care which sides he can kill for. As long as he can ...

Tal vez, brother. He doesn't back down, you are right on that. A long sigh like a whistle came from Benjamin's mouth. Maybe, he'll do like you say, make himself fit into the mess Nicaragua has become. No sé, hermano.

Luis paused, his certainties inside him, ones he could only feel, not able yet to articulate—torture, rape, and murder, the government's entitlement to claim, and justify.

Nicaragua, like all the other central American countries surrounding it, whether run by left or right winged bodies, drank from the same clouded water—an antidote that kept them from feeling, denying humans the right to live, their lives—worthless lives to them, and easy to dispose of. Julián wouldn't care, would he? What was right for him? I don't want to be like him, he said. Maybe ... Nicaragua hasn't changed at all.

What choice do we have?

Easy for you to say, you two are alike. He bit his lower lip. During the civil war, remember all the children he recruited for the cause. He fell in love with them, you know.

Brave children, he always said.

Not all of them

I know, but most.

What about them?

I am not like them. Luis shook his head. Something is not right, Mino.

Everything is perfect big brother.

Stop lying. Mamá is changing. She barely sees me. Only has eyes for you. Says you remind her of Papi at the same age.

Don't be jealous.

No. It's not that, Mino.

The boys stayed silent.

I'm afraid. Of both of them. He wrung his hands. They are both mad … for different types of bleeding …

With an elbow supporting the side of his body, Luis raised his torso and looked up, imagining Benjamin on his back. I was born undone, and you know it. But you, Mino, you came out ready for this world. This one, here, now.

You mean damaged, like him.

The word tumbling inside his head, Luis closed his eyes, the soft touch of the milliped crawling over is forearm, his breathing becoming short. This fear, he thought, is going to kill me. He dropped a hand to the floor, sending the insect to the ground, his fingers searching for the cortisone filled pump placed below the bed. Finding it, he brought it to his mouth and pressed the release button. Then he closed his eyes.

Tipitapa is located on the river of the same name, Julián said, walking to the shore ahead of where they were. It leaves lake Managua about twenty-two kilometers northeast of the city of Managua and flows into lake Nicaragua to the southeast. It connects both lakes. He pointed to the right. Look at those falls, boys. Paradise. A perfect place to be.

The rain had ceased, and the air, moist and oppressive, had drawn from their pores large circles of sweat now imprinting their shirts. Benjamin removed his, tucking it at the waist, inside the back of his Bermuda shorts, and Luis did the same.

Are there any crocodiles in there? Luis asked his father.

Bull sharks, mostly, when they leave Lake Managua, Julián replied, staring at the two women soaking in a pool of water not far from the shore. Hot springs. Tourists love them.

There's barely anyone, Benjamin said, pointing at the four groups of young men and women dispersed among the series of natural hot pools.

Our lucky day, isn't it? the father whispered.

The three men looked over to where the two women seemed to be floating, their heads just above the water, and speaking a language unrecognizable to the boys.

Swedish, Julián, whispered, that or Dutch. Norwegian, maybe.

How do you know? Luis asked.

Just look at their hair. Shiny. Platinum blonde.

Hair can't talk.

Yes, Luis, it can, and swiftly he turned toward him, his eyes mocking. You don't think your nigger hair says anything about you? That there isn't a story, a sad narrative inside each of your dry and prickly black stubs? He continued to walk. Your hair is a passport to nowhere, hijo. But theirs— just like skin.

What about *your* hair? Benjamin asked.

Julián moved his hand over his mane. It causes confusion in most people I meet. It's always been my ally.

And … what about mine?

Julián laughed and tapped the top of Benjamin's head. All I can say about your hair, hijo, is that one day, unlike your brother, and God knows why, the top of your cranium will be shinier than my combat boots.

Benjamin shrugged his shoulders. But they were always dirty, Papi, your boots.

Exchanging a short glance, in silence, they continued, their pace slow, reaching a small group of tall palm trees, their roots like hands grabbing the grassy soil. Lifting his head, Benjamin noticed a heron leaving its rookery, the nest firmly built inside the bushes adjacent to the current of the river. He watched it fly a short flight, the bulky bird skimming the water's surface until plunging into it. He watched it fly back to its nest, a fish in its mouth.

Are we there yet, Papi? Luis asked, nervously.

Julián pointed to a narrow beach, 200 meters from where the women were bathing.

We'll hide behind the bushes, behind that small dune.

Hide?

Hide.

We're spending the rest of the afternoon here?

Julián turned to his son, his eyes beaming, inflating his chest. Yes, Luis.

The boy's face became stern, a warning settling inside his belly.

Once at the dunes, contouring debris littering the shore, they stepped over elevated tree roots, and avoiding the small mound a colony of termites had started to edify, they spotted a set of rocks. Carefully, they each chose one on which to sit on, and as if knowing what to do, they waited, staring at Julián removing his shirt—the same rosary, idle, pink and red beads clinging to the wet ones pearling from his sternum. A familiar sight. Bringing the old straw-made Christ hanging on the cross to his mouth, he kissed the crucifix.

Now fifty-six years old, Julián's physique still commanded, his posture, a long erection of the body, sinewy, and never tilting. Over time, through spartan regimes imposed by the rigor of the training camps devised to infuse men, women, and children with grit, supply his country with strong nationalist vittles, Julián's body had remained lean yet robust, his face structure, just as obtuse. But the blue of his eyes, clear and deep, compounded with the leathery sheen of his skin and the flaxen of his straight hair, had always been the lure. And like a novel motif, exotic and rare, reinforced by the man's awareness; of what catches; of what yields—together, the features arrested the feminine eye, still.

He smoked, one after the other, a never-ending hurricane of smoke, stale and waiting around his head, and from their safe distance, he observed the women talking, their words inaudible. We will continue to wait from here.

Wait for what?

For the right one to leave. For the right one to stay. Luis. In the meantime, just look. Dive in.

The boy brought a hand to his chest, the other, he slid inside his Bermuda front pocket. I can't breathe, Papi.

Julián turned to him, annoyed. Take a puff now, Luis, I don't want any noise coming from your pussy mouth. You hear me?

Luis, unable to move, started to shake, and looked at Benjamin with pleading eyes.

Without a word, Benjamin stood from his rock, walked the few meters separating them. Here, he said, as he slid a hand inside Luis' pockets, retrieving the pump and placing it against his brother's dry lips. Don't fuck up, he whispered.

The late afternoon was nearing, and the ceiling of clouds, low and homogeneous, was stretching furthermore over the sky's dark tint. It's going to rain, Luis whispered, as he stood from his rock. We should head back home. Mamá is waiting.

The voice—harsher. We are not done. I'll tell you when its time, hijo. Sit the fuck down.

I wish I could understand them, Benjamin said, undeterred by his father's tone, and looking at the young women.

What for? Julián asked. What they have to say is never important. Wherever they come from.

I'd like to understand, mumbled Luis, confused.

A riddle dancing in his eyes, Julián laughed. And what would you possibly do with your understanding? Try and court them, marry one of them, even? You think they want to have anything to do with you?

I would, Benjamin said, pensive, and both, at the same time. Marry them.

Then why bring me here? Luis replied, ignoring Benjamin's comment.

To punish them, Luis. For their ignorance.

The sound of laughter caught their attention, redirecting their thoughts. The women they could see from between the branches and the bushes, were sitting on the edge of the spring, its soil damp, their feet remaining inside the steaming water. They continued talking, delight marking their faces. Unable to stifle more of the heat, the girls removed their bikini tops unknowing of the masculine gazes contemplating their curves—their juvenile breasts, unaltered by time, pale colored nipples, engorged, rippled by air infusing dents, their dancing hips, and their lips rouged more by the heat.

How old do you think they are, Papi? Benjamin asked, unable to remove his eyes from the tallest one.

I'd say around twenty-five. Maybe younger. Intrigued, Julián looked at Benjamin, noting how immobile he had become. I'm here, for Luis, he thought to himself, not for him, not yet.

The short and stubbier looking one raised a finger, mumbling staccato filled words, and slid back into the pool, disappearing into the water's murkiness. Crouching, her body fully submerged, she unfolded with her hands glued to her belly. Still oblivious to the men's presence, their laughter carefree sounding, the young women continued to talk, the girls painting each of their faces with the gathered mud. Spreading the earth onto the blinding white of their skin, they proceeded to draw, on each of their cheeks. This squarish shape.

Julián slid a cigarette from behind his ear, and lighting it up, travelled an improvised travel to the mornings of his youth, a time with Marisol and Luna. Round and rosy visages appeared to him, long hair, too, like wavy ropes, black and shiny, as if he could touch it, the scent of lilies floating from the creases of their necks. Those mornings had a song in them, a song that was with him now, and resounding. A stability. A completeness. Peace. Antonio's face appeared to him. Alberto's, too. Unwanted apparitions, sending him into another space.

If the boys had looked at him, they would have thought their father locked inside his usual vacancies. But the man, inclined to nothing but effusive thinking, became pensive, his forehead lined deeper, a set of grooves piled from the bridge of his nose to the edge of his hairline. He brought a finger to his face, caressing his sagging cheek, and when he did, he brushed its tip against the hide it had become. A stealth motion unnoticed by his sons.

Benjamin, absorbed by the women's gesture, became entranced, too, and focused on the space the one woman's finger had drawn. A son unknowingly inhabiting the same instant as his genitor, and he continued to fixate on the tall woman, her hair braided into tresses she was bringing up and pinning to the back of her head.

For two hours they waited for the youngish crowd around them to leave and for the night to come. For dusk to fall like an old cape.

Julián had known—his prediction, reliable and telling, manifesting itself. Everyone had left except for the two girls they had stalked. They waited more, until satisfied no one was left to see them, and Julián stood, oblivious to the swarm of mosquitoes that had formed around them. Luis, your birthday present, here before you: vanilla cakes.

You are late, Philomena said, visibly concerned. Dinner has been ready for four hours, Julián.

Benjamin pulling a chair to the table, sat. We went to the lake instead of the river, Mamá. Took a boat up, went fishing. Then we came across a cockfight. Papi insisted we go.

Slowly, she scanned their expressions. Did you win?

Yes, we did, Mamá. We won big.

Philomena turned to her husband, disheveled and shirtless, still, like Benjamin, and he returned her stare. In his eyes, something less was worming, something she had rarely witnessed before. The stare of a defeated man. She looked over to Benjamin. The boy was beaming, a new assurance in his eyes—yet more extinction in its light. Your chest, Julián, she said, the scratches.

With an index finger, Julián traced the numerous marks, long and deep lacerations, now exposed on his torso. Branches along the shore, he said.

Benjamin and his father looked at one another.

She felt her body stiffen, her face aged by fate, hard and unforgiving, by time, used and misunderstood. She propped her frizzy gray hair into a soft bun, eyes askance. Where is Luis?

In his room, Benjamin, said. You didn't hear him go up? Said he felt sick, not to wait.

The mother looked at the table, set with all things celebratory, including the cake placed in the middle. A small lifetime of candles waiting to be lit.

When Benjamin entered the bedroom, Luis, seated on the top of the bunkbed, his back against the wall, was looking at his unwashed hands. I told you, he whispered, his voice shaky.

Benjamin, pulling himself onto the top mattress, sat next to Luis, but he did not speak, feeling stamped by the dawn of something alien taking life inside of him. There is no use in fighting it, he thought. He looked at his brother, at his hands, too. But if you want to survive Papi, you need to do better, Luis. He will never change.

Starting to cry, the boy dropped his head on Benjamin's shoulders. I couldn't do what he asked me to do. Pass his test. I can't take someone's life. He lifted his eyes. You saved me tonight, Mino.

What choice did I have?

Did you know he had a knife on him?

Yes, I did. I do. He usually has it with him, Luis.

And you know this …

I guess I do, yes.

The rain had resumed, the jungle's symphony matted by the relentlessness of its fall. Stretching an arm to the window, his fingers playing with the horizontals slats, Benjamin thought about the absence he felt, yet, when looking at Luis, a filament of sadness tugged at him. He has me, Luis. He knows it.

You liked it, Benjamin, I could tell. It came easy.

Benjamin nodded, the pallid color of the girls' bodies flooding his mind—like funeral carnations, and his father, tall and assured, approaching the girls—these libidinal youths, as they were leaving, topless, buoyant, carefree, walking back toward the land. Eyes fixating on the calendar pinned before him—another year, another month—the picture of the Virgin Mary praying, eyes folded to the unseen ground and not looking at him. Why is it we love the Virgin so much, he thought, yet hate the women that walk our life? He arched his neck back. Luis, I may have crossed his line.

What line?

Benjamin brought his hands together, slowly intertwining his fingers.

When Papi approached them, before they realized the bad dream about to come real, they looked at me. They were busy scanning me—not him. They thought we were coming to play, *their* play. They were drunk.

We never noticed they had been drinking, the bottles thrown on the other side of the pool. That's what made it easy. He swallowed. They tried to use approximate Spanish with me—flirting—you saw it—when one grabbed my hand, playfully. He struck them both. Benjamin paused. The second one never had time to move.

I know, Mino …

Papi is a jealous man, Benjamin replied. He usually gets to toy with them first, you know, before …

Raping them?

I guess so.

How do you know all that?

Benjamin looked away yet feeling unashamed. I followed him once and hid in the back of the truck.

You saw him?

Benjamin nodded.

His breathing short, Luis brought his hands to his temple, grabbing his ears. Stop it, he whispered. No more. *No more.*

Slowly, Benjamin took his brother's hands, pulling them down. Listen to me, Luis, you need to get a hold of yourself.

Luis started to shake—a small bird trying to fight winds. We're going to get caught, Mino. I know we will.

Of course, we won't, stupido.

Luis closed his eyes, his lips quivering. What about the bodies?

Better than anyone, he knows what to do. Wildlife will take care of them. They were hippies. Vagrant girls. They won't be missed, and if they are … no one will find their remains. And anyone can be blamed. The Contras as much as the leftists.

Luis looked at his brother. There was so much blood, Mino. So much.

Benjamin sat up, an arm stretched to the ceiling, and he pulled the string to the light bulb toward the ground, the room becoming black. You need to rest. Fatigue nesting inside his chest, Benjamin placed himself behind Luis, sliding underneath the damp sheets with him. A hand caressing his brother's brittle coils, he wondered—about death, about birthdays. Today was about celebrating the arrival of a soul, he thought, a soul replete with hope. Yet, it felt as though the Greeks had been right—birthdays also welcome evil spirits. Isn't that what sister Bettina had told them, not so long ago in English class?

From a distance he heard a monkey's howl, guttural and primitive, their father's voice, too, in tandem with Philomena's screaming, biblical incantations, dictums, delivered in high-pitched uncontrolled tones. And then Benjamin remembered a different moment with his father: Hijo, mírame, Mira, cómo se hace, his father had ordered. He had watched as the whole of Andie, the nakedness of her, lay on the bed, pinned down. Like a rare butterfly, he thought. And her hair, so much of it, tarnished reflections of reds and yellows, swallowed by his father's hands. She likes it. Yes, she does, his father had whispered. Because she doesn't see, she feels so much, you see. Watch carefully, Benjamin. See our hands, hers in mine, and look at her skin. Look at mine. The contrast. That intersection that bleeds into me from her. The white river that seeps into my steeled veins. Benjamin had looked, wondering why his father had chosen him, and not Luis. To be this witness. Give me your hand, son. Touch what I touch, feel what I feel.

Leaving a hand to rest along the side of Luis's face, Benjamin, in the dark, lightly pressed his finger against his brother's cheek, fleshy and tender, and fell into a dead man's sleep.

He left the villa that day with its scents and recesses moving inside his own. He walked amidst the marble and the crystals and the Persian rugs and all things that made this abode what it was—a newly refreshed monument of Spanish colonialism. In his mind, as he left, he carried images of Philomena spread on the couch Julián had placed underneath the large fruit tree years ago, her legs scissoring pillows, their cases soiled with her blood. It must be a miracle, he thought, these continuous late-in-life pregnancies. But he knew better. His mother had been cursed. All in the village knew it. And now, Andie would be hovering above his mother, asking: Would the señora need anything else? His mother, reaching between her legs with her hands, saying, no, that she could go. He could imagine her now, for he had witnessed it often. Andie clenching the silver top of her cane, her nails feeling the intricacies of the carvings, a female wolf nursing her young, as the cane kissed the floors and its surrounding.

Always kissing her way into their lives.

Fifteen-year-old Benjamin walked steadily, a sense of doom leaving him like it did every morning he walked to school—this fleeing from his father's ways, reminders of who he was.

Everything about their relationship had changed that night. He can't forgive me, he thought, thinking of the mixture of sweat and puss dribbling from the sores on his back, the top of his shirt clinging to them. He will torture me until I leave—or die. And let him … He made the barn my house, the critters living inside, my roommates. And as Shaunny came to mind, he thought, at least I have you.

He cleared a path with his feet, crunching dead leaves, the scent of the jungle descending upon him. The morning dew had lifted, the dampness still lathering the air, and he breathed, thick and forceful breaths. Above him a flock of scarlet macaws flew tree to tree, their low-pitch and throaty squawks ruling over the jungle's symphony.

He continued walking, the sun's rays finding a way through the canopy to him. Nestled under his armpit, a small, grey nylon case filled with what his teacher had asked him to bring the day before, his charcoal drawings. Strange and precise they offered a look into a chaotic mind. Sister Bettina Winter had said, I need to see, Mino. The government wants to promote more of the country's folklore, with music, and through literature. It wants to make peace with the world. A form of redemption. And, of course, through art, too. The prize is a full bursary, Mino, to Spain. I think you should send in some of your drawings. His work, she had told Julián and Philomena at the last school meeting, is not often seen. I should know, she had added, I studied art in Berlin before joining the convent. Bauhaus University. And art will quiet him, compensate for his lack of reading ability, she had said. Upon hearing Sister Bettina's praising of her son, Philomena had squeezed her husband's forearm, and feeling the starch of his military coat, she had dug further into the cloth, chipping the nail polish from her freshly manicured hand. Amor, mira, nuestro hijo, un artista … Julián avoided the missionary's eyes, and turning away from her, considered the red markings his wife had made on his sleeve. Gracias, he had said from afar, impatience in his step. Reading is overrated in this land, he said to his wife. Around here, one simply needs to hear. Obey. Philomena. Ahora.

The American School began to emerge between the branches, a one-story building surrounded by students dressed in the blue and white school uniform, like him, and waiting for the sound of the bell to make them move.

Benjamin slowed his pace. The first period of the day was English—poetry.

The first bell rang.

Slowly writing the week's cursus on the upper left side of the blackboard, the teacher stood, her white and long wimple swaying to the back of the room. The students settled, about twenty of them, unphased by the cursive flowing out from her fingers, uncaring of the week's work being spelled out for them. Turning around, she pointed to one of the girls seated at the end of the room by the windows. Victoria, she said, close all the blinds. Today will be a cloudless day, sun filled and hot, she thought, as she scanned the room. And listening to the Monday morning sound—the boisterous talk, the exuberant laughter, and the clatter of chairs—she smiled.

The second bell rang.

She pushed her head up and saw Benjamin seated at his desk, his usual place, the front row. Looking beyond him, she lifted her index finger to her lips and mouthed—Salvador Juárez, "Puro guanaco". Someone of my choosing will recite this poem within the hour. Page fifty. Quietly, inside your brain, she whispered more.

She lowered her head and sat at her desk and looked at the two drawings. She scrutinized the strokes, the blends and the forms. She smiled. The subjects before her, one of a cylinder-shaped vase holding a bouquet of long-stemmed forks, the other a portrait of a choir boy, singing, his eyes endeared by what one imagines he is witnessing, the boy's mouth twisted. Protruding from underneath one of the drawings, the vase one, was the corner of a curled page. She pulled it out, slowly revealing another drawing. A third sketch. Quickly sliding it back underneath, she looked up at Benjamin staring at her. Sweat quickly appeared at the front of her neck and she felt it dribbling down the crease of her breasts. She brought her hand to her chest, pushing the fabric of her habit to it, and then, speaking as if to no one, she told her students she had to go, now, that she would return, that Victoria would be the one reciting Juárez' poem.

Benjamin opened the bathroom door and walked to where his teacher was, bent over the sink, heaving. You don't like my drawings ...

Her mouth dribbled with vomit and with the corner of her wet wimple she cleaned it, brushing her fingers along the borders of her lips. This drawing, Benjamin, she started,

It's my favorite, Sister.

Benjamin …

You told me to go beyond, and I did. I did exactly what you said I should do. Draw my inner life. Dreams of being myself.

From inside her habit, she pulled a piece of paper and unfolded it. Go back to class and fill in the application. We will submit two of your drawings. The other—please burn. She took his face between her hands and told him all would be fine. I am here, she said. I can recognize luminescence long before it reaches God's earth, and I will make sure you leave this infection called Nicaragua.

From the tree's roots she still grew—and yes, ever since the soil became one with pieces of her, she roamed inside the wood's hardness; its dents; its rings. Benjamin leaned on it, this tree, unaware of its past; of the future—the ones it was a witness to and would be always. He caressed its bark with the soft palm of his hand and looked at the maid sweeping the pavement, fascinated by her quasi blindness. Today is here, Andie, he said, I don't want it to be here. Tomorrow is new. I want tomorrow to be here.

She stretched her neck toward him and taking hold of her cane she walked to him, feeling her way through the yard, the light reaching the back of her eye a little more. Come here, Mino, come.

His eyes looked around, feeling space, hoping she would anchor into his own, hoping he could hook on to something—someone. He crossed his arms tightly bringing them to his chest, and he clenched his belly. The ache was always unsettling inside his stomach, a well he kept digging into. He pushed her away. Where is Shaunny?

I don't know, Mino. Maybe ask Luis?

He scanned the property grounds. The pigpen was empty. He descended the stairs to the backyard and pushed the barn door open, and he walked inside.

Dusted light sprinkled the dark, bathing the inside of the old barn, his own quarters. The gap between the ceiling planks allowed some brightness to guide him. He held on to his case, stuffing the drawings back inside that threatened to escape. The letter, too. His eyes shifted everywhere as he walked slowly through the stewed air, remembering how he had toyed with Andie's world, pretending to be her, trying to understand her plight.

He stopped walking, hearing high pitched whimpers. His eyes followed the sound until the rawness arrested him, there—bright drippings of fleshed out flesh. Shaunny had pulled a blanket far to the corner, his snout-less face trembling, his open flanks shiny red, and still pulsing. Benjamin kneeled and locked onto the animal's dying gaze. Father, he whispered, as he lay beside the animal.

He stayed there until the end.

Two days.

Upon waking, only the blanket was left for him to hold onto, a brownish rag soiled with maggot-filled pulp, and slices of cooked meat on a soggy paper plate had been placed on the floor. Feeling observed he looked up at his father holding the school envelope, looking at his son, and smiling. Benjamin returning the stare, smiled the way he always did when alive with rebellion. Yes, he said, I will eat him. Only because I loved him. And hate you.

A welcoming solace inside the hole inside the boy's body, a space that somehow kept him full. Maybe he would bury himself there, too, one day. Maybe, after all, it was the safest place in the world to breathe, the safest place in the world to be.

Eyes fluttering, he opened his mouth and slid the meat inside of it.

From the other side of the window, standing, his mother watched him. She should have walked to him, offered him something, rocked him into another oblivion, a more comfortable one. But she simply looked on.

The courtyard beat to the rain's needling of the soil, a sound the country was used to dance to, just like Philomena was.

Standing in the middle of the yard, cleaning his wounds, she asked her man-boy what it was that compelled him to draw all the time? This life, their life. ¿Y por qué, Mino? Didn't you want to keep our secret intact, Mino?

Benjamin, sitting immobile inside a basin filled with water, vivified by its coldness, thought of Sister Bettina, of her words. No, he said. I didn't want to, I didn't see the point, either.

She moved the sponge over his large upper back, across the width of his hairless chest, too. The blood distilling into a lesser version of itself, by the rain, and by her. You must do what Julián tells you to do, she continued, and go where he tells you to go, Mino. Y quédate donde necesitas quedarte. Escúchalo a él. Stay where you need to and listen to him. Just like Luis always does. Or else he'll continue to beat you. She brushed a finger along the contours of his wounds, old and new. Yes, I know, Amorito. You won the art contest, Mino, and you can let this triumph live secretly in your belly—because he wants you here, as something else. Better. He will not let you go. There is no winning. He loves you. He hates you, too. Upon hearing her words, Benjamin, clenching his teeth, grabbed the rim of the basin with his hands. If you don't bend, she whispered, he will kill you. I know he will. That is how he loves. Her eyes remained on him, a body now embraced by water, translucent and pink. I can't lose you. I've already lost Luis to a permanent sadness ... the girls ... You are all I have left.

For Philomena, loneliness's only lair had become fantasy ... until fantasy meshed with her buoys. Driftwood that would never see land. Her world, a dirt-filled one—the harshness of men, the clutter of chaos, the weight of knowing it will always be and never changing. You'll see, she whispered.

The rain suddenly stopped, and she looked up. No movement above her, only a firmament seen through space the leaves allowed her to see. Gray spaces filled with an infinity of black at their edge. She cried, her fingernails digging into her abdomen, the moment leaving as quickly as it had appeared, and painting a new face onto her. Ponerse de pie, hijo. Benjamin obeyed and stood. Eso. He covered his shoulders with the towel she handed him, and hopped onto the soil, dark and muddy. Philomena took his hand. Sígueme, Mino. Tonight, you are with me. Conmigo, solo.

They walked to the house and climbed the stairs to her bedroom. In silence they lay on the large bed, unaware Julián was watching them. The father looked on, recognizing pain swimming inside two bodies wishing to be elsewhere—he didn't understand. Te amo hijo mio, he thought. I love you the same way Alberto loved me, holding me by the hand while we followed the making of our markings, which were dark always, and heaving inside our brains. Your grandfather didn't understand them, Benjamin, and like him, like me, you won't either. What I know is you must lean into them to survive. I will try to help you as best I can. As best I know.

Inside the house, more dimness, settling and reaching, the sound of the rain coming, again, ever present. Julián remained, letter in hand, reading it one last time.

No, son. You are staying here—

Julián walked through the corridors, and down the stairs, sensing time would start spiraling into its own, from now on. He felt those days coming and knew they would take hold of his son, just as they had taken hold of him, before—oscillations between two selves, the false one dominating over the pure.

Hijo, he whispered, you cannot escape your destiny. It's just impossible.

Anyhow, what can possibly be done? You are already whole. And you will surpass me. I just hope I will continue to love you, when you do.

The Rodriguez villa, otherwise known as la casa del General Azul, referring to the color of Julián Rodriguez' eyes, eyes known to roam, had over time become the heart of the neighborhood, one that was devasted, like the rest of the country, by the large and murderous earthquake of 1972 and a two-decade-long, bloody civil war—Sandinista socialism against Somoza's Liberal right that left in its wake 35,000 men, women, and children dead.

Once the Sandinistas' revolutionary movement successfully overthrew Somoza and his men in 1979, eradicating a forty-three-year-old dynasty in the process, and the 1984 general election democratically confirmed Ortega to the Nicaraguan Presidency, Julián's world remained a world needing to be purged by the same perceived red colored evil.

While the National Guard, a group of men and women highly trained by the American military, foraged the country for young minds willing to die for Somoza's ideology, Julián's ways—efficient and non— were noticed by the American military who fought the Sandinistas in all their forms. General Rodriguez, they had reported back home, was loyal to the cause and displayed charisma that lulled all who worked with him. A snake capable of disguising as a mouse.

The United States of America knew the fight against the leftist movement would need to continue following Somoza's defeat. They wanted to root communism out completely—the Central Intelligence Agency needing someone inside the walls of the Casa Presidencial. Someone to relay information. A reliable insider.

On a sunny morning, as he walked the muddy streets of his barrio to the local café where his daily poker game waited for him, two white men accosted him. Flanking Julián, they told him the game had been cancelled, to follow them to the Jeep parked in front of the gates to his villa. A gun pointed to the side of his torso, Julián obeyed.

For two hours, seated in the back, Julián listened, his eyes taking in the landscape he knew inside and out, the jungle and his soul—the one and the same. We know, General Rodriguez, everything about you, the driver said. The angel, the monster—we have hardcore evidence. Proof. If you want us to keep it a secret—and maybe continue feeding your nasty ways—your son's?—we need you at the presidential office, the other one continued.

And so, General Rodriguez, another American-made puppet, through a series of subtle modifications—a change of name only known to him, Frederico Castillo, the issuing of a new Nicaraguan passport, the dying of his hair black, and the creation of a new life story that made a single man out of him, was able to infiltrate the ranks of those that worked closely with President Ortega. Versed in the art shapeshifting, he would forever be kept in place, remaining faithful to none, even through Chamorro's reign, the winning candidate of the 1990 general election.

And while Julián Rodriguez slowly faded away, giving birth to another identity, no one in the household dared questioned the new look and the repeated absences, his travels to America, Miami—his demeanor had remained the same.

Just like the dancing inside the blue of his eyes.

Inside the villa, this new hope—Marxist fed, one that spread through Nicaragua, where its people moved and lived to the pulse of belief-filled wills, eager to live peacefully within the soft confines joy and equality were promised, their coexistence, a true-thought reality—was never felt.

Luis had become almost mute, almost catatonic, only speaking to Benjamin the few times Benjamin was home. Having abandoned high school, unable to function, Luis became a human foulbrood, walking the small circumference of the courtyard, morning to night, anxious for his brother to return from law school.

On her good days, Philomena, wanting to escape a life burdened by Julián's repeated abuse, had returned to spreading the word of her catholic God to the small barrios and the poverty-stricken villages that still crawled on the land. But when reality would find her again, equally bruising flesh and spirit, the woman retreated into her head, watched and cared for by the housemaid acquired on the day of the large earthquake in 1972. Anita the hunchbacked, they called her. By Andie, too, who would prove loyal until her very end.

Contrary to Luis, since that night by the river, Benjamin's ruses had sharpened. A new man born, a man with a better understanding of himself. An acceptance cautioned by the sword that would be his forever, his lack of conscience, the profundity of an absence even Julián would only come to envy. Despise, too.

While pursuing law, following his graduation from the American school, the seed grew, yet not fully exploited, its stem seeking the sun, bright and warm with fertility. Benjamin continued what had come to him so naturally: the will to haunt; to kill; to collect what had become his obsession: white squares of skin; scales of white; hues of clouds—silver lined, maybe.

Julián had watched over his son's deeds from a distance, witnessing Benjamin's recklessness, understanding he would need to interfere, if not distract the pulsion he knew he had directed.

For years, when home for dinner, Julián pestered Benjamin. Settle down, marry, hijo. Give yourself the gift of a child. Of a woman. It was following a family dinner wrought with the same insistence, soon after abandoning his law degree, that Benjamin announced he had fallen in love, the neighbor's daughter, he said, the farmer we all love. Shoving a spoonful of crispy rice in his mouth, grains dropping from his plump lips, Benjamin continued, we are getting married next month—she is expecting.

Six-month-pregnant Desirée Zafón, ten years older than her groom, married Benjamin Rodriguez surrounded by her sisters and a medicated Luis Rodriguez, Benjamin's best man. In the middle of her father's cornfield, they held the small ceremony, the rain that day replaced by the piercing of a stable sun. It could have been a new beginning, Julián would think later when alone and missing his son, but like any beginnings, false starts can await, too.

One stormy day, following a dispute concerning the concealing of Benjamin's on-going violence: dead, white women—tourists, found with mutilated faces—Julián decided he had to be stopped. Something was bound to become unmanageable, consequences that could be far reaching, unavoidable threats needing to be mitigated.

Seated at the table, as Philomena cleared the table, Julián slid a hand inside his jacket pocket, retrieving a leathered-like card. I've had a word with someone high-placed in my network, Benjamin. Here, he said, eyes into Benjamin's, look. The father handed his son a new passport. I want you out of the country, by the end of the month, hijo.

Benjamin read the document, and raising his eyes to his father, asked, what am I to do, *Papi*, in the Dominican Republic?

The army, *Mino*. You will be happy there. I know you will. My contacts will be waiting for you at the airport. They will take good care of you. They promised. They owe me ...

A hot and steamy July morning, and Benjamin Rodriguez woke up, a grackle nestled at the bottom of his bed and staring at him. Desirée stood above him, too, tears in her eyes.

Lifting an arm, stretching to her hand, he pulled his wife to him. I'll be fine, Amor. I swear to you, I will come back to you and the boy before the year is over.

The lure of adventure enticing him, Benjamin left his country for the first time, leaving behind his four-year-old son Alejandro to be raised by his wife Desirée, living in the Rodriguez household.

The year was 1999.

He trained in the Dominican Republic for four years as part of the Special Operations Brigade, 1st Special Forces Battalion, and later, integrated into a European unit called the Ultra Plus Brigade. Captain Benjamin Rodriguez was deployed to Iraq in 2003.

To this war, the country of Nicaragua sent 302 soldiers, together with troops from Salvador and Honduras: Brigada Hispanoamerican.

In May 2004, when the Dominican Republic withdrew its men and women from the Iraqi war effort, Benjamin Rodriguez and a few of his men were asked to stay an additional month at the U.S. military base situated in Andalucía, southern Spain—Rota.

Entering the restaurant, Benjamin ambled to the bar, head up, and chest wide. A Caipirinha, he asked, ignoring the waitress.

From across the room, he watched his men, vermouths in hand, green olives twirling inside their mouths. He walked to them, holding his drink, proud and stern. Without saying a word, he pulled a chair out and sat, intrigued, as usual, by the banter that bonded them. He sipped his drink and listened quietly to their voices, the ups and the downs of them, like a roller coaster he knew he would never climb into, being not tall enough, the mind too small.

It's good to leave the base, one of the soldiers said. It's suffocating with all the GIs running around us. No?

Muchas gracias, Captain, for this trip, one of his men said. Freedom for a night. And lifting their glass, the soldiers downed their drinks.

More and more, the flow of words and their intonations puzzled him, confronting him, the sterility of his mind and its inability to decipher joy from pain, or to weed the genuine out from the not so real. Stiff and alert, he swerved on the barstool, and he told himself, I am a simple ghost, a ghost addicted to mirrors, and what my mirrors make real.

He looked around, scrutinizing more faces, complimenting himself on his chosen method of choreographing expressions, his study of curated glossy images, magazine faces. Inside his travel bags, and inside his home, moirés of guises collected to survive a world devoid of direction. He taped them around looking glasses, above each one, and written in black—a sense, an emotion, perfectly spelled out in square black letters. For each one, he rehearsed tirelessly, life's infinite parts, until satisfied, the mirror happy, his face was ready to improvise, exist and express itself according to the laws of a world that were not his nor ever would be—the mimicking of humans. And how is it possible to keep dying—all the time, repeatedly, without ever having been born? The shadow of the phoenix's ashes; his life, an ashtray, overflowing and smoldering.

This wasn't war's doing—just a true self holding a flag.

Captain Rodriguez, the smaller man yelled, mira …

He looked at the waitress standing beside him, then to his shoes, the shiny black of them so comforting, and he picked at the lint stuck to his uniform. He stood, and as the young girl slipped her hand into his, her dark hair dangling on her shoulders, he said, Plaza de Lorca, the bus leaves at 1:00 P.M. See you back there, fellows. And make sure to have fun.

The neighborhood of Lagunillas, a Málaga graffiti filled alley, and he took her quickly, senselessly, leaving her there scrambling for her purse and underwear.

When done, he walked on, his chipped Movado watch indicating he still had two hours to spare before meeting his men. He adjusted his uniform and decided to linger Málaga's streets more, loving the sound of his heels clicking the tile-made street—the echoing of his presence bouncing within of the city's buildings. Rota, he loved. But in Rota, he rationalized, they know too much about me, the military base does, that's for sure. He looked around, lost in his thoughts. War was an answer for death. A legitimate answer. Maybe Papi, after all, knew exactly what he was doing.

The ice cream stand was set before a tall office building on the Christian side of town. It was hot, so very hot. He decided to enter, to cool his instincts, the marble bench inside the lobby too inviting to ignore. Sitting down, cone in hand, he licked the flavored gelato, and watched a woman exit the emergency door. Tall and lean, light-colored hair rolled into a soft bun. The features, arresting all of him. Delicate and fragile, or so he thought.

He watched her long legs extend as she walked past him. Standing, he followed her, to a party. A bachelorette soirée.

This flawless ballerina for his musical box.

From across the street leaning against a decaying wall, he watched her more through the restaurant's window, and he waited.

Eventually, she left, alone, a little drunk, and he watched her trip over a broken tile, losing her shoe. He hurried, and he caught her by the elbow, then by the waist.

She grabbed both his arms. Lo siento, she simply said, her hair falling on her shoulders.

De nada, Amor. De nada.

The pull to him had been instantaneous. Literal. A soft touch, yet firm—protective.

Don't worry, he kept repeating. I have you. *I have you.*

It had been as simple as that.

The promise of a suave climb, the pursuit of a soft rappel.

The draw.

And in silence, their world had collided.

Within a few weeks, Benjamin brought this woman, Sylvia Lopez, back home to Managua, braving Julián's certitudes, hoping them not flayed; by time; by the memory of a son, and knowing—now indifferent to her—Desirée had left him for another man. Her last letters had been clear: love is gone—you never kept your promise. I've met some other man.

The newly formed couple arrived, deciding to live in a barrio not far from his parent's villa. Eager to please, for a time, Benjamin found work as an assistant for prosecution's office and for a while, a limerence weaved itself, intense as it always is, between Sylvia and Benjamin, one all lovers in the world drink from—a potion laced with infatuation.

But soon enough, limerence transformed into acrimony Benjamin had been bred to cultivate.

The *accident*.

Babe, he had said, possessiveness tugging at his core, you are coming with me, to visit some friends, you know I can't let you be here on your own. Your parents would hate me for it.

She had pushed back, refusing to go, preferring to dive into the solitude he denied her. Everyday. The cooking, the cleaning, the fucking. On demand.

You are mine, Sylvia, he had told her. And as he had repeated to her the very words that had boxed her into a life, so desolate and barren and unkind, away from her beloved Spanish land, she had pleaded in her mind for her father, for her mother to come and save her.

Retrieve me from this hell.

Her lids lifting on their own, without warning, she looked at the white of the ceiling, unsure of where she was—a hospital?

She tried to move her head. It was stuck. Pain shouting through her body, she squinted her eyes, sifting the yellow of a light that blinded, coming from under the curtains. He appeared as if on cue, standing tall, erect at the end of her bed. She stared at him, with questions hovering

157

over her, until she remembered—the feel of the speeding wind, the noise and smell of screeching tires, her voice, distorted, crushed metal banging in her head, the road trip through Nicaragua. Sinuous turns, bends followed by more bends as they ascended mid-way to the volcano. The green vegetation, so vibrant, and so inviting, had hypnotized her. Recalling the smell of it, that place where sulfur met with the humid air, carving sculptures of scents she would never forget, she felt bile crawling up her throat. She had been yanked out of that place—slow down, she had yelled, suddenly aware of the danger, *slow the fuck down*. Turning to her and smiling, he had shifted gears, from third, to fourth, to fifth. Her screams, coming from a deformed mouth, faded, her nails digging into his thigh as she pushed into the dashboard with her feet.

Stop, she had tried to tell him.

Stop.

From her bed, closing her eyes, immobilized by steel contraptions, no choice other than to summon the mind, the memory of a road she should have never taken, she cried and she prayed for his stare to go away, for him to stop looking at her, in awe, smiling his intumescent smile, there every day, suspended over her until she became to him a beautiful gargoyle, a curiosity-filled creature. For she understood underneath crushed bones, slashed flesh, broken capillaries, and blackened skin, squirmed a beauty that was only his to know. A secret beauty that could not be shared.

The last day before being dismissed from the hospital, the test results came. No children will be had, the woman doctor told her. Ever.

Soon after, came the day when the fount of stability Benjamin sought hard to secure, disappeared. All I am doing is returning to God what I borrowed from him, he told himself, walking the tarmac to the push-up stairs, Sylvia's hands grabbing his shoulders for stability. *Stability.* I got you, he said. *I got you.*

He turned away from the plane, shaking the image of her body away. Another image to store. Easy as that—little morsels of death, he thought, little breath by little breath. And he asked himself, what can possibly be easier than that?

The Boing 727 took off as he stepped into his old Ford, Sylvia returning to Spain, was now part of a past, recent and old, as if she had never counted, as if an existence dismissed. He turned the radio on, listening. A lack-luster bachata was playing, common, yet inviting. Bobbing his head, his fingers tapping on the wheel, he started to sing of love; of passion; of nostalgia. Nothing but him on his mind.

Wrought with a tempo he loved to move to, he thought of the night to come. A club he would go to. Or maybe ... a visit to the lake?

Hold her head properly, he breathed out through his teeth. Luis, fuck, stabilize your fucking hands. I thought you were healed, he whispered under his breath. Benjamin sat back and considered his brother's volatile state. You simply wanted to prove Papi wrong, didn't you? He slowly scanned the lakeshore of Lake Managua, the tepid smell evaporating from the water soothing his mind, bringing him back home, a chaotic thinking that made sense.

Breathe, buddy, breathe, he coaxed him, watching Luis's hands finally quiet themselves around her neck. There we go. Benjamin contemplated the face before him, satisfied to see her eyes had left for another world. He caressed her cheeks one by one, circling the soft white skin with the tip of his fingers. The tingling sensations he loved so much, the ones he sought, managing to pierce through his callused fingertips. How amazingly reliable, he thought, as he grabbed his knife. You can go now, Luis. Wait for me by the road.

Luis, anticipating the usual command, already had started to remove himself from the scene. As he walked toward the road, he suddenly stopped. Noises were coming from the lake. Motors. Voices. His eyes settled—boats, like fireflies bouncing off the water. Mino, he yelled, we must go. Someone's coming!

No, not yet, I just started, Benjamin said calmly, but I'll be quick. With surgical precision, he drew the lines that would guide the execution.

We have three minutes at most, ¡vamos!

Ignoring his brother's request, Benjamin proceeded with his favorite part of the deed. And it was effortless. I am done, he whispered with relief as he delicately unpeeled the last corner off the porcelain-colored skin.

He stood, placed the soft tissue in a plastic bag making sure to keep it flat, and placed the bag inside his pocket and looked to the lake. He looked at her. You'll join the others, he whispered, examining the mark of his passage. You are my fifth worshipper of gods that never existed.

With a mix of peace and excitement spreading through every inch of his sick, neural pathways, he looked at Luis, and they started to run toward the jungle, into which they disappeared.

Breathless, damp, and muddied, Luis and Benjamin set foot inside the maid's quarters located at the far end of the house, leading to the kitchen.

Looking beyond their father's large silhouette, they all searched for hesitation, groundless composure, wishing to see Benjamin lose some of it. Become human.

Even Luis did.

Mostly Luis.

How many times did I tell you, to not get caught, and to clean after yourself? Julián seethed.

I did all of that, like usual, Papi, Benjamin said. I'm always careful.

Luis, nervous, eyed both men, remaining silent.

Then, why the fuck did I get a call from the President's office, Benjamin? They followed both of you, once they got to shore. They were right behind you. Saw the body.

He turned to Luis. You dropped your wallet, you fucking idiot.

Luis, head bent retreated to the kitchen table, sitting down.

And they had time to see the make of your car, Benjamin. A part of your plate.

Go to hell old man, Benjamin thought, noticing Julián's rosary had fallen to the floor, somehow unclasping itself as Julián was gesticulating. Quickly kneeling, he smiled a triumphant smile, and picking the strand of rose gems, placed the rosary into his coat pocket. Hecho, he thought, fuck you.

He turned and walked toward his mother now folded into a chair in the corner, Anita by her side. As he approached closer to her, his stance softened. Mamá, look at me, he said. Mamá, stop it. Ahora.

She lifted her head slowly to meet his eyes, her tears having settled mid-cheek, the eyes he wanted to quiet. He dropped to his knees, pushing Anita aside, seeing questions alive in shadows on Philomena's face. It had to come to this, Mamá, he answered, knowing he had gone too far, and you knew it would. I tried, so hard. Across his face, a hint of sincerity sauntered. Law school, he continued. The military, D.R., Rota. I married Desirée for you. I did it all. I even gave you a grandson. And what for?

Philomena slumped her head. She had tried, had she not, to infuse him with all of herself.

An unstable permanence.

And now this final crossing. December 2004.

She grabbed his hands and pulled him to her, kissing his face profusely, knowing absolute faith would have to be forgotten, forever. Muted, she knew. He had to leave, and soon. This thirty-two-year-old man, her beloved son, about to vanish and never to return.

He turned and looked at his brother who understood that helplessness was something that one feeds on. Time and again.

The blood.

The screams.

The skins.

How often had Luis secretly dreamt of this? Of the disappearance of Benjamin, a crutch that kept tripping him. Yet, he could feel his heart sink—an ambivalence he had never been able to subjugate.

And he remembered how Iraq had been the key to a temporary freedom, Benjamin's carte blanche to play in a field made of wicked dreams. The pictures he had brought back, Luis now recalled, of all the civilians accidently killed by the fighting, of this pregnant woman, dead, her fully formed fetus hanging from a butchered abdomen, its eyes welded forever—by the murder of a birth.

Brother, Benjamin said, I will miss you.

Luis heard him from afar. He glanced at him, circling the rim of a glass, leaving his fingers to drop along its curve, cold and smooth. In a flash, he upturned the table, pain firing inside his sight. We will see, won't we?

Then, the brushing of clothes that sent a portion of the silence in the corners of everyone's mind. Andie. She caught Benjamin's attention. How he knew she was aware of the untouchables poking at his mind. Because she had to have known—more than most.

He contemplated her face, and he brushed her shoulder with his hand, as if asking for forgiveness. He picked up the military bag his father had prepared for him, and he headed toward the door.

Feeling defeated, Philomena stood and slowly walked to the tree, the old couch waiting. I will pray, she thought, until it kills me, and that is all I can do.

Saliva pooled at the bottom of Benjamin's throat, he summoned it forward, and lowering the window, he spat it out. He looked to the mountains before him, feeling his body recalling souvenirs meant to be buried. His right hand reached the top of his back pushing to feel his dented skin, the burning familiarity too present for him to forget, his fingers mindfully rubbing the scars. His ears started to buzz to the beat of rodent's wings and the squeaking coming from their tiny mouths—the barn. He shook his head. Okay, he whispered to himself, tranquilo.

Behind him as they sped through the early morning, he saw his life—oranges and blues and silvers that sketched the anonymity of a nature that never cared.

But he hadn't cared, either.

Here, his father said, still driving, as he shoved a brown envelope onto Benjamin's chest. All you need to facilitate your immigration. But this time ... this time, you leave this family for good, you leave the country. Nunca volver.

Benjamin tilted his head back, the nape of his neck arched against the cold leathered headrest. He kept repeating it to himself, what the world around him whispered: A failed man. And he thought, aliases are meant to kill. I will get one. Just like he did.

I'll swallow you some day, somehow, piece by piece, he thought, I swear I will, like I did Shaunny, and I will never return to see your body burned by your own men, father, he thought. Abroad—wherever I will land, I will lie. I will tell all who want to be part of me what a great father you were. I will tell beautiful tales of you taking my hand when sick, of those times in the warm evenings when you defended me from strangers who put their cigarettes out on my thigh, and how you fed me as I sat on your knees, caressing my hair, my back, soft and patient, and not how you locked me into a cave full of flying bats to teach me the quiet of pain. I will tell these tales, father, fill them up with memories I never had, to look like I should, to seem breezy to all who need this feeling from me, knowing that you were just another me, broken and brittle, fleeing beyond what we really are. Yes, you will die, and I will say that I ran to your hearse crying, and grieving. I will say it, but I won't do it. Not for you. Not even for Mamá.

With a pasty and dry mouth, with dusky eyes and anxious fingers, he opened the envelope and took the American papers out, opening the documents to its first page. You little fuck, he thought, reading the delivery date. You got this ready for me a month ago. Before all of this happened. He looked to his side, at Julián. You've been waiting for this, he whispered. All along.

Smiling, non-plussed, quickly understanding America was a gift to Nicaraguan men like him, he looked out the window. I'm good, he thought. A new start.

With the tip of his fingers, he brushed that place just below the eyes where dark circles would never form. Always so dry. And he wondered, why had his own eyes never leaked like the rest of the world's eyes?

The mystery behind the production of tears.

She had not been easy, he kept thinking. They all had cried, all but her—the plump, one-legged bitch—looking meek and tasteless. Maimed by a tractor's blade when she was little, somewhere on a grain farm in Georgia, an ugly duckling, and limping like all lame ducklings do, he would later understand, reading the papers.

I was ready to go back home, he thought, I was ready to let that one go and go be with Mamá. But just as they were about to leave the lake, he had seen the improvised substitute take a cigarette out of a cheap fanny pack and place it between her thin pale lips. Squatting beside him, in the thickness of the tropical forest's knots, hidden by the abundance of its underground thickets, Luis had said no, let's go back home, this is not the meal plan. Benjamin would never know the trigger, Luis even less. Had it been the cigarette, the womanish vulgarity he believed it to be? The unsightly image of a botched tattoo curling on the side of her thigh, wrapped with the tentacles of a thorny rose? This other one, unaware of the craziness boiling behind her, had stood in the water, lifting her long, grey skirt above her knees, exposing more of the womanish impurities that defied his rules.

Nothing virgin-like about her.

An irk impossible to ignore—a voice yelling inside of him, surging.

He watched more of this girl lost in the tangles of a moment.

Unsteadied by the softness of the lake's bottom, the girl's one foot toyed with the wet sand, her toes wiggling inside it like worms wanting to hide, her other leg, a prosthetic leg, the ill adjusted device having slid under her knee, red and raw, pulling the leg's ghost into a painful nowhere. Isn't it what physical pain must do to justify its existence, she had asked herself, becoming a time-capsule in which wounded souls embark and travel through time's wake? Pain opens the present, veils the past and steels the future, sucking goodness out of those tenses like incest burns the flesh's light. She had looked at the horizon and, tethered to it, she had thought about her place inside this place, this cultish group formed to save the world, part of it anyway, of the mall where they had recruited her seated on the floor facing the McDonald's, begging for something other than the life she was living. Away from her worries, waiting, she let herself feel the breeze, warmish and still, caressing her face. She had dallied a little, listening to the jungle's dark hums—the clicks and howls and chirps—a noise like a song sucked into the humid air.

The crackling of dried leaves, the stirring of the soil, the steadiness of fate coming—the flicking of its knife.

She had heard nothing.

I am so lucky, the teenager had thought, to join the Elders in their incantations tonight, so lucky Roxane is sick. I am the replacement, young and promising. Her, the rookie, now allowed to be there and partake in a ritual she knew nothing about, a ritual where prayers and dances rule minds, hers in the making. Lost in her thoughts, and waiting for the rest of the group, she had let go of her skirt, letting its flayed seam fall into the lake.

But another ritual instead had greeted her, for the members of the cult she had joined and wanted to impress had never shown up, and her feverish roommate, sick Roxane having never been notified of the ceremony's postponement.

No, she had not been easy. She had fought back, defied his fingers, the roughness of hands that could speak and yell and rip, and tried to push him away.

He opened his eyes.

Luis yelled, you fucked up, bro.

Did I? Did I really fuck up? Are you kidding me? No, I don't think so. You did, Luis. Your wallet, stupido …

You didn't follow the plan … how could you not follow the fucking plan? Wasn't it clear enough from the start? To leave if it wasn't her. If we hadn't done it, losing my wallet would not have gotten you where you deserve to be anyway.

They had stayed. They had wanted the pretty blonde one, Roxane, the one that had never showed up, her pulse never to take, never to stop, in its place a facsimile. They had been taught to wait for the right moment, so often in their sick lives, until the perfect one would be alone, there by the waves, doing what all her kind did.

Pray.

To Lords drenched in absurdity. Mute and deaf and numb to the world of humans, for Gods are for Gods only.

Luis sank into the seat of the car, shaking his head. Simple enough, no? To get to that place where we knew she would be. Only her.

Shut up, cállate la mierda, los dos, Julián yelled, as he stopped to park on the side of the road and turned around to look at them. His gaze landed on Benjamin's hands, unsure for a moment of who exactly to be.

You. You, he continued, you and your hands. You got that fucking Dominican bad luck in them, that fucking fuku. And even the D.R. doesn't want you back. Did you know that? They found you out, didn't they? he said, rage stretching his old and wrinkled face. You finally got caught, you dumb fuck. Serves me right … should have sent you to Haiti instead. Where you belong, with them no-good niggers.

Benjamin bit his tongue, looking straight ahead to the control tower.

An agitated silence fell over the three of them as they approached the entry to the airport. Stone faced, the personnel at the gatehouse, notified of their arrival, waved them in. Julián was assured all would be cleared, that the transfer would be smooth. A one-way ticket, the government man had said, nothing more. And make it quick, so quick my American contact won't be able to kill him with his own two hands.

The father scanned the area and drove slowly inside the private perimeter, stopping at the edge of the unfolded staircase. Waiting for them, the loud hum of a private Embraer's engines revving up, signaling the end of a time.

All this for me, he thought, his wide eyes smiling.

That's it, Luis said, tapping Benjamin's shoulder from the back seat, time to go. Benjamin turned around, stared. Leaning forward, his face livid, and taking Benjamin's face in his hand, Luis told him, this farewell, te amo, Mino, and for those times when you took my hand, those times when you held me, thank you. Benjamin nodded, and remained, looking at Luis. Be careful, Mino, please.

Satchel in hand, Benjamin stepped out of the car and walked to the edge of the plane's stairs. There, he stilled but for a moment, giving his heart the chance to pound less—less of him, more of another one coming.

And, no, he never turned around, never bowed to his father's power, soaking what he thought was his due.

But even if he had turned, even if he had succumbed to the pull of a wanted love that would never be his to have anyway—never to give either—he would have seen nothing other than taillights blending into the dust.

Leaving the road, passing through the gates, Julián continued rolling into the morning, a too obedient son by his side, yet—tears threatening to pierce.

Papi, aren't you afraid for him?

That he may die? Julián replied quickly.

Yes ... Sooner than *you* will ...

I see. You're afraid of dying, Luis. Yet, you, like me, have seen souls lifting from bodies.

Luis' eyes fell to his lap.

And Julián recalled, and it tumbled inside his brain: Spain, his women; the sound of his own flesh falling into the Atlantic Ocean; the orphanage; the wars—the sound of death—of winds pushing a small and lifeless body from a tree; Sophia's gaze—the feeling of being loved, and hated, too, for a moment, wanting it, wanting to give it.

Was God ever frightened of the void men could bring to him? he asked himself.

I sure was never afraid of the ones He brought to me.

As he rolled silently onto the driveway, a microburst, reaching him.

Mangoes dropping from his tree.

At the passenger door, Benjamin took in the smell of the jet fuel and stepped into the plane.

Hello señor, he heard, welcome aboard.

The pilots, headsets over their ears, extended their neck to greet their client. We will be leaving shortly, they yelled in tandem, fifteen minutes.

Benjamin nodded as his eyes absentmindedly scanned their dashboard.

So happy to have you with us today, señor, a feminine voice floated to him. Would you please follow me?

To his left, another woman, a tall, young and slim, was pointing to the empty seats. Please.

The sound of her struck him, her accent, pushing in images, images alive with a freshness that dizzied. He couldn't forget, that beach, a few hours ago.

He had been so close, he thought. Too close.

To let her go.

Almost—but no.

He politely smiled and walked behind her to the back of the plane.

Once seated, he pulled the screen down, closing the porthole, not wanting to see the sun; not wanting to feel its warmth on any part of him, especially his hands. He felt his twisted knowledge come to the surface of his mind. He smiled, and knew then for sure, that unlike the sun that disappears and returns to the world everyday with its failed promises of new beginnings, the stings never fade.

Or do they?

For his kind? A canopy of all fallacies and truths.

The tall stewardess approached, cabaret in hand, the slenderness he ached for—an ivory-colored creature designed for his pleasure—and he wondered if she was his father's farewell gift?

I know it's early, she said, as she lowered his tray, can we offer a glass of champagne?

Gray eyes so gray.

No, he whispered, I don't drink. I never drink. Just an apple juice or if you have a hot chocolate.

Apple juice or hot chocolate, she thought to herself, cute. Give me a moment.

There was something unsettling about him, she thought, walking back to the small galley adjacent to the cockpit. With him, there would be no ass or pussy grabbing, no reaching for the breasts with impunity and dismissiveness, no humiliating demands. With him, vulgarity would be replaced by a politeness stiffened by the wanting of something holier. She had seen it in his eyes. Tray in hand, she returned to his seat. Here you go, sir.

He nodded.

It was then she noticed his hands. A mixture of fresh and dried blood, barely perceptible against the bronze of his skin, streaking both of their sides with an Asian-like motif. She stilled, fighting the impulse to question.

Benjamin gently took the washcloth from her hands. I'll keep it if you don't mind, as a souvenir.

She acknowledged, unflinching. Very well, sir. Let me know when you wish your meal to be served.

The mirror inside the bathroom welcomed him with the sight of a wanted man. He blinked at his reflection, seeing nothing, and remained motionless. With a breathing slow and deep, deathbed-like, he proceeded to scrub the blood from his hands, leaving the towel out of the cleaning process. No trace of anything, he thought, as he unzipped his pants.

The captain's voice suddenly echoed against the steel walls. Taxiing would start, take-off was imminent.

* * *

Benjamin looked out the restaurant window, curving his neck up. It's like even the sky is made of cement, the thought. To his right, immigration papers were spread, and he took his pen and doodled; faces of women, many, and differently shaped. Stopping to draw, he placed the pen down on the table, took a sip of his hot chocolate, and recalling what the immigration officer had told him. You need to work on your reading abilities, Mr. Rodriguez, if you eventually plan on obtaining your naturalization, going all the way, you see. You appear to me almost illiterate—even in Spanish. Yeah, he thought, remembering how sister Bettina had pleaded for Philomena and Julián to help him learn how to read. And money was all that it took for me to attend the best of schools Managua had to offer.

But it wouldn't do here. I have to become enough.

He looked at the Spanish note the officer had written, circled the few recommended school phone numbers. Mindfully, his back straight to the bench he was seated on, and scooping a fork of mashed plantain and fried chicken in his mouth, he thought of what he should do.

For two months he had been staying at a New York City shelter. For two months he had slept inside a room filled with strangers that would stay strangers, at the bottom of a bunkbed filled with fleas and bedbugs, feeling the remnants of men whose lonely passages had starched and stained his mattress, his sheets, too. Roaming the streets of the city, looking for work, searching for handles, new handles that would help him make sense of his new life, Benjamin's mind had been rolling, just as it was now. I didn't think it be this hard, he thought more.

He stood and walked to the diner's cash register and placed his bill on the countertop. Here, he told the waitress. Pulling money out from his wallet, he looked at his face reflected in the rectangle mirror that hung behind the young girl. Not hearing her words, he took the change, leaving her a small tip. I need to go to the barber's, he told her, as he scratched the top of his head, his military haircut long gone, an afro threatening to push too high. Any place I should go?

The barber, clipper in hand, kept pressing on Benjamin's head, as if playing with a doll, and clipped the brittle coils that made his client more negro than he wanted. Finishing the flat top, he expertly sculpted the hairline into a straight edge that met with the two-sided fades.

Thank God, Benjamin said, my skin is not black.

It doesn't matter, man, around here, brown is just as black. Twirling the chair, and moving on to Benjamin's neck, he said, you say you were a lawyer back home?

Never finished. Military was my thing. Iraq.

Hum. Was it? It wouldn't matter, anyways, he laughed, if you had finished. Swirling the chair back to the front of the mirror, the barber examined his work. Here, you're not at the bottom of the ladder, you are the ladder. What'd you do when in Managua?

A landscape artist, he lied.

Did you? Then you'll fit right into someone's undeclared pay roll. That's the power of your color. Visible to the eye, but invisible to authorities—all authorities. That's the recipe.

Dipping his fingers inside a jar of transparent gel, the barber then lathered his client hair with shine, careful not to leave any clumps. There you go, he said, snapping the black plastic cape from Benjamin's shoulders. You said you wanted to go dancing tonight? Listo, my man, I guarantee you—with this cut, they'll be falling on your lap.

Dressed in black slacks and shirt, wearing a stiff, distressed leather jacket he had bought at a second hand Puerta Rican boutique close to the shelter, Benjamin climbed the long and narrow staircase leading to the entry of the club. There, fourth client in line, he waited five minutes until his turn to be let in came. The bouncer, nodding, directed him to the table to his left. Five dollars the seated woman said, a stamp in her hand.

Right, of course. Here.

She took the five-dollar bill, placing it inside the bottom of a small gray case. You're new around here?

Yes, I am. He smiled. My name is Benjamin Rodriguez.

The music faded, the salsa running low, and the D.J.'s voice towered over the crowd, reminding them they needed to be present to claim their raffle prize. At midnight, he said, and he slowly increased the music's volume.

She held her hand out. Janelle Rivera, she yelled.

A bachata, he thought, looking to the dance floor, rippling with moving bodies. You dance, Janelle Rivera? he yelled back.

What on earth do you think I'm doing here, vaquero? She looked over to the bouncer. The Jamaican man, convincingly obstructive, was chatting with a customer waiting to pay his cover charge. She looked back at Benjamin, and extending her arm to reach the bouncer's jacket, she pulled his sleeve. His eyes turned to hers'. Find me Sheila, her lips said, my shift is done. Turning her attention back to Benjamin, she stood. Come on, we don't have all night, do we? She pointed to the coat check. I'll be waiting for you.

Benjamin watched her walk to the dance floor, unsure of what had happened. Her blonde haired up in a bee-hive—yellow against a skin he wanted nothing of. Blackish skin on a frame, muscular—too firm, a female version of me, he thought, and this way of walking, as if she owned the ground. He removed his leather jacket, walked to the coat check. Without saying a word, he paid the young man and placed his ticket inside his back pocket. His eyes filtering the room, adjusted to the lights, pinks, green, and blue, stroboscopic and disorienting, spotting the bar. Right, he said to no one. Walking to it, his gait slow, his posture soaring, he felt the music crawl up from his legs, tantalizing his hips.

A Caipirinha, he yelled. No ice. More lime.

No ice?

Impassive, he looked at the man. You heard right.

Pushing his back against the bar, foot crossing over ankle, he sipped his drink, the citrus tingling the sides of his tongue. Lime, he thought to himself, the taste of home. From the middle of the dance floor, Janelle Rivera moved amidst the crowd of dancers, a youngish woman in her arms. He observed them until, his drink empty and returning to the counter, he walked, faster this time, to her. When he reached her, he gently tossed the dancing partner away, and moved in, his hands grabbing hers, taking charge of Janelle Rivera's pace, her rhythm.

So was his hope.

She took a bite, leaving a lump of cream cheese at the corner of her mouth. You've never had a bagel before? she asked, wiping it off.

Benjamin stared at the bread-like donut placed at the center of his plate, as if contemplating the accomplishment of an impossible task. No, I haven't.

Some say Montreal has the best ones in the world. I don't know about that … Try it with the smoked salmon. You will love it.

Benjamin didn't move. It's okay, Janelle. I'm not that hungry. He pushed the plate to the side, looking around the diner. You live nearby?

Yes and no, she said. I'm here for the weekend. I'm staying at my friend Sheila's, around the corner. Once a month, I like to come here, mingle, help with the running of the place. It's a new one.

And dance … I must say you're quite the dancer.

You know the steps to all the dances, Mr. Rodriguez. Just like I do. She took another bite, quickly cleaning her mouth up with the side of her napkin. I hate to stay still. Just hate it. And coming here, you know, it's like a small vacay from work.

And where is work exactly?

Where I live. Far Rockaway.

WHEN I BECAME NEVER

Benjamin's brows lifted. Never heard of it.

It's in a neat New York borough called Queens.

Ah. And what does a beautiful woman like you do in Far Rockaway?

Slow down, vaquero, with your charming words, she said, half smiling. You're definitely not my first rodeo … Picking at the capers on her plate, her eyes intermittently lifting, she assessed him, this expression morphing into an impatient rictus. Unphased by it, she continued. I've been working as a nurse at the local hospital for five years now. Night shifts mostly. The E.R.

The E.R.? he asks, inquisition in his eyes.

The emergency room, you know, the front lines. I help fix the minimum, stabilize the patients, before we send them away to the proper department.

You are from Puerto Rico …?

Ah. Well, as I told you while we were dancing, yes, I'm form Puerto Rico, born and bred. And I fell in love with an American, followed him here. A doctor that had interned where I was studying. And the rest, the usual … it didn't work out so well. I decided to stay in and finish my nursing here.

Why stay in Far Rockaway?

The beach. I was a surfer back home. Competitive one, too. Far Rockaway has a small surfing community that's quite vibrant. They adopted me. She tossed her head back, sending her beehive to the side. I did, too.

It's quite the doo, he laughed. A smile. Affable—comforting.

Janelle brought her long fingers to her head, Benjamin staring at her nails, long and painted pink and jeweled with sprinkles. Diamonds? he asked, playfully.

Sliding a small Coke bottle closer to her, she brought the straw to her lips, and biting its tip, said she wished, but that diamonds in the end, like anything else, are disposable, that they mean nothing. And the hair well, I like to vary my looks. She pulled the wig from her head, revealing her shock of blonde-dyed hair. What do you think?

You're just as beautiful ...

Of course, she said, batting her Cover Girl lashes. And what about you? You didn't say much in the club.

No future for me where I come from. Nicaragua is a continuous implosion. His head slightly tilted, he told her about the country's civil war, about his failed schooling, about Iraq. It's where I shined, he told her.

She stilled. Why did you leave the army, then? You had a future there, no?

My father needed me. My brother, too.

Ah, and it didn't work out after your return?

Not so much. It's not something I enjoy talking about. It's kind of messed up.

Oh. I'm sorry. I didn't want to intrude.

What happened with your doctor?

I have endometriosis. He wanted kids.

Endo ...?

The long and the short Benjamin, is I can't have kids. It became a problem. He left me for a younger nurse—I am older, too. Moved to Connecticut. Never heard of him after he left New York. Feeling tears about to come, she snapped a napkin from the dispenser, dabbing the rim of her eyes with it. You have any kids?

Benjamin, paused, pulling his plate back to him. One son. Alejandro.

Still in Managua, is he?

With his mother.

You're still married?

No.

You want more children?

No, I don't.

The neon lights above them, white and defective, flickered. With her neck arched, fixating on them, she smiled. You know, I won't sleep with you, Benjamin. I'm not that kind of girl. Not the first night, anyway. She unzipped her purse, nestling her wig at the bottom of it, retrieved a pen, and wrote her number down on the corner of the placemat.

Here, she said, carefully ripping the piece of paper. Get your shit together, your basic paperwork, the English classes you mentioned, and when you do, Benjamin, maybe, I'll be able to get you some work.

Listening to her, he realized her tone was unknown to him, for he had never met such poise, such control—these were not the makings of the women he had been with.

Okay, Janelle Rivera, I'll do my homework, and then—ring your doorbell.

* * *

The train climbed to an elevated station, moving from Brooklyn to Queens. In between the never-ending rows of houses, the mesh of plastic sidings and red bricks paving the way to his new home, that's where he heard her voice—the contralto hooking into him, bringing with it a pull that promised more of something. Caught between two strangers reeking of sweat and cigarettes, his eyes escaped into the now speed-blurred landscape.

It came from the third or fourth row behind him: jazziness peppered with that want-to-fuck-me-call men so easily hear. The words had surprised him, mundane yet pain-filled, as if she had known, and spoken the words, you know I'm no good.

It was the sight of her image, not her music, which would haunt his hunts. Skinny and white, blue blood white, the skim milk type of royalty. That's what he had ached for all his life, the kind of trophy that would throne above all the others.

His gold standard. Amy Winehouse.

And from that moment on, almost two years into his American life, Benjamin Rodriguez knew he would have to prowl in a different way, and never succumb to the pull of killing, but instead, keep them alive—just vary the prizes a little more.

Hey, Janelle said, tapping the mattress, seems you're back where you belong. How was your train ride back home, Amor?

How he hated her for that. The arrogance, the entitlement. She treats me like I'm her little man, he thought, like she wants to carry all of me, right there in the huge back pocket covering her dark culo. Long and tiring, he said, walking to her, normal.

Stretched on her side, an elbow to the mattress, she sighed. You remember when we met, what you told me, Ben?

I told you nothing you didn't already know. You are the blonde reina of my dreams, perfect for me and Alejandro, he said, and sitting beside her, his fingers now curling into her straw-colored hairdo.

She closed her eyes and toyed with her ring. You're never here anymore, baby. Either working at that garage or taxiing all those people around. And those English classes all the way up in New York city ... Since we got married, Benjamin, you're mine even less.

There is no point in living here if I don't learn the language, mi Boricua, properly, he said, dropping his index finger in between her breasts. Besides, it means better jobs for me. More money for us. No more living here.

The place is small, Ben, small, yes, but fine for the three of us.

It puzzled her.

Cramped spaces where promiscuity bloomed, those were what he had learned to love the hard way. In Santo Domingo, in Rota. Holes. Her fully furnished two and a half should be plenty. And his English was fine. More than fine.

You will go to the beach with Alejandro today, Amor, no?

Today is Saturday, Benjamin, I've made plans for all of us. Again. And to her mind came the preceding week's load of wobbly explanations: the English class that ran longer, the missing of his train, the cell phone, out of reach. All these excuses, like a record, repeated and scratched.

Today, he said, renovation contracting.

Let me guess, New Haven, Bangor, Lowell? And she thought, nothing ever around our home, Far Rockaway.

I have no choice, Janelle. I have to go where the big money is ... He stood, his eyes brow arching. I'm going to clean myself up now, and that is it. No more discussing this.

He leaned over her and placed a dry kiss on her cheek, understanding his wife was now writing a narrative inside her mind, one which held the possibility of messing with his life, and his plans. And how I hate to see a woman thinking, he whispered to himself, as he walked to the bathroom. It always means trouble.

Quickly undressing, leaving his clothes to fall on the moldy carpet, he stepped into the small shower area, anticipating the scalding heat of the water. Ablutions needed to hurt, he had always told himself. And more pain was needed now.

Standing in the doorway, still dripping, a towel hugging from his waist, he examined her, his eyes like lasers, as if wanting to pierce the inside of her head, poke and pry and know—all about her; her schemes; an incursion to her thoughts. Alert with rehearsed ease, his lips drew a curved line. He knew this pattern—bitches whining, repeatedly, their cries and their tears—a red flag telling him to regroup and slow down. That's when he felt the urge to appear as he truly wasn't. Pretend. It wasn't time to let go, he thought. No. She hadn't delivered yet. Citizenship. Passport. In the meantime, however, there was an abundance of white asses to fuck.

He approached the bed, released the towel from his hips and hopped over her. Janelle, look at me.

Her mouth began to form what could only have been a sharp retort. Catching her cheeks between his thumb and his index, he told her, no, not a word, and squeezed a little more. Just enough. The index made its way to her lips, parting them. Then, slowly, the hand followed down as he started to kiss her neck. Janelle, immobilized by fear as much as desire, obeyed. He painted her face with the drippings from the pool inside his mouth, pushing his hands further down the throat as he split her legs open.

Now, he said as he removed his hand, not a word.

Alejandro Rodriguez sneaked his hands inside Janelle's, mesmerized as always by the plastic jewels, zircon-like trinkets glued to her pink-colored nails. He stretched his neck looking at her; her touch; her voice; her presence, her goodness. He had never known any of it—his own mother having immigrated like he had, and moving near-by, with another man, other children, too, yet ignoring him.

He squeezed Janelle's hand a little harder then let go. Tripping over his feet, his knee caught the edge of a rock. Janelle lifted him by the armpits and brushed her lips against his cheek. Surfing class, she said, what do you say?

Forcing back his tears from the pain, he nodded.

She knelt and as she did, she wondered, about his time in places he could barely call his own. This boy, one that made no sense. His curly Negro hair, his chocolate skin.

His blue eyes. An oddity.

It still hurts, he said, here, pointing to his kneecap.

Janelle frowned as she assessed his knees, both covered with dirt. You'll be fine, she said. You can move your knee, right, Amor? And the ocean water will clean it all up.

The boy remained silent, took the woman's hand and pulled her forward off the boardwalk and into the warm sand.

The surf stand was busy, as the summer was coming to its end. The air was still warm, pushed around by a soft breeze, and while hurricane season was lurking, the day promised nothing more than a few capillary waves. She watched him wiggle into his wetsuit like she had done so many times when his age. Middles Beach. Puerto Rico. Home.

You're going in, today, señora Rivera, the instructor asked, haven't seen you since the championship.

They both laughed, as she pointed to the relative tranquility before them. I see, Miss mermaid of the sea, too boring for you today? All right buddy, the instructor said, turning to the boy, time for the safety recap and the warmup. Let me see those nose to toes. You gonna pop them for me today?

Alejandro smiled. Yes, I will.

All right, son, let's start, so we can play, and the man smiled.

The beach was starting to fill with the usual weekenders from the cities. Blue collars, hipsters, women dressed in skimpy bikinis and men flexing what needed to be flexed. Magicians of the moment, and seeking more from time. She took her tee off, fixed her halter top, and keeping her shorts on, spread her towel on the sand and sat. From there, she watched the son she would never keep, but always love. She watched him learn about stances, swells, about waves, about rocks.

About perfect danger.

Detailing his body, his gait and his stance, she recognized from afar the bipedal swagger that came from deep inside his genes. Benjamin.

Women stay with men they don't belong to for reasons that don't belong to them either. Her thoughts circled until they settled, there in a wiser place. Just then, Alejandro climbed onto his large beginner's board. She looked on as the boy caught his first wave of the day. She couldn't see it, but she guessed the boy was laughing.

Finally.

Alejandro had become just that, she thought, watching him disappear into the white foam. A reason that shouldn't be hers.

Benjamin squirmed on his stool while waiting for the lesson to start. More of this, he thought, discouraged, but better this than going back home to Janelle. He looked around, a small smile hanging from the bottom of his otherwise empty face. Too busy settling into their own space, the other students hadn't given him a first look, let alone a second one. They had spaced evenly across the floor, easels and large black cases marking their territory. He didn't care. Not this time anyway. He scanned the room. So, he thought, this is what a real art room looks like.

On each of the walls encasing the classroom, tall shelves were erected. From floor to ceiling, the racks were stuffed with objects meant to inspire the artist, vases and potteries, mostly, of all sizes, some made of metal, some porcelain, others made of raw plastic, trinkets inviting eyes and hands to discover the play of shadows, all waiting to teach.

Directly behind him was an assortment of paint brushes, stacks of paper, new and recycled. Further up on the same shelves, baskets filled with what appeared to be lumps of unfolded fabrics. A small section to his right pulled him in. Peach tinted depression tableware, cups and saucers that summoned rain-filled images—Philomena's home. This place, an open-air treasure chest to the artist, a pile of rubbish to the rest of the world, he thought.

At the Institute for Immigrant Concerns where he studied English as a second language since his arrival in the United States, the year before, they told him to continue elsewhere. Your English is quite good, his teacher had said. You stay here and you will be bored to death.

She had taken his workbook, flipping through its pages, stopping here and there. Inside, aplomb and fluidity, mastery of portraitures, a pencil stroke that poetized the human face.

I see you drawing in class. You even drew me, didn't you? I'm no art expert, she had continued, scribbling an address on the inside of the workbook cover, but I think you would enjoy this class.

And perfect my English?

Sí, Benjamin, and perfect your English.

The classroom chatter stopped as music started to play. The week before, he had skipped the introduction lesson, preferring a tryst to his new class, the one the teacher had recommended. The whole trip had been demanding—the girl, unwilling to let him go. Stay, she had pleaded, stay the night, just this once. Okay, he had said, just this once. Unable to find sleep, he had kept an eye on a phone that didn't stop lighting up with messages. Janelle. The girl, young and unstable, had clenched to his body for fear of being alone. He had left, though, in a hurry to flee clinginess he didn't care to understand. Too tired to go on driving, he had parked his car on the shoulder of the I-95 somewhere between Lowell and Chicopee. There, he had resumed his sleep until refreshed enough to continue, his art class but just a thought.

The art class, its second week, and he decided to attend it.

Today, the teacher, an older woman, said, I want you to practice trusting your intuition. Last week was about technique. Today is not.

A voice coming from the back. So, forget last week, forget everything Dr. Rubenstein has taught you. Gingerly, she made her entrance, reddish hair floating around her shoulders, her skin Scandinavian white. He watched her walk to the front and plant a few kisses on the old woman's cheeks. Dr. Rubenstein, she said, so sorry. My plane was late, but here I am.

Claudia Balasco pulled her hair in a loose chignon and quickly explained her background. New Jersey girl, she said. Rutgers for undergrad. Chicago for doctorate. Spend half of my time between homes, San Salvador and New York.

Benjamin stared, suddenly transported to the day he had set foot on American soil. The J.F.K. airport, her, descending the air stairs, and wearing the same Chanel pantsuit. Except now its tweed wasn't blue, it was pink. His eyes had followed her figure strolling onto the carpeted pathway leading to the VIP section of the terminal. But there had been no time to follow through with what his mind was devising. There would be other opportunities. There always were. And sure enough, here she was.

Go on and choose any object that speaks to you, she said, pointing to her left.

There's more in the back room. Two minutes to choose.

Dr. Rubenstein watched the class of twenty disperse as she walked to Benjamin.

You weren't here last week. Mind if I take a look at your portfolio?

Benjamin shrugged, pulled the folder out of its black case and handed it to her.

Little sketches, really. Nothing much, he said.

The teacher thumbed her way through the drawings. Claudia, she said, lifting her head to find her, come take a look at this.

As students around them came back from their treasure hunt, the older woman paused, studying the last piece he had drawn. Claudia's manicured hands gently slid another sketch from its cover. As she dove into the portrait, Benjamin dove into her, equally disturbed. Premium fuel, he thought, brimming with joy. Intelligence. Empathy.

An imperial beacon—like in Spain.

The beginning of an end.

Poland Spring with lime, she said, as she poured the water into his glass. What you asked for.

Benjamin took the tumbler and circled its rim, the finger firm. The glass, its intricacies, was something he had only seen once before in his life. Sylvia, Spain, the bar, popped into his head again. Discreetly shaking his head, tossing the memory out, he walked around the living room, soaking in the view. Entering a new territory was like opening a gift box, filling him with a new sense of purpose, with the hope that he had found his missing link—this time, the ability to attach.

Show me again, she said. Show me first then let me tell you what it is I see. Claudia Balasco removed her blazer and placed it on the edge of the glass coffee table. Please, she insisted, tapping on the seat of the sofa.

Benjamin grabbed his case and sauntered to her, eyes beyond the window, the Manhattan skyline.

I've never done this before, you know. Brought a student here. Kind of a no-no. But then again, this isn't exactly University, is it? But now. You.

Benjamin, remaining silent, sat by her side, removed the portfolio from its black case, and again, handed her his work.

You have talent, Benjamin. My guess is you already know that.

Her tone changed, he could tell, mellowed most likely by the dark rum she was twirling inside her mouth.

Sister Bettina, who had believed in him, in his promise to be more, appeared to him, brandishing a document. Running around like a teenager, she kept screaming it had been signed by the President, that Benjamin had won the contest, that he would leave this country.

She took the second drawing out and let her finger hover over the drawing. Now that she could, with unhurried eyes, she absorbed it. Here, mastery of shades, she told him. But then again, a penchant for the dark. Much mystery. So much evocation, she thought. Of the forbidden. You know, Benjamin, you remind me of one of my idols. Yes, Sargent. But the theme you seem to prefer puts you closer to Henry Moore. You. It's never about less, is it? Devious. Hard core demands for retributions. From under the coffee table, she pulled a large book out—Charcoal Through the Ages, an anthology, and she retrieved the bookmark and opened it. Mother and child. A timeless theme.

Yes, he let out. I guess that's why I'm here.

She stood, walked to the window and pushed the curtains a little farther away to the side.

He followed, stopping behind her, far enough, but still close. He looked at her feet, focusing on the back of her black patent leather shoes. He took a step closer.

I am with oil, now, sometimes anyway, she went on, pointing to the nightlights staring at them, painted landscapes the likes of what we see here. Used to be obsessed by all shades of white, too. They ruled my life for a time. Then Miguel died, she whispered. I needed color. Color needed me, too. I studied some, across the Hudson, she continued. New Jersey. But I eventually discovered I preferred sculpting—went on to Chicago— more satisfying to my senses. Yet, as you can tell, she said, a finger loosely pointing everywhere and nowhere, I have none of my work at home. I'm still learning—not ready to showcase this new side of me. She pushed some hair away from her face, turned around. I see the same infant, the same mother in all your work, Benjamin. Portraits of Mary and Jesus with a twist. Let me just say I have a place in mind for it. I'd love to buy it from you.

Taking her in, he smiled.

Claudia, feeling her body relax, walked to the large wall-to-wall window to her right, and swaying to the music playing in her ear, rolled her head back and forth. Lightness, where have you been, she whispered to herself, finally.

He followed her, hoping this crusade would be the one yielding, the last one. Always the same hope, the same chagrin. Wrapping Claudia's waist with his arms, he let his fingers crawl. I guess sculptures are more satisfying to the touch, Claudia.

Like a doll, young and malleable, she let her head drop to his chest.

Novelty's curse had been unleashed.

She leaned closer to the mirror, searching. I'm not sure anymore, she thought, leaving a finger to move across her face. And taking the Poland Spring water bottle left on her bathroom counter into her hand, sipping its left-over, she closed her eyes. It's been so long, she thought. To want. To want to please a man. A pastel-like feeling she carried since her husband's death. Something of a saturated blandness had swum inside her, since then, finding its way inside her paintings, even. Was she not letting go of her addiction to all shades of white?

She tilted her head slightly, the smell of her dead husband coming to her. A strange Salvadorian, a businessman dealing in rum and precious wood imports, a collector of all things with a cunt. Miguel Balasco had plucked her out of her zombie land like a gardener weeds his grass—with fervor and disgust, he had transformed her into his version of a wildflower that wouldn't spoil his earth.

Claudia Russo, third generation Neapolitan from New Jersey, hair drawn into two tresses, had appeared magically before room 347 of the iconic Hotel del Coronado. Flanked by two large canvases and a small case containing what Miguel would later discover were art accessories, she had returned the wide stare. Dressed in a white scruffy t-shirt, a pair of overalls and some form of loosely fitted tool belt, Claudia had winced at the sight of the puzzled man whose hand was scratching a day-old beard nervously. She had smiled. They told me you signed up for a one-on-one art class. The black velvet peignoir that greeted Claudia, half open, barely restrained the bush of hair springing toward her. I have the wrong room, she had laughed, or you've had a really, really hard change of heart.

That evening, Miguel had asked the hotel concierge to prepare a picnic basket filled with his favorite: sushi topped with uni, foie gras and bubbles of the Laurent Perrier kind. Pink, she had demanded. A thick Navajo blanket safely spread on the beach, just where the grass chased the sand away, far enough from the Pacific's soft surges, and with the effusion of time, they had fallen in love.

The idea had come to her following her second visit to San Salvador, just a few weeks before the wedding. The creation of an art school for the women of the country, the ones unjustly incarcerated, the ones whose miscarriages had been distorted into abortions, the ones whose abortions had been mislabeled as murder. She had understood. That the powers at play felt untouched by the plight of the women prisoners, indifferent to their destiny. As long as they got to dip their stubby little fingers into some form of sticky nectar, all was well on the land of the self-righteous.

And so, she dreamt the dream of a hopeful, for the hopeless, and it was fine, Miguel had thought proudly, let her shine. Let her shine, there in this man-made prison called El Salvador. Let her shine because I love her.

And he had loved her, becoming versed in the art of holding her— her tentative ways of being fragile and broken. Her and Miguel, two worlds meshing into a life that breathed lust into a paracosm needing some form of realness. Them—the artist made of white, the wife made of flesh, the husband meant to simply be.

A story lit by warmth, soon to disappear.

The nightmare—

Miguel Balasco's body was found floating on the turquoise water of a turbulent sea, his head tied to the propeller of his beloved yacht, *la Mujer*. No one ever found out exactly why the man's life had been taken away, only suspecting the official culprits of corruption, betrayal, or this common currency, one's association to a wrong political party.

As death had arrived in Claudia's life, so had little Aitana, the daughter made of many dreams, and left now, rich beyond her aspirations. Sebastián, too.

Enough, she whispered, eyes still glued to the mirror. Enough. You must get ready, Claudia Balasco, you have another date with him.

And it is making you happy.

She removed her coat, placed it on her lap. It was difficult to say no, Benjamin.

I made it impossible, wouldn't you say? Benjamin replied with a smile.

Claudia looked around, and catching the waiter's attention, waved at him to come to their table. We're ready, she lip-synced.

You're always so forward with men?

He's our waiter, Benjamin … And no, I've never been forward with men.

He might be our waiter, but you are my guest, Amor, let me do the honors, let me get us the drinks at the bar.

Claudia nodded and folded her coat tighter, pushing it against her belly. A timid smile, almost grateful. Thank you, Benjamin.

A Caipirinha for me, and for you .. ?

She pointed to the bar menu before her. This Bordeaux. Half a bottle, please.

Benjamin stood, and walking across the table, he lifted her chin, kissing her forehead, his eyes lost, as if in a blur. Coming up.

Watching him walk to the bar, his legs like a long and calculated drawl, Claudia wondered about this man who had fallen on her lap three weeks before. Our third date only, she thought, and it's like I know all of him, and nothing. Removing her phone from her purse, she opened it and pressed the green message icon.

Connected to Benjamin Rodriguez' name, the day's date showed forty messages. Forty messages, she thought more, just today. And it's been the same every day, since the beginning. Raising her head to where Benjamin stood, his large back to her and facing the bartender, Claudia's stance hardened. An apprehensiveness arising from the onset of their relationship, one she hadn't been able to understand. It came and it went, this presage—words and gestures, passion-drenched—epochal.

Benjamin turned to her, eyes dancing, and he raised the glasses, as if to say this is for you my love, just for you, the reina of my life.

Another moment chasing her fears, and Claudia sank into it, the moment. As she sipped from her wine, feelings carried by images came to her, settling in her body—the quieting of a small storm. Miguel, she thought, I've been alone for so long now.

I am lonely. So are the children …

This is my favorite, she said, playing with the glass and twirling the wine inside it. I just love the richness of the Bordeaux. Did you know the wine's name comes from the Bordeaux-color itself not the other way around? Holding the glass' fine stem, she looked at the liquid, intent. You see, the beauty of all colors is that they can walk away from their saturated self and mingle with the world and transform it. Just like us. And see here, she said, pointing to the glass, when you look at its robe … The depth of it. The taste, even more. She sipped, closing her eyes. Colors that never disappoint.

Neither does white, Benjamin thought.

Examining her hands, as they manipulated the glass, her fingers, too, gliding over its shine, he lifted his eyes to her features, harmonious yet imperfect, a pointy nose, eyes a dull-browned-color and recessed, a mouth too full. Her face, he thought, she keeps touching it, every five minutes. Reaching for her, he found her fingers, and he delicately laid them on the table, curling his into hers. You are beautiful, you know, Claudia, the most beautiful woman I've ever met.

Her skin, a flush of pink. Benjamin, she mumbled.

You are my sunshine, Claudia Balasco. And I know what I have in my hands, Amor, he continued, as he stroked the red hair surrounding her rosy cheeks. My sun.

As suddenly as Claudia had blushed, blood now, evanescing from her face.

What is it?

She slipped off her stool. Maybe we should go.

But the bottle …

She looked to the waiter, a finger circling the air. The bill it said. They know me around here, Benjamin. We can bring it back home or leave it her for next time. Let's leave it.

In silence, they left, holding hands.

I will never get tired of New York, she said, her body clinging to his. The buzzing sounds, the people. Even its funky perfume, she laughed.

You've been here for so long.

Ever since Aitana was born. 1991.

Fourteen years.

But we shuttle between El Salvador and here, too. She has to know her roots. It's a promise I made to Miguel. At his grave. Same for Sebastián, this orphaned teenager I adopted soon following Aitana's birth.

Bringing her closer to him, Benjamin's muscles tightened. I can't wait to meet them, Claudia. And stopping in the middle of the street, the flow of night pedestrians brushing against them, Benjamin, cupping her face, told her she would never find anyone like him, that she was his everything. Forever.

Claudia looked up, pointed to the moon mingling with the New York lights. I don't know why Benjamin, but sometimes you make feel like I'm in a movie. A fast-paced romantic one, she thought, again feeling unsure. Maybe, still, he will tell me nothing in life is ever enough—certainly not me. And Miguel came to mind, his words, soothing. How you held me, Miguel, she thought. You reassured me, didn't you? Always. This patience of yours. Telling me stories about this beauty you know I never had, of its sprouting from every single part of her body. How can it be, that I still love you, after all this time.

I can tell you're thinking of him, Benjamin said. Were you?

I'll be honest, Benjamin. I miss him. I miss our evenings when following dinner, we walked to the art studio, glass of rum in hand, to discuss the intricacies of my work. She laughed. I don't understand, he would sometimes risk, what are you trying to say? And turning momentarily to Benjamin, she continued. Other times, I simply knew he understood—maybe my beauty lives between the hues I chose to layer, and he decided to make them his, too. She glanced at Benjamin. Maybe he will make them his as well. She brought his hand to her chest. I'm sorry, she said. Maybe I shouldn't have.

Do you still love him?

Do I still love him? She paused. I don't know if it's love. Everyone that we cared for and loved, our past, will land inside our earth, our flesh.

It's another kind of burial. So yes, I must be carrying him, somewhere. She pointed to their right. We're here. Stopping and turning, she kissed him on the cheek. But so you know, there is room for you. A big space.

217 West 57th Street, Benjamin said, pointing to the address.

The valet opened the tall building's door, the gesture soft, reverential. Good evening, Miss Claudia. You'll be happy to know, Mr. Sebastián has just dropped Miss Aitana from the train, said to tell you he had to go back to San Salvador. Something about the house. The man bowed, more, and as he did, he wished the couple a goodnight.

When they entered the apartment, Claudia's confidence had withered. In her head, a voice telling her not to go ahead, to give it more time. Yet, she walked in and joining her daughter standing in the kitchen near the refrigerator dressed in a yellow onesie. She told her, I'd like you to meet someone, sweetie. Aitana Balasco, meet Benjamin Rodriguez.

It's 2:30. You're not sleeping.

Claudia remained, naked and on her back, her arms thin and exposed stretched along her small body. How do you think she took it?

Aitana, he thought. Pretty Aitana. She seemed happy to me, no?

Yes, she did, I know, it surprised me.

Extending an arm, and bringing her closer to him, he gently pushed her head against his chest. Why did we leave abruptly, tonight, Amor?

She clenched her teeth. Pushing her hands into the mattress, lifting herself from his chest, she pressed her back against the headboard. And looking straight ahead, to the wall, papered, where green-colored peacocks stood against a background shimmering with gold, she opened herself. She told him about her hauntings and about the vivid images running to her, of New Jersey, a home wrecked by destiny—a return from the museum, her parents, seated on the subway, tired, arguing over the mundane that make a couple lose itself, distracted, her sister moving through the gaps of standing bodies, statues waiting to get off their stop—five-year-old Julia skipping out of the subway. Of that door that closed too fast. A door that would never reopen. And Julia was never found, she said. And I became, then and now, the poor substitute. That was her, she said, as she pulled a picture from the side table's drawing. We were three years old. She was my twin.

Benjamin now, too, his back against the headboard, listened. Attentive.

We abruptly left the restaurant because of the words you spoke. Julia and I were fraternal twins, not identical. Her fingers caressed the picture and stoked the image of her sister. She had blue eyes, she had blonde hair, she was the vivacious one. I was nothing like her. Sliding the frame back on the drawer, she continued. My parents' grief became complicated, the doctors said. And so, they never forgave me for not being the one to vanish. It came from their mouths, you see, constant slew of words, telling me I was nothing like her. They had missed the mark with me. They had wanted me to be the one to be gone.

When I told you that you are beautiful?

Her eyes fixated the tip of the bed. Yes. A trigger.

They never found her?

Never.

I see.

I got sick from it. The words. The abuse. For fifteen years. No one intervened, until … the depression got so bad … psychosis, suicide attempts … I had a fit at a Walmart somewhere in Clifton. She smiled, shook her head. Aisle five is where the drama happened. The last thing I remember is seeing the row of razor blades looking at me.

Looking at her profile, at her lips moving, at her eyes now closed, he saw Claudia had morphed into a study of human pain, of roads mapping her body, offering an entrance to a well of vulnerabilities. Tender ammunitions. I see, he simply said, again.

I was hospitalized until the right cocktail was found. She pointed to the medication bottles standing on her night table.

How long did you remain at the hospital?

Three six months stays. And you know, it was there that I got into drawing, painting. Dropping her head on his shoulders she spoke about this man, an art professor from NYU struggling with early onset dementia. He noticed something in me, she said. And when they discharged me, I went back home for a few months, then escaped—art school, California, El Salvador, New York. And I never saw my parents again.

Benjamin pointed to the digital clock. What do you say we watch the sunrise, Amor?

She turned to him, her eyebrows softening, smiled. We have two hours at least until then …

He moved his body over her small frame, pulling the covers down, a descent, slow and controlled—a pressure to come. I know, he said, as he started to kiss her. And fuck your parents. Fuck everyone.

Now, you have me.

Two weeks velociously passing, dreamlike and soothing, her angst filling lacunas of the mind. Benjamin Rodriguez moved in, now with Claudia, and continuing to shuttle between New York and the various renovation jobs he had contracted. Upstate New York, he said—Fallsburgh, Bethel, Monticello—some in Brooklyn, too.

Janelle, busy with work, having picked up more shifts at the hospital, had noticed nothing but the usual: Her man was never there. Never had been. And somehow, she had become fine with it, welcoming the hiatus—the strange peacefulness.

With Claudia, the pace, while unconventional, imposed itself, stretching into months, and with it, twisting inside her, a bond, intense as much as unescapable. Aitana came and went from her college in

Connecticut, most of the time chauffeured by Sebastián. Sebastián, shuttling between New York and El Salvador, continued taking care of his mother's real estate affairs. A routine settling in their lives. A hint of normalcy … for now.

Busy with her classes, Claudia, at first, didn't feel the shift occur, the initial shocks remaining unfelt. Benjamin evaporating into the early morning, as if a feather transported by an invisible calm, his absences, more frequent, becoming longer. Her phone calls, ignored, ill returned, and directed to his voicemail. But it was the sensation of feeling dropped, in-between texts, now discontinuous, repetitive in their shallowness; love grenades thrown at her—rehearsed. And in-between them, a chasm into which she fell. Her phone, now, always glued to her hip, yet, never vibrating, never ringing. And this Hello Kitty key chain, a childish bauble, hanging off his own set of many keys. A gift from a client's daughter, he had said. The reprimands, too, stealth, insidious shots to the soul, about her ways of doing things, her art, her mothering, her teaching.

About her physique.

Here son. Here, she pointed, here Sebastián.

She slammed the Maybach's door like she always did, violence feeding her swing. I'll see you in three hours, she said through the open window, then melted into the mess of New York's overflowing sidewalks.

He watched her black dress heave amidst other moving garments, pushed the tip of his tongue on his palate, the sound of it, this tic—toc.

She swallowed, and straightened her body, aware of a shift, a promising one. She continued onto 5th Avenue, to Valentino's. Inside the boutique she let her fingers dawdle on everything she touched: silks, crepes, tulles, and leathers her fingers intimately knew. The time had come, to push them outside her mind, for Benjamin didn't like them, these ostentatious bearings of hers. She chose a simple one, a long and white Claudine collar that showcased her delicate shoulders, a small opening at the cleavage, a reminder of what she was after all. No bows. A fitted silhouette. Red, of course. Red.

Bag in hand, she left and sauntered to Angel's, two blocks over from where she was. Before entering the hair salon, she stopped and looked at the rust of her hair reflected in the glass. She would transform into the color of his dream, she smiled. Then, Emilio's for Italian take-out, wine at Claremont's, Aitana at the airport.

Labor Day weekend with her new family.

I'll miss Aitana, she said. I'm never sure, Benjamin, to what extent she misses me. To what extent I did the right thing to send her to boarding school. I don't know ...

But Deerhill Academy isn't so far, he said. We can visit. And I can do that when working the area ... would you like me too?

Claudia paused. She had observed her daughter interact with Benjamin at dinner. There was restraint, politeness, yet her daughter seemed genuinely interested. His humor, his knowledge about war— Central America, the land they understood. And him, well, she thought, Benjamin was forthcoming, affable even. And Aitana never had said anything. Never had complained. Yes, maybe, it could be a good idea.

Sebastián, though ...

He's shy. He always was shy. Give him time.

I never asked you before ... What happened to him?

An orphan, you know that, already.

Why did you adopt him just as Aitana was born, though?

For some time, I taught art to his mother in prison—she was killed her husband, a violent man who beat her and Sebastián almost every day, with nothing less than a machete. But for his tattoo, he was unrecognizable when they found him ... Her and I became friends, and when she died—

breast cancer—while he was under her care, living inside the prison, with her, I took him in. All this happened around the time my life imploded.

Aitana and him?

The bond has solidified over time, I like to think, over these years. So much older than her, really. But yes, the boy has had his issues, still does, some bad case of paranoia, anxiety, mostly. She smiled. They should take care of one another when I'm gone. My hope, anyways. Any mother's really.

Right, he thought, thinking of how the stocky young man observed his every move.

And he's going back tomorrow?

Yes. The house needs him back in El Salvador. Renovations.

Good riddance, he thought, as he stared at her. Your hair, he said, letting a blonde strand glide inside his mouth, it tastes of unripe fruit. It's bitter.

She laughed, surprised. Really?

He dived in, a dramatic gesture, intimidating even, unknotting a mouthful of balm into her neck, into the flurries that had started to swirl inside her head. Bitterness is just as good as sugar, Claudia. The strands of her hair he proceeded to swallow, saliva wetting the length of them. Releasing them for his mouth, slowly, he turned around, dropping his feet to the ground.

Must you go, Benjamin, it's four in the morning, she mumbled, understanding the moment was as rhetorical as the question. How I hate the dawns now, she thought—its amorphous light, inimical at its core, a twisted brightness that fucked her day, towering over her ever so diligently.

Yes, I need to, he said, as he dressed into his attire. Work, baby, work. Another drop.

But when I return, I would love to take you and Aitana to the Six Flags in Springfield. We can pick her up from her school in Deerhill, then head there for a couple of days.

And just like that, everything continued to be believable.

Something inside her continued to descend farther down, tentacles, poking, unfriendly to her mind. And now, when alone, because of it, the ground archived stories of drunkenness, of her slides to the floors, the slightly slippery part of the evenings when her feet hit the marble floor differently, deploying slowly, the heel extending to the ball of the foot, much, much too mindfully. Once the gait failed, she had discovered, the floors become promiscuous.

That night was no different than the others, following another unexplained absence, these new vanillas of her nights. Still drunk, and heavily medicated, attentive to the weight of the oversized wine glass she was holding, her palm detected the perfect wobble inside the ballon of red, the perfect pitch of the swish telling her all was good. Because it had to be. No matter what. For her. For Aitana. Sebastián, too. Dizzied by fatigue, she dawdled inside her living room, the scent of Benjamin still lingering. Mont-Blanc. She looked out, bored by the skyline, and sipped more. She let herself fall, a slow, controlled fall, glass in hand, stilling by a miracle onto the carpet. Body stretched, arms extended, the fingers twirled the red, calibrating the relevancy of what was left inside the glass. Always so practical to have such built-in sensors when you can't open your eyes anymore, she thought with a smile.

Inside her head, a constant bashing conducted by him, a soundtrack on repeat. I want your flesh to move as I move into you, he said. I want it to speak to me, when I fuck you, he yelled. Yet, in the same breath, as if disconnected to the preceding moment—scathing words.

Your too skinny, Amor, a fucking flaca, not enough curves, too. Running the tip of is finger over the bridge of her nose, he told her about this thing in the middle of her face was all wrong, too long, that it needed to be shortened. And kissing her, a strange look hanging from his face, he spoke about her mouth, her lips.

I prefer the mouths I kiss to be heart shaped.

She pushed the air out of her lungs, the last comment resounding in her mind. And how grateful I am Aitana inherited your complexion, my love—and not Miguel's.

Her feet led her to the shore, telling her to stop on the cold wet of an empty beach, somewhere between Jacob Riis Park and Rockaway Beach. There, Claudia thought, pushing the medicine bottle against the side of her thigh, this is where I found you Benjamin Rodriguez—from her handbag, a bottle of water, and twice she tilted her head, twice she swallowed, sending the pills, painkillers, tumbling to the back of the mouth, her throat barely fighting their bitterness.

Standing straight, feeling her body sinking into the sand, she closed her eyes and screamed a silent scream. You are married, Benjamin. All along, while with me, you were married.

The wind was gone, the air humid. Sweat, she felt it run between her shoulder blades, sponging her scalp, at the back of her knees. Her dress clung to her, and when she felt it mold her body, her pores wet and wide, she thought of him, of how she had clung to him, and with the warm rise of the tears, she paused. What am I? she asked herself.

An ugly doll—mushy fleshed, mushy minded, is what I am.

And a stupefaction, soft, deep, spread just like she had wished it would.

She looked at the faint sea line swimming into the sky's, aware more than she should have been—of the parasite that had laid its nits inside her.

They wiggle inside of me. They twist underneath my skin. I feel them. I see them, too. I need to pull them out, she repeated, convinced, her voice to the ocean.

When the warmest of breeze slid into her, she removed her clothing. She took out the razor from her pocket, shiny chromed and stained by the white of his shaving cream, shaved the hairs on her body, removing with intent—all of it, the bushes, the strands, from every possible place on her skin. The hour passed, and once done, for the longest of time, she hooked her eyes onto the liquid void facing her, waves swirling, calling.

She caressed her scalp and smiled.

Groggy and fighting the urge to surrender to sleep, the painkillers anchoring into her brain, making pain bearable—she took out the scalpel from her bag. No hesitation. A firm intent. To reach beyond the skin; beyond the muscle; beyond the flesh—to the bone. And carefully, she started to puncture her body. From the sleek and taunt surface of her ankles, she pierced and carved, because that's what he had said— everything must start from the bottom, always. Leave the top for the end.

The first stab sent excruciating pain into her body. A long scream, an exhale. And for a moment, hesitation did come, asking, will you go on, is this what you want?

A second stab. A third. A fourth one, too, this time more bearable.

She let go, determined to accelerate the shedding, for shedding meant discarding the parts he disliked the most. New skin, she wanted. And so, she dug feverishly into a worn-out body—calves, hips, abdomen, breast, buttocks—stopping at the base of her neck. There, she took a breath, took in the high of the pain, a pain so high, so alive, endorphins brass-stroking into her.

The high, pain-induced, tall and fierce—reliable.

One last time, she closed her eyes and let her blood-soaked fingers run over its once flawless skin. Her face—a visage, gone and re-imagined.

Her naked body was found early morning on the beach, face to the sand. From that redefined body, incontinent pores and holes, her fluids snaking the ground.

All flowing to a sea that would never care.

Pockets of time were filling the night with a strange quiet, cutting into her shift's 'all you can eat' tragedies, the buffets that paid her bills. Janelle Rivera settled onto the floor and closed her eyes. She would meditate, something she recently started to do.

The night shift was the shift she loved best. The swish of the uniforms so dizzying during the day, reassured her nights. It meant she wasn't totally alone, or just alone enough.

Slow night, nurse Rivera?

She heard the words coming from above her, momentarily unsure of where she was. Her brain had confused meditation with sleep. Again. But the coldness of the floor brought her back, helped by Devon's tone.

He sat beside her, cup of coffee in hand.

I need your opinion on a patient, Janelle. I feel like poking at your knowledge, he laughed, just for the sake of it. Besides, you'll need to clean the wounds.

She opened her eyes.

I've also called for the psychiatrist. And the plastic surgeon. They'll be here first thing in the morning.

She followed Doctor Byrne—the Devon they all wanted to land, in scrubs and all, mostly without them—excited to spend some time with the tall Irish man.

Hey Janelle, the nurse at the desk let out with a wink, enjoying your shift?

They all knew about her. Her failed tattoo stories, the piercings, Benjamin, the sex, the fights, her love for Alejandro. Which meant they all knew about her crush on the bearded man, her penchant for freckles and reddish hair.

Funny, Emily, she replied, batting her eyelashes à la Marilyn, you know very well that Doctor Byrne and I make the best duo on this floor. Contain your jealousy, sister!

The banter could have gone on, but it didn't. Doctor Byrne's face became stern as he pushed in the door. Room number twenty-eight, and they walked in.

The hospital room—white walls shaded by machines meant to monitor her heart, so broken.

Janelle's voice, its velvety inflections now swimming to her ears—it's okay dear, we're taking care of you, I am here, all will be fine—undulating to her with a motherly intent she couldn't understand. Accept, either. Her eyes, clogged by sleepiness, had stopped seeing. I can't see you, she thought, but I know it's you, Janelle. The smell of iodine suddenly climbed her nostrils, jolting her. And lying in her hospital bed, Claudia moved her head in the direction of the voice she had come to hear. She wanted to warn her, speak, about his evil; about this absence of soul, but her mouth wouldn't move. I followed him to you, she thought—you were just a number on his phone, like all the others, and an easy one to trace. You are a nothing. Just like me.

And not long after Janelle's departure from the room, the scent of him reaching her, another door closing.

Quietly, Benjamin sat by her side on the hospital mattress and scrutinized her face. How beautiful you are Claudia, he said. So perfect. Finally. And upon hearing his voice, the tone strangely loving and low, she thought, wanting to shout, hidden beauty is your drug, the only thing you can possess without the fear of it being snatched away from you.

Tears squeezing out from her tender eyes and burning her wounds—she heard another sound, that of his hands brushing against the paper, meshing the whites and the blacks with the side of his hand and the tip of his fingers, the sound of a pencil grinding the paper, pounding it with hard lead like he used to fuck her. I am this skillful duotone, aren't I? A passage in your hole. And I have multiplied them, your holes, she thought more, random punctures all sutured with a black thread. A seam that will never hold anything in.

Nothing is more beautiful than what I see, he said to her as he stood over her. Goodbye, mi Amor.

No longer in a trance, wide awake, he hurried to the door—what if Janelle saw him?—and without looking back, he told her to rot. Rot my beautiful, Claudia, rot. Then, he left the room, the sound of her crying, too.

Janelle looked to the bits of dried cocoa powder floating on top of his cup. The sun's morning rays ran across the kitchen table, landing on the frayed carpet. From all corners of their building, morning shows, morning news, morning music meant to awaken, seemed to converge inside her ears, telling her to snap out of it.

She tried as much as she could to decant what she had seen. Her brain, like a sponge, was engorged—she needed to wring it out, and so she shared, the way she always did with Benjamin, thinning the pain out, diluting the powerlessness she often brought home. The millions of craters, drilled into skin with consistency and purpose, she said. Mini volcanoes oozing with blood like pus. The body, she told Benjamin, as she picked the toast crumbs from the table, you could see she was toned, muscular even, and perfect in an odd way, even though so much of it was wounded. But her face, Benjamin.

Inside her bedroom, she undressed, throwing her bloodied scrubs into the basket, and walked to the bathroom. She brushed her teeth, grabbed the hand towel and hesitated for a moment, dizzy. She leaned toward the mirror the way one searches for what could be, looking at her own pores. Could I do that to myself? Could I? And for what? She lowered her head, and as she did, spat the name out loud, the minty foam dripping from her mouth.

She hadn't heard him, didn't notice his silhouette in the doorframe, just as she hadn't noticed the bed she had slid into had not been slept in.

She stretched over to his side of the bed to flick the noisemaker on and pulled the sleep mask over her eyes. She felt the warmth, the light piercing through the satiny fabric from underneath—the curtains had been forgotten. She sighed. Baby, you mind pulling the curtains shut?

Benjamin seemed stuck in the doorway, just like a right-side hanging bat, lost, bearings floating around. He walked to the window drawing the curtains, and coming back to her, unbuckled his belt, removed his jeans, keeping his white tee on, and slid beside her. Janelle motioned to remove her eye-mask, Benjamin catching her hand and placing it inside of his, firmly. Okay, she said, okay.

On your stomach, Janelle. That way, he thought, she really won't see. Glee.

He parted her thighs and grabbed her from under, one hand pulling a breast, the other caressing her lips—a transactional motion. He smiled. What did you say her name was again?

Balasco, baby, she moaned, Claudia Balasco.

But he knew, for he had been there. Seen her. He felt himself go limp, and closing his eyes, he tried to continue his push into her, alone, as always, her body a masturbatory tool that would eventually yield. Becoming hard again, Benjamin let go, lathering her back, spreading his warmth thick and wide. From behind her, with knees planted in the mattress, he looked straight at the wall before him, to the portrait that hung above the headboard.

Janelle rolled to her side wondering about this absence waving between the two of them—it had captured her, again.

He stood from the bed, slid a pair of sweatpants on and told her he had to go. Pushing the mask up to her forehead, she watched him exit the room, the posture loose, yet without a hint of poise.

She slid herself up, turning toward the portrait, her neck bent backward, eyes looking up, as if pleading. So many shades of gray, she thought, and without them, you wouldn't be alive, and without them I wouldn't be able to see you. I don't know what it is, chica, and I don't know you, yet, I do see you. And because I do, I must go, too, she whispered. Something so wrong is here, yet I don't know what it is.

The room was dark for there were no windows, only white walls onto which a broken Tiffany lamp shined its mosaic of shades.

It needs to be refreshed, she thought. And so, Janelle whipped the red bedspread, thinned out and holed, and the sheets from Alejandro's bed like she did each time he was set to return to them. From visiting his mother. And she knew, he would arrive feeling half orphaned. Like always. You're mine for a while, Janelle thought out loud. You'll see, Alejandro, I'll fix things, like luminous tides coming your way.

Something about Alejandro had called out to her the moment she had met him. Polite, restrained and so obedient, like a child soldier responding to life's imperative to survive. Survive to what? There had been something else, hints of loneliness floating in his gaze, feeding the slump in his stance. Or so she had thought. She had no children of her own except for the children she cared for at the hospital. Maybe I see distress in them too readily? Maybe it's me? And so, she had dismissed the unease, preferring to wallow in the conjugal bliss that had been knocking at her heart. Benjamin. Besides, Alejandro would prove easy to love. So very easy.

She sat on Alejandro's mattress and remembered—I gained a son when I fucked that peasant woman, that is all, and everything, Benjamin had said to her, there in a field ruffled by the warm wind. Desirée was her name. Janelle had listened to his remembering of the past while washing the dinner dishes, pretending to understand, pretending to be what he wanted her to be: obedient; submissive. That's what the pollen did to her, he had continued. The fucking wind must have fucked her, not me. Because only the wind could have given me a son darker than me. Scratching the top of his head, he had spoken of her stocky body, of her legs, strong and muscular, of that hairy pussy, the culprit. A wet dish towel hanging off her shoulder, and she had turned to him, watching him scrutinizing his own skin, his hand, the abrasiveness of it, looking for the specks of white he wanted, somewhere there, pixelating the surface—the white that made him a milky bronze of a wicked man.

To appease my father's worries, the gossip, I married her. To give comfort to a family that needed it. Craved it. He had started to pace in the kitchen, his mind gone, pointing at her, as if she had been a frustration to beat up. A woman meant to quiet my urges, they all said. Yes, I married her. Then I let her go, he said, never talking about Sylvia. Divorced the black-ass lady. Left Alejandro behind. I had to flee. To war. For a moment, Benjamin and Janelle had stood, staring at one another, her the only one alive with fertile quiet. Why, she had risked, why did you have to really go, Benjamin? Leave Nicaragua? He had exploded the way a man explodes when feeling empty and knows he is missing—something. She remembered the yells as he told her Alejandro would come to him, to America. Soon. Then, he had run out the door of the apartment, disappeared, for seven days, reappearing with Alejandro by the hand—the first time meeting the boy. And the mother, Desirée, too, deciding—able—to marry an American, had moved near-by.

Yet.

Janelle stood up from the bed and wiped her tears away. She shook the sheets off the mattress, rounded them up and kicked the loose ball into the corner. She thought of the weekend ahead. Of surfing. Of the three of them.

She tidied his closet, pairing the sneakers, suspending the few belts snaking the ground, picking up the dirty clothes piled at the back, behind a set of three stacked boxes.

As she motioned to retrieve one of Alejandro's water shoes, she inadvertently knocked the top box off, sending its content to the floor. Shards of glass-like gems, sundries, of all sizes and many-hued had fallen out, clinging to the shag carpet with nowhere to go. She examined them, and then took a few to roll between her fingers. Plastic. Angular but soft edged. Alejandro was a collector of peculiar things—the top shelves of the kitchen cupboards were full of them. Simple Yu-gi-oh!, Pokémon, baseball or hockey cards never appealed to him. What the eleven-year boy brought home was an ode to his burgeoning eccentricities. Herbs from everywhere in Central America, some comestibles, others not, rock salts of different provenances, coffee beans, most of which he catalogued like a philatelist would his stamps. Of late, there had been a newfound interest for the Middle Ages, Europe and its monarchies. From England to Spain, Austria to Russia, like the herbs, the rock salts and the beans, portraits of the women and men from this period were glued inside the pages of a makeshift scrapbook.

What are they, Amor? she had asked him.

Beige-colored terrains. My lovelies.

Oh.

Their wedding picture was hanging above his night table, lopsided. Leveling it, she looked at herself. Not at him, the vacuum of him. Less even—Alejandro. The white chiffon cold shoulder dress, her hands, soft and surrendered inside of his, her smile, tentative but willful, the only one gracing anyone's face. The day had been dreadful, she now could admit. Nothing any bride could have wished for. Nothing. Yet, she had pretended. Hoped.

She started to walk back and forth inside the bedroom, not wanting to look more, but knowing she had to—face it. Her cowardice. Why had she not said anything, why had she let him do it?

Approaching the wall again, she raised her head to the portrait, and lifting her eyes, she decided it was time to look. See. No cara pina at my wedding Benjamin had said. No acne-faced riddling my moment. And with these words pinballing inside her head, she looked on to the small black face in the portrait, not staring, not looking at anything or anyone, a small black face whose eyes had capitulated.

A small black face, half hidden—half covered with peach-colored band aids.

The day was bright. The waves, promising. And walking toward the sea was always my cure, Alejandro. And I hope I will pass this balm on to you, she thought.

A toneless whisper inside his questions as they walked to the beach. You think Papi loves you? You think he loves me?

Janelle stopped and turned to him, the wind blowing on her face. Sometimes I do. Sometimes I don't, Alejandro. She took his hand and pulled him against her, slowly walking on the boardwalk, parallel to the shore.

I can't tell you because you are not allowed to know, he thought. When I feel his hands on mine, when I feel my own on his body, I think he does. Especially in that corner. The garage. But in another corner, the web of a childhood spun like a funnel that has no end. Inside it, images of a mother who was slowly erasing herself, words and gestures of a father who teaches that everything in this life is made of rights and open passages that you claim. Without impunity. Take what you want. Especially when on your hands and knees, pillars that can never cave in. Then blood trickling. No stops for him.

His father's tentacles poked at him. He felt it, felt them while his hands moved inside Janelle's, knowing—knowing that in a near future, the quest for trying to be more would take a new turn. Because ignorance takes many forms. Because sometimes it is sweet. Because sometimes, it just is.

He says that we cause suffering to the ones we love, only them. As proof of love. Do you believe that we do? Quien te quiere, te aporrea, he always says.

No, Alejandro.

Okay.

She led him toward the ocean, the wind pushing onto their back. The conditions are perfect today she whispered to herself.

On the sand, they removed their shoes and walked on as frozen frames of hurt rushed to replace the blue combers before her. Aggressions meant to tease, bites meant to tickle, slaps meant to brush. That was Benjamin.

A fleeting moment, a filtered present. She stared at the eternity ring he had given her, turquoise and diamonds circling her finger. She didn't understand.

He is leaving me, the boy said.

Maybe, Alejandro. But he never arrived …

If he loved me, Papi would be here.

She stared ahead. There's a big bruise inside his brain, Alejandro. An invisible one. It bleeds like a sore from a birth mark. Hidden, you know? But it's there. He feels it every day. A deep itch he can't flee from.

I'm hungry.

Me, too, she replied. Let's grab a taco before you hit the waves.

He nodded, as they walked back toward the boardwalk to their favorite stand. The crowd around them was buoyant and loud. They joined the end of the line that was long and filled with parents and children his age. Eyes filled with smiles that were real, and the touch and tones of a love he wanted.

She slapped saliva onto her thumb, reprieving the sound of her sorrow, and removing the blood that had formed at the corner of his mouth, she tried a smile. Let's take our tacos for a walk, then, time for class.

Uneasy, he rubbed his knees, the reddish thickness of them.

They seem better, yeah?

Maybe.

The scabs have almost gone.

Almost.

Okay, then. It's settled. Listo, Amorito?

Sí.

The wind flagged her towel in the air, sending sand into her face. Unfazed, she settled in, the slow boom of the sea welcoming them. She dug in the sand with her feet, creating pockets of comfort for the few protruding parts of her body that needed it. He kissed her cheek then walked to his instructor, placing the board above his head. He liked the shadow it made. Some shadows protect, others haunt, that much he had understood.

As the water circled his skinny ankles, he felt an urge to tell her, and dropping the board he ran back to her. Breathless, he wrapped his arms around her shoulders, his head facing the taco stand they just had left. Te amo, Janelle.

He turned around and moved back toward the tidal flats. Mouth agape, she looked ahead, pulling the strings of her hoodie tighter around her neck. As if summoned, tears appeared.

Through them, leaden skies melting into leaden seas.

No horizon but him splitting the gloom in two.

She watched Alejandro tackle the waves, remembering Benjamin, sweetness's failed understudy stamped all over this one's young skin. She knew the truth.

That he was common.

Salty soot.

Never caviar.

Benjamin's retina captured what he sought, eidolons that wafted above the eventides.

2005, now. The birth of a grief, deep; the obsession feeding the need to understand the inconceivable.

Alejandro walking back to the water, never saw she was crying, tears that punctuated the decision she had come to, just then. This newfound understanding—to live, she would have to leave him behind. Alejandro.

BOOK THREE

I slowly rock in this chair and hear nothing but the soft buzzing of flies that have found an opening through the screen's broken mesh. All it takes is one opening and the leak introduces itself, uninvited, flies buzzing.

I look through the glass, look at the frame of the window, watch its wet paint slowly dry, and see the landscape made of greens that whisper of jealousy to me. Is it jealousy? I really don't know. At the very least, it is envy, I think.

I rock a little faster and start humming this song, this sentence stuck inside my head, a virus that reaches the deepest grey of my brain. Or has it become black? And I think of him, of the bar, of that other song that reminds me, yes, it's a good life if you don't weaken.

And when I wet my lips, I taste his vodka.

I am weak, I finally understand.

Yes, I am.

Made of a weakness.

I have disappeared in the back and forth of my chair's motion, looking not so still, but I am. I close my eyes and remember the ceiling, the fan and the heat I almost returned to.

Let me say, I come to you from a place that reeks of sterility.

Why am I here, exactly? Sometimes I understand, sometimes I don't.

All I know is that my thinking is no longer under my control, that images—soft and out of focus, snapshots of what life there was, of what life *and its soothing mundaneness were—loops without end like a rusty trap, one that bites and grips and swallows you whole, bloody and all.*

And blood there was. So much of it.

But not mine.

I heard the doctors give it a name the other day. I heard them talk about me, not far from where I usually rock, close to the nurses' station. It's called survivor's guilt, they said, that I have it bad, like a case of it rarely seen.

At the miso plant, though, usually, I'm okay. It's when I leave that place that the rumination starts. To the beat of Rachmaninov and now this group the barman told me about, these words that speak of the night's shades and the fog in one's life, of the instability inside a body, in all the movements we improvise—God knows, I did, and I will some more—of those collective whispers that tell us to stay here now and stay whole, of getting along every day in dreamlike states where our sorrows compensate for all our woes, everywhere we are. That's what I hear, this other loop that rings inside my head, a melody pulled by the melancholy of a twelve-string guitar. And in the end, this lesson, to be learned and absorbed and lived, that we will go where we are needed, that we will grow where we are needed—that it will be a good life if I don't weaken.

But weak, I am.

I look at my feet now and see I forgot to slip my shoes on. But they are used to the forgetfulness that is often me. They don't know that sometimes, though, I do remember. It is a secret; I am a secret.

I think I am.

Isabelle

The start of her nightmare—pictures sent by her husband's mistress, of the two of them. In all sorts of angles. Positions.

December 2015.

After seeing the pictures, Isabelle had sought revenge—a revenge made of flesh, one that should have lasted a night, a weekend, maybe, never eighteen months. But it had and with it, self-harm made of tolerated deceptions.

Benjamin Rodriguez.

Sitting in her apartment in Montreal, Isabelle Duval remembered it vividly. You want something to eat? Benjamin had asked her casually after they had finished making love—their first night together following a right swipe: January 2016. She had been high on the wanting of lust—the wanting of satisfaction, to even the score. She had been absent from her mind for too long, and now, driven by her desire to numb the pain, she had done ... the unthinkable. At least to her, at one point, it would have seemed unthinkable.

Benjamin had insisted they stay naked after their lovemaking, and despite being cold, she had not cared. Looking back, understanding he was never who he said he was, she could still feel the iciness of the kitchen counter against the backs of her thighs. Cutting an apple, he had sternly looked at her over his shoulder, knife in hand. His gaze had held Isabelle's a few seconds too long.

She knew now what she had instinctively felt then. What she had known but had dismissed. For a second, she had been a temptation ... an option ... a risk ... that he did not take. He had offered her, with precise intent—to kill?—a piece of apple planted on the tip of his knife. What saved me? she had wondered. The lighting. The lighting hitting her white skin had been her savior. It had uncovered the pastiness he so loved, exposing her veins snaking under her skin, the fodder his eyes needed to feed his sick mind.

She had been a keeper.

One of many.

Spare, or otherwise.

She thought of Alice, caught between a mother's urge to live at the cost of dying, and the cost of her daughter's life.

A monumental betrayal.

And of course: the box.

Time holds power, its passing filled with promises of cures, dilutes memories and transforms them into palatable pieces of semi-truths.

But she does not know this, yet.

After one long year had passed, unhealed and damaged, Isabelle Duval sought for more than what she had discovered the year before, 2017, when leaving Benjamin Rodriguez behind. Trying to understand, too, the crimes.

The criminal.

The two men are suspected of killing that girl, Peter Cowans had said, that and many more. Staring at the screen, looking at this woman, wilted and muted, not understanding—yet, the Canadian military consultant living in Managua, continued. The newspaper article. The revelations—both are linked to an old General, a rightist, and influencing the 2003-2004 military mission in Spain. Iraq. They were his sons, Isabelle.

Luis Marco Rodriguez.

Mateo Patrick Diez. Patrick—that alias created just for her. Or was it?

The pain lingering still, unable to shed it—she needed to go back, she thought, figure things out.

An unhealthy thirst for knowledge that had rooted itself deep within her.

She lifted her body from another sleepless night, slipped into the clothes she had chosen for the trip, simple leggings and hoodie all meant to conceal. She looked at herself as she waited for her Uber to arrive, placed her buds in the nook of her ears, and swayed to Sinead O'Connor's music—this soft singing of such abundant meanings. She stared at the long, black-framed mirror planted against the bedroom wall, barely able to confront everything reflecting to her. Was it Monroe or Bacall who had said it, she tried to remember, that looking into a mirror to see oneself, isn't the study of a life. What is it then? Lives are made of choices that design and define our moments. And moments can melt into one, erase and remold whatever had been, at some point.

The goodness of me, and the good goodness of all of me.

One moment had altered the course of my life, she acknowledged. I can see its reflection following me wherever I go, never letting go, right there, always, another stalker, asking why?

Waiting still, and now seated on the floor, she travelled to the year she had turned eighteen, when walking to school dressed in her pink jeans, her pink polo and white topsiders, she felt so light, unreachable because fierce in her belief that life would always be like this, never faltering, never defaulting on her. Yes, she had come to understand, somehow, that everything has an expiration date, but then, she didn't want to believe it. A yellow Walkman to her waist playing some Duran Duran song—or was it, The Stranglers? Sucking on a strand of her hair, her steps grounded, her head so very light, she had thought, nothing good or bad should be bottled, lives can be short or long, they also can never be, never breathe—maybe for but one moment. One long, single, never-ending moment.

And she thought, I won't cry. Not for him anymore.

She heard the Uber notification push from her phone, stood, took one last look at herself and rubbed the numbness from her eyes. The ear buds had fallen, dangling to her chest. She tucked them back in, white plastic peas meant to stem, cranked the volume, and left the apartment with Sinead telling her she is the chosen one, that she will soak the sea—to let the night fall into the day. I'm a heroine.

Leaving her home, Isabelle quickly turned to the table placed at the entrance and looked. On it, this reminder, the book she had just published, *Inhaled*. The story of her and him. Uncensored.

She smiled. Yes, that is what I am. A heroine.

The warm air whipped at the back of her throat as she stepped out of the plane. No transition between the metal bird and the outside world, no corridor to buffer the heat's aggression.

She let go of the stair ramp and grabbed at her neck, jolted out of balance onto the tarmac. She smiled, like only she could, embracing this particular brand of strangeness; this wicked urge of wanting to dig deeper; this well to dip her pen in called revenge. She gathered her belongings, straightened, and spotted him standing next to the "Welcome to Nicaragua" sign.

There you are, Isa. How are you? he asked, as he removed both earphones.

Scanning him slowly, indecently really, her lips half opened, she tittered. Once immobile, facing him, she turned her head, bowing to the fragrance that was reaching for her. The air had been tamed, leaving the bougainvillea's nectareous scent to rule the space around her. Far from her past, closer to herself, she had decided it would be him, that being there was the first step—the first real one. How am I? Thirsty, she said, very thirsty.

Peter took hold of her with his eyes and laughed a hearty laugh that crystallizes moments preceding a human collision, the one you never knew you had wished for.

She continued, looked at him with intent, studied a face weathered by life, chiseled by loss.

Isabelle.

Peter.

Hold on tight, Peter yelled, as he brought her hand against his chest, I don't want you to fall.

She let him take it, and feeling the squeeze, let her head fall between his shoulder blades, the noise of the engine buzzing inside her brain. Here, he continued, releasing her hand to point to the ocean, we've almost arrived. The wind was breaking his words, but her eyes followed his finger, extending her gaze further on until she saw the roof of the tiki bar appear. She smiled, anticipating the first sip of the day. It was 2:00 P.M somewhere in Nicaragua, a somewhere only known to the year—October 2018.

He slowed the motorcycle, turned right into the sand filled parking lot, and chose a spot to land his bike. He took his pack and grabbed her hand, and as he did, he looked at her, and he smiled. I'm so glad you're here, Isa, to finally see you again. He stared more at a mind hostage to hopelessness, a wound loving its own freshness.

Still gone.

Time for a drink, she said.

Is it, now? he laughed.

A terrace floating above the sea, a table perched at the end of the pier-like platform.

Two Jamieson's, he ordered, as they each pulled a chair out, with lots of ice. He turned to her and said something about the heat needing more heat, to be tamed and fought, something about the ice being safe here, that the water was clean, that she wouldn't get sick. If she had heard him, she would have thought, it's fine Peter, all of it works for me. I want to get sick, with something new, the new that kills the old.

Tired and dulled by her travels, she sat, immobile, on the bamboo of the wobbly chair. Head down, she stuck a finger inside her drink.

The art of the stir.

The outside as much as the inside of her drinks had become a world of its own. In them—on them, she would get lost in the absence of measure, tapping mindlessly at their rims, their ice, puncturing their garnish, aware of the unease she was leaving behind. She didn't care for pacing, unity, or harmony. The souvenir of this trip, of her time with Peter, would remain vague for years to come, she knew, filled with alcohol induced memory gaps and images scratched by excess—two tippers creating a world in which their existence made sense, the conviction somehow destiny could sometimes be right.

Are you all right, Isa?

She looked away, her chin up, her eyes to the ground.

You have to stop these travels. Move on, Isa. It will kill you if you don't.

Her face gaunt, her hair thinned out. I know.

Nodding, Peter stood up, grabbing the drinks, and motioned her to the same. Let's go for a walk.

In silence, she removed her sandals and walked to the edge of the wooden floor, stepping onto the sand, feeling it burn the sole of her feet. Hands barely touching, they walked to the edge of the ocean. There, she looked through her glass, the thickness of its diamond shaped carvings distorting the horizon in front of it. She sipped her drink, looked around, her shoulders loosened by the heat and by the alcohol, a wanting body that was letting go. They walked farther up where the sand was moist and cool and sat far enough away from the small crowd gathered at the bar.

You will survive this, he said.

I fear my mind, you know. I didn't know myself before all this. I do now. These obsessions. And I'm afraid of me, Peter. Me. Has that ever happened to you? She paused, not expecting an answer. What I can't tell, explain, is how low I can go, or how high. This potential. So corrosive. Maybe I knew it all along and chose a life of boredom to make sure I wouldn't explode. She looked at him, her smile a funny grimace. Boom. Time to pick up the shrapnel.

She stood, pulled him by the hand. Let's walk more.

You came ... because ...? he asked.

My life is like a night that won't lift. I'm here because of that.

Time, Isa.

The tears. Too familiar. Time is making me think, too much, Peter. What I did to myself. The selfishness. The lust, narrow and inconsequential. And all for what? Because I was wronged? Why is my pain different than the woman's next door. And Alice ...

Alice?

Yes. Alice.

The sea, moving and lapping the shore with calm, Isabelle walked to the edge of the water. The obscurity must rise, she thought. Somehow it has to.

The perfect night came, the one she had dreamed of while staring at the ceiling of her bedroom in Montreal, unable to sleep. She had hinted to it a few times, her plan, thinking their intemperance kept him from grasping what she was saying And so, two days into her trip to Managua,

225

Peter felt her absence, a space, still warm, beside him and got out of the bed, there in his loft. From the window he watched her hurry into the taxi. Some words were exchanged, all inaudible. A sense of urgency took hold of him, and quickly sliding into his jeans, he shook his head in disbelief looking at his watch. 2:00 A.M. What the fuck Isabelle, what the fuck.

Managua at night is like a lost bullet looking for its mark. A Latino filled effervescence that simmers below the cheap cologne, and the rum lathered air, just enough to let one know their safety is not to be taken for granted. But danger was what had brought her there—the thrill of looking for what she should flee.

Wait for me, she told the driver, do not move and do not shut your headlights.

Her feet struggled to make their way through the sludgy beach. She stopped and scanned the ground some more, taking in the shore on which, some fifteen years before, more than garbage had washed up. Her head lifted to a horizon she didn't understand. Everything about this place was foul, she thought, suddenly aware of the acrid smell grazing her throat. Polluted by eighty years of raw sewage and effluent pouring into its waters, lake Managua stood before her.

Stars shone for a second on her, and she let go of her shivers, coming back to the purpose of her trip, to verify with the mind's eye—an eye no longer wanting to close its lids, or its junction to her brain—somehow lessening the assault of the lake's smell. She let the fetid breeze caress her cheeks as tears veiled her eyes. So, this is where it happened, where they were found, she whispered to herself. Barrio El Fondo.

She walked around, careful not to step on the carpet of half opened cans, plastic bags, and dead fish. So much vegetation around, she thought, as she scanned the shoreline, yet so much deadness. It must have buffered the sounds, she suddenly realized.

Pulled by the sparsely lit horizon, she moved toward the tall pier that unfolded above the murky water. She stopped at its edge, but barely, fighting the absurd urge to dive in. This is not a lake, noticing the sea like waves, this is an ocean of lifelessness—water from the under-life.

With a body swaying to the rhythm of the past, she stayed.

With a mind unwilling to let go of it.

She didn't struggle to comprehend most of it—all those girls had died a death imagined by wickedness. I just want the pain to leave, she thought. The fucking pain, always there, following me like a sick puppy.

And she cried this time, just long enough.

She walked to one of many large concrete blocks littering the area planted at the front end of the pier, its base partially lathered by the waves.

An altar.

She remained seated there for an hour, her feet dangling above the shoreline, her eyes feeling and hearing what needed to be felt and heard.

Because when confronted with darkness, that is all the eyes can do. Listen.

She had read about them: The Nahuas, an indigenous people found in Mexico, and most parts of Central America, believed in their God's power to push the sun's rays into the infernal world. Xolotl was the God's name, the name given to the lake. And where were you Xolotl, you pimp? she yelled. Out fucking the moon's dark side?

Her mind brought her back there, like it had so many times before, inside Benjamin's bedroom closet, to that corner—to that box, an image haunting her days more than her nights. Had it really happened? Did it exist at all?

The glare of the headlights startled her. She turned around and saw Peter get out of his car, sending the taxi away. She stood, slowly, Peter walking toward her.

They stopped where they met and said nothing, there in an intersection wrought with unanswered questions. Her head, drawn down by gloom, placed on the nook of his shoulders. She couldn't weep, she couldn't sob. Everything inside her was dry.

I'm ready to go home.

Okay, he said, let's get out of this dump.

During the next two months, with each of his visits to Montreal—a taste of the past dissolving, parts of her present found new roots to sprout from, shaky but willing, life re-emerging from her body.

They acknowledged one another, as an evening came to stay, in the promise of a fall's night embrace, their readiness to cross over. Hand-in-hand, in silence, they strolled to the elevator up to his hotel room, walking into its dimness, the scent of her guiding him, Peter turning around slowly, taking her face inside his large hands. The kiss soft, tender, all too foreign to Isabelle's senses. Unhurriedly, they undressed each other, their rhythm synchronized, both tentative, yet wanting to trust.

At the sight of Peter's body, Isabelle became unsure, suddenly questioning her desire to be with him. Eyes closed while lying on the bed, naked, she brought Benjamin's body to mind, her brain flashing images of him. All of him.

The truth, unavoidable, impossible to ignore, comforted her: It is my skin that is grieving, she thought, as she looked away from Peter's questioning gaze. Not the heart.

Not the soul. The skin.

They made love for the first time that night, a love born out of the wanting to hold. But, used to being used, she felt lost inside this newfound sensation—this tenderness that moved like ammunition under her skin—and unable to absorb the meaning of it, she cried, her back nestled inside his arms.

Peter fast asleep, she stood from the bed, suddenly craving her own space, wanting to leave. With the plush of the carpet, her toes played for a time. It was warm. Soothing. But she had decided to go, and so, she dressed herself quietly. Her eyes had adjusted to the dark of the room, and so, confident Peter wouldn't wake up, she allowed herself to fully look at his body; his breathing, the minutiae inside of it. For the longest of time, she remained, until shreds of light appeared from the bottom of the black-out curtains, foretelling, of a new day, a brighter one, she hoped.

She walked to the small secretary located by the bed beside the window, and gently tore a page from the night menu the clerk had handed them the evening before. I'll see you tomorrow night, she wrote in cursive as loopy as her thoughts had become. My place—yours, too. Then, she slipped out of the room.

The end of November, and she sauntered back to her apartment through the empty streets of the city, her silhouette slicing the fog floating around. I did it, she thought, triumphant. I broke the crazy man's spell.

That next night, at her apartment, he asked, what are you thinking of?

She turned her head slowly toward him, met his eyes, glacier-like turquoise, transparent as crystal, seeing her for who she was, she was certain. The absence of an abyss in his gaze also unsettled her. The depth she was seeing was welcoming, yet unfamiliar to her here amidst the bed sheets.

Still.

That your body scares me, she thought. That I am unsure of my response to you. My physical response. That I still feel as if I am betraying someone. Not Patrick, because I killed him. No, not him. His alter ego. It. Benjamin.

229

Nothing, she said, caressing his back. Nothing. And she stared at him wondering still: Does the body talk, can it keep secrets?

Not wanting her words to weigh on a moment already so burdened by awkwardness, she let her mind move away from her confused state and told him how happy she was he had come to visit, again. Of how she had missed him, this closeness.

As Peter took her hand, she remembered the savage bites seeded by Benjamin's teeth along the contours of her hand. Loving aggression, they call it, the animalistic instinct to play—the sexual way. In that instant, she imagined Peter's benevolence softly carving deeper into her palm's lifeline, changing its course.

This is what I want.

To be diverted.

Like a wild river.

She got up reaching for the clothes scattered on her bedroom floor. I'll go and make us some coffee.

Wait, not so fast. I am not done with you yet.

He pulled her back to bed, teasing the inside of her forearm, the way she liked. She resisted, stiffening as his fingers feathered her skin. The alcohol emanating from his breath was repelling her. Or was it hers? She didn't know any more, remembering how they both doused themselves in wine the night before.

No, she smiled, a hand to her forehead, if I don't get some coffee now … And don't forget your meds. She pointed to his shaky hands wondering why she fell for the head-fucked army guys? What is it I want from them?

She slid into her jeans, the ones she loved so much, the ones that made her feel eternally young, and grabbed a soft, pink sweater.

She dawdled through the corridor leading to the kitchen area, her body brushing against the wall, clipping some of the cracked paint along the way. A stubborn nail sticking out of the floor caught her foot. Again.

She clung to the pain, oblivious to the train of blood now staining the old wood surface. Something must drive me to this nail, she often thought, because this hurt feels good. Necessary.

She made her way through the dishes and made coffee. Waiting for the cups to fill, she fed her cat, James, pushing him away from the empty wine bottles he had started to toy with.

Isa, she heard, come over here.

She froze. The words in her head ringing, echoing the past, ramming into her mercilessly. Images of Benjamin asking and demanding and expecting. How she had obeyed. A virus in her head—ven aca, baby—come over here.

Isa, he said your foot. It's bleeding. He walked to the sink, ripped a tissue from the roll and wet it.

I didn't hear you come, she said, startled by his presence in the kitchen. It's okay, I'll do it. She smiled and gently took the tissue from his trembling hands. She kissed his cheek and stared beyond him the way one wishes not to see. There is nothing animalistic about him, she thought.

So kind.

Too human.

Peter had become used to her leaving for a world filled with hostile ghosts. He could feel Isabelle swimming inside her past, guarded, secretive almost, with unabated agility, alone, always. Who is she protecting? Herself?

Me?

You keep disappearing when I'm with you, he said, as he lifted her up, it's been almost one year …

She took a step back. You're like the others, Peter. Turn the page. Move on. As if…

I didn't mean—

Peter, I know it's been a year. No need to remind me. I'm a big girl, I remind myself of that very fact all the time. Trust me. I do. A million times a day. Yes, she thought, each day is crossed. I don't feel they mark a victory. I feel they mark a countdown. And I know no one understands me, no one can, she continued, and I hate them for it. They understand from that comfortable place made of pains and sufferings they can fathom and dismiss. Everyday loss. Everyday grief. Normal pain. Decipherable pain. Emotions and reactions empathy can ease into. But not this. Look at me, she said tearfully. Look-at-me. My face. My hair, shedding non-stop … Gone and lost.

He brought her close to him, harder, and caressing her hair. You are beautiful, Frenchie. To me.

Her head dropped onto his chest, and with aches slowly retreating, pushing her breath closer to her core, she lifted her head, her eyes moist. Bagels with hummus? she risked, her smile, valiant as much as pleading.

Breakfast is on me, he said, as he kissed both her eyes.

Okay, she whispered, and please, do brush your teeth before you leave.

Come on, Frenchie, killer breath is part of my repertoire. I am a military man after all, you know that. I kill with all I've got. And that includes my mouth, he added, motioning again to kiss her.

Isabelle pushed his shoulders back with her hand, her shakes subsiding, and brushed the back of his neck with fingers eager to dismiss as much as to keep. Just go, she laughed, just go.

He strolled along the main street, his head tucked inside a parka, his eyes to the sky. Mouth opened, eyes closed, he let the flakes melt on his tongue. It'll freshen my breath, he thought with a smile. He ungloved, wanting to feel the slivers of white cool the top of his hands. Maybe it'll stop the trembling, too.

Grocery bag in hand, he glanced into the bedroom as he headed to the kitchen. Isabelle was lying on her side, resting on the bed. Leaving the bag on the kitchen floor, he stared at the pots and pans piled up on the stove. He turned to face the sink. A jumble of sauce-stained plates and half eaten salad bowls were spread precariously on the countertop, waiting to be washed. Champagne flutes and wine glasses, their stems intertwined, filled the sink. We kind of outdid ourselves, last night, Isa, and he laughed.

He opened the cupboards above his head, confronting the tussle inside his brain, a daily ordeal that had marked his life since leaving the military. He looked at the liquid dancing inside the stillness of a wanted bottle. Yes, it said. Yes, he simply heard.

Each morning holding so many possibilities, possibilities flying inside of seconds preceding the first swig, escaping his will. He reached for the bottle hidden behind the summer dishes, uncapped it and poured the flames greedily. Eyes closed, he let the fire spin inside his mouth—an untamable frailty—quietly placing the bottle back behind the packed set of plates.

He walked to the bedroom carrying the food tray. Bagels and hummus, he said, just like the diva ordered.

Isabelle steadied herself, leaning against the headboard, and laid the tray on her lap. He couldn't read Isabelle most of the time, and now was no different, her eyes had hardened, her shoulders had dropped. A paradox.

She twisted the soft curls that hung sideways, framing the right side of her face, that lock of hair so often mocked by her daughters Alice and Catherine—the hair that hadn't been pulled for a while, and plucked one by one by the violence of trauma. I'm thinking, her speech now composed, since the girls aren't with me this Christmas—a skiing holiday?

Not waiting for Peter's response, she took a quick bite of her bagel, and flipping the duvet off her lap, walked to her closet, grabbing a towel hanging inside its door.

I'm taking a shower, she said, as she walked out the room. And in the meantime, Peter Cowans, check Mt. Tremblant out. I need to get out of here.

The lockdown is over, she thought.

No more invisible hands to fight off.

I am exhaling at last.

Putrid air.

From all of me.

Slicing into the icy patches with ease, digging the sharpened edges of her skis into the cold ground, reminded her of what she had once been: strong. The run had been easy enough, and as she tackled the vertical that suddenly appeared, her mind filled with thoughts of Alice and Catherine. Daughters that reminded of her purpose.

She scanned the view before her, eyes taking in the quiet of the trees bordering the ski run. I can do this. She bent her knees a little more, let her quadriceps answer the urge to aggress and simultaneously tame the slope. Planting her poles and skis with the sole purpose of killing the frozen ground, she felt alive. She felt free.

How I crave this.

Speed. More speed.

She felt herself fly above the white of the hardened snow, and she heard her laugh echo inside a heart that needed buoyancy, and she remembered then, that to survive life's race, whatever it is, she had to learn to halt her body and her mind on demand.

Before the loss of control.

That if she gave in to the arousal of the moment, she could die.

Now was time to stop.

At the bottom of the ski hill, she lifted her head, searching through the crowd for his red ski jacket. She saw him, waving his arms in the air as he watched her glide to him. Kiss me, she giggled, as she wiped off her nose with the outside of her mitten, puckering her lips, warm these up.

You awake, Isa?

She turned over to face him, smiling.

He moved closer and kissed her forehead gently. We have to talk.

The bright light piercing through the curtains hinted the morning had well arrived. The room, located on the first floor of a three-story hotel, reeked of brown. Yes, she thought, colors do smell and this one smells of mold and dust and of starched hopelessness. She reached for Peter's chest and as she heard skiers getting ready to attack First Tracks, she slid her hand further down and looked at him, the urge to cling to him arriving. She removed her hand and propped herself up, rearranged the layers of blankets making sure to cover her feet. I'm listening. Her head leaned somewhat toward him, the window framing his upper body, letting in the light she sought. She knew. The face she inspected told her that, yes, a velvety certainty, so present, so warm, was there to make her feel safe.

Seen.

Secure.

Well, you know, for the better part of the last twelve months, I have respected your silence …

She squirmed onto herself, wanting to fold and fold and fold some more. She watched the light flicker below the television set, and travel deep into the recent past, back to Benjamin's closet. An extemporized cleaning of his bedroom; the box—the necklace. The beige leather-like charms. Human skins? Maybe little Jocelyne Rodriguez had simply gifted those squares hanging from that steel thread. Maybe they had been improvised childish baubles given to a father she so wanted to have. Maybe the box only contained mementos and trophies of digested conquests. Whatever they were, she knew they highlighted Benjamin's craziness—undeniable obsessions with his idea of love, of proof of its passage in his life. Tucked in beside Peter, feeling the beat of his heart crawl everywhere over her skin, she wasn't sure anymore. Suede, silk, leather, or plastic? Her own memory, she feared, like his, had maybe erased the impossible, only choosing what the mind could see—tolerate. Because memory is a form of imagination, isn't it? Memories move, sculpted, sometimes by dangerous understandings, sometimes by the consistency of our wants. Memory—a shapeshifter made of unreliable truths.

There was, there is, nothing to say, nothing to add. What would I be hiding? Everything you and I already have exposed, she lied. No proof of anything. Nothing sufficient to incriminate.

For she had never shared about the box.

Isa, we could have asked for more. There are ways to get closure on this for you. And just so you know, the newspapers were wrong. One girl had been found the last time. Not two.

Yet, she knew, more than one girl had been murdered. The necklace had spoken.

Hints of anger scratched the back of her throat. Closure? What business is it to you? You don't get to decide when hurt and betrayal comes to a stop for me. Not you, not my friends, not the girls. No one gets to tell me when it's over. No one.

The girls, she thought. Catherine in Argentina, with her new beau. Fuck you, Mom, she had told her before leaving the year before, you deserve everything that's happening to you. She had called Isabelle a whore, a lying wife, a mother made of clay. A fake. Isabelle remembered the words, the delivery of them, disgust filled. You turned around so quickly from Dad when he cheated. You never loved him, did you? How convenient for you to turn around and fuck the first guy ...

Isabelle looked ahead. Alice. Gone to live with her father. No disgust there, just pure suffering thrown at a mother who had failed to stay one.

You left me alone with this man, suspecting he had killed. And when Dad left you, *Mother,* you left me, too. Abandoned me. For them. Him and his children.

The shame, so heavy, deserved, yet unwearable. It came in waves, and the waves carried with them refusals to let go. One clutches to that wave, one tackles its wall, sometimes hoping it will never find shore, she had learned. Swim in pathos girl. Just don't sink. She shook her head. I'm sorry, Peter. It's been difficult for me to get here with you, to this place. I know I owe you much. But all I can give you is ... what I can give you.

He wanted to tell her. So much. To shout it out. That he had continued to enquire, a deeper dive, that some of his contacts in Managua had been tasked to dig for more. Other options exist Isa, that's all you should know.

As he got up to open yet another cupboard in this other kitchen, he decided there, in the middle of coldness he wanted to flee, that he would continue to harrow. Alone. Maybe, maybe I'm the one who needs closure. Let go.

She thought, I want you to ski with me, be more than a snowflake melting on my skin. Please.

Peter took his eyes off the road to look at her. She was glowing, different. The Christmas ski trip had done its thing, he thought, and the road back home has infused this otherness into her. Somebody else, somebody new. Perhaps.

She knew it was transient, that this moment was a small opening to enjoy and leap from. Like a nervous bunny, she thought, still smiling. Right. Who are your clients anyways? You never talk about them ...

Peter paused for a moment. I can't baby, kind of confidential, it's in the contract, but even if it weren't, I still wouldn't tell you. Pointing to the cup holder, he told her to drink her tea, took her hand to his lips and softly kissed it. No choice, Isa. Better for you anyway.

Says who?

Says me.

Isabelle turned to the window and fell silent.

Because trust is a precious material that should never be bent.

She closed her eyes and slowly shook her head. I do think I know you. But I also thought I knew him.

She also had trusted her parents, her sister, John.

Fueled by a desire to please everyone, pushed by an urge to barter her legitimacy into the world, she had chosen to trust, trust that kindness existed in equal amounts inside all humans. Worse, she had forgiven as much as she had trusted, her boundaries left unattended, invisible to the guiltless takers.

Betrayals, deceptions—abuse of the secret kind.

Sometimes all of it hits love in the face, other times it infiltrates the skin where the emotional beatings linger, spreading in-between the layers, undetected—more lethal than a melanoma. Snap out of it, Isabelle. Like now.

I say your clients are British, she let out.

Peter smiled. She is pretending, I know she is. The battle played on her pretty face where the eyes, shifting, sought to quiet the mind, where the eyebrows, arched, betraying her confusion. Like a kettle of hawks. Whatever thoughts were swarming in her head, she had the option of ignoring them. She just hadn't figured out the exits. Nope, not British, he said. He placed his hand tenderly on her thigh, searching for her hand. Everything will be all right, he quietly let out.

She stared at their fingers, noting how they had gently intertwined, touching but barely. With Benjamin, sleeping, walking, or watching television—doing life—she had gently formed a ball with her hand, placing it inside of his, his fingers wrapping her trust inside the only pastiche he could offer. It told of the story of her abdication, of her surrendering of power. Here with Peter, their fingers gently laced to one another, sketching the possibility of something she didn't understand. It's me, Peter. It's not so much about trusting others anymore. I got my own way of dealing with it for now. It's about believing in me, my ability to discern. She stared ahead, beyond the windshield of the car. My capacity to trust myself is gone.

That is my cancer.

The night was just about to burst, the evening light so ready to come. A Tuesday night, a holiday night, absent of traffic. At another time, not far from where they stood in that contentment, these two humans, starving for nothing they ever knew, bonded by the mystery inside their newfound complicity, would have suspected something.

The car following them, never heeded.

I'll be away a little longer than usual this time. The training will be stretched out. We're bringing them into the jungle.

Oh, so now you're sharing, Isabelle mumbled, as they walked back up the set of stairs with her ski equipment.

Still, it's a first for me, Peter continued, I usually train from Managua. Basic self-defense methods and common-sense education from the comfort of our offices. This time we're going to El Salvador. And material needs to be bought, checked, the cars selected. Most importantly, the men that will help us choose the trails need to be reassessed. That and more workers are needed to be hired. So much shit can happen. I'll be honest, not sure it's the idea of the century.

Then why do it, baby, she asked, suddenly becoming serious. Why put yourself and your clients in harm's way?

He continued to pack. Money. And harm is the name of the game, it's at the very heart of what we do. Breathing danger is the business. The kidnapping business.

I know, I've been there, she said.

Right. Guatemala. El Salvador.

She paused, her head shaking. About ten years ago, we were returning to Guatemala City from a visit to Iztapa, a small town located on the shores of the Pacific Ocean. John and I and the kids got lost. We didn't understand the highway system, and we took the wrong route, the one reserved for semis and heavy trucks only. It was crazy. The two-way road was so narrow, winding, precariously hugging the edge of ravines. And John, so fucking reckless, tried to pass the trucks ahead of him. I can't tell you how many collisions we avoided.

An asshole.

Yeah. First class one. But he didn't care. Never did, because—his reptilian brain never registered our fear. We all panicked. The kids yelled. But then—mistake, we stopped.

He looked at her. Yeah, well. Not the thing to do, there. You always want to move. Some urban legends are steeped in truth, you know. The gangs, their killing at random. The initiation fee. And never flash your high beams, and never stop until you have reached your destination. There is truth to all of that.

She nodded. We got sandwiched between two trailer trucks. And when we looked out. This human fauna, Peter. A spectacle. Naked children were glaring back at us. But the worst, Peter. Those three men, shirtless, lying side by side, shot. Their bodies limp. Disjointed. Testicles gone, cocks, gone, ears ripped off, eye sockets looking at us.

I know, Isa. He stared at her. So unruly, that land. Lives seem to be disposable to them. The women's mostly. The birthing place of the term feminicide, you know. Think of that. And fucking Americans, too, Peter blurted out. They come to Central America not understanding where exactly they have landed. I am there to remind them.

What a lovely team we make. Tolerance, our middle name, she softly said, opening the night table's drawer. Here, she offered, placing a little straw-made box full of tiny dolls in his hands. It's from Guatemala. Trouble dolls, muñeca quitapena. Alice places them under her pillow to shoo her worries away. Do the same. And think of me.

Peter took the miniature charms, manipulating them, intrigued by their size.

What about Alice?

It's called Lexapro, Peter …

Right, he smiled.

His fingers, slowly moving, played with the intricately made miniature characters dressed in traditional Mayan costume—all children. His hands had become her sole point of interest. Tremors, agitating of the wrists, had waved onto the palms, crashing onto the fingers.

Here, she said again, as she picked up the fallen dolls from the floor. Make sure you pack enough meds. She replaced the talisman inside the palm of his hand and kissed him gently. Isabelle considered Peter for a moment, contemplating his physique. Tall and athletic, he exuded steel-like strength, a presence that exacted as much as deterred—but he was not bulletproof.

She grabbed his hands tightly, wanting to infuse them, him, with some of her tranquility. Some. She lifted her face and pulled him closer to her, her nose now caressing his. I'll miss you.

Muted by the intensity of the moment, she slowly undressed him and caressed his body, a body she so wanted to confront and tame. The skin had been the first hurdle to tackle. For so long she had bathed in scents and colors that had redefined the make of her own senses. Now, there with him, she wanted to understand the white of Peter's skin and touch a different fluidity.

The second hurdle, to lead, to let go.

Dive into him, she thought.

She gently led him to lie on his back, wanting to capture him, snap an image that would carry her at will, anywhere, everywhere.

Stay still.

I am him. I control. I decide.

She placed her hands into his, lifting both their arms above his head. Her mouth first started to draw soft circles around his temple, descending slowly to his ear, wetting its inside, softly. She turned her head to face him, letting her fine hair dangle over his face, brushing it with lightness. You know I hate it when you don't shave, she whispered, her smile hidden.

He motioned to grab her face, wanting to kiss her but she gently pushed back.

With her hair still caressing his body, she lowered herself, hovering over his stomach, her warm saliva painting his skin. Sensing his excitement, she lowered her face yet again, her tongue dawdling slightly above his pelvis. She raised her eyes, searching. Lust she saw, lust and a plea for indulgence.

I have become him. Sit up, she said.

Inserting into him slowly, she steadied herself, her head melting in his neck, her hips sinking into his a little more, farther, and with Peter's arms wrapped around her waist, she absorbed his jolts. They were strong, immutable, almost painful. But she knew about pain, she had learned to bend to and transform it into new thresholds, and new possibilities.

And pain—it could be passed on after all.

Ticket in hand, Peter walked down the aisle to his seat, 21-E, just above the wing. He placed his carry-on above, pushing it to the end, leaving the bin's door open for the steward to close, excused himself to his neighbors, and hopped into his place. There, in the middle of the middle, the story of a life, so he thought.

The plane took off from Managua, and as it did, he felt the small push of the passenger's feet behind him. Annoyed, he turned around and told her, his face caught between the cracks of the backseats, to ease up. Ease up, girl. The pushing stopped.

The flight was short, uneventful, and he welcomed it, feeling drained from the eve's bingeing. He hadn't slept. He slowly stretched out the soreness from his body, aches he never would get used to.

Crosswinds, and the landing, abrupt and loud pulled him out of a dreamless torpor. The plane came to a full stop, and around him, waiting to deplane, men, women, and children stood in relative silence. Peter remained seated, unhurried. Last to leave, he walked the aisle, thanking the crew standing at the top of the airstairs. Below him as he descended, the tarmac, dark and steaming hot. He stepped onto it, his feet as heavy as his mind, his heart unwanting of this, as if resisting.

Once at the small carrousel, he spotted the grey rectangular box filled with training equipment slowly coming his way, strangely standing upright, like a soldier standing guard, unaltered by war. He picked it up and walked to the taxi station.

Behind him as the car rolled out from the airport, a commotion, noisier than usual. But in this country, commotions were like the country's currency—devalued, worthless. No one took heed.

No one ever did.

He tapped on the man's shoulder.

Me llamo Peter …

The man looked up into the rear-view mirror and smiled a welcoming smile.

Lo sé, señor Peter. Mucho gusto. Sebastián. Bienvenido en mi paìs. Toc.

Peter sat back, surprised by the sound that came from the man's mouth, the clicking of his tongue—toc toc toc—amused, and shooing the feeling of surprise away, he asked for some quiet to spread inside the car. La música, Sebastián. No quiero …

Sebastián nodded politely without saying a word and extended his finger to the radio's power button. Hecho.

Peter closed his eyes. They had spoken almost every day since his departure from Montreal, two days before, their conversation tiptoeing around the subject of them, but never addressing fully the Benjamin factor. He wanted to tell Isabelle about what he had started.

Señor Peter, there is water for you if you wish … Just look inside the arm support … agua fría, señor.

He opened his eyes. Sebastián's tone, flat and polite, contrasted with the usual conviviality Latinos are known for, although his English was stellar with barely any trace of an accent. Yes, Sebastián, gracias. He opened the top of what turned out to be a miniature cooler and took out a bottle of Evian. Your English is quite impeccable, Sebastián. Where did you learn it?

The man directed his eyes to the rear-view mirror. Me madre, señor, mi madre.

Hum. I see. And your father?

This time Sebastián kept his eyes on the road. Dead, señor, está muerto. Toc.

Peter mused over this response. Instinctively, he knew better than to push further. So many Central Americans, from Guatemala, Nicaragua, or Honduras had lost a loved one to either gangs or civil wars.

Mi madre tambìen, Sebastián suddenly whispered, mi madre tambìen. Muerta. Toc. Pero, the señora is my mother, he thought.

Yes, Peter gently repeated. He popped the cap off the bottle and took a few sips, realizing how parched his throat was. I drank too much, he thought, recalling the previous night with Steve. The celebration of their new venture—lectures, kidnaping simulations, workplace-shooting enactments, interrogation dry runs—this time outside of a class environment. What do you think? Peter had asked him, five months before, in the middle of their hike on Volcán Concepción. What better place to feel alive than in a real-life abduction situation? Let's bring them in the jungle. Make them feel the real deal. Maybe feeling one could get shot in the head would parallel climbing Everest.

Peter's mind came back to the car and the rhythm of the asphalted road. He looked out the window, the highway leading to his new client's house was quiet, eerily so. The landscape flat, the horizon stretching into a deep nowhere, and Peter pored over this tranquility that had taken root amidst a country steeped in violence. A land devoid of humans, Peter thought, would be a land devoid of bedlam.

Sebastián …?

Una hora, señor. Toc.

Peter fidgeted on his seat. In these tropical countries, heat was to be kept inside the barrel of a gun, not inside a car. Nonetheless, despite the air conditioning blasting a breeze capable of making gelato out of bone marrow, Peter was covered in sweat. He had barely curbed the drinking and had popped the proper medication in his mouth to help control the tremors that would give him away. He had indulged the night before and now his body ruled, and his nerve wirings were calling the shots. He took a larger sip of his water and stared at Sebastián's back seat. Breathe it out. That's what Isabelle had told him to do.

Green eyes appeared, floating around him in a cloud of soft laughter. He had held, caressed, and rocked her torments away. He had given while she had demanded of nothing, not then, and not now. She had licked her wounds in his presence, ugliness pulsing out of the pain. Over exposed, Isabelle had stopped caring about everything that was less than her. You divulge not to impress, and you keep in what alleviates the pain, she said, but you can't truly hide. Ever.

Dialing her number first, he slid the computer out of its pouch to scan the proposition written for his client and waited for Isabelle to pick up. They had spoken the night before. Mellowed by wine, Isabelle had called Peter. I miss you, she had said, and there's a storm blowing over here, and I wish you were here with me. Permeated by the best scotch he was able to dig out from the city, Peter had listened, there amid a fiesta held in an Irish pub with no name. Something had changed in her voice, and more, he had wanted—tried—to tell her. Isa, he had yelled while stuffing a finger in his ear, I have something to tell you. Carried by the rapture filled moment, he had decided it was time. He was about to explain they would now know. So much more. He found someone. An informant. An Ex American diplomat now living somewhere in the Dominican Republic. That he would be meeting him in the next few days, after the meeting in San Salvador. That he missed her.

That he loved her.

Isabelle, hearing nothing but an echo of interwoven static sounds, herself drunk, had laughed and hung up.

Now, seated from the backseat of a limousine, Peter listened to her voicemail greeting. The message had been changed—in English this time. I will be away for an indeterminate period. Leave me a message in case of emergency only. He swallowed, nervous, his tongue playing with the inside of his mouth. More sweat pushing through his pores, and he wondered, if he, Peter Cowans, would count as an emergency. He stared at the other number, the unidentified number appearing on his list of recent phone calls received. Leave a message next time buddy, he whispered.

Sebastián slowed and turned right onto a dirt road. Human-like scarecrows, disseminated here and there throughout his client's property, saluted them subtly, stiffened by the machine guns they flaunted with a straight smile, something Peter was used to seeing. The only exception here was the number of men planted on this landscape. There were many—too many?

The armed guards acknowledged Peter's driver with unrestrained deference, waving him to the top of the road. They climbed the wide trail for two miles, wheels over dry gravel. Sebastián's silence came to a halt when the villa appeared through a thin layer of fog. Estamos aquí.

Perched on the edge of a ravine overlooking a small valley, the house was a spectacular work of contemporary architecture—another anomaly detonating in the scenery. Sebastián stationed the truck in an empty parking area the size of two basketball courts. Peter moved out of the car, baggage in hand, and examined the marble pavement on which his feet had stepped on to. A microclimate filled with money.

The stairs wrapped around the villa, leading them to the last level of the four-story house. The air, flooded with humidity, carried with it a wood scent whose spice tone, while not unpleasant, overwhelmed Peter's senses. It's too much, he thought, and shaking his head lightly, as if to repel the perfume away.

Awaiting them at the top of the curvy tall stairway was a template from which a gauzy shawl breezed along a white bodysuit, around its neck, a pinkish Hermes scarf wrapped à la rosette. Flanked by what appeared to be westernized valets—all from an art deco tableau—she smiled.

Peter Cowans, he said, extending a hand.

She took it. Claudia Balasco. Just Claudia is fine. Come on in.

Looking around, Peter stepped farther into the room. This place is quite the architectural feat, he said.

She nodded. How was your trip?

A short one, but never short enough. I'm not so fond of planes. A necessary obstacle. But I tackle it.

Oh, I see. I must confess, I love the doting I'm subjected to when flying.

Not sure we fly the same airlines, he laughed. Or planes for that matter.

The smile, fond, endeared almost. Would you like to head to your room, or join me for a drink? You seem ... worn out ... The smile disappeared.

He looked at her, now closer to her scent, and so uncomfortable, feeling the flow of her hair—a rusty red, thickened by waves of unruliness. It's her face, he thought.

A drink is fine.

Claudia swiftly disposed of Sebastián, but still lent him a smile. The short man bowed, then descended the stairs, retreating to his quarters with the others. Toc. She turned toward her guest, her lips slightly parted, welcoming him. Come and sit.

He approached slowly, the smell floating inside the capacious room. Sweet and spicy, rosewood from Honduras, precious and rare, was everywhere he looked. The staircase leading downstairs, the wainscotings, the furniture, a monochromatic symphony. The art furnishing the walls, whites floating on white, and sometimes brought to life by large specks of black. The one that stood out made him look away, a woman and a man— a child maybe?

He turned toward the bar, a rectangle composed of marble and some form of pink ivory wood trimming. He let his hands caress its cold silkiness. Pink, he thought smiling, the color of tepid loves.

Peter, hear this, she suddenly said. "Despacito." Sung by the woman who co-wrote it. Erika Ender. Listen ... much better than that Bieber guy from your country, she laughed.

Peter laughed along, too. Not my cup of tea either.

Hearing the words, Claudia Balasco started to dance, as if alone, twirling her body, her hands above her hand. Her eyes wide open. Oh. You must tell me, she said, suddenly stopping in front of the counter, and placing her hand on top of the counter, what is your cup of tea, exactly? Dainty and gold rimmed, or slick and simple? She stared at him, eyes lingering on his mouth for a few seconds.

Peter, not returning the inquisitive stare, avoided looking at Claudia. You don't quite strike me as a tea lady yourself.

She shook her head and placed two shot glasses in front of them. Touché. First, she said, the real deal.

The bottle she poured the amber liquid from was long and elegant, its outside embossed at the bottom with a cactus, and at its neck, detailed with a Louis XIV-like sun. Barrique de Ponciano Porfido, a special edition. Tequila. To the now, and to our tea, she winked, as she lifted her glass.

Yes, to the fleeting now. And long life to all strong teas.

Peter walked on the elongated structure powering the room, drink in hand, fighting the sun's rays scratching his eyes. Overhanging above a cliff, the balcony was large and majestic. Feeling his core being diluted by the pre-prandial liquid, he dropped his body onto the large couch facing the vista.

You are tired, I can see, she said, standing at the bar.

It's true, I am, he replied. But I'll be fine.

Her steps, soft and gliding, and she joined him on the couch. She looked ahead, at the triangle-shaped mountain of lava, the fog surrounding their peaks, and slowly evaporating. The sunsets are not to be missed, Peter.

Like all sunsets, he softly said.

Untrue. Sunsets are like humans. You of all people should know that. They are unique, unique and flawed. And sometimes, they simply don't show up.

You of a people, he repeated in his head.

Claudia Balasco unfolded slowly, bringing her scarf closer to her face.

His back to her, Peter didn't move, listening to the sound of her walking back to the bar.

I would offer you another drink, but I know you need to rest. I, though, will indulge some more. She poured herself a larger amount of the liquid, and letting the liquid loosen her mind, she reminded herself why Peter Cowans was there, inside her house, in El Salvador.

The wind pushed her laced, cape-like covering, Peter following her with his eyes as she walked around the bar. Dinner will be served at six, she said, impatience now in her thinned-out voice. Continuing to the large colimaçon stairs leading down to her bedroom, she started to wave her arms and hands, insisting on each whispered word, as if sculpting abstractions into the damp air, none of it audible to him. Six, Peter. Dinner.

Sprawled over the middle of the large bed, he brought his hands underneath his head, wondering about what he had seen, and what he had felt. Such strangeness. Discomfort. He looked at his phone—5:00 P.M. His bag beside him, he reached into it, retrieving the notes Steve had redacted for him the day before the trip. On the tab of the folder: Claudia Balasco. He opened it, giving it another glance. Reading on, he thought, why me? All this money. And she's been around El Salvador for a long time. She must have connections. Better than mine. He closed the file. Later, he told himself, after dinner.

Fatigued and achy, he rolled over to his side, pulled the cover to his chin, and bringing his phone close to him, he texted Isabelle. I'm somewhere in the middle of El Salvador, Isa. I miss you, Frenchie. And *where* are you?

The phone to his chest, he closed his eyes pushing his mind to rest. Now get a hang of yourself and close the deal, Cowans. For 200 hundred thousand dollars, you can suck this nonsense up.

All of it.

Claudia was waiting for him, glass of champagne in hand. Smiling, now dressed in a black sleeveless maxi dress, the base of her neck embraced by a black satin scarf wrapping her shoulders, too, she took his hand and led him to the balcony running around the vast property. See, just for you, and she pointed to the flawless sunset. Can you synchronize to it, you think, she asked, smiling a new smile.

She is right, Peter thought, ignoring the question. The sun's rays welded into the Chingo, violets, reds, and oranges, all saturated, and together unreal to the eye—the volcano waiting, under sun and moon, for its life to be seen and felt. Dormancy is relative, he thought, eyes on Claudia, and nature will only deceive the human willing to romanticize the sight of what it covets. What do you want to know, señora Balasco, he added, so many men littering your property, armed and trained, at your disposition. They know more than I ever will or can teach.

I don't trust them. I have money. They know I have money. Ironically, I have security watching over my own security. Her hands rising, a finger circling the air. Trust is something you buy around here. And if you happen to touch it for a while, you soon are reminded that it's a fleeting thing. Claudia looked ahead and absorbed the view she had tamed long ago. The expressions on her over-painted face betraying the existence of passages, transitions, with no place to settle in. You are good, I've been told. She shook her head, her locks falling. She took a strand and brought it to her mouth, wrapping her lips around it, and wetting it. If I am to surrender my life to your abled body, and hopefully equally equipped mind, why should I? Sanity landing back in her gaze. What happened, Cowans? Why couldn't you have saved her?

Peter's throat tightened, and recognizing a shift, a sudden and rational one, directed his eyes to his hands. You are making me travel to the land where randomness was Goddess, Claudia.

You understand if I'm to go into this jungle training, I need to know to what extent reality will be joining us.

If I understand correctly, you have been afraid of the jungle most of your life. You've never wandered past your houses.

Correct.

A phobia.

Maybe.

You want to paint, draw, everyday atrocities, common place central American deficiencies. Peasant life. You want to document.

Yes.

In the depth of the jungle.

Yes.

And you want my services.

Yes.

Let me lay down my own law, then, señora Balasco. Let me be the first to shoot straight. Your daughter had an abortion in a country that despises women just for breathing. You and your late husband have corrupted your way to the top of a country that doesn't even belong to you. You're an American from Jersey City, an elegant dump in the middle of another nowhere, was married to a man, as seedy as they come in this neck of the world. If you still need to know what happened in Afghanistan, if you still need me to delve into a past that, as I am sure you will agree, has no true relevance to your decision to hire me, if not to reassure you, if you still want to know how I manage my failures, look at me and check it out. This is how I manage, and how it manages me as well. Peter pointed to the sun, settling behind the mountains. Even nature agrees this conversation is over.

He walked to the bar, walked behind it to face the display of alcohol and spirits spread on the shelves. Full disclosure, he said, as he pulled a bottle of Bowmore out, and poured himself a generous glass. This is how I manage, this and the pills I need to pop every morning to keep myself from indulging furthermore, to keep my hands stable, and my core momentarily impervious to life's petty jokes.

Claudia, stoic, watched as he threw the liquid in his mouth, softly placing the glass inside the clean sink.

You know all you need to know, now. Your insurance validated my program. The references have been spotless, even if your gig is the first of its kind for me. You want me to give you guarantees. But my business thrives on the notion of harm, risk, and imminent death. So, no. Your call, not mine.

Claudia, a body filled with a presence, wavy but constant, approached him and took his hand. Time to eat.

They walked in silence to the outdoor eating area, a small balcony where a round table for two had been prepared. Claudia extended her arm, inviting Peter to sit, her hand dragging and catching some of the silverware, knocking a water glass off the table. Looking at it, she tossed it aside with her foot, pushing it underneath the table.

She leaned into the mesh of the rattan chair and pushed her hair across the right side of her face. Look, she said, sliding a cigarette from her leather case and tapping it gently on the table, at this face. What is it you don't see, when you look at me? Her body straight and her neck stretched, as if pulled by an unseen wire. There used to be so much on it, life, she continued, a sensuous whole. Perfection.

A few tobacco leaves, humid and rusty looking, feathered the linen tablecloth, and she blew them across the table. I wasn't born like this, you know. Just like you were, Peter, I was sculpted after, not before I was born. Her mouth wrapped around her stick, she took a long, slow drag, pushing hollowed circles into the air. Let me tell you what *I* see. What *I* know.

Born 1970. An alcoholic father who worked in the Royal Canadian Mounted Police, an older sister who died from leukemia at five. Your father, a bastard you loved and hated, while hating yourself for loving what could never exist. You retreated, God knows where for a time. And survived. You found solace in Psychology studies at the University of British Columbia, but never finished. That's when you joined the Canadian Armed forces. 1995.

Peter detailed her face, the awkwardness he saw there. Well, he said, there you have it, it seems. Most of it ...

That's the whole point of you being here, darling.

Is it, really, Claudia?

A long inhale and squishing the base of her cigarette she told him that no, she didn't know everything.

What do you mean? he asked, and looking at straight at her.

Claudia Balasco's face, now a distortion, and the woman traveled to her own sands, to the saltiness of her fogs, since then and now coming to stay. She had left her own mind. I-sa-belle, she articulated, her voice changed.

Peter paused, absorbing what he had just heard. This is insane, he whispered, as he pushed himself up from the chair. None of this is making sense.

Why Isabelle Duval, Peter? she yelled. Why choose her?

What in the fucking hell does Isabelle have anything to do with here—with you? Me? Why did you really ask me to come here?

I needed to see you, to try and understand her, what you saw in her—to know what *he* saw in her. She looked away. That wasn't me. That wasn't good enough for him.

Claudia's gaze became cold, absent. Her smile, a rictus telling insanity's doors had been opened. Wider. The words came quickly. Everything, Peter Cowans. I, like her, at one time had Benjamin in my life; in my arms. In my bed. She never lost him, did she? She got a piece of his heart. I wanted to know why? How?

Peter scanned the room, looking for Sebastián. Alerted by the tone of their voices, the man, seated at the end of the large room, was running to them. Watching him move toward the table, it was as if Peter was seeing Sebastián for the first time, this overweight man, balding and vulnerable looking. Such weakness, he thought. And even though the man's face showed alarm, his gait had remained tentative, unsure. Peter looked at Claudia stunned. Isabelle's face came rushing to him—that first day when they had met. Her eyes holding the same distress, this obsession. And Claudia, now, fingers spread across her face, crying, spitting, too. Nonsensical words. Guttural sound. I will be leaving in the morning, Claudia, he said flatly. Obviously, the deal is off. And turning to Sebastián who had rushed to Claudia's side, Peter said to have the car ready. In the morning. I'm fucking out of here at dawn, Sebastián. At dawn.

Once inside his room, from behind the door, Claudia's screams coming to him. I need to know, Sebastián. I need to know. The sound of Sebastián's tongue clicking, echoing to him, too.

Toc. Toc. Toc. Toc. Toc.

Her fingers removing her fake eyelashes, she thought, another black-out. But now, I am fine, she thought, as she popped medication in her mouth. And I don't need him.

Just Janelle.

Claudia stroked her face, leaving her index to test the stickiness on her skin, and playing with the depth of a protective layer she had become addicted to. That's what she did each time she entered her room—any room.

Her self-soothing.

In public, she had trained her fingers to probe with restraint, their tips, sensors warning her of the overexposure she feared so much. Those fingers knew how to behave, when to push, when to wane, living in a world that intersected with an out of synch Claudia Balasco.

The world will find out, she thought. It always does.

She looked at the rim of the golden mirror, almost dodging the looking glass, remembering nothing of the evening, of a certain past, too. But she conjured Aitana's face to appear, and she did—make her appear, from somewhere far; her long hair; her pasty looking face; her warm eyes, brown, deep; all her waning, more and more, the frailty of memories foreshadowing the extinction of Claudia's own flesh. You are safe my daughter, there in Switzerland, far from him. But I can't carry you in my head anymore, not like I used to.

Stepping out from her dress, removing her underthings, she let a finger travel to her crotch. It lingered there, for a long second. Naked, her head loosening, she tipped it forward and scanned her body like she did every night, cursing him, wanting him—her holes, her scars. But also, now—wanting her, to study her, touch her, even. That girl from Montreal. And Peter, a failed gateway, it seemed, to her. To Isabelle. I messed up, she told herself. I know.

She unknotted her scarf and removed its clasp. She pulled the middle drawer out and spread it flat above the thick pile of silky garments, placing the clasp, with the other ones, inside a large, yellow velvet covered box. Tomorrow, she thought, the Bisous Bow Tie. She closed her drawer and moved on to the next step.

WHEN I BECAME NEVER

The bottles, below the mirror frame, lined up, their sequence predetermined, rigid—beauty creams meant for the wounded. She dug into the first jar, wobbled her fingers into the bespoke concoction, and slapped her skin with a youthful bite. Her evening prayer.

All these punctures—everywhere.

Dig and slap.

That's what she did each time the hospital staff untied the webbings of her straitjacket, a useless corset only squeezing a body, nothing else. Seated, head tilted, and pretending to heal, pretending the treatment was finally yielding, she had looked at the turquoise-colored walls, her so-called home, her so-called safety, and the hell she lived in, too, roaming the wide avenues of an imagination, now bereft and stale.

Eleven years of being gone, hounded by her imaginings.

To dig and slap, to feel alive, more alive, that's what she did when they had believed she was sedated enough to be trusted—dig and slap.

That last time, waiting for their voices to fade into the far end of the narrow corridors, she had slowly counted to 100, a weak shelling of time, biting the sides of her tongue in between counts. And reaching the ninety-nine count, she had slowly brought her fingers to her face. Again, and again. And even though they had trimmed her fingernails into brittle pieces of streaked death, she still had found a way. To dig far enough, to push into the rawness of unhealed scars, stripping layer after layer of skin, until the never healed wounds had gushed. Then, the time to paint her pain on the white of her loosened jacket, on the turquoise of her walls— a sea smeared and dotted by shades of browns.

2006 to 2017.

They had called Aitana, and told her mother should go, that it had been too long, that maybe somewhere else, somewhere in her adopted land, maybe, she would heal, better, more, that they didn't want her anymore, that she wasn't good for the other patients. Only good for the agitation of what they wanted tamed.

Aitana flew back, temporarily leaving the life she had made for herself in the Geneva she loved. Inside her central American villa, she had tended to her mother, rocked her, this time inside her own arms, mending the torments, all of them, deep and hollow, zigzags most of the time, straight lines, never. Like her own. Concerned, she collected the luminaries needed to heal her mother's health: plastic surgeons who remolded the body, psychiatrists known to reprogram the brain.

Then, one day, she left her mother for good, unable to witness history unfolding, yet again, different, but same. She had to protect herself, too—six months ago.

Inside her mother, malignant hope continuing to live, carving abstractions.

Claudia grabbed the second bottle, letting it mold the inside of her hand, its cold soothing the warmth that had spread to her fingers, appeasing them. She stared into the mirror and slowly angulated her face both left and right, observing her skin millimeter per millimeter, attentive to all blemishes and open pores, eyes trained to spot, wrongs, subtle but deep. She knew, she had become a familiar alien to the outside world, an intimate partner to herself—a woman striving to morph into whatever notion of perfection reality was demanding of her. What she saw, her vanishing, and replacement, too—Isabelle.

Peter—a bad impulse. Janelle Rivera, a better one.

She walked to her closet, a large walk-in filled with one-piece bodysuits and lounge wear, and grabbed a black dressing gown made of Chinese silk and slipped it on. She took her phone from her purse and took two steps back and let herself fall onto the bed. Holding it above her head, she scrolled, images of the three of them inside a rollercoaster ride, the one where he had unbuckled her seat mid-way; a short-lived family.

She knew nothing would be forgiven, the grieving of the baby Benjamin and Aitana had made. The abortion, the only solution.

The Jersey girl disappeared more, lucidity moving, less and less, and threatening to settle away from the dreads of sanity still trying to fight.

The door opened, and Sebastián walked to where Claudia was, laying on her back, her eyes to the ceiling. Mamá. La última día, aquí, ahora. It cannot go on this way.

Amorito, she said, it's going to be fine.

Toc.

Naked, and still dripping from the shower, Peter was at the window watching the night skies—never skies, clouded and dark, and he wondered, questions invading his mind, is a moonless night more dangerous than a sunless day?

Claudia's mention of Isabelle was eerie, ominous, and it made no sense, he thought. Or did it? Disquieted by the evening's turn of events, he wondered: What had Steve and him misread? The woman, clearly, was crazy.

He walked to the bed, picked up the folder, and removing the last page of the report, he read—this gap in time, her life, staring at him. On the bedside table, the phone, and he took it, hands shaky. No voicemail. Not Steve. Not even Isabelle.

Fingers on his phone, ready to text Isabelle, he saw the guitar in the corner, leaning on the wall, as if waiting for him. He picked it up, examining it, and feeling its awkward heaviness, wondered, does she know I play? A smile stretched across his face. Only the rich and the eccentric, he whispered to no one, would use an Eric Clapton version of some sort— the very expensive kind, as decoration. Still, he let his fingers scratch the guitar tentatively, making the strings sing, tremors freed to walk across the air.

Uneasiness caught up to his muscles, tightening them. A few words left his mouth, notes and tones framing the poem he had started to write for her.

The visions I drew,

The plays I imagined,

To get you through—

To you.

He felt his core give out, swaying almost. I need to sleep, he thought, as he walked back to the bed and slid under the sheet, linens raw and abrasive. He placed the guitar by his side, the wooden fuselage spooning his fleshy one. His lids dropped and he travelled to all the spaces that came rushing, triggered by Claudia's words and insinuations.

Flashes of dust-filled winds, images of blood-soaked sands.

Aadela's body distorted, her face looking up at him, asking: Had the bullets been for both? No, just for her, his informant, and lover. He had tried, yelled for help, cursing this sea-less beach, in that fucking Afghani hell. He lost her just as the medics had arrived. You couldn't have saved her Peter, they had repeated.

He never believed them.

His heart squeezed just a little more than usual, there in the middle of a bed meant for a king. The walk into the past became ever more fluid, vivid images stippled with a mixture of relief and sorrow—Emma, his sister, seemingly sleeping in an austere hospital room, dressed as Dorothy's Wizard. The braided hair, the grayest of faces, the rosy lips. Protecting her feet: red slippers glittering, calling out to the angels, to bring her home, his drunken mother had whispered. A Halloween night never to forget, a true Halloween—full of death, full of grief, for an already broken family.

And then there was Francis, the child he had abandoned. The child he had wanted. Because, sometimes, the best of fathers must disappear.

Peter felt his breath quicken, the guitar close to him, hugging its waist, the sound hole facing the other way. Isabelle. Such intensity inside of her, he thought.

The sound of a notification came from his phone, its provenance only guessed. My contact he thought. Santo Domingo. He read on and when he finished, understanding, he decided he had to tell Isabelle. Now.

All the girl's bodies were cremated, need to stop looking, he copied from his contact's text, and sent it to her with somewhat shaky hands.

He then texted her a message of his own.

We now know that we have nothing, there are no traces of anything leading to Benjamin or his brother. You can't go on, Isa, we've been warned. Stop looking. Put it behind you. And call me soon. I need to talk to you about this crazy woman, here. Coming back sooner than planned. And I love you, Frenchie. And where the fuck are you?

The shaking subsided, waves stilling in every cell of his heart. I love you, he whispered.

But the message, lost to another cloud, stuck somewhere, would never reach her, stuck in time's purgatory.

His vision, a blurry fogginess, like cotton sealing his mind. And Peter would dream of her; of cold sands; of warm embraces and death—the kind that does not surprise you.

It slithered out of the guitar, all so stealthily, as it is known to do, muskiness and acridity, the only warning sign that would not be heeded. It would have gone to settle in a corner of the room had Peter's body not jerked and twitched so much, or had his phone remained off. A second before the snake struck, Peter opened his eyes, alerted by the funky smell that impregnated the room.

The last thing he thought of before feeling his blood thicken was that, yes, moonless nights are more dangerous than sunless days.

The hospital, a hovel in the middle of a jungle, somewhere in the middle of El Salvador.

Steve walked to Peter's room, the smell of the place clogging his brain: Vomit. Shit. Bleach.

Follow me, the doctor said, he's semi-conscious. Brought to us yesterday morning. Left out in front, like we told you.

Like trash, he thought, eyes scratching the dirt off walls that wanted to peel away.

Steve saw him, just as the doctor pushed the door open, on his back, his neck blue and black and red and distended.

Don't ask, she pre-empted, we don't know.

Steve stared at the doctor. Phone?

No. No phone. Just this.

He took the plastic bag. A piece of paper.

Prognostic?

The Fer-de-lance, it spits its torture to all humans who cross its path. It's hard to tell.

Steve turned to Peter as he took the paper out, eyes on the blood-soaked bandages wrapping Peter's abdomen. He read. *What does it matter, anyway? For the burials will be had. And I will get to her, one way or the other. Claudia.*

He folded the message, confused, as Peter's hands motioned for his friend to approach. Okay, Steve said, I'm here, and look what I brought you. From the inside pocket of his jacket, he drew a small bottle of whiskey. He uncapped it, and lifting Peter's head he brought the amber liquid to his lips. Peter, unable to speak, tried to open his mouth. Here, Steve said again, as he parted Peter's lips with his fingers, let me help you.

He sat against Peter, and for a long moment remained silent until Peter eyes' fully reopened. He placed his hand on his, alarmed. I don't know what happened, but I'll find out. The policia came to me at the hotel last night. They want to know what I knew and seemed eager to help. Bad publicity for this country is never a good idea. So … Also, weird calls from unknown numbers. Something about Lake Managua. They also mentioned Isabelle.

Peter tried to move, tried to talk, but everything in him was immobile and stiff.

I've tried her and left her a message. She won't answer her phone … I'm off to the Canadian embassy tomorrow, and we'll figure this shit out.

A whisper. And Claudia?

Her and another man were seen leaving by helicopter the day you were found.

Peter's eyes closed, his mouth as well, his hand limp and cold let go of Steve's.

Doctor, Steve called, turning his head to the door.

He watched her lift Peter's arm, the one tied to the intravenous bag. He watched her quickly remove the capsule where a needle full of antidote would be inserted, again.

All we can do now is wait, she said, but don't hold your breath.

Steve left the hospital room, and walked by the reception area behind which a male nurse was seated, a cell phone to his ear, silent. As he stepped outside, he looked up. The sky felt strange to him—stranger than usual in this country where rain pouring ruled the land more than the skies—the whiteness of it, heavy and bland. The taxi was still there, waiting for him. He opened the door, threw his bag on the car's backseat. As he leaned toward the front of the car, wanting to ask the cab driver about the nearest watering hole he knew of, and drive him there—the last thing he would ever hear: The whistle of a stray bullet that would settle inside his brain, and delivering death.

Isabelle thought of him, now in Managua, of how she missed him, their mornings spent lazily in bed, his hands, so strong, his shoulders—stronger even. Of the tattoo on his forearm that welcomed the future, any kind … *come and get me* … I hope he'll be fine, she thought.

Because I need you.

And because she loved him.

A drape of white twirled into the thin windowpanes, pushing the cold air through its cracks. She extended her hand and caressed the sharp edges with the tip of her index finger.

Isabelle sat back and watched as a fine powder glided over the glass, leaving nothing but minute traces of dryness behind—wet-less snowflakes. Hurled up inside her den, wrapped around a fur poncho, she let herself fuse with the winter's temper.

Ever since a child, storms had fascinated her. The sound of thunder, the anticipation of faraway lightning strikes, the rain sheets carried by the wind, always lulling her into a welcome trance. She remembered living in Taipei with John, lying in their bed, listening to the wind gusts fueling her Typhoons. There, amid nature's uncompromising folly, she felt alive and safe—at home. How interesting I stayed so long with him, breathing stale air, she mused.

Only when Isabelle had met Benjamin did she understand she had been strung along a river of life-killing seconds. Storms, she grasped, she had wanted to chase them, moved by this need to live. Walled in domesticity, she had failed to do so.

Then, Benjamin.

An undoing—of her.

Being stalked by an unsound mind, a man she thought she knew, a man she had loved deeply, she thought then, had pushed her into confused state. A changeover pushed by the twisted forces that curl inside human existence—human made storms. What had been the truest of traumas? A death-defying ennui at the heart of her worn out relationship with John? Lifesaving vibrant lies at the center of a deceptive bond she had with her madman? Or her self-betrayal?

She stood, stumbling, as if sawed in two, there in the middle of the night, walking half bent through her apartment, holding herself, the ache replete with sadness. Another glass, she needed. And in her mind, she claimed remembered moments, again: a watch left on a night table; working shirts littering dirty floors; the ringing of notifications startling her nights—flashbacks triggered by the little wonders of a life that had slipped away from her.

The rosary, never far.

Yes, she thought, the horrifying narratives they carry.

Left to loneliness, she had wondered not too long before now, if pain, her pain, was like the one Benjamin carried within himself? Was their loneliness equal in despair? Is this what it feels like to be him? she had asked herself.

But love had gone.

And she recalled yet again, troubled by this guilt—this suffocating guilt—that along the way, confused, she somehow had decided to remain in a twisted and dangerous relationship, betting against herself. How she hated all of her, of a hate that holds no possibility for forgiveness. Transfixed by a visceral need to stay and observe him, she had allowed herself to become an unapologetic voyeur. She knew he was crazy, that everything about him spelled danger. Yet, she had wanted to see if the monster was real or just an illusion. She had wanted to dust off his mask and remove it from his face, all from the comfort of his den. It was all so unreal—impossible to exist. A monstrosity. An overzealous anthropologist is what she had transformed into.

And beautiful Alice.

The images of him standing erect at the edge Alice's bedroom door, back in Northampton, the sight of his flaring nostrils, the cove of his nose moving, smelling, the scent of her daughter. His hard-on, she had seen, his hand grabbing her hand, loose and numb, to place on it.

She reprieved the urge to vomit, to cry, to scream.

A limbo dematerialized—unmooring from the known, when the known is soaked in suffering, it can be brutal. The power alive inside a storm unleashes the powers dormant inside anyone willing to embrace it, she thought, a truism no one should flee. Or possibly survive.

Seated on the couch, she reached for her wine glass, careful not to disturb James who had hopped onto her lap. The red liquid, sturdy and dry, slid down her throat, its warmth familiar. I should feel victorious, she thought to herself.

After all, I left.

But did I win?

What?

She slowly snaked her fingers into the cat's fur, looking beyond the snow flurries. The storm had intensified, its wind now forcefully whipping the window. Time to head to bed.

Walking toward her room, she sipped more of her wine, wide-eyes on the hands holding the stem-less glass, a glass bubble she wished she could float in. Feeling dizzy, she grabbed the bedroom's doorframe, grounding herself as she took sight of her unmade bed, that she slid inside of. Twisting around the sheets, she wondered, did he remember the smell of her breath, the taste of the sweat he licked off her breasts, the color of her eyes? What parts of her had he kept? Discarded? Who exactly was the Isabelle that remained alive in his sick mind? Or had she died in the worst way, no longer part of any past, or memories?

Dead to the heart, dead in the mind.

But did all this really matter?

Peter, she thought. I need to call Peter.

7:00 A.M. and she broke free from her bed, surprised by an energy she couldn't account for. It must be Peter, she recalled, with a smile. The feeling of him. His voice last night, soothing and still resonating in her mind.

She sauntered to coffee, sat on the high stool facing the round wooden table on which her laptop had been left the night before, and she checked her emails, her texts, and the news. James scratched at her leg, demanding food, leading her to the pantry. James James James, she whispered, as she picked him up to kiss the top of his head only to throw him back on the floor.

The door to the pantry jammed as she tried to push it with her hands, and, resorting to kicking it open, she felt a want for lightness, the simple mortal aching for an irreverence that seldom came. She bent to retrieve the cat food, and there on the floor she saw it.

John's belongings: suitcases, lamps, book stacks, tacky Asian souvenirs, and boxes bursting with tax papers. Somehow, the open door, her kick, had dislodged this single piece of paper from its hiding place. She picked it up, unsure. The folds of the paper were numerous, and surgically precise, their angles needle sharp.

She stepped out of the room, closed the door behind her, and remained still while her hands played with the prickly construction. Delicately, she unfolded the puzzle, a corner at a time. Apprehensive, Isabelle fixated on the flattened sheet of paper. This wasn't a gift she had unwrapped, she thought. Written at the top right of the sheet, in crisp, capitalized letters, a simple question: WHY? Her eyes slid to the bottom and stilled at the sight of a sketch. Her—Benjamin had outlined her, all of her, that suggested all her contours and what whispered inside of her for him to see—an essence that mingles with emotions too powerful to let go of. Everything he lacked within himself was there, staring, the words at the bottom, striking at her. You are the sweetest drawing I never drew.

She took one step back, feeling the door against her back dissolve, as if it had been made of wet sand begging to liquefy. She slid to the ground and turned the paper over. Looking at her, filling the whole of the page, the drawing of a one-eyed man—a cowboy? Benjamin, what are you trying to tell me that I don't already know?

Everything about the portrait was loose, yet precise. Erasures, crossed out lines, and hardening of the pencil irked Isabelle by their absence. Had he lifted his pencil off the page but even once? She knew of his talent, had seen strange drawings litter that hellish place he called his home, a tidy garage-like space Isabelle had learned to hate, the meekness of it nauseating. Abstracts drawings filled with surrealist strokes, charcoal renditions of his children, and sketches, so many.

Of her.

Oftentimes, after sliding off from her body, Benjamin had asked Isabelle to still, to die really, so he could capture her, forever. She had obeyed and hushed her bones, frightened, yes, but smitten by the attention she so rarely received and craved. She recalled just then that moment in Northampton, in her bedroom, ethereal as ever. The morning light illuminating the floating flecks of dust, as if fallen stars resisted their fate. Her leg, resting on his, swinging. The seductive silence hovering over satiny latte and snow-white-colored skins—a marbled cake, really. His eyes taking in the moment, fascinated by the black nail polish shining at the end of her toes. His head facing the ceiling, his eyes split by whatever was running though his mind. Something had transported him somewhere else.

Somewhere far from her.

And that rosary shining always, swaying on his chest, above her.

A smelly crucifix falling inside her mouth.

Sitting on the floor, eyes on this cowboy, she tried to understand.

While the portrait was reminiscent of a naïve style bordering on the cartoonish, there was something dead serious about its execution. The perforated cowboy hat, the wide eye patch, the sutured scar, all half-assed iconographies begging to tell his story, she thought.

A pirate?

Cyclops?

A battered soul?

You were making your coming out, Benjamin? she laughed nervously.

She examined the details of the portrait, wanting to remove the eye patch, the sutures. You should have disclosed, baby. You should have let me caress that shiny head of yours, let me soothe that slash, let me fill the hole inside your mind.

And she asked herself, whispering it almost, her lips close to a sketched-out face full of so many things she knew, how does one know of the omens inside a portent, how does one recognize them?

That one day, she recalled still, he had drawn her, moving her arms, positioning her head, directing his shoot, weaving the sheets tightly around her. She didn't know where the sketch had landed, she had only seen it once, but the image was alive inside her brain. Benjamin had drawn a moment, a warning she had never heeded only because she couldn't have imagined the truth, let alone believed it.

The sheets spun around her, her face, quasi expressionless, a blissful smile cracking the white celadon face—a cocoon?

I dreamt of you last night, he had replied, impassive, as he continued to sketch, all of you, the whole of you, every inch of your body, made of chocolate.

She had propped herself up, back straight, everything in her stiffened by the expression on Benjamin's face. You hate chocolate, Benjamin. You hate anything black. Maybe it was white chocolate, she had risked, with a fake smile.

In my dream, he had pursued, ignoring her question, I licked you with my tongue and dug in with my teeth … ate the chocolate. Ate it all.

Isabelle had frozen upon hearing the soft-spoken words, words that had moistened his lips, almost dripping from his mouth. It was the wildness inside his eyes though, their violent void, which had struck her with fear, a fear she had quickly dismissed as nonsense—to demystify deliriums, to dig out the tunnels that mapped his despair was something she had decided to forgo. Instead, she had chosen to float, dangle between warped realities and ignore the insanity of it all.

And she remembered again, those links he had denied sending to her, the title of the article burnt in her brain: "13 Gory details about what it's like to be skinned alive."

But that was then.

So now Isabelle Duval, she whispered to herself, shame-filled tears menacing to flee, heal well and wide and deep.

The box, its content—the obsession to tame.

Or not.

One single drop of rain splashing the pavement can mislead anyone into thinking two things: one, that a storm is coming, two, that it's just that, one fat bubble of water, a delinquent drop that couldn't hang on to its mother cloud.

Isabelle had never been able to tell the difference.

She packed the carry-on with the essentials, retrieved all the papers required to pass the border to prove she no longer resided in Massachusetts—her lease, hydro, and cell phone bills—dropped James with her neighbor Estelle, and after checking her messages, closed her phone.

This was her mission, no one else's.

Then, with delight, she opened her bedroom drawer and fetched Benjamin's set of house keys.

Silly, silly man.

The uniformed man, overweight and slow-moving, looked at her inquisitively from the other side of the car window. My destination? she asked with a smile. A friend's house in Petersham, Massachusetts. The duration of my stay, sir? Four days. At the very least, she thought to herself.

Keep that smile on, pretty lady, the custom officer said, as he handed her passport back with a wink.

How inconsistent they all are, she thought, recalling the randomness of her border crossings when living on US territory. You fool, you saw nothing, nothing at all. Because she hid it all, the shame, the excitement, there, underneath a face where simpers danced hard enough to pierce her skin and show the world, she could do it, too, she could trick. And the restraining order I filed twelve months ago, well maybe, you, Rodriguez, should have done the same, she said out loud.

She started the playlist prepared for this journey, her foot relaxing off the gas pedal, just enough for her to blend onto the road.

Coming to her, thoughts of Patricia, the old woman who had become the strangest of friends, a relic in her heart. Benjamin had stalked her, this seventy-two-year-old woman, pressuring her into selling him her house. For a little more than three years, in her mind, they had dated, Patricia had believed it, negating, like Isabelle had—the obvious. It was the sex, the attention received, the sincerity of it all, the old woman had said. Yet, it had been predictable, the moment the sale had been closed, Benjamin had discarded Patricia, denying their relationship to Isabelle and to all who had witnessed it, even while keeping her belongings trapped in the basement of his new house.

Her eyes to the white line of the roads, there was a feeling of unfamiliar release carried in her being, a freedom, however strange the circumstances. Medications, some very special ones, will do that to you, she thought, noticing how her emotional mind had been reconfigured by her migraine medication. So strong, she smiled. Reliable.

Flakes started to fall from the sky, weighted by the clouds' heaviness, flakes, big and plump, forming a tunnel as the car sped. She looked beyond, feeling the transience of each white shaving. There was no rush to get to him, was there? No body to caress, no liquids to soak in, no lips to gnaw at, only the will to appease one's conscience—hers. The trauma, she knew, was fading, the fog a little less opaque. She felt it, sometimes saddened by the loss of intensity she had become addicted to, the lust, the cravings that had fed her for so long, all vanishing. Throughout the last year, she had resisted the man's attempts to lure her back to him. Emails, text messages, all sent from anonymous accounts that had failed to bring her back into his cave. This time, the familiar destination offered new gifts yet to be revealed.

She sank back into her seat, and one hand steering the wheel, she felt a comfortable numbness seeping from Nora Jones' music—Happy Pills.

Shadows moving, shapeless forms, and despite the flurries whitening her sight, she magically saw them, all four of them, and stopped on the shoulder of the road. Why, she asked out loud, why am I here? She walked on the wayside, feeling the push of the wind against her shoulders, and she stopped, and the deer stared back at her, and like her, wondering— maybe? About what to do in the face of suffering that was unwanted and so unfair.

But it just is, isn't it?

Unavoidable.

Just like breathing.

The pain of living as we die.

On the edge of the forest, a limping wolf with fading brown eyes, dragged its body. The rare sighting of a common fear. A chain and a closed trap hanging from his left hind leg.

So that's why I'm here, she whispered. To expose the unseen, a wolf now so visible. Added to this oddity, she saw a young doe moving toward the stranded wolf, bending to the wound and slowly trying to clean it. Such a reckless doe, she thought. The wolf stilled and stared back, angry but too weak to growl, waiting for his heart to give out. The small doe looked on still, surely understanding the strong usually win, whether good or bad.

Don't do it, Isabelle yelled, licking its wound won't change a thing.

Startled, the deer simultaneously stretched their necks toward her voice and ran away, dispersing beyond the edge of the woods.

The wolf let his head sink into the snow and closed its eyes.

Good luck, she screamed through the wind. And if you do find a place up there, keep it warm. But it won't be for me.

She walked back to her car, ignoring all the weaknesses the moment had borrowed from itself, more than ready to leave the scene, her mind now directed to a recent past.

She slid back on her seat, so very lucid, buckled up and pressed the pedal slowly, as if readying to taste what she had finally come to understand: That prey don't always mingle with their own demise.

Before arriving in Lowell, she stopped in Concord, New Hampshire to fill her car up. The buzz from her medication had faded, in its place a feeling of quiet angst. The contrast was sharp but welcome—like a bearable contraction mimicking a reprieve. I know what's ahead, she thought, as she felt moisture return to her mouth, I just need to be on top of my game.

Once back in her seat, with precision and discretion, she took the wig out of her purse and let her stealth fingers quickly secure the clips to clump her hair. She had practiced enough, first the front, then the back, and then the sides. She checked herself in the rearview mirror, adjusted it, and finally tugging at it from the top to test its stability. Perfect, she acknowledged, just perfect.

The motel room she rented was in the small city of Methuen, just a few miles out from Lowell. A true Latino ghetto, and comparable to its sister city, Lawrence, in that poverty, drugs, and crime, the holy trinity of a certain hell, hovered over Latino souls. Yeah, she thought, the great U.S. of A. … the ultimate destination.

She parked in the small area located at the back of the building and slowly stretched her legs outside of the car. Inside her body, pain had returned, a migraine promising to flare. Her eyes dropped.

She sluggishly walked toward the entrance, scanning the surroundings with purpose, as if wanting to reacquaint herself with the bearings that had once misled her into a pit. I don't care if it's too soon, she thought, I'll be fine.

A tiny Latina woman greeted her at the reception desk with approximate English. When Isabelle said she had left her passport inside the glove compartment of her car, and that no, she would not go back for it, the woman replied, esta okay, señora Colins, no problema. Isabelle's lips synched a thank you then suddenly stilled. To a script, she remembered, Benjamin had improvised when checking into a similar motel with her in Charlestown, New Hampshire, two years back. Yes, he had said, we just travelled from Ottawa on our way to Amherst, the road was long, and my wife is exhausted. Isabelle had stared at him, absorbing the useless lie knowing full well they simply had decided to take a night off from the everyday bustles. Why on earth, lie about this, she had asked him once inside the room. Why not, he had replied, who the fuck cares? All is okay, señora, she replied, as Isabelle landed back in the moment. She faced the worried clerk, estoy cansada, solamente.

After returning the car and renting a new one—the Canadian car plate number, a potential telltale sign—once inside the room, Isabelle let everything drop to the floor, unsteadied by the day's drive, its swaying motion still affecting her balance. She sat on the bed and took her phone out. It was time to call Patricia, again, and tell her she had arrived, that she was planning on visiting her. She dialed, listened to the voice: The number you have reached is unavailable.

How odd, she thought.

She looked around, detailing the walls surrounding her, impervious to the same odor she had learned to tame when at his house, mold mixed with bleach. I did it, she thought, studying the room's tasteless greenish décor, I'm back here, in his world.

The elation only lasted a few seconds, as she felt the weight of her day fall upon her. She slid under the brown quilt hoping nothing would crawl onto her.

The time was 7:00 P.M.

The exit came up, the one she had taken so many times, the one she had mistaken for an entry countless time. She tugged at her hoody, took a sip from her coffee, and fought the emotions that whipped at her. How often had she swerved into this exit, barely unable to contain the delirium it provoked? Going to him had always felt like a delicious tease that stopped the moment she saw him—a bare wall on which she had projected life. Then, like a meaningless orgasm, her world would deflate.

City hall, the Big Ben like town clock and, just before turning on his street, the CVS. She felt her senses sharpen, as she saw the boutique where she had brought little Jocelyne, his young daughter, to get her nails done. She blinked and continued to the end of the road, then turned right.

14 Blackwell Street.

Isabelle held her breath. There would be no rushing up the stairs, no hearing the sound of her carry-on marking her arrival on their edges, no landing in his arms. She sped up instinctively, forgetting no one would ever recognize her.

The house, which materialized before her, was the same, but for the added plastic porch extended from the front and the asphalted driveway where grass had been. She drove around the block trying to figure out who, if anyone, was still inside the house. Alejandro had redirected from studying medicine into business at University of Massachusetts, Boston, and Jocelyne was usually picked up from her mother's place, in Lawrence, on Friday nights, and returned on Sundays or Mondays. Monday was here. And Alejandro's old black Toyota Corolla was absent.

The new parking area created along the house hosted many vehicles Isabelle couldn't identify. Audis, Mercedes, and the likes stood awkwardly, protruding. Moreover, the junkyard adjacent to the garage hosted a fleet of trucks she had never seen. She remembered then, that just before escaping the Latino man, he had evicted all his tenants to build more rooms inside his triplex and therefore increase his rental income. Still, she thought, whatever you will add to your life, will always be as plastic as you—Proteus is your only ruler.

As she scanned the area, an acceptance settled inside her head: Randomness and luck would play a huge part in her plans to enter his house and not get caught. Nothing in Benjamin's choices and behaviors could be predicted, everything in his life was dictated by whims and impulses meant to manage his urges to do what he pleased, when it pleased him—the man, at his core, was a petulant child hostage to destructive fantasies. Who knows, she wished, maybe he's landed a contract that is sending him far from Lowell, the only choice was to watch from afar and observe. She nervously looked at her phone. 10:30 A.M.

Folding into her seat, she felt the pastiness inside her mouth slowly spread. A warning, she wondered. And for a few, but long seconds, doubt descended into her stomach. She had missed him—moving images slowly unveiled themselves to her, and eyes wide open, she took in their flow. I'm solid, she repeated to herself.

Solid.

Twelve hours into her version of a stake out, after watching only men walk in and out of the side of his house, he appeared. She saw him step out of a white GMC truck. Some form of quiet surging in her veins. And as he walked fifty feet from her, she stared. The paint-stained jeans. The white tee showing from underneath the stiff leather coat. Blunt coldness— his face.

The likes of him only come alive when feeling seen, she recalled, as their day trip to Far Rockaway came to mind. A dealership, he had mentioned, a used Audi I want to buy. Okay, she had agreed, fully aware no choice had been given. She recalled the flow of her silk dress, short and flowered with tones of yellows, slit in the front, and how he had grabbed the back of her arm with firmness as she walked past a salesman who had looked at her with too much interest. The layover preceding the long return home, the visit to a favorite place in the Brooklyn neighborhood he once had lived in. She remembered as well, The Seaport Buffet, a large restaurant located not too far from the shoreline. Seafood, Chinese American staples, cheap and delicious, Benjamin had said, walking in, his infamous trot threatening to overtake the whole of his body. And heading for the smorgasbord filled counters, he had continued, sit down Isabelle, I'll bring you some of my faves.

Midway through their tuck-in—more awkwardness, dressed in plain jeans and black tee, he had abruptly stood and called for her to look at the crowd of patrons, and pointing at them, said, see how everyone is looking at me. Quickly, with a gait meant to compel, he had transformed into a mobile lounge lizard. Is this a joke, she had thought, or is he really serious? But buffets, she now recalled, were a stage to his void.

Like all his stages.

Staring at the man now, she saw what very few people had ever seen, his raw and unmistakable loneliness on a visage accustomed to performing. She knew him, she knew that with the glare of the far away streetlights barely slicing the obscurity, there was no one to impress—no need for a mask.

Detached, she watched him unload tools from his truck and place them haphazardly inside his garage. This isn't fatigue, she told herself, as she watched him enter his house and letting the door slam on itself.

There simply is no one there.

She rubbed her temples, tossing on the motel's mattress, feeling the pain return, between her shoulder blades and running up to her head—the dullness she hated.

Pain held her mind—another migraine, an intense banging inside her skull, unannounced, as usual, fueled by thoughts of him, about what she wanted to accomplish—her body hostage to time's stretched out drips over which she had no control, and the absence of pain a curse just as well. For in that space, the enormity of what she was missing, the life that had been there, but untouchable, became visible. What am I going to do? What would Peter do, she asked herself, wondering if she shouldn't at the very least call him. What about Alice or Catherine? she pushed further in her mind, as she popped a few painkillers in her mouth. No, she decided, it'll be short. Easy. All I need to do is to gather more information. Reaching a comfortable decision space, she thought, no, this is my business. I will do all of this on my own.

What she observed for the following two days revealed there was a good chance Benjamin was travelling far enough for her to risk exploring his closet. He left every morning around 7:30 to return every night at 10:30, the five other Latino men who lived there were gone by 9:30 A.M. Charleston, Lebanon, Keene were places he often had worked in while with Isabelle, small cities all located a good sixty miles from Lowell. He must be waiting for the weekend to get his fix of targets to play with, she mused, noting no women had stepped into the house yet.

A smile grew on her tired face as images of her attire came to mind. Her shorthaired wig, messy, her loose fitting and stained clothes; the antithesis of Benjamin's numerous mainstays. There, from the comfort of her car, as she watched him disappear again inside his house, the decision was made. It had been four days and three nights. The time had arrived.

Tomorrow. I'm going in.

The keyring felt awkward, almost like a metal contraption meant to prick the inside of her hands. She examined the five keys hooked to the pink studded metal device he had welded. Which one is it already, she asked herself, nervously looking around the neighborhood. She played around with the zebra-striped one, making sure to avoid the edges of the ring, remembering, as she wiggled it, that it was the key to the inside door, not the outside one. She zeroed in on one of the two plain silver ones, her wrist swiveling gently to the right, releasing the lock.

The familiar sound of the fire detector beeping, the unkempt and shared entryway, the frayed wallpaper, all welcomed her with nauseating familiarity. Nothing had changed, everything had remained. All right, she thought, rushing to the main door, let's do this.

Can I help you, she heard from the back of the door.

She froze.

You must be Augusto's new girlfriend, the feminine voice let out. Isabelle stared. Fuck fuck fuck. She had run her plan inside her head many times the night before and she had never seen any women coming in or out of the house. But it hadn't even felt like a plan, had it? she admitted to herself—more like a structured improvisation guided by a wobbly fate.

I'm Lola, Ben's novia, she added, extending her hand. You must be Caroline.

Isabelle stilled. Caroline was not part of her scheme. Neither was Lola.

Lola … How beautiful you are, the thought so instant. And so young. Yes, of course, Augusto said you might be here, Isabelle blurted out. Breathe Isabelle, and pray Augusto is not inside. Who the fuck is Augusto anyhow? Is he in? she suddenly thought of asking, turning to face the teenage girl. You see, I wanted to surprise him … Lola …

The Latina woman smiled timidly as she motioned for the doorknob. All the men are out today. That's why I came. To give them a hand you know, to cook … laundry.

Isabelle took it in, dumbfounded. How do you do it, Benjamin? How exactly do you teach our little fingers to play house, our legs to run at the sound of your ven acas? She stepped aside, leaving the girl to unlock the second door, transfixed.

She should have walked out, she should have escaped while holding on to her synthetic wig, pretexting anything, while there was still time. Maybe it was a built-in penchant for inertia, one for euphoria, too, maybe a mix of both, but looking back at herself, her choices—her failures of the mind, deciphering her decision to faun and not flee, then—a cold stain inside the beating heat of her heart, she would not forgive herself.

And it—time ill spent, wouldn't be forgiving.

She stayed and followed the sweet looking Lola into the kingdom Isabelle had once ruled over. But a ruler of nothing, is no ruler at all, she reminded herself.

You see, Caroline, no one is here.

She stared at the woman-child—slit-eyed, permed-haired, and docile looking—long enough to know she would go through with it. Get to him somehow. Make him pay.

With soothing affability, Lola took Isabelle's hand and pulled her farther into the twisted dominion, unaware something was amiss, that Caroline was gone, and did not, in fact, exist.

As she entered the house, Isabelle's mind became blurry. The scent of spices she knew too well, reaching her, star anise and cinnamon cutting into her, everywhere into her. This perfume he manufactured with attention and care, religiously, a perfume with the power to transport her far away. But now, there was nowhere to be transported. She didn't need them anymore—she was already there.

Lola walked through the small kitchen, placing her purse onto the dining room table. Isabelle shifted her eyes while moving toward the girl, looking behind her.

Isabelle knew all would pour from Lola's sweet mouth, the teenager telling the tale of a stranger named Caroline, whose foot, entangled with the camera cable, had caused the fall, sending her body to the floor, the hardness of the metal chair meeting her right temple. Rolling and moaning like a hurt animal, she asked for coffee—a migraine to fend off, she said. The woman's eyes, Lola will tell him, they were unsteady, they frightened me, Benjamin. His eyebrows arching, eyes askance, he will listen attentively, and ask nothing, for he will know, in the coming days, the amplitude, long-lasting, of this apparition, for he will feel the certainty in his heart, and in his mind, too. And so, she will tell him, I left her there, went to Dunkin', to get her a coffee.

Head placed on a pillow, Isabelle saw she had succeeded in unplugging the camera system, for there was no red or green lights flickering anywhere on the control board, no images divided the screen into four equal segments: the basement, the dining room, both front and back porches—his preferred rooms to survey.

Benjamin was a paranoid man addicted to all kinds of devices, a man obsessed by the blank spaces he couldn't fill out, by what he couldn't see, distracted by life, its negative space: imaginations that took hold of him; his imaginations, confusing because brimming with filth. A map never accurately represents a territory, she thought, only a very skewed image of it, and that very fact gnawed at him.

She scanned the bedroom. The usual display of colognes was still there on his commode, huddled to the right, a congregation of fragrances meant to capture. Time. There is little time, she thought. She hurried to his closet, stepping over the laundry he had prepared for Lola to wash.

Confronting her were visions of her own clothes touching his years before, hanging beside his—a proximity of sorts. She stood in front of pseudo silhouettes, shirts hanging still and waiting to be chosen, sequenced by color, sequenced by season—pinks, whites, and blacks staring back at her. Isabelle's breathing increased. Okay, she said, center yourself.

She slowly bent inside the closet and knelt, her arms extending, her long fingers, the tip of them surveying the state of the floor, and summoning her memory to guide her hands—the white wooden handles protruding at the bottom of the closet, one foot from the floor, a set of makeshift cupboard doors she had seen, and wanting to see again because a large shoe box lived there, and inside of it, she recalled now: the unseeable—suede like in feeling, leathery to the touch.

They had to be there.

Her hands probing, amidst fallen clothes and belts and orphaned shoes—she saw the small knobs, dull, the wood flaking. She pulled them toward her.

It was empty.

Sitting atop the dirty laundry, Isabelle fixated on the textured off-white carpeted floor. I should have known, she repeated to herself, and why would he have kept it there, still? Dumb girl, she thought, water swelling in her eyes. The police? she thought. A long thought. No. I tried that before. Lowell Police Department on Arcand Drive. Yeah, they all had said, we know about your guy. Trouble, they had said. Serious trouble, but nothing to back it up.

Defeat morphing into fatigue, visceral and sudden, she looked to the digital clock placed in the middle of the bedroom commode: Ten minutes had passed since Lola's departure. She had to gather herself, leave as soon as possible.

She sat up, rubbing her temples, real pain threatening to strike her way. In the corner, the candle was burning on the altar, improvised, uninspiring, too—a shaky pine-made box over which a photo had been pinned to the wall with blue sticky tack—a light pretending it irradiated truth, on him. A reflection of him.

This photo, Isabelle thought, forgetting time, and walking to the corner to kneel. It's not his mother's anymore. Who are you? she asked the blonde-haired girl—this sadness-filled expression, inlayed, as if trapped, forever by this aperture, wanting of nothing this girl wanted. And to the right, nailed to the wall, she saw someone she had known through Benjamin's stories—this family, a past, recounted and believed—of men: Julián Rodriguez dressed in his military whites, Alberto Rodriguez, a beret propped on his head, a priest by his side. A woman there, too, squinting. Dolores, is that you, she whispered to herself, entranced by the woman's beauty. I finally see you. He was right, she thought, you are not to be forgotten. And just below, wrapping the altar with its gems, his pink gemmed rosary. Her eyes widened. Oh, Benjamin. The thought came quickly, and she ripped the necklace away from the makeshift shrine. I know this will hurt you, she thought, as she stood and placed the beads inside her pocket. It belonged to your father, yes. I remember how you told me. The story. How proud you were, too. Your turn, now—to start hurting.

Outside, winter called, still and again, as flakes drifted to the ground, contrasting with her state of mind. Nothing gentle waved inside of her, only edges sharpened by doubt. This house, she thought, dark, cold, cursed with staleness and rot.

She quickly walked to Jocelyne's room, unable to resist—Augusto's room now, it seemed. An odd sight, she thought, noticing how Jocelyne's toys mingled with steel-toed boots and other items belonging to a man's cave.

She recalled then, his seven-year-old daughter, Jocelyne, of how she slept with Benjamin when under his care during the weekends, and how he took his women while his daughter slept beside him.

To mind, came that moment she had repressed. They had made love on a Sunday morning drenched in such quietness. She remembered how, upon getting dressed, she had walked to the little girl's bedroom, thinking Benjamin gone to the garage, and opened the door, wanting to kiss her good morning. Startled by what she saw, and she had looked away, not wanting to see, and now, almost two years later, the same impulse overtook her. The image was still too fresh, assaulting her. For one second, her eyes had registered, then discarded, the sight of Benjamin, fully dressed, lying on his daughter's little body—she was lying on her stomach, looking at a picture book—his hands holding on to hers. The rosary, twirling above her. Startled, he had jumped to his feet, an undeniable guilt she had placed inside her mind's drawer. Or was it really hers? What are you doing? she had asked him, as she watched him leave the bedroom. She had then turned to Jocelyne, her heart beating inside her throat.

What was Papi doing, sweetie?

WHEN I BECAME NEVER

Helping me learn to count by playing with my fingers. The young eyes spoke of nothing. It had silenced Isabelle.

She stayed there, leaving her tears sign the betrayal of a chosen absence, her decision to say nothing—the glaring of her idleness. She could have made a difference. She had loved her like her own. Like no one possibly ever would again.

Isabelle backed away, gently closing the door, and looking farther down, she walked to the third bedroom. Unusually, Alejandro's door was unlocked.

No images this time only words, Benjamin's voice flowing to her: Walk to Alejandro's bedroom, slide beside him, slide your hands over his skin, because, Isabelle, Alejandro told me—tells me—he wants you to kiss him; to fuck him. He loves you. The middle the night, and Benjamin had pushed her naked body off the bed, to the floor, the whole of him wired, the back of his eyes taunt with blotches of ink that told of his own blankness.

Alejandro. The other one she could have saved.

But I did call the children's services, she thought, consoling herself. Twice. They just never came. And I had to flee.

She entered his small room, flicked the light open. Black painted slabs of J-Prock onto which posters of cars had been hung. Jaguar. Porsche. Ferrari. She walked farther in, reached his night table. Five books had been stacked beside his wiry lamp, the spines facing her: Henry Mintzberg, Barak Obama, Sam Shepard, Oscar Wilde. The top one, wobbly, as if wanting to fall, The Prince—Machiavelli. Isabelle smiled. Of course, Machiavelli. Who else?

She picked the book up, went to the only dog-eared page, and read what was highlighted. "Necessity is what impels men to take action, and once necessity is gone, only rot and decay are left." She let herself fall in laughter, the bed behind catching her. Her head sank into the cheapness of the mattress, and as it did, flickers of dust hovered over her. A reminder, she thought, that everything here is outdated—Medieval in feeling. She caressed the top of the red bed cover, let her fingers dig into the tracks of its frayed corduroy make, and closed her eyes. Alejandro, I am sorry. So sorry.

Just before leaving his room, her feet searched the floor, wanting balance, wanting to go, and there, under the bed—the worn-out corners of their black and white glossiness.

Pictures of her. With Benjamin. With her girls. This other woman, too. Black.

She left the room, shut the light off, and closed the door.

Time passing, as if caught in a warp, a tunnel, a slow speed she couldn't feel—the danger of being caught and herself brought to the authorities for trespassing, an afterthought.

Isabelle continued through the house, and her heart squeezed at the thought of that delicate woman now roaming this place. She saw what she had seen in his other novias, the ones she knew about—Patricia, Lydia, Felicia—when uncovering Benjamin's parallel lives. Like them, kindness, empathy, and generosity abounded from Lola, a young girl too young to know about limits and boundaries and the predators who get their fix from encroaching on them. Isabelle sighed. Lola's youthfulness had a short shelf life, an expiration date. Like the other ones before her passage in his life, hers would eventually wither away, hatched at carefully. Then, a young girl gone and never to come back, the innocence Benjamin sought in her dissipating, sucked into him, by him. Isabelle had seen it under her eyes, and above them, also, marking his presence, the dark circles. Maybe he hadn't murdered people, she thought, but he dispirited humans, carving out the good to leave husks behind.

It struck at her.

She was there now, wasn't she? Far from Peter, and far from the girls, out of touch with her world, back into his. Just like before. I need to go, she suddenly realized, sensing his barbs catching hold—if I want to live. I fought so hard, I climbed back, I wrote my own damn cautionary tale. Face it, she told herself, you found nothing—nothing to prove his guilt, or link him to the murders.

Heading for the door, she stopped at the sink, looking out the window still framed by the starchy brown curtains she hated so much. She stood firm, eyes fixating on the blur in front of her, the neighbor's house, her two feet standing on the kitchen mat.

It was real to me, she whispered.

But maybe I did dream it? Made it up? Maybe I saw nothing because there was nothing to see? But what of—the box.

I need to leave this place, remove it from my head, and just then, the sound of agitated voices and the clinking of keys from the outside door. She froze. Either climb the stairs to the second or third floor or go to the basement, she thought, provided the door is unlocked.

It was.

Holding her breath, she opened the inside door, quietly descended to the first landing leading to the basement. There, she stopped, nudging herself into a faraway corner of the landing, invisible. I didn't hear the door close behind me, she whispered to herself. She squinted her eyes hoping they would work in tandem with her ears, making the chaos unfolding upstairs comprehensible. Two feminine voices, she recognized, both Latina sounding, both infused with a mix of English and Spanish. Fuck, she thought, as the words gashed out of their mouths at machine gun speed, I understand nada. Then one voice rose, submerging the others, piercing the air. Soy Caroline, soy Caroline, soy Caroline, damn it, Isabelle heard, unable to reprieve a smile. Okay, she heard Lola say, come in and see for yourself, there is a woman here, says she *is* Caroline.

The footsteps, determined and quick, reached Isabelle as the two women headed for Benjamin's bedroom. Surprise, she thought, there's your magic for the day, and may the real Caroline rise.

Amused as much as relieved, Isabelle quickly started for the top, believing the exit now possible. But another voice emerged, a voice filled with anger, dominance, and rage.

The door, ajar as she had feared, allowed for a sliver of air to flow to her. The scent of him, bold and crude, reached her, and in that instant, she felt the deadbeat of his heart trying to cool her own. Eyes peeled on the knob, petrified to be caught, she waited.

Que paso chicas, Benjamin said, as he closed the door shut, sealing it with a skeleton key. What happened?

Turning quickly, she ran down the two levels of stairs, passing both washer and dryer and veered to the right. Inside the alcove, she hid in yet another corner, hoping Benjamin hadn't plugged his system back in, that the system didn't reach that deep inside his basement. Above her, a mix of wires hanging from beams made it impossible to locate the placement of a camera.

She lifted her eyes, extending them to the right of the ceiling, and knew exactly what would be unraveling above her. The chair pulled to face the screen, the inquisitive stance as his ass only caressed the seat's edge, his torso extended toward the screen filled with nothing but snow, eyes bulging. She could imagine him clicking away on each frame, his mouth looking for something to spit at. But tonight, Benjamin, she thought, you'll see nothing of substance. Lola will tell you about this other Caroline you see appearing on the back porch from your screen—my gift to you. You will zoom in and out on me, look closely at my clothes, my hair, and analyze my gait as I walk up your stairs. You won't recognize me, not now, anyhow, Benjamin, nothing will be triggered inside your memory, but for one simple reason: You never really saw me in the first place.

Searching inside her purse to retrieve, this time, her migraine nasal spray, she started to feel it, the beating inside her head. First things first, she thought, as the inside of her nostrils absorbed the shot of quick relief. She looked at the time, it was 7:00 P.M., and the January sky had darkened. Unsure of what she should do, she curled up in the corner and rested her head on her knees, hoping Benjamin believed she had left the premises. He knew the cameras had been turned off. If I were him, I'd inspect the whole house for anything, and that includes the basement. Okay, she thought, feeling the pain leave her temples, I have no choice, and I must get out of here, one way or another.

She mentally scanned the basement, her mind remapping an area she had often snooped in while going through Benjamin's belongings, looking for clues—looking for him, the real him.

The basement, typical of many unfinished basements, felt like a large rectangle encased in cement and wood beams. Divided in two by a stopgap wall made of old wood planks in its middle, most of the space was unkempt and messy. Facing the laundry room located at the bottom of the stairs was the alcove in which Isabelle was hiding. Benjamin used this half of the basement to store tools and construction material. There, carpeting, dried up gallons of paint, paint accessories, tiles, tires, and machinery were strewn across the floor. A toddler in a playpen made of cement.

The other half was accessible through a makeshift door that stood in the center of the temporary wall. One thing she remembered was Benjamin did not watch over the space that went beyond the wall, no cameras were pointed to the deeper end of the basement.

That's where I need to go, she thought, understanding she had to find a way to get to the other side without being seen. She slowly straightened out from her corner and pressed her back against the wall to test its solidity. A tower of boxes she hadn't noticed before shook, catching her attention. Quietly, she approached them, letting her hand touch the back of the wall they had been placed against. That's when she felt it, a literal hole in the wall. She carefully pushed the boxes away from the wall and examined the small gash where a plank used to be. Rotten wood, she concluded with her hands.

It took her no less than fifteen minutes to worm herself through the hole, backwards, as she pulled the stack of boxes back into place, arms extended. Easy enough, she thought. Until the top box toppled over, its content spreading on the cement floor.

She held her breath, on the lookout, her body, starfished. Hearing nothing, Isabelle turned over and surveyed this part of his crypt-like space, this time using her phone's flashlight. Some of Patricia's belongings were still there, to Isabelle's surprise. Two long clothing racks on which Patricia's suits, knits, and pants were hanging, all vestiges of her youthful past ruling over the dump. Surrounding those racks were boxes of old board games yellowed by time, and piles of knitting patterns from another era. Benjamin was to donate them to some charity or dispose of them in some way. So he had said.

She got up and walked around the display, her hands caressing the fabrics that had withstood a life only known to Patricia. It seemed Benjamin wanted a piece of it, not wanting to let go.

Isabelle's eyes fell on the basement Hopper windows behind the racks. Some form of glee hit her stomach. My only way out of here, she thought, as she tried to open one.

Lucky for her, these windows were old, and their mechanism opened from the top and not the bottom. Needing something to climb on, she started for old suitcases piled up in a corner. One by one she brought them below the window, smiling to herself, reassured. But her exit would have to wait—his voice floated to her, followed by his steps, then the flick of the light. There was no time except to slide in between the suspended clothing and crouch. The last thing she did before the door opened was to pull a suitcase toward her to hide her feet.

He appeared phone in hand, looking around, his face unreadable as ever. She held her breath as she saw him nestle into the far corner where the suitcases had been. He propped himself onto the antique built-in counter and looked around, unknowingly staring at her. He should have seen her, he should have noticed the suitcases had been moved, but not knowing what to look for, he redirected his stare to his phone. Curiously, she felt safe, untouchable. Look at him, she thought to herself. See. And wincing, she realized—I've become immune to you. That's what happens when you tire of chasing the deceptive, when you come to demystify it. The magic leaves and the ordinary takes over the deity one loves to project.

She watched his fingers tap. She watched him dial a number. Amor, she heard him say, seemingly on a voicemail, I can't come tonight, but I will tomorrow, I promise. I miss your culo, Amor, like crazy.

Benjamin jumped to the ground. It's over, she thought, he's leaving. I'll be going shortly. But he turned around, kneeled and opened the old cupboard door. From deep into the back of the wooden structure, he pulled three bags. One by one, he untied them, checking each of their content with care. As if on cue, princess Lola appeared at the open doorway.

Coming right up, he said, as he walked up the stairs. Ven aca, Amor.

He approached her, his hands removing one strand of hair from her face, tenderly.

Isabelle watched. She should have ached. The ven acas should have commanded her as much as they had Lola. No. There was only music playing inside her head, one beat, one melody, and a simple chorus that kept coming and going, like an armed pendulum. Honey, she thought, don't chew so hard. Fear acidifies all meat.

The couple walked through the door and closed it behind them, pulling its lock into place and switching the light off. I'm hungry, baby, she overheard Benjamin say, baiting his plaything as they climbed the stairs. Lola's response was inaudible, but Isabelle already knew whatever the timid girl had said, was of no consequence to Benjamin. He didn't hear as much as he didn't see.

Eyes glued to the counter, the image of his seated silhouette still lurking in her brain, Isabelle waited patiently for time to pass before pushing away from the mothball scent she had been breathing. Surrounded by Patricia's past, Isabelle remembered the night she had helped Benjamin fix the broken boiler, here in his basement. He had demanded she help him, waking her up in the middle of the night, screaming that partners needed to help each other. What the hell did she know about boilers, she had said, laughing, I'm afraid to light the fucking barbeque. To buy peace, she had followed him down to his catacombs, half asleep. Hold the flashlight, he had ordered. Point it at the bottom. Stop shaking. Can't you do this right? And now it came to her. A box full of Patricia's old tableware had caught her attention as she had stood by the boiler. Orange and green depression eras glasses, dainty serving trays, thick gold-rimmed wine glasses stacked inside a large plastic container. Without saying a word, she had told Benjamin she was taking a break, that really honey, you don't need me at all. As she was starting to poke into the treasure chest, Benjamin had become nervous, suddenly yelling not to touch anything, that she was right, that he didn't need her after all, that she should wait for him upstairs. Startled, she had obeyed, too tired to care.

Can a house keep its secrets?

The phone beamed to the back of the cabinet. She pushed through the bags and looked for the shoebox she obsessed over, quietly sounding out the space—hoping. Still nothing. Removing the three bags, she felt the time had come. I'm guessing that's where you shoved some of your other truths, she whispered to herself. Let me unwrap more of your life.

But not here, honey, no.

At the motel.

She retreated to the far corner with her loot—the bedtime release would be happening soon enough. You fondle and bite at the same time every night, Benjamin, like a ritual, she thought, and fully absorbed, your door closed, you won't hear a noise. She looked at the closed windows. She would tackle them at 1:00 A.M. Until then she would rest.

The sound of water running through the pipes woke her up gradually from the bed she had improvised on Patricia's vintage coats. Stretching her body, she knew what was happening. She looked at her watch. 2:00 A.M. Yes, she thought, the follow up to all his fucks, the proverbial ablutions, the washing down of liquid with liquid.

Now, go.

The piled-up suitcases staring at her called for movement. She climbed on them, fighting the unsteadiness. From there, she opened the window, swirling its crank and praying the rusty hinges would give in easily. Then, with force, she neatly jerked the frame down. After the third attempt the window surrendered, dropping on the pads of clothing she had spread over the floor. Okay, she thought, carefully removing the screen.

One by one, she threw the bags out the window, hearing them fall on the snow. Feeling the tower of suitcases about to crumble, she stepped down and repositioned them as quickly as she could, then climbed back up. Adrenaline is a wonderful thing, she thought as she pulled herself up to the edge of what was left of the frame.

The air stiffened her bones with a hit of humidity, and she welcomed it. It woke her. She looked up to the first floor and saw someone had switched the light on, flashing a shadow through the kitchen window. She worried that same someone was about to go downstairs and call the police.

Alert, she gathered her bags and ran to the left of the house, creating a blind spot for the cameras. Looking back, unsure, she rushed into the backyard that offered some shelter.

Eventually, silence called her out of hiding.

She walked through Lowell's empty streets, her purse safely worn across her body, the bags in her hands. You wouldn't recognize me she told herself, stroking her own hair and pulling on the blue hoodie she had changed into while hiding.

Part of her expected to see a cop car emerge from anywhere, looking for her. The other part understood it wouldn't happen. The local police knew Benjamin the wolf crier; the cops hated and avoided him. They probably thought this entitled asshole deserved to be broken into.

There was some otherness about her now, for she had really seen Benjamin for what he was, the extent of his affliction. Because, she thought, to see is to believe, to see the hunter and stab the lies away, the only logical faith one should adhere to.

Peter came to mind, his soothing kindness, his infallible vulnerabilities. A strong and gentle bohemian looking, like her, for a shelter she could trust, she thought. I miss him, she suddenly acknowledged, as if the loosening of Benjamin's grip on her mind freed her nucleus, making space.

She continued to walk, letting some poise come in, bit by bit, understanding it was too late to go back. But she didn't know, did she? How all would unfold. Yet she felt it, the motion, the coming and going of her sanity. Would it always return from its soiled travels? she had started to ask herself, more aware. I don't know. I don't know if what I am doing is wrong, she whispered to herself, but I don't know if it's not right, either. And as she pulled herself into her own form of Socratic hell, a small rat, brown and scabby, crossed the sidewalk, sauntered to its feet, and raised on its hind legs, stared at her. Your spirit animal, she thought, as she walked around it.

She looked up—the sky was clear, star-filled, and snowless, and she kept on, staring at the apartment buildings, tall and industrial-like, bricks and mortars from another era, oppressiveness erected and worshipped, still framing the lives of the desperate. She remembered, Quebecers, her people, leaving their land, back then referred to as Lower Canada, to look for work during the mid 1850's and on. This diaspora seeking solace here in Lowell. They had abandoned their lives and their lands to better secure their families' wellbeing, these very textile buildings goading them into the industrial era. Isabelle had hoped to settle somewhere on the east coast, like them, looking to resurge from chaos and transition into a new world. Ever since her parents had brought her to Maine, Rhode Island, and Vermont, either to sun-up on the East coast beaches, or ski the Green Mountains, she had been seduced. By what, she never could tell. Now, as she examined the bleakness of this disheveled town, she wondered how disheartened she had been to consider up-rooting her life to live here— because of him, and his fantasies. How desperate must you have been to come and die here, she thought, absorbing the town's absence.

She walked more and finally reached her car, parked at the edge of a vacant lot near an old, abandoned mill. The brown monument blending with the night.

Just like she had.

To get out of bed felt like pulling her body out of quicksand. Seated on the edge of her mattress, she shook the stiffness away, stretching her limbs in every direction, like a shredded map.

Naked, she walked to her small carry-on, picked a clean pair of underwear, then walked to the bathroom. Her hands underneath the faucet, the feel of the warm water soothing the cold of her hands, and she did not lift her face to the mirror, to the etching of new lines at the crease of her eyes, around her mouth, above her eyes, to her hair, wispy and scantier, falling, and falling more.

Her feet in a puddle of water, she arched her neck, facing the pummel vomiting more liquid, and opened her mouth leaving water submerge the inside of it, bubbling with the taste of chlorine and metal. She stepped out of the shower, grabbed a towel, and walked back to the bed. I am cold, she thought, sliding back into bed. So cold. My mind, too.

Sleep came, again, and when she woke, the side of her face pressed against the bleached smelling sheet, she saw—the bags, gospel-filled.

One more attempt, to clothe herself, to freshen her mouth. Her spirit. She unplugged her phone from the charger located near her head, sat on the carpet, and stared at the CVS bags, brittle and torn.

Randomly, she chose the bag from which she could guess a black contour punctured the opaque plastic. She retrieved it and opened it. Neatly tucked inside the inner pouches of the folder, official documents, all written in Spanish. Isabelle leafed through them, scanning the dates, the headings, and the signatures. Legal documents from the military, she realized. She took pictures of each one and smiled. Got ya.

She proceeded to open the heavier bag, the one containing the letters Benjamin's mother had written to him while he was in Iraq and America. She had seen them before, piled at the bottom of the altar he had erected—the shanty to his genesis. There, beside the letters, in the corner of his bedroom, pictures of him and his mother had been slid to the front of a wooden box. Laughter suddenly flew out of her mouth. Liquorice, she remembered, Liquorice was the name engraved on a brass plate glued to the top of the small box. That evening, wrapped into a bedsheet, and sitting on his bed, she had lifted the cover and examined it. Where did you get this? she had asked. The flea market near Manchester. You have no clue, Benjamin, she had said, this is an urn, there are ashes in here, and judging by the name, not a human's ... A feline spirit released, he feared. Yes, a cat's, she had said, smirk unseen, for she had known his aversion to them, the fright of death it summoned and the ghosts he said appeared to him. Human ghosts. He saw them: Patricia's late husband who was said to have been found dead in a pool of his blood down in the basement. A heart attack. The hitting of a head against the cement. He would randomly appear anywhere in the house, at night mostly, he said. And this little girl, too, wearing a white gown, her pinkish hair waving above her head. When I wake, she is there floating above me, as if waiting, her lips moving, her arms stretched out to me with fingers that keep curling. Right, she had replied with a smile. Now, they have a cat to keep them company.

She undid the long shoestring holding the letters together and carefully picked four or five from the top. As she did, a picture of Philomena standing at the stove slipped out from between them, and inscribed behind the matted photo: April 2016, Managua. You told me your mother had died, she thought, shaking her head. Non-plussed, redirecting her attention to the letters, it surprised her, Philomena's cursive, neat and consistent, readable. Her fingers touching and fanning through the letters, she recognized a texture, rough and dented, one she had played with a few days before, pulling it out of the bundle. Unfolding it slowly, she stared, the image sinking into her like an anchor looking for any kind of silt to sink into. No. No. No. The drawing—never burnt.

I need to rest.

The light woke her up, finding her on the floor. She raised herself to a seated position, and with a sigh, deep and shaky, she read them—all of them. Thank God for Grade ten Spanish lessons, she thought, nervously. Before her eyes, deluges of love, unswayable laments. News of a mango tree, thriving. She is still there, Philomena had written. Still, and waiting for Julián.

Isabelle stared more at the sketch, puzzled; at the woman and the child, locked together and forming an intersection where promiscuity hinted to incest. So, you are still alive, Philomena Rodriguez. And I wonder, are you just as unwell as he is? Were you part of the seed, too?

She folded the sketch, placed it back inside the bag. Pausing for a moment, she thought, such freshness inside this pain, I can almost touch it.

Coming back, slowly, she spread more of the content on the bed.

Another folder. Just as black.

Her fingers felt it waiting at the bottom. A passport. Not Nicaraguan. No. From the Dominican Republic. When she opened it, a legal document telling of things she had never known.

Capitán de Corbeta, Benjamin Rodriguez

Republica Dominicana

MARINA DE GUERRA

Base Naval "27 de Febrero"

She paused. So, you were born in Nicaragua, but somehow served the military of the Dominican Republic. Okay. And so what?

Skimming more, a small carton popped out of the loot.

An appointment confirmation.

COURT HOUSE OF LOWELL

Benjamin Rodriguez

October 14th, 2014.

11:00 A.M.

Lawrence, Massachusetts.

Isabelle studied the information, recalling a conversation she had with Valeria, Benjamin's sister-in-law, two years before. The conversation had been drenched in predictable moan-like complaints about her life and its emptiness. Valeria had seen in Isabelle the perfect outlet, the stranger in the room to whom one could confide their burdens to; their sins; their family's secrets, all with impunity. Isabelle would never know Valeria's true intentions, but she liked to think Benjamin's sister-in-law had wanted to warn her, protect her from the danger she had refused to acknowledge. Whatever the motivation, one July afternoon, while sipping tea, Valeria nonchalantly spilled the beans. Benjamin, she had said, spent six months in jail … and always thought he was guilty.

Isabelle circled the court's phone number.

Five counts, the clerk said to her, matter of fact, one for each of the following: Obscure matter to a minor, assault and battery, open and gross lewdness, criminal harassment. And sexual assault, with the intention of killing.

A gasp filled with more shame and Isabelle closed her eyes and swallowed heavily.

What was I thinking, she whispered to herself, shame in her heart.

Alice.

The time, phone to her ear, she never felt it slip. Coiled, her body sideways on the bed, she remained, walking through a door, now open in her mind—a point of no return in the making. Ma'am, she heard, are you still there? And she came to, her head spinning in all directions, as she tried to make sense of what was revealed. Why was he released?

All I can see is that the victim, the clerk had said, a female, pleaded the fifth. And I can't tell you why she did.

Or who she is, Isabelle had risked.

That's correct, ma'am.

Okay.

Thirsty for water, she rose, walking to the bathroom sink. She returned, water in hand, repositioning herself on the mattress. She played with the court notice, then the black folder again. More documents.

Copies of birth certificates belonging to Benjamin and his parents, Philomena Diez and Julián Rodriguez.

She read on.

Both his parent's legal documents stated the usual: place of birth, address, status, and date of birth. The handwritten documents had been signed, stamped, and certified. Her eyes widened as she read Benjamin's own formal information. Yes, Philomena and Julián were identified as his parents, yes, Managua was said to be the place of birth, yes, madrina and padrina were there, identified, failed magic wands in hand, she could only assume.

Two other birth certificates stared at her. The first one, dated 1992, stated Benjamin Diez-Rodriguez was born December 23, 1972; the other, dated December 1984, stated Benjamin Diez-Rodriguez was born September 8th, 1975.

Two birthdates.

One man.

Or no one at all.

For two years, this man had been a stranger to her—and why is she still surprised?

Hidden inside the pouch, his military graduation picture, his wide eyes, his crooked smile. Who could possibly have resisted you, Benjamin, she thought, transfixed by the shine of his skin against the shine of his costume, at least, not me, anyway. But I know, she said, her voice lean and soft, the shine is narrating a story made of artifices meant to fool and play.

She slid out a two-page letter dated November 2004. The title left no doubt as to what she was going to find. The investigation had been coordinated under the umbrella of FISCALIA, procedura fiscal, abuso sexual. The accused's name was thirty-two-year-old Benjamin Diez-Rodriguez, the victim, a fourteen-year-old named Olivia. The location of the crime remained undisclosed. As she read the handwritten report, Isabelle understood the relationship Benjamin had held with this teenager lasted six months, its ending precipitated when Olivia confided in a friend she had been raped multiple times by Benjamin. The friend, alarmed, had quickly informed the parents, who then had filed a complaint.

Then, another document, pointing to something similar, albeit more formally. Addressed to a magistrate, copied to the procuror fiscal adjunto del departamento de abusos sexuales de la policia national, the five-page typewritten document blunted Isabelle's stomach. Succinctly stated, the facts exposed the predator living inside Benjamin's psyche. On May 5th, 2005, on kilometer 9 de la Autopista Duarte, D.R., Capitán de Corbeta, Benjamin Rodriguez had raped at gunpoint. The victim, unidentified, had been lured by a bola.

A fucking ball.

How old had she been?

She clenched her stomach, reading further. Follar con el puño. Follar con el puño. The fisting of a child ... The fuck-fisting of a child!

The sudden threat of a mental fatigue she was fighting to dismiss, came, or was it sanity simply leaving—again? A long breath. A longer stretch of the mind. She stopped breathing, her hands looking for the bottle placed at the bottom of the bed, the sip of rum spreading its warmth everywhere ice had threatened to form. She poured herself a second shot and read on.

Re-examining Benjamin's incriminating documents, her eyes dropped on his signatures, their complex loops. Someone should have made sense of the nature displayed, the swirls, the dots, the superimpositions, understanding it as an admission of unconscious guilt—the psychopathic kind. She remembered clearly how each time he had signed a credit card receipt in her presence, it was as if a kindergartner had drawn his name at the bottom of a finger painting. A doodle, matchstick strokes barely touching, barely making sense. The given name had been there.

Just the given name.

Benjamin.

Then, hauntingly spread at the bottom of the documents, a signature, intricate and so artful. The other personae's plea to be seen. A coming out, so timely and bubbling to try and seal perceptions. This pseudo human wanted to be seen as a star. Didn't he know that what shines in the sky is already dead?

A new version of Cotard syndrome.

Isabelle looked out the window and was lost in a hole from what she had seen. Everything in that closet was real, she now knew. Nothing had been imagined.

Yet, the box—gone.

She steadied herself, closed her eyes. Quietly, she returned to her task, almost in a trance. She reshuffled the papers, ready to close the folder she was holding, when Polaroid photos fell to the ground.

Girls, in his bed, all different, some smiling, mostly not.

And this one, too.

She retrieved her phone. Made the call.

And still, the same recorded message—there was no one at the number she had dialed.

Nauseated, Isabelle played with the border of a picture, staring at the naked body of an old woman sprawled on a bed, in disarray, lust mingling on her face, wrinkled and paper thin. Patricia, she whispered.

Placing the Polaroid on her chest, Isabelle thought of the old woman, of how she had fallen for Patricia quickly, seduced by the Irish feistiness simmering underneath her heart, that and the Armenian warmth her late husband had infused her with.

Patricia, such strength, she thought, her heart squeezing. And where else was I to pour my story? she asked herself. Where others had stoically displayed their judgement at her inability to see Benjamin, Patricia had understood her distress. With compassion and concern, she had kept her tethered to the facts, thereby ensuring Isabelle wouldn't give in to the fabricated memories Benjamin had planted in her mind.

A mother saving a daughter.

And now the leanings inside life's reciprocities.

I'm coming to you, Patricia, she said to no one, as she started to pack everything away.

I know where you are—the place I once spent a weekend with you. Your family cottage.

The small cabin was located thirty minutes from Lowell, in Atkinson, New Hampshire. Surrounded by a dense forest of pine, the small farmhouse, with its wind battered shingles and dangling gutters, felt abandoned.

Isabelle parked her car beside Patricia's white Honda CR-V and walked to the front porch with apprehension, the crackling of the ice under her boots, the only sound carving into the air, glacial and dry. The door was unlocked. An invitation, she thought. Or more additional neglect. She pushed it open more, unsure, and stepped in, almost tripping over the curled welcome mat.

The constricting of her throat. The burning of her eyes. Ammonia rushing to her lungs, threatening her breathing, she pulled her scarf, covering her nose. She looked around, holding her breath, barely recognizing—

The layout, reminiscent of a tiny bungalow, offered the eye no definite place to land. Pinkish vertical shades were drawn, blocking out whatever was left of the day, giving Isabelle nothing to hang on to. Her eyes tamed the dimness. Dishes, their hardened mess now visible, strewn on all the counters over which the cupboard doors towered, all opened. On the stove, pots, more dishes, and traces of sauce that seemed to form their own continent. The sink, filled with garbage, appeared useless, out of order, misused—like the rest.

From the back room, the only room fitted with a door, three guinea pigs rushed up to her. What on the fucking earth?

The soft sound of wood rocking answered her.

Patricia, she yelled out, walking toward the doorway, pushing the rodents away, is that you?

She entered.

Stumbling over the open cages, graffiti hit her retina as she eased herself in, welcomed by drawings that spelled someone's devoutness to a master, lighting the room with their fluorescence: orange crosses drawn sideways, green rosaries disguised as snakes, purple, eyeless virgin Marys, crying pink tears, all had been drawn over a black wall. She lost herself inside them, feeling as though she was part of a black light poster that celebrated something nebulous, yet unsurprising. Motionless in the middle of the bedroom, she recognized the loops, the fonts, and the iconography. Dizzied by the show, she knew that she knew.

Benjamin.

Don't look, she thought.

There were guinea pigs everywhere, fifty at the very least, their purring and whistling diffusing the pungency suspended in the air and brushing against her leg. Quickly, she placed a hand over her nose again, leaving her eyes to rest on what she assumed to be Patricia. Seated in her rocking chair, the old woman swayed, her face impassive, looking straight at her. My God, she said, my God, what happened to you?! Patricia, she yelled, approaching as she removed her wig, it's me, Isabelle. I'm here!

Then she saw it, the large knit meshes covering her white skin.

Her nipples, her crotch.

What the fuck.

From Patricia' skeletal frame, hung a white oddity meant to represent someone's version of seduction. Isabelle knelt by her side, her knees crunching the mix of dried feces and litter the cavies had kicked everywhere. No, she thought, don't throw up. Not yet.

As her fingers recognized the woolly texture, Isabelle understood the knitted two-piece set Patricia wore—the halter-top and the short skirt—was unfinished. Motioning back and forth, sitting in her soiled diaper, Patricia still was knitting the top part of what looked like a baby doll outfit. With her hand, Isabelle followed the moving strand of wool attached to Patricia's needles and reached the white wool ball slowly unrolling. How does this work exactly, she asked herself, it almost feels like feeding upon oneself.

She got up and snapped a sheet off the bed and covered Patricia's shoulders. Everything swelled inside Isabelle, a tide of some sort running her over as she now acknowledged the orange glow of a Himalayan salt lamp thrown on the walls. She turned around and saw it, the same one, a reminder Patricia was his.

Above the wicker headboard a black and white blow up of Patricia. Nude. She closed her eyes and turned to Patricia. Hey, she softly said, regaining some composure, look at me. Please.

The chin started to tremble as she stilled her needles and took Isabelle's hand. Isabelle looked at her in disbelief, unsure of her presence there with her. The pale turquoise of Patricia's eyes told the story of an ocean one could trust. But something else was now at play inside of them.

Isabelle helped her up, her hand scooping hers. Let's get you cleaned up and into bed, she finally said, and get some warm clothes on that skinny body of yours. What do you say? From far away, Patricia smiled.

Isabelle sat Patricia on a plastic chair placed in the middle of the bathtub and gently cleansed her body, washed her short hair, curiously cut and greasy, talking to her, whispering all would be okay, that she was there.

The elderly lady remained still, feeling the water drip from the old shower head. Slowly rolling over her parched skin, the water felt as though spring droplets announced the arrival of a promise she had prayed for. Moments of lucidity had become sparse, but there with Isabelle, she touched upon one. Not so long ago, she could feel it, she had ached for the normal, the humdrum of everyday life to coat her with safety. Looking at Isabelle's hands moving up and down her sagging skin, washing weeks of secretions that had niched inside all her creases, in all their form, she thought of how that place had found her. With Isabelle by her side, she could feel it, the soft push of the summer wind impregnating the intricate lace of her mother's curtains, the touch of a stranger kindly tucking in the unsightly tag hanging from her shirt while walking on the street, the sound of her young father's accordion playing as she nestled inside her bed, listening to the laughter of a party.

Isabelle brought it all back for a long second. Patricia hung on to it. Until the water carried them to the drain. With the rest of her. Hugging herself, she started mumbling, repeatedly she was allowed to keep them, but he said to get rid of the cats, and replace them with mini pigs, that I could, that I could keep those, she stuttered.

Yes, Isabelle responded, disturbed, yes ...

After securing her diapers and pulling a nightgown over Patricia's head, Isabelle gently lowered her onto the bed, refusing to acknowledge the grotesque art hanging over them. Sleep a bit while I clean up and make us something to eat, she told her.

Patricia, exhausted from the effort, was already asleep.

Isabelle corralled and caged the rodents, then cleaned as much as she could, as much as she could tolerate, haunted by the bedlam she had discovered. Thoughts slayed her mind, armed by representations of what she had seen. The props, the décor, the costume—the starlet. An improvised play, she thought, a barren script. Then, images of Patricia's body, of her back full of little marks, indents resembling the ones she had seen on Benjamin's back. He never had let me caress any of them, she recalled. Injuries from the army, he had said, shrapnel. And she had let it alone, his explanation, just like she had done with most of the rest. She swallowed and shook her head. And with the image of Patricia too alive in her mind, her skeleton framed, she walked to the kitchen. A sandwich. She needs to eat.

Walking back into the kitchen, and waiting for her: the dinner table, covered with receipts, bills, and blank checks.

What first caught her attention were the medical bills overflowing from a ripped manila envelope. She took them out. Dementia the doctors had written. Advanced. I should have seen it coming, Isabelle thought sadly, recalling their last phone conversations, in July—the repetition of Patricia's questions, the retelling of events, the seldom remembered answers. She should have known.

She tiptoed to the bedroom to see if any medication had been placed in either of the night tables. Finding nothing, she stepped into the bathroom to open the pharmacy. There, only the usual array of over-the-counter lifesavers: Tylenol, Pepto Bismol, used lip balm, and some cheap make-up. Isabelle kneeled to check under the sink. It was empty, other than some cleaning detergent.

In the kitchen, hidden behind the piled-up dishes, Isabelle found one set of tablets. Memantine, a medication prescribed to Patricia the previous September. The packet was still unopened. Either she refuses to take them, or someone believes she doesn't need them. She read the dosage, called the pharmacy and walked back to Patricia's bedroom.

She was told they wouldn't take effect before some time, but still, Patricia had to start somewhere. She walked to the bedroom, placing a plate of buttered toast on the bedside table, and bent over the sleeping woman. Patricia, she said, lifting the heavy head, open your mouth, take a bite. The woman obeyed, eyes closed, chewing slowly what she could. Unable to finish the improvised meal, she raised her hand—no more. Still, Isabelle softly said, this, Patricia. And try hard. Your medication.

Waiting for some life to re-enter Patricia's body and mind, and to wake up, Isabelle roamed her space, absorbing the reality she had stepped into. Whatever was unfolding here should have been seen and reported. How was it Patricia had slipped away from the world, unnoticed, as if the cracks in her life had become invisible chasms? Fucking Benjamin, she thought, you're the one who disconnected her phone. Authorized it, somehow. It makes sense.

Phased, she let herself fall on the loveseat's ragged cushions. Denim, she guessed as she looked on. On each end of the sofa, a small, whitish altar, candle-less, had been erected. What they displayed Isabelle recognized immediately, jeans and plastic beaded rosaries, all his. How did I miss that? she asked herself, her fingers clutching the rosary she had stolen from the altar in his bedroom.

And then the scent—unmistakable—her head turning.

Cinnamon, star anise, and cloves. The tea recipe.

She got up, and there, spread on the tiles, their composition, randomly strewn, resembled that of a wave. How curious, she thought. She bent to pick them up, the stars, the cinnamon sticks, the dot-like cloves. Looking more, she saw their folds, piled underneath the shrine— a dozen of them. One at a time she opened the mementos, birthday cards, Christmas cards, Valentines' Day cards.

All bearing the juvenile signature she had so often seen.

All addressed to the same person.

Mother. Patricia—Mother.

Whispers of hope and perversion artfully threading together. Bloodletting, the name of your game, she thought, eyeing Patricia's bedroom door.

The last night coming, and she helped Patricia ease into her pink pajamas, one bony limb at a time, then slid her body next to hers, as she had done since her arrival, every night for three nights.

Lily-of-the-valley, the sweetness ... Patricia said, her words soft, you found it ...

Yes, yes, I did. It was inside your night table ... Just a few sprays of your Dior perfume. I thought you would like it ...

It reminds me of the Armenian springs, you know. Of him. My husband. She paused, stretching her mind, retrieving slivers of her past. I fell in love with them on our honeymoon. Armenia in the springtime. Closing her eyes, she fought the fog that threatened to return. Every Friday after work, she whispered, I would get home to a fresh bouquet. He used to tell me that spring was our only season. Because in it, all the seasons live. Like us. Like we did. Miss Patricia Dior, he used to say. She brought the bed cover to her chest. That was me.

Isabelle listened to the winter's slamming of the window shutters. I never really liked spring, she whispered to her, it carries uncertainty, and it weighs me down with expectations. Hope is a seed sowed in the fall, not something you reap, not something that you take either, like the raping of the land. Hope lives inside fog's murkiness of the skies, inside the cold rain that pushes the fall leaves down to the ground, inside the quiescence the winters impose.

Isabelle took Patricia in her arms, her petite body resting against hers, feeling the weight of her head on her shoulder. I can't stay Patricia, I have to go tomorrow, she said, her throat knotted. I need to go home, she thought. I can't do this anymore. Tomorrow, social services will come, to check up on you, she continued. I've arranged for some volunteers to come and take care of your little friends and help you start knitting again. They will also drive you to your medical appointments. Maybe find you another place to live in, she hoped.

Patricia's eyes opened, her hand squeezing Isabelle's softly. She spoke, her voice, thin—a filament. Will you come back?

Isabelle swallowed her sadness. Yes, she lied.

Will he be back?

Isabelle turned her head to meet her gaze. No. No he won't Patricia. Social services will see to it. The authorities, too.

They stilled, listening to the rodents' whistle, to the wind's howls, to the strange symphony floating in the room.

Kissing her forehead gently, Isabelle stroked her hair, caressed the nails she had polished with red while Patricia had slept, and she left the room.

Benjamin—everywhere he had been, the bitter taste of his insanity hidden by the sweetness moving inside his words. She knew. She had sucked on it, sapped it from the bark—willingly.

Unlike Patricia, she had escaped.

Seated on the sofa, Isabelle picked up the rosary and played with the beads. You always carried a plastic mock-up of these little hardened pieces of shit with you, and this one is no different. But now, the real one is with me. Around my neck.

She replaced the plastic rosary back on the altar and when she did, she spoke to him, as if he was there, his face to hers, shining his usual schadenfreude smile. You think you know how to dance better than the rest of us, fool us with your steps, Benjamin. We shall see, fucking asshole, we shall see. It's called the contrapasso.

310

The punishment of souls.

In that instant, her mind travelling to foreign land, inured by what she had seen, she knew the malevolence brewing inside her would never be as somber as the ink running inside his veins.

But maybe, it would be dark enough.

She walked the Moakley Bridge, huddled inside her coat. Water below the deck. She stopped and looked at the cold flow of the moving water, crystals of ice the slow current kept undoing. In her head were such dark thoughts. Darker, now. It should have been a movement forward this quest for satiation. The wanting of a better conscience. But no—Isabelle walked for two hours, oblivious to the icy air, the delivering of dullness. Flecks of snow doted the hoary of the sky, falling lightly, as if suspended, as if randomness was the trajectory to follow. The purpose gone, and redefined.

She walked to a café across Boston Harbor. Choosing a table facing the large window she ordered a hot cup of coffee. Christmas decorations still hanging, Nothing But the Girl coming from the speakers. All these moments now, the slew of them; a change had glided, modifying her course. The coffee feels good, she thought. Around my hands.

Scanning the establishment, she noticed it was half empty. The waitress, alone serving, was speaking to a couple standing at the counter.

I did what I could, Isabelle thought. Two weeks of running around.

The motel.

Patricia.

The authorities.

Looking at her phone, Peter came to mind, and she dialed his number, hands shaking, needing to hear—to speak with him, but the call would not go through. Breathe, she told herself, and anyway, she rationalized, you had wanted to do this by yourself. Not involve him—

more. She sipped her drink, feeling dizzy, and she left her money on the table.

A foot outside the door, she heard the waitress thanking her, a goodbye. Come again. She turned around and smiled. I am heading back—home.

Her car was parked two blocks up from the harbor, away from the shore. The walk slow and somewhat slippery. The snow now falling sideways, plumped by the sea's proximity, the air so wet; her eye lashes, a dream catcher made of winter's tears kept her from noticing the sidewalk's depressions, and her feet caught a cavity, hollow and snow filled. A slow-motion fall, the skipping of a heartbeat. Spread on her back, her head to the ground, she looked up. A hand hovered over her, fingers like stars. A kind voice came. Let me help you, and she took his hand, nodded and continued to her car. The ticket was flapping beneath her right windshield wiper. She tore it out from underneath and dropped it on the sidewalk, the wind blowing it away.

Once seated, Isabelle turned the key. Three attempts and the engine was heard. Inside her mittens, her fingers intertwined, her thumbs removed from their slot, joining them. Let me in, she smiled. She adjusted the vents first, away for her, wanting to avoid the first wave of air that would be pushed out, always so cold. Waiting for the heat to permeate the inside of the car, she stared at the office building facing her, made of brute cement, men and woman leaving for lunch, their steps hurried and brisk. The heat finally reached her, prompting Isabelle to remove her mittens and her beret and slide her arms from the sleeves of her coat, leaving it to gather behind her.

As she left the city's parameters, she thought of Alice. Of Catherine. But not too long. The pain was wider than before. It wants to unsee and unhear, she thought. The sounds, the words. So many images. How can I kill them? Will I ever?

Once on the highway, the absence of a wanted numbness. I am tired of claiming what I think belongs to me. Maybe nothing belongs to me. And anyhow, it is life that claims, not the other way around. And am I not, an ordinary, claimable subject? I miss the not knowing, she thought more, the drifting inside excessive comforts.

I miss my innocence.

The sense of things, leaving and coming. Skidding.

Thoughts—so frontal.

I simply wanted to understand what happened to me.

Will the world ever understand that—me?

Why.

BOOK FOUR

I come to you, this moment, dressed in white, a white somewhat stained, my hair held up by two French braids. She did them for me this morning. *Like every morning.*

Today, I listened to her more than I should have—more than usual. I told you. I sat at her feet, feet as bare as mine and I let her braid my hair again, one braid down the middle of my head, thick and heavy, tickling the middle of my spine.

The morning is bright, and the sun is ploughing through the windows and is landing on both our legs, burning and not moving. And it feels good. As I listen to her, I ask myself: How is it we are here, the both of us, stuck in time—the same time? What were the chances, her, me—me, her.

Here.

And still this other song, now echoing softly inside my head. Did I really say no, it asks me, did I really mean it, or was it fate that decided for me? That or destiny? And what about those shadows in my hair, and the flowers on my dress? All I know is that the only flowers on my dress are made of stains. Wild stains that remind me of my childhood, somewhere on a well-kept lawn.

But she is here. And it all makes sense.

These shadows on my hair.

I know, now, that I will walk my corridors with the intent to fool. A fool that fools, there but unseen, just about to slide to that place all fools go to. Family dinners, schoolyards. Bedrooms.

That hotel room. Managua.

Sandy.

I will walk through them with guilt living inside my head. Words pin-balling against its bony walls, making my cranium ache for more relief.

Images of them—that man, the one I never really knew. The one I was meant for.

And this question that keeps coming: Why me?

There had to be a beginning.

I am tired now, and I must go back to my room.

The black woman had blonde-dyed hair, a face that reminded me of Donyale Luna's and a body akin to that of a body builder. None of it worked together, but the attractiveness was there, in her strut, light and uncaring, inside her eyes, intelligent and aware. She carried in her arms a large portfolio bag, black beat-up leather, its handle broken. Right here, I heard her say to the tall red-head walking with her as she pushed the half-opened door in with her foot.

Just before entering the room, the red head turned around, looked at me, her eyes, almond shaped, became rounder, the green of them turning blue. In that instant when we saw it all, she dropped what she had in her hands. Freed but for a moment, they curled onto the floor, little snake-like necklaces, beaded. I heard them, these wooden beings, the sound of them bouncing on the freshly washed tiles. Come on, the other one said, we need to say goodbye. And she took her hand and pulled her in.

I survived, I tell myself. Most of us did anyway.

In some way.

And still, it's a good life if you don't weaken.

I know it to be true. I heard it on the radio.

Beige Livings

Come on, Jocelyne, Alejandro said, as he tapped the stiff leather of the couch Papi will return later tonight. We have time to watch your movie.

Jocelyne ran from her bedroom, her doll Elsa in the other.

Sitting down, she moved closer to Alejandro. Is Malaika coming tonight? The rim of her dress, frayed, its body stained of brownishes and whites. I miss her, she continued. And she reminds me of Isabelle, too, Alejandro. Her eyes lowered for a moment, only to stare back at her brother. She never came back.

No, he said, she never did. And that's okay.

He examined her hair, the state of it uncomfortable to see and to smell. So thin and oily, it exposed an already larger than normal forehead. That's why she's so smart, he thought—everything's buzzing in there, with an ability to remember and sing every word of the songs we play in the car. Tonight is French poetry night at the Spoken Word Café in Boston, Jocelyne. Malaika is set to recite her slam. The one you heard practice the other night.

Oh. Okay

She'll be back for the weekend, he smiled.

I want to go to her country, Alejandro, she said, wide-eyed and looking at him. I want to see the lions. At school, I drew them today, you know.

You did?

Yes, and the teacher told me it looked like me.

Did she, now? Nodding, Alejandro pressed on the remote and selected the movie that had taken his home hostage. Just lions, Jocelyne?

Just the lions. And I want to learn French, too, speak it, like her.

I know, he said.

Alejandro watched as the opening of the movie lit the room, the bias lighting spraying pink onto the wall behind the large screen. He smiled more, watching his sister disappear in this land of hers—Frozen. Then, he looked away.

The month before. The sage had been burning, he recalled, the weed, too, and the room, dusky lit and fusing with the smoke. But the mushrooms, so many, rushing to his brain—and his fantasies had meshed with reality. Malaika had said it was beautiful, the land of her birth, that they all should go, this place where magic lived for the dead more than for the living. West Africa. It stayed with him, and the thought would bloom.

The dinner, now, too, vivid in his mind, when he had introduced Malaika to his father, who was unable not to stare, while examining her, her beauty rising from raven-colored skinned, dark, almost blue. Alejandro, his father had said, pointing at her, undeterred by her presence, you can do better. I came here, to America, not to brew more of the life we fled. We need to move. She won't help. That skin will never help.

She might not help you. But she will help me.

Asleep on his shoulder, Alejandro carried Jocelyne to her room, and removing the toys from the top of her bed, he jerked the fleeced cover away from her. Here, he whispered, I'll see you tomorrow morning, baby girl.

Her bright, brown eyes opened, and he saw, the asking, her confusion. What of me? And will you stop it? Pulling her dress down, he saw them again, the traces of his father's passage.

He pulled the fleece back up to her neck.

Te amo, Alejandro.

Te amo, también, little sister.

Let it go, she whispered in a song, as he closed the door behind him. Let me go.

He should have done something before this—and why hadn't he? But now? Yes, the time was now.

He had packed both suitcases. He had gathered the papers, the passports, forged legal documents: proxies; consents. And to her school he had said, she is moving to another country. No one had showed concern—the teacher, the principal, the afterschool supervisor—trusting so easily the brother they knew him to be. Not even the mother.

They left early in the morning, the two of them.

Come Jocelyne, he said, take my hand. We are going home.

On his birthday almost every year since she left him, Janelle Rivera would park her car at the corner of Blackwell and Main Street. Every February 10 at midnight, driving from Far Rockaway to Lowell, along the I-95. Three hours, a blurred vision of Alejandro pulling her, hope etched in the frost of her windshield, a hallucination—maybe. The intent? To take back what in her heart belonged to her.

Parked, she would wait for Alejandro to appear, this gift she gave herself, the sight of him, a long-distance love, never known, requited in absence only.

Huddled inside her car, the engine running, she would tap her fingers on the steering wheel. Feliz cumpleaños hijo mío, te extraño.

5:00 A.M. and she watched a taxi pull over, waiting in front of 14 Blackwell St.

From the house, Alejandro appeared holding Jocelyne's hand, hurrying inside the taxicab, and as they did, she saw Alejandro's eyes, no longer blue, she thought. No. Not even at dawn.

The roads were mostly empty, traffic about to swell. Before her, the morning sun appearing, a pale orange bulb—a low light, as she followed the taxi.

Logan airport, and she parked three cars behind them, watching Alejandro walking into the airport, holding Jocelyne by the hand, Jocelyne's doll squeezed against her small frame.

She watched the taxi driver exit his car, leaving the motor running, and join the other drivers gathered on the curb.

From her seat, she waited a few minutes, unsure, then decided to step outside. She walked to the drivers. In them, she could see joyful surrender—daily morning levities. The conversations were animated; they were talking over themselves, yelling above the morning bustle: about the Celtic's new point guard; the Bruins' first line; the Patriots' next season.

I'm sorry, she said, as she approached them, focusing on the one driver. The man looked at her. Where are they going? she asked.

Their driver considered her, rubbing his hands, deciding not to care. West Africa, he said. Bénin.

It was not the smell of breakfast that woke Benjamin the next morning, it was Jocelyne's perfume, apple and vanilla, something the girl's mother had given her for her ninth birthday. Looking at the ceiling, he remembered the night, the sight of Alejandro standing in the doorway holding his sister's pleading eyes. He had backed away, whispering, hold Elsa tight, very tight, and talk to her, sing her that song, Jocelyne, sing it to her and all will go away.

324

Benjamin got up slowly, placing his feet on the carpet, and he remained still, trying to understand what he was sensing. The absence of voices that would usually greet him during the morning weekends, his planned time with his daughter.

He made his way to his daughter's bedroom, and he scanned the room, toys of all kinds scattering the carpet, little pieces of Lego princesses and Barbies and porcelain tea sets, and her clothes, pink underwear with Elsa's picture stamped on the front, shorts and dresses, all glittering with some sort of pink dust. Walmart trash. He hurried to her closet. On the top shelf, his hands moved over three large fleece blankets, hanging, ready to fall, her little suitcase gone.

He hurried to Alejandro's closet. The same thing, and many of his clothes, too. Gone.

He walked to the living room and sat on the brown leather couch they all had known, unsure of what was happening, knowing only that they had gone. He thought of Isabelle beside him that one time not long before her vanishing. He hadn't noticed when embracing her that she had seen—really seen him, and through him, the non-existence of him, a fallacy as deep as they come, that Isabelle had observed him try to mimic crying, watching his face contort and transform into disfigured and primitive expressions—of what?

Unexpressed sadness, like he was feeling now.

And rage.

Isabelle left the following day, he recalled, a year-and-a-half ago, for good. His last sight of her, she was laying on his bed her head buried in the pillow, her shoes barely hanging from her feet. Her dress to her hips.

Turning his head to the window, he watched the snow dropping, straight and abundant, and he cursed it, a curse that lay inside of him—born from those days' past: fucking fuku, he heard repeating. Papi, you were right. The fucking fuku is there. It never left me. He turned from the window and tried to recall Isabelle's scent, notes of her that had already begun to dissipate, diluted by the smell of failure. His. As he did, mechanically, he reached for his rosary, yet knowing she had removed it from his altar. Nothing was hanging from his neck. Nothing from Julián, anymore. A steal, he thought, as he clenched his jaw—even Alejandro had not been allowed to touch it. Just like Jocelyne.

He fell asleep on the couch, this witness, clean and tidy and without a trace of a living soul gracing its premises. When he woke, fragments of Isabelle flooded his mind again, because he never wondered about the others, for he had consumed them like a flower spider liquifies the greens and the colors, leaving behind appearances of life about to flake.

Benjamin stood from the couch and stretched his forearm, and extending it to the ceiling, he dropped his hand to his upper back, stretching it further and sliding it beneath his shirt, his fingers feeling these markers of a time, dents inside his flesh. Caressing them as if a birth mark, he smiled.

Like so many other times, blankness of his mind, on repeat, reliable, emerged now without warning. White psychosis, some call it—that wide space he checked into, undetected, craziness disguised behind a slew of rehearsed patterns, of well-practiced postures and poses and words and kisses and timely fucks. Yes, white psychosis merging with his craving for absolute light.

He walked to the kitchen. Once at the sink, he drew the curtains in and retrieved a pot from the drying tray. He poured water into it, and placing it on the counter, opened the cupboard to his left. From the bottom shelf, he removed a metal box containing a mix of star anise, cloves, and cinnamon, and from it he plucked three stars, two sticks, and four dried cloves. Dropping the spices inside the pot, he remained nowhere but there, his mind empty. Ginger, he suddenly remembered, and he turned to the refrigerator, opened it and retrieved a block of it, throwing it in with the other spices inside the pot.

On his way to the basement, tea in hand, he stopped in front of the shelves propped on the landing. Gallons of paint, saws, drills, and tires, all bunched up. He didn't have to put his tea down, no, he knew where to look—where the box was. With one hand he reached, and finding it easily, hidden like a chameleon never to be noticed, hidden in plain sight, as the saying went. He continued down the stairs, the box in his hands and thought, Isabelle never got to this one, that she had nothing on him, or so very little.

He walked to the end of the basement, pushing Patricia's clothes rack away from his path, feeling nauseated but for a second, then turned to the right. In front of the antique armoire, he sat. There, at the bottom, everything made sense.

He lifted the cover of the box and retrieved an unopened letter. Philomena's.

Managua, December 2009
Mino my love,

Did you ever know I walk the street of our lives with the conviction that God is in me more than ever when you are gone? For you and Him, I remove my shoes and feel the earth, hoping to feel your own, wherever it is that you are.

When I walk, I look at the tree. Yes, all the time, I raise my head to the branches, and I sway with them. With her, this little ghost star that hung only to become the fruit Julián was always seeking. It never could have been me. We all know. Yet, I tried to replace her, didn't I?

And this sketch of us, Mino, when I stare at it, I see your hands moving across the paper, creating. Us.

I cry.

But my tears have never counted, have they? For if they had, God would have come down and saved me.

And did you know, these years that I have walked in my bare feet everywhere in the village, feeling the breeze, that is like your breath hovering over me. Like you used to blow your warm wind on me, my fingers, my lips, deep in my old neck. You remember? For it is the only way to be with you, as you will never come back.

To your country. To me.

I know you won't.

Now. I need to tell you—they wanted another leader, his men, a leader that wouldn't prey on the weak, on their women, on their daughters. The President found out about his double life and ordered, to purge the past, to give it a real chance. I told him not to go, Mino. That his men hate him, that Nicaragua has had enough of him, that this ceremony to honor his so-called achievements, was a lure. Still, he went, and I watched him leave. Andie, too.

They came back with his body, yesterday, walking through the courtyard stopping at the tree. We all looked up, at the branches weighted by the fruits, ripe and not, some waiting, others too far from the soil. We laid him on the couch by his tree.

Julián is gone, Amorito, and so is Luis—who decided to leave us soon after.

Too much pain. Too much waiting for you.

You've been gone so long … But the sky will be there, as always. They will be there, too. And you will be soon as well. I can feel it. And when that day comes, I will climb to all of you, the past and the future.

The ladder will be waiting.

And I will climb it with all of you around my neck.

So very tight, and raw.

- Mamá.

Impassive, he replaced the letter inside the envelope and put it back inside the shoebox. He turned his attention to the box and smiled.

The necklace, his fingers brushed over it delicately, and he lifted it to his cheek, knowing what to expect—the remembering of the feel of them. He blinked. But they must all go, he thought, as he pulled a lighter from his back pocket. It's them or me.

The flame rose, brushing against the first square of leather, the first kill, the smell of burnt skin rising. Each one, one after the other, a sequence, and he watched them burn, carefully, kissing them goodbye, making sure the order was right, remembering who, remembering where. All non-believers. All white. And, in all honesty—just because.

1989—Cassandra Smith

1990—Alida Bakker

1991—Emma Smith

1992—Sabina Pachon

2003—Sandy Hansen

Sandy, the last one in his hand, and he paused, scrutinizing its particularities. The skin, lighter than the others', younger, too. How ironic it was you, he thought. Chosen—unlucky. And yet, if your face hadn't been so much like Andie's, I would have let you go.

From inside the box, he saw a picture of himself dressed in military whites. He picked it up gently, eyes gushing over himself, wishing he had never left Spain. He placed it back and he thought of her, remembering that night he walked onto the plaza. Sylvia, her climbing the air stairs, the painful limp, his gift.

Pensive, absorbed, Benjamin watched the flame climb this last relic, making its way to the edge of the peel, dry and soft, until it, too, was burnt down to nothing. Gone.

From the earth. From his memory. The smell of it running to is head.

A beautiful anchor to the past.

Like my tea, he thought, as be brought the cup to his lips.

Colder still, honeyed, always, bitterness staying.

But still one more thing to look at and waiting at the bottom of the box: Isabelle's book, *Inhaled,* How dare you, disturbed woman, do this to me. All fucking lies.

A sound shook him—the doorbell ringing, and he heard himself saying, I'm coming, his rage fleeting like it always would. I'm coming.

In a trance, unaware time had turned, against him, catching up, he opened the door to a young cop. Are you Benjamin Rodriguez?

It had happened so many times before in his life, these encounters with men of order. In Nicaragua, in Rota, in the Dominican Republic. It meant nothing to him, to be detained, to be accused, to be found guilty. He always had emerged, unscathed. Untouched.

Sí, soy Benjamin Rodriguez, he said, with obvious pride on his face.

All right, muchacho, the other cop said, I believe you know a certain Patricia Dermijian, yeah? We got some questions for you, and he reached for a picture he had in his jacket pocket. Is that you?

Benjamin smirked. Proud, still. Maybe.

All right, well, you're taking a ride with us. We'll wait, get ready.

Getting into the back of the cop car, a hat with New York written on front and precariously perched on top of his bald head, he looked up and waved at his upstairs tenant.

I'm coming back later today buddy, no worries, he yelled.

This is your house? the one cop asked.

The urge to say, to speak. Pretend. Lie. And he does. My home, yes. I've lived here all my life, you know. I have a beautiful wife—a lawyer—three kids, the cutest in the whole world. Lots of money, too. He looked at the snow clinging to the passenger window. She's the best cook, too. The very best.

A nice life, the younger cop blankly said.

Never boring. Never.

What's her name, exactly?

Isabelle Rodriguez. Canadian. She's got her papers and everything.

Ah. Good to know.

Benjamin wedged his head between the two front seats. It's Taco night, Tuesday. Then bowling. I need to be back by six, so you know.

Really, muchacho? the cop driving said, glancing at his partner. We'll see about that, won't we? Just remember, he laughed, as he pressed on the accelerator. There's always a Taco Tuesday ... waiting somewhere else.

Frozen

J ocelyne's tired eyes opened wide, in front of her the sea, the wildness of its surf the only filler of silence. Here, Alejandro said, looking in the distance, is our home. Our real home.

The huts were few, spread unevenly, thirty feet from the water breaking. Having removed their shoes, Alejandro carrying the only backpack, they walked to the hut they had been told was theirs. When they entered the small space, pushing the beaded curtains aside, Jocelyne laughed. I've always wanted to have this, she told her brother, her fingers caressing the strands. It's cold. It's soft. And when it moves, it makes music.

He looked at her, this happiness. I have no choice. All right, he said, taking note of the jug placed at the side of their bed. Time to rest, Jocelyne Rodriguez. The night has arrived. Time to sleep.

Sleep.

We can play tomorrow.

Tomorrow.

But first this.

But I don't feel tired, she said.

Your eyes tell another story.

Then they are lying.

Impossible, Jocelyne. Eyes never lie.

No?

No.

He leaned to her, kissing her forehead, the sound of the sea reaching them. It's been a long trip little sister, and this will quiet you until the morning.

Until your morning.

Still standing, she watched as Alejandro lifted the jug from the ground and pouring the clear liquid into a plastic cup. Here.

It tastes of grape.

Does' it now, he said, sadness on his face. Here, he continued, it's time.

All Time.

He helped her lay down, placed the sheet, light and humid, over her, pulling it up to her chest, her thin arms above them. I love you, Alejandro, she said, her eyes drooping. And I know you love me, too.

More than you can ever know, little one. Now sleep.

It came quickly, this shutting down, as if she had helped it, this ending to her; of her dreams, and her nightmares. And when she fell for her last sleep, inside his arms—a sun shining for a child and only for a child, now and forever, at the door.

Sitting on the mattress, he lifted her limp body, rocking her, and waiting for her little breaths to fade, the rhythm quieted by the drugs, so many of them. He waited, hovering over her, eyes tender, blue lips; frozen lips, before him—how I have loved you little sister, he whispered. Please, understand ... and he remembered, her little bum, naked, the day before leaving—in the air, her face deep in the yellow pillow Isabelle had left for her to hold when scared, at night when alone; a little girl whose body was being violated to the beat of a man ramming his flesh into hers. A little girl who had survived another moment. Her last one. She had turned to him—her brother, her eyes blinking and blinking some more, and she had scrunched up her nose and ground her teeth and squeezed her doll Elsa against her heart. It always helps, she had whispered to him.

No more, Jocelyne.

I'll make you a snowman, he sang, caressing her hair, I will, I promise, and make me one, too, he continued, as he uncapped the bottle of bleach. Made of snow. Made of sand. And with a brush made of steel, pouring the liquid over her naked body, he cleaned her as much as he could, words of the winters she loved coming from his mouth, distorted with grief.

The night fell quickly, and he heard the shuffle soft steps in the sand, men walking to him. The tall stranger standing guard, bowed to the men dressed to kill and resuscitate, in colors speaking of truces and certainties that will carry her innocence and her soul to the heavens. Sorcerers and apprentices and believers. He had told them her story. Of the denial of her being, of the taking of her short-lived purities, of the blood-soaked sheets welcoming each morning, of a father that was a monster, a teenage mother who had fled. Lurid details to a talisman meant to save her. Bénin. The place I want to root myself into. Its soil. His tears still falling, he let her go, letting them take her away, yet following them until they reached the altar placed by the shore, isolated and lonely.

He watched, in the distance, the long burning of her small body, the African men then grinding her bones to a fine powder, compressing ashes of her into small pearls, coating each one in a mixture of silver and gold dust. And in the late hours of the next day, they handed him a box made of raw teak.

He walked barefoot, listening to the road's murmurs. Stop, they told him, here. A restaurant by the road, a small Tata Somba. Some yams with tambo chili, tomatoes, onion, chicken consommé, and peanuts with beef, he asked. He placed the box to his left, on the wooden table. He stared at it, a soft prayer sliding inside his mind. Lifting the cover, he held his breath, and he remembered why he was where he was. In so many places, all at once.

Long and black skinned phalanges came gripping the edge of his plate. He saw the lines above her hand where dust had settled, and running too, inside her palm, a pinkish white where life, love, and death were carved, suspected but never acknowledged. There, the old woman said in broken English, your meal.

He played with his food awhile, then, when hunger called, he proceeded to eat with his hands. As he brought the lump of pounded yams to his mouth, he knew he had done well, penitence and guilt weaving into that space where the world needed to absolve its sins. He needed to save her—a blessing she needed. Deserved. Her death, a malemort made right by the sanctity of their ritual.

She was the branch that had sprouted not too far from his. And looking at the necklace the men had given him, he caressed the beads. I became this: The one branch that had to break. You as well, he whispered. We were keeping it alive, weren't we, Jocelyne?

That tree. Born sick. Born to stay rotten.

Seeking another soil; seeking but never finding.

He took a sip of his tea, and he took the new talisman and wrapped his neck with it and left on the table whatever money he had on him.

He continued to walk, uncertain but quiet, carried by the dryness of the heat that never failed to follow you on this land. He gripped the necklace, an incomplete rosary made of her. Papi, you did this.

The dust clogging his breathing, staining the inside of his nostrils the color of blood. Ahead of him, the land meeting the sky, saturated blues meeting saturated crimsons.

A color-blocked landscape.

As he walked on, he saw nothing of importance, only what lived inside his head. Running is all I can do, strangely, as every cell in my body has ossified. Stranger even, I have no destination, not even Malaika.

He didn't hear the old Pajero stop, and he didn't hear the white man ask if he needed a ride. Alejandro simply watched the car speed ahead of him.

We both had become anvils, Jocelyne, me, being the heaviest, he thought again. You need to understand, baby sister, there are parts of the past that belong to some more than to others. The ones that are oblivious, the ones who flee, the ones who wallow, they float like the top note of a scent meant to be forgotten. The ephemeral, blown away by the base and the core of absolute perfumes. Our core weighed us down.

He stopped by the road, and let himself fall to the ground, and he fell asleep, dreaming of her, of the days winning over the nights.

Decayed radicles.

Albino heaven is what he dreamed of, there in Africa. Dotted pinkish skin wrapped around lanky bodies. Rust-colored hair extending to the heavens. Men and women and children who fluoresce through the days as much as the nights, gentle zombies who don't understand their relevance to the world, the worming of their own magic, the power simmering under their skin.

He woke, steeped inside the dream still, gripping the necklace, and looked up and saw the moon. It felt so close, this moon. He lifted his arms, stretching his fingers to the roundness of it. She pulls tides, pushes them away, too. And that's been us, never permitted to be settled, one way or the other.

He stood up from the road's shoulder, and as he did, headlights beamed ahead of him. The old school bus stopped, its door already open. Where are you going? the old driver asked, seated, staring behind tinted, shattered glass, his hair made of kink and unruly curls, white and grey and not black anymore. Alejandro climbed up and said to the man, any airport will do.

Alejandro got home, the empty house waiting, smelling of the funk left behind by a lifetime of absences. Papi, he yelled to no one. Papi? He walked to his bedroom door, unlocked it and walked in, understanding all would have to wait to the morning. I need to sleep.

The ringing of his phone, a voice, soft and recognized. Where have you been?

A long pause.

Wharton State Forest, Janelle said to him, dress warm and bring a sleeping bag, I know where to go. And he thought, yes, finally, his mother now back, with him, like the good old days when they escaped Far Rockaway and fled the weight of his words as much as the weight of his hands. Their love of winter, an oddity that had saved them. What took you so long?

Mullica River, where we used to go, she told him, and take the bus.

From the window, the snowy landscape swished by, frames that moved quickly, too quickly, never halting the mind, their motions not stilling it. He walked the bus aisle, looked at the back of the driver's head, a shiny and bumpy head. Africa came to mind. Jocelyne came to mind. Benjamin. He clutched his necklace.

You're lucky, boy, the driver said, Alejandro descending and stepping onto the mushy ground. It's a warm winter day today. Like spring.

Alejandro, nodding, started to walk.

He reached the path leading to his meeting place with Janelle, walking slowly, untouched by the quiet of the trees, oblivious to the life inside the forest's humming and soft cracklings, his mind was stuck in a mud of his own making. I will have to tell her. Everything.

He walked to the campground, wild and isolated, inside this forest made of skinny trees, the only witness to him. To what he had done.

A black face, like his, against a whitish background. She was there waiting. Huddled inside her blanket, sitting on a log, teasing the fire. She stared at the sky so busy with its glows and shining and promises of real norths. And she asked herself, how is it we live under the same lights? Yet most cannot find even one, and when found, whatever the shape of it, whatever the strength of its beam, how to use it remains unknown, and unfelt.

He spotted another log, and picking it up, he placed it by her side. He sat.

For one hour, they remained quiet, not looking at one another.

I missed you, Janelle, he finally said.

Me too, hijo. También.

Why so long?

She paused, looking at her lap. I don't know, Alejandro. The fear of him, I suppose, the fear of me, too. I became unwell, too. Very unwell. I just hid it better than the others.

He looked away from her, to the coming night. They all do, he said. Become unwell.

Yes. I know. She swallowed. Before your father, my life had been like a quiet river, steady. With him, constant upheavals, a rhythm that left no space—no place for thinking, for existing, truly. The exhilaration was real, never stopping, which in itself is not real, and so very destructive. Two years of it. Full time.

You left.

I saw too much of what he was.

You could have saved us, you know.

I know.

You save everyone.

I had to save myself first.

And still, it almost killed you.

A fog setting above them, between the trees. Like a thin river. She looked to it. Yes, and the boredom, the floating around, aimlessly. The boredom, Alejandro. It stole from me. I was lost inside this wanting of wanting. Never having. Holding. Like I was dead. My life became some form of suspension where nothing began, nothing started. I moved away to Toronto for some time. My brother's. I didn't work. Just volunteered where I could. The Puerto-Rican community is vibrant there, you know. Then, I came back here.

Same apartment?

Same apartment.

Still at the same hospital?

Yes.

After you left, he went ... mad ... crazier—for a while. He looked for you. Even in Puerto Rico. He hates to lose. Cannot bear the humiliation of it.

Alejandro, listen to me now carefully, try to understand. Her eyes turned to the snowy ground—shame filled eyes. I followed you. I've been following you for the last month. Followed Isabelle, too. She paused, and raising her eyes, she summoned his own. I started to have dreams, Alejandro. Alive with blood. I needed to know if you are like him. Are you like him? Did you become him?

From his pocket, he retrieved a plastic bag. I need to take one, Janelle. I just do. Popping a candied mushroom into his mouth, he said, I think I am like him, but different, Janelle. I feel it, sometimes. Some say we have no soul. It's false. All of us have souls. Ours is just different. In consistency. In substance. I think the world and I are equal, or at the very least, both creatively equidistant from our personal notion of what is, what should be. Two circles that rarely intersect. The world does not possess my difference, and I do not possess its own. We both envy one another. Like you, I want what I do not understand.

And I think, Janelle, like others, you envy my lack of remorse and conscience, the pure awareness of being what I am, the conviction all the better. Unrestrained, unforgiving, and forever immobile. And yet, I understand love. At least, the love for a sister. He looked at her. A sister now gone.

A sister now in peace.

I don't envy anything. I will never envy you. You or your father.

You say that. But I don't believe you. Aren't you curious? Don't you want to know what it would like to do anything you wish to do without any regards to the consequences? A better kind of neurosis. He removed his gloves and retrieved a picture from his pocket of Jocelyne. Eyes closed. Janelle, I have the same sickness. You were right, and now you can stop wondering.

Her eyes widened. I saw you leave with her. Your birthday. Where is she?

The nocturnal winds, wintery in sounds, will not bury the rest of his story, and he said, Africa.

Africa?

He handed her the picture. A voice coming from his bones. I killed her, Janelle.

She stared at the sight of the little girl, the trees, even the sleepy ones, witnessing her thoughts. Would her violence trickle down to their roots, stunt their reach? Oh, God, Alejandro, no, she whispered. Why?

He ruined her forever, destroyed her.

She could do nothing, now, and she gathered her belongings, not looking at him. Walking back from the campground—from him, in her mind, she placed his body on a pyramid of wood, behind an old, abandoned cabin, and waited for his body to become bone, and nothing more than just bone. She would have taken the charred remains with her, delicately placing them inside the bags she had brought with her, crushing them into pearls, like Jocelyne. She would have walked the trails back to the car, recalling the beginning of his beginnings, his ending now, forever, for she had been part of both.

When they parted, she didn't stop, walking on, saying only: Be well, Alejandro.

The no caller I.D. notifications kept appearing and ringing. Isabelle looked at the screen. Ignore it, she thought, the police again. She bit her lip. What if they can't send him back to D.R., like they said they would— could. What if all I provided isn't enough?

The wind blew the car sideways, and she slowed down, one hand on the wheel, the other placed on her belly. The conversations with the deportation agent and the lawyers had been clear, though, she recalled. Easy. Too easy? Maybe. Sometimes, she wondered, can ease and fairness not happen together, like a tango gone mad? And she thought, yes, they do—they can—had. Because all is possible in the United States. Invoke the right argument and tug at its principles and—

She bit harder this time, unpeeling a half piece of skin from her lip, her teeth pulling and stretching at the dried-up skin, the blood beading and dribbling down.

She tugged more at her belly. There had been Patricia, the last straw, old and soiled and abused, Benjamin's utter stupidity laid bare, enabling Damocles sword to drop, like a guillotine on himself—his own head. The system, made to protect the country as much as the immigration seeker, had been contoured by Benjamin one too many times. This clause you never read, understood, you fucking illiterate—there was nothing vouching for your moral character, was there? And both the lawyer and the agent, Latino like him, had been duped.

Benjamin Rodriguez had falsified answers, and falsified documents. You stupid fuck, Benjamin.

Her phone rang and she picked it up. Hello?

Mrs. Duval? Isabelle ...

Who is—

His ex-wife, Janelle Rivera.

Janelle? she replied quietly.

I need to talk to you. It's about Alejandro, and ... Jocelyne. I need to see you, Isabelle. Nothing over the phone.

I'm about one hour from crossing back into Canada ...

You need to double back. You need to ...

But I'm so close, Isabelle, thought. So close to getting away from all this.

Isabelle, are you still there?

I am ...

Please ...?

Isabelle, in a daze, took the next exit, her breathing the only thing Janelle was hearing, loud and steady.

Isabelle, Janelle continued, I texted you my address. I'll see you in five hours.

In Far Rockaway, she parked her car, started to move to Janelle's apartment, stopping in front of a city garbage pail, and vomited, again. Some spew stuck to her lips, and she said, fuck, as she tried to wipe it off.

Fuck.

Nobody can win, she thought. Nobody. Why can't I just let it go, all of this? With shaky hands she retrieved her cell phone nestled in the back pocket of her jeans. She texted Janelle that she was here and that she needed help, to come and get her there by the pail, that she couldn't move more, and then ... nothing but white and black fuzziness.

The landlord and I managed to get you up to my place, she heard. You fainted. You've been out for two hours.

The light was harsh and unavoidable. Finally, Isabelle said, squinting, I've always wondered about you. She tried to push herself up, flattening her back to the headboard. Photographs spread under Alejandro's bed came to her. I always wanted you to write back to me. You never did. Why didn't you? she asked, her voice weary.

Janelle played with her nails, chipped and jewel free. I couldn't then.

A black and stalky silhouette is all Isabelle could see. She blinked and rubbed her eyes, calling her focus in, revealing the details of a face she had just been able to imagine.

Chemical straightened blonde hair, large brown eyes framed by pencil-drawn brows, a nose wide at the base, and full red lips. I had just discovered you, last year, your existence before me. I hated you for it, you know. I needed more information …

Here, Janelle said, drink this. Always makes life more digestible.

Isabelle scanned the room as she took the tumbler to her nose.

Rum?

Rum.

Janelle stood looking around, too, her eyes sad, as if gates to a grief that will always stay. This used to be Alejandro's room, you know. I haven't touched it much. It's all I have left.

Isabelle stretched her neck and looked at the framed portraits of Alejandro everywhere—an Alejandro she had never seen or met, his science fair, pictures of surfing competitions, holding a medal. With Janelle always. And this one reigning over the others, framed in a rococo style, an anachronism as much as a revelation. The three of them, Benjamin, Janelle, and Alejandro.

All of these were taken before Jocelyne was born, Janelle told her. I never met her, you know. I was tempted to. I only know of the mother, a teenager Benjamin impregnated sometime during his so-called necessary travels. Could never stay put, you know. Felt dead when immobile, alive when moving. But a deadly alive, obviously. Another type of movement. But things have changed since then, Janelle added, her eyes lowering.

How so?

No, no. Not now. You need to eat and wash up. Then …there's much to say. And I think, do.

She pointed to the bathroom adjacent to the room. I left some clothes for you to wear while your stuff is being washed. And there's an ointment on the counter. Use it, she added, your lips …

Isabelle walked to the kitchen table, eyeing the bottle, her empty tumbler in hand. Her senses on alert. The open window. The lack of sunlight. The sounds of a salsa coming to her from outside.

Janelle looked up at Isabelle entering the room. How do you feel?

I'm not sure, Janelle. You tell me.

Sit.

Isabelle, dressed in Janelle's too large sweat suit, hair still wet, licked her lips, and waited.

Did the rum sting?

Bringing her hand to her mouth, she said, yes, that it stung, that she didn't care.

Good then. Let's get you some more.

Isabelle pulled the chair up, sat, and watched Janelle pour more of the rum into her glass. Just then, Janelle, as she did, weakened by the memory of him—of them, started to share about Alajandro, this son, and his sister, Jocelyne. In disbelief, Isabelle listened, her body vacillating, and matching her mind. Jocelyne. Her little hands, her voice, so soft. Brittle almost. This little person throwing her arms around Isabelle's neck, every time she had come back from leaving Benjamin. Alejandro … If I am going crazy, she is already there, waiting for me to join her, she thought, tears rolling on her cheeks.

And more, coming at her.

I followed you Isabelle, you know, Janelle continued. Those two years. Mostly in the last month. From the moment you entered Benjamin's life. Out of spite, but then it became out of curiosity. Something to quiet a rage filled jealousy. And I started to follow him after I found out about Claudia Balasco. Many years ago, but still. His betrayal. It's a form of pain, betrayal, so acute, time can barely cure the damage it leaves in its wake. It took me years. Years. Stalking helped dose the rage, most important to me, made it possible to see with my own eyes how Alejandro was doing. And I did, from a distance. He is poet you know, a part-time one, the only type, really. But yeah. So easy these days to know everything. About a past, any past. She looked to the window. But Alejandro is gone.

Memories of Benjamin's son, came, of the many times he had sought her advice while baking, the three of them huddled in the corner of that small kitchen. Alejandro. Jocelyne—her. Gone? she asked.

Gone.

She looked at Janelle, the sadness that had fallen on her, and decided to leave the subject of Alejandro behind. He was gone, whatever that meant, and while she felt the heart's remembering of him, warm and achy, she couldn't help him anymore. She didn't want to. Why am I here, Janelle?

Because I need to talk to someone who will understand …

I'm listening.

Claudia. The hospital.

Who is this Claudia?

Not now.

Isabelle turned to the window and felt the air, compressed by the wet of the sea, and cooled by the winds, and she tasted its salt, the burnings in her mouth. She motioned for her phone. Peter—

No use. I tried already.

Isabelle shivered. You tried already? What do you mean? And why?

It's quite simple Isabelle, Janelle quickly said, I am planning a little trip. For you, me … and Claudia Balasco. Benjamin has left for D.R., yesterday, did you know? Deported. Denaturalized. You helped undo what I accidently help create when I married him.

He has? Isabelle asked, fixating on Janelle.

Yes, return to sender as we say. My uncle happens to be working at the prison he will be sent to. In fact, he's the head of it. Married a local, moved from San Juan to Santo Domingo after his law degree. So, we go there. I'll fill you in on the plane. After, go see Peter.

Peter, Isabelle said, tears still coming. What do you know? Is he okay?

We don't know.

We? Panic grabbed her stomach. What is there to know exactly?

Janelle spoke softly but focused on the topic at hand. We will need to visit Claudia first, tomorrow. And you will see then, pretty white girl, forgiveness, too often, is taken as a permission to continue. A mistake. And when that mistake occurs, something happens to us.

But I have no money. None at all.

It's on the house, Isabelle. Blood, from where I come from, is thicker than over here in America. Blood helps, at times. Janelle watched Isabelle's eyes, the docility in them, never wondering about what was to be. She took a last sip, stood, and walked to the kitchen counter to pick her purse up. She looked back at Isabelle, time for lunch, she said. There's a great seafood place I know of by the boardwalk. Buffet style. You will love it.

The room was dressed in her preferred shade of light—a calm reminiscent of the seas that crashed the inside of her worlds, and yet, she couldn't move, overtaken by the images on the walls—images of herself. Photos taken while she lived in Northampton, and Montreal, large blow ups of her face, scarred by Claudia's strokes, white and black, intimate charcoal portraits of herself and Benjamin.

Of herself and Peter. Peter, she thought, I need to get to him. And fast.

What is this? she cried. Disoriented, she turned to Janelle. You brought me here knowing about this? You said nothing about this—

Yes, I'm sorry, but it was necessary. There was so much for you to take in, yesterday…

How long has she been here for? Isabelle asked, looking at Claudia's absent gaze.

Thirteen years, give or take, I think. She left for one year, then relapsed. She was readmitted a week ago. That's why we're here. There was a long pause, followed by her sigh. We did it together, for a time anyhow, this last year. Followed you.

Her breathing was short, the intake shallow, and Isabelle backed into the wall behind her, displacing one of the blow ups of her face.

She was let out a year ago, still quite dysfunctional, Janelle continued. The doctors here thought some time back in El Salvador, with her daughter, would help. And during that time, her son, adopted, Sebastián—she's been estranged from her daughter Aitana for some time, now forgotten it seems—told me she did get better. But he soon realized the reason behind her so-called improvement had to do with this obsession over you. She wanted to be you, become you, wanted to understand what it was in you Benjamin loved more, more than all she had to offer. It had kept her alive, until it was no longer enough.

And what happened, exactly?

Inhaled, your book, Isabelle, that was her drop. She saw the book on display in a bookstore window, your name, of course. Bought it. Janelle shrugged. You see, in her mind you became real, and so ... she had you followed, you and Peter ... Before that, you and Benjamin ...

She is obsessed.

Aren't we all ...?

Peter ...?

Peter, yes. Getting close to him, the training a pretext, his client, an opportunity, I suppose. I never knew what she had arranged until she informed me of what had unfolded. She paused, her eyes softer—her eyes: guilty eyes. We were told he is back Managua, quite sick, she said softly. A viper bit him repeatedly. That, and his partner was killed while leaving the hospital where Peter was admitted. A lost bullet, the local authorities claim.

You told me yesterday you didn't know. Isabelle's eyes, large and probing. She stood. You knew. She swallowed. I am leaving. Now.

Janelle blocked her path. No. Not now. Sit. You will see him. Two days. Maybe three.

Isabelle remained silent, standing. Angry.

She wanted to study you, Janelle continued, as if nothing of consequence had been said.

Isabelle began to shake, sliding along the wall, and she began to cry, bringing her hands to her face. She looked up at Janelle. This is crazy, all of this. You both are.

Center yourself, Janelle said, and she moved toward Claudia. And look at yourself, too. What you did to get here. You are no different than either one of us. No different at all.

Stunned, Isabelle watched Janelle, carrying a large case, walk toward this other woman, grossly disfigured, yet smiling. Claudia ignored her and turned toward Isabelle instead. Isabelle, she said, oddness in her gaze, and moving toward her, moving slowly through the air, through her notion of time, repeating her name, her mouth barely moving, her eyes focusing, searching. Stopping inches from Isabelle's mouth, she lifted her hand, and with fingertips stained by a lifetime of painting and drawing and cursing, she palpated Isabelle's face; her neck; her jawline; her lips; her nose; her eyes. Consciousness' stream, now heard by all. Questions. What was it about you that he wanted? What did you have that I didn't? I saw the two of you, I spied, and I saw—if it wasn't love, it was the closest thing to love he would ever know. With you. Not with me.

Isabelle, not moving, watched tears falling over Claudia's face, collecting in her crater-like scars, pools brimming with water. Lifting her hand, scared, she allowed herself to touch Claudia's face, too, her fingers feeling the woman-made holes, the urge to quell, deep inside her, strangling her throat. Isabelle spoke of nothing, madness looking at her. Taking Claudia in her arms, resting her head against her shoulder, Peter in her heart, and she, too, cried.

Janelle laid the first drawing on the tiled-floor, Isabelle abdicating, refusing to look.

Claudia stood, and walked to it, the space, waiting, floating above a portrait drawn by astuteness, her own sight recovering its balance. Like a ripple it came to Claudia—the strokes, the brushes, spelling it out for her, pulling her out of the torpor she had chosen to live in. She rubbed her delicate wrists as she started to tiptoe around the images. There, in the middle of her small universe, her dress untrimmed and layered with pink and orange and fuchsia-tinted patches, there she stood like a flower shredded by the winds of her own making.

It will bring her back, Janelle said.

Impatience taking hold of her. This senselessness. A mistake. And why do we need to? She seems to be in a better place, here, is she not?

Because I promised her, Isabelle. Once.

What?

Revenge. Revenge, now.

Isabelle, not speaking, studied Janelle. She looked at Claudia. In silence, the woman was dancing. She looked back at Janelle. How?

Janelle walked to Claudia and took her hand, pulling her toward the bed. Here, she said, lay down. Claudia let herself be guided; her words replete with gratefulness. Thank you, she said, thank you. There was a passage across her face, it seemed as though sanity had returned, a somewhat faraway softness surfacing.

I told you I would help you, and Janelle covered her frail body with a large Navajo blanket. She opened the window adjacent to her bed, and then kissed her goodbye. You need to rest. So, rest. We will see you tomorrow, Claudia, and be ready. You are going on a field trip, remember? We've arranged it with the hospital staff. We've got the green light.

They walked the corridors of the hospital ward leading to the reception area, men and women walking and talking and dancing and yelling around them, Isabelle thinking.

I am not sure anymore, Isabelle said, as she sat on the driver seat. We are summoning more pain for all of us. All of it feels wrong. So wrong.

Then why are you still here?

Isabelle, stunned by everything that had been unveiled, ignited the motor and as she did, said she didn't know anymore, that maybe, one grief can never stand on its own, its healing a calling of others, that the quest for healing is futile, for it can murder beyond what one wishes to kill. And where does it even stop?

This grief.

For the first time since leaving Montreal two weeks before, wearing Janelle Rivera's clothes, large and synthetic in feel, the scent of Claudia Balasco's craziness caught in them, she felt like surrendering. I am moving, still, yet my purpose, I don't understand—my bearings; my heart; my brain—all of these things surrounding me now—melted plastic.

And Peter, she thought, where are you?

I need you.

To hear your voice.

To feel your shoulders.

I don't want to do this alone.

Not anymore.

The man's body, tall and jerky, betrayed the face, impassive and stern. Hurry up, Jorge Rivera said, not much time, we only have a six-hour window.

The women obeyed and quickly settled in the back of the van, silent.

We should be there in about an hour's time. There's water and some food in the back of the seats. When I tell you to, hide under the covers at your feet, and stay like that until I tell you it's okay to come up.

Claudia, seated in the middle, took Janelle's hand, we are seeing him today? We are doing this?

Janelle brought her closer to her, and said that yes, today is the day, finally. She then opened her satchel and retrieved a small plastic bottle. Take your meds, it'll make your moment shine.

Make sure she swallows them, Isabelle suddenly said, feeling nervous. She glimpsed at Claudia, then looked back at Janelle, her eyes shifty. Maybe we should take some, too.

Janelle, looking through the windshield of the car, said that no, she didn't need anything, that she wanted to fully see and fully feel all that is planned, that lucidity will make her come alive.

Are you sure we should do this, that we won't get caught? Isabelle insisted.

I am sure the man replied. You reached the right people. The whole of Santo Domingo wants him gone—deep tracks of his passage are here, fresh, still easily seen, and fortunately for you, remembered—and it is us who should be paying you, bringing him to us, a child motherfucking molesting bastard among us. Not here. He pressed farther down on the gas pedal, the car reaching a dangerous speed. He paused, smiling. Everything has been arranged. The space. The tools. The privacy. The cleaning. Most importantly, the compliance—by everyone needed. Security will be escorting all of you back to your planes as soon as it's finished. Janelle and the crazy one, back to the States. And for you, green-eyed girl, I've arranged a plane to Managua.

Isabelle sank her back further into her seat and thought of Peter. Soon, she thought. Soon.

Wrought iron gates, tall and rusty, appeared, and beyond them, beyond the barbed wire that laced and twirled along the edge of the walls, the maximum-security prison, pale yellow and dirty. From the prison's tower, a stomp made of grey concrete, guards walking and looking, machine guns ready.

Time to hide, he said.

They crouched and placed the blankets over their heads.

Madness, Isabelle whispered. I feel its roots inside me, as if my brain has been ploughed and seeded just for this moment.

Yes, Janelle smiled, harvest season has arrived.

And Claudia started to laugh.

He seemed stranger than a sterling stranger—like someone never met, never imagined. The three of them letting their eyes decipher, anchor to the past, not asking anything more from the moment.

But he was there, seated in a patched-up leather chair meant for the curbside of a ghetto. A lazy boy for the unstill one, Isabelle thought, triggered.

She started from the bottom up. Yes, she thought, going up to the last floor. A penthouse with no vista. An old looking man—but he is not old, he is young, had looked young for most of his life, until—now, waiting for them. What he dreaded from the start, she thought. If old people were a thing, they would be like dust bunnies, that's what old people looked like. Frail and light, they dawdle in angular spots willing to be sucked up and spit out to another universe.

His shoes, distressed patent leather foot wraps, heavy, grey-colored cotton socks springing from their lips. The mid part of him called to her, the bulge of the stomach hanging over a beltless pair of white polyester pants. Suffocated skin. The death of him, that much she knew. Around the crotch, off white plaques that didn't make her wonder. She dismissed the certainties and climbed higher. To the chest. She stared and recalled its moving, the tranquil nature of a killer's breath as her head had followed him when awake.

He looked at Claudia first, her face so pulling. A disfigured face inviting a defeated soul.

You shut me down, she whispered to him.

He continued to look at her; at her disfigurement, and then he looked at the others, Janelle, first, then Isabelle. I am still there, he said, his eye lids heavy, resigned to his coming fate. I can see it, inside of you; inside your heads. I know I do. I always will.

All three women remained silent, until Janelle said quietly, no.

They let you go, Claudia, he said. How are you, tell me, really?

She looked at him, images of the institution's green and white corridors flooding her mind. The straps, the pain, the waving feeling of never existing enough. Or too much. The sea, mostly. It came from the bottom of her throat without warning, a flying wetness to land on his face. He smiled and travelled back to the villa, remembering how Julián had set him up against the neighborhood kids. To fight until the end. Fists and arms swung out by fear, and legs and feet kicking anyone, anything. To win. To win what? A wad of Julián's saliva being dropped inside of his mouth. Proof of my love, his father would always say. He smiled, welcomed it, leaving it there to drip, the wetness. Thank you.

Claudia motioned the guards to leave them.

Patricia died, Isabelle said.

Patricia, the elderly slave meant to subdue his urges; Patricia, found, gnawed at by her rodents, dead, three days following her departure. A heart attack they said. I should have stayed, she whispered. Waited.

Did she?

Yes.

You came here to tell me that?

Yes and no. It was us, her and me, that's why you're here.

Shrugging his shoulder, he kept quiet, looking at her lips, expectant.

I always wondered why you held on to all that incriminated you, Benjamin. You clung to your mementos like a death row inmate clinging to his chair. So, willingly. Stupido, she let out. How easy it was to alert the authorities. To trace the immigration officials and denounce your fraudulent papers, the blatant lies about your past. But Patricia. You outdid yourself. So did I, she thought, because now, you are back where you belong. The human statue, the imperfect bronze, finally caged.

A series of twitches betraying the nomad's mind, the fallacies and all their trimmings. I knew it was you in the basement that night. I saw you leave; you know. I saw you hide, change your clothes. Preferred to let you go and risk. Catch up to you on my terms.

A failure, she smiled. This time, epic. She walked to him, pulling his rosary from underneath her shirt. His eyes unblinking. His mouth a rictus.

357

She lifted it to his face and placed it on his cheek. And yet, you didn't, and now you're here. And missing a piece of skin, mine, aren't you? Why did you let me go? she asked. Why not draw and cut and thread my skin like you did with the others?

He shrugged his shoulders, looking away from her.

Examining him—she understood. He knew. That night, the apple, the knife. Have it, he had commanded. But like many performers, he was not yet ready to allow her to walk off the stage. Not then. Not yet.

I trusted you, Isabelle. To come back. Eventually.

Why not Claudia? Why not Janelle? she continued.

He turned and looked at Janelle and Claudia. Them, I needed alive. For other reasons.

Janelle stepped forward. I am here to tell you myself, Jocelyne is dead. The hate in her eyes for him, unconcealed. Alejandro killed her, your own flesh. He has disappeared. Africa. And that ... is your doing, and I hope you rot in hell for eternity. But even that, would be too good for you. She turned to Isabelle, then to Claudia, then back to him. You deserve nothing, Benjamin Rodriguez. An eternity of nothingness.

He stiffened, his eyes shifting, his body starting to twitch. He cleared his throat, the smacking of dryness resounding inside his mouth, and he tried to speak the word, no.

Yes, Benjamin, she said, she is gone, just as you will be soon enough.

Before dusk, within the gray walls of his cell, his naked body will be nailed to the wall, paralyzed by pain—a last canvas over which Claudia will sign her name. An abstraction made of cuts. And while he will moan in pain, she will not say a word. She will stand, stare at him the way an artist studies her creation. Janelle will walk to Claudia and stand beside her, her eyes following the lines—precise incisions, narrow in their execution, deep in their intentions—left by the sharp edge of a scalpel.

She will not look at him, she will avoid the dropping of his mask, under which—this never seen face, novel expressions detailing the presence of a human, one who feels as though he was being born for the first time. She will take her metal and plant it where nothing had ever existed, a soil, maggot filled.

He will scream. But no one will care. No one will come.

From the corner of the room, seated on the leather chair, Isabelle will watch, and think—Alice. She will stand and walk to the women, their eyes drowning into the sight of their vengeance; retaliation; ultion; revenge. Justice. Together they will witness the coming of his death, breath-by-breath, the scent of who he was when hovering over their presence.

Levitating in front of himself, he will see the outlines of his many false selves, the ones he has portrayed so convincingly, the ones that hide him from the world, invoking the need to protect.

The ones he hid from himself.

Isabelle will remove the rosary from around her neck, placing it around the large base of his own. May it bring you to hell, she will whisper, a special one. Reaching for Claudia's hand, she will retrieve the scalpel. Feel, she will say, digging into his scrotum and moving up to the testicles, slowly dividing them. More blood pooling at their feet. And stepping into the pool, Janelle will take the scalpel, and twisting it into is left eye, she will talk of Alejandro; of his wounds; of the curse of being born a Rodriguez. This is to make sure even in hell, you will never get to see anything, even its flames. And removing the scalpel from his left eye, she planted it deep into his right one.

Isabelle will take both women's hands and she will tell them it is time to go. They will look at her—seeing her, and say, yes, and together they will walk out of the cell, hand-in-hand, and they will not look back.

At the airport terminal, all three women stood in front of a bathroom mirror and stared at one another, searching their faces for something new. But everything old was still there. Fingers tickling the water, fingers rubbing and scrubbing, hands and wrists twisting. Eyes not looking anymore. We need to go.

Isabelle turned around once at the top of the air stairs and waved, the others waving back. She slowly walked past a slender blonde and took her seat. How long is the flight?

Our flight to Managua will be just under six hours, the flight attendant replied.

Tightly pulling her coat around her waist, Isabelle slid her hands inside her pockets.

Just wake me up one hour before, please. No meal. No anything. I just want to dream of him in peace, she whispered, looking out the porthole. Peter.

All right, Ms. Duval. Enjoy the flight.

The medical staff told her the venom had stifled all his organs. That, yes, they had been able to put off the end, but that the end was inevitable.

Isabelle took his hand, pressed it against her chest. Peter, she whispered.

She stayed with him, lying against his body. For ten days she stayed. Then, on the tenth one, he opened his eyes and saw her, knees to her chin, pushing against his torso, a body depleted and emaciated.

Well, she said. There you are.

He raised his eyes, at first unsure, then convinced. I made it back, he told her.

She looked at the machines' telling of a different story. The truth always lies inside numbers, she thought. She took his hand, and brought the palm up to caress her cheek. It was warm, moisten by the thought of death.

What happened to you, he asked. I tried calling you.

A finger to her lips. Shhhh. I'm okay. I'm with you.

The breath released from him, stale, tepid, reaching her. Her lips soft to his forehead, caressing, she slowly dragged her fingers through his hair. My breath, he started, still a killer, eh? A tentative smile came on her face. Removing the rogue strands from between her fingers, she looked at him, reality settling in. Images of them, in Montreal, Managua. Their last night together. You need to rest, Peter.

The skin sagging from his lid, heavy, and he closed his eyes. It was Claudia, he said. The snake, she did it.

She said that it was not. That they never found out. That Claudia doesn't remember much of anything anymore.

His eyes opened.

An accident, most likely, Peter. Happenstance gone wrong.

I had started something, you know, he whispered, to help you find the truth. Help you bring him to justice.

Justice is done, Peter. Trust me. And don't ask.

Sebastián, he mumbled.

Her son brought you to the hospital before bringing Claudia back to the mental ward in New Jersey. All she wanted was for you to lead her to me. You were a decoy.

The last conversation with Claudia, still a blur. He lifted his head. You?

Yes, me. She was jealous. Wanted to get even, it seems. A sick mind.

No training ... I remember now ...

She shook her head. The training was just a pretext. She paused. Her face, you know.

Yes, he said, her face. I remember.

He tried to sit up, but the pain, too acute, halted his attempt. He swallowed, his eyes blinking it away. I want you to reach Francis.

Francis?

My son.

Oh.

I tried to tell you the other night. Once we get out of here, were heading to Vancouver.

Okay, Peter, her eyes dropping.

The sigh was loud and born from the life that was leaving him. She kissed him more, on the mouth this time, then placed her hands on his chest. I love you, she said, her palms running underneath his shirt. He squirmed, wanting to look at to where his right leg had been.

And Steve …

Steve, she whispered, is gone. A lost bullet took him in the head when he left the hospital. An accident, it appears. She looked at him. I'm so sorry, Peter. I thought they had already told you …

No, he whispered, and half bent, he let himself fall into her arms. I'm so tired, Isa.

I know you are, my love. I know. She caressed the top of his large shoulders, then lowered her hand to his abdomen, circling the bandages wrapped around his wounds, her touch so light yet unbearable for him to endure. She pulled his head to her shoulder and listened to his breathing, closing her eyes. I owe you, she said. I will always remember. My life.

The voice was soft, coming from far away—the haze inside a nightmare. Isabelle, he said. Then silence. Not a loud one, no. Just the way it is meant to be heard, filled with truths, suffused with unbearable answers.

The nurse walked slowly toward the edge of the makeshift hospital bed. Here, she said, it's for you, and she handed Isabelle a manila envelope.

Dawn had arrived, Peter's stiff body next to her. The smell of him, she recalled, the ruggedness of his unshaved face against hers, the way he would hold her, how the reveal of their bodies had been slow, steady. A safe place coming ... A safe place now gone.

Propped onto the mattress, the new cold of him behind her and hugging her back, she let her legs dangle as she felt the outside of the package. Weightless, she thought. Slowly, she unsealed the envelope. She pushed her hand inside of it, moved by the knowledge of what was there. Little dolls, she whispered, still together.

Inside the palm of her hand, she put the trouble dolls away, wondering about Alice, about Catherine, about this Francis. She placed them flat onto him, within the valley of his abdomen. Beside them, she laid her head, her tears telling of unfulfilled quests that became blessings, of triumphs that became curses.

She took a long look at him.

She took the dolls.

Do wait for me, my love. I will come back, somehow.

BOOK FIVE

*T*he subway station, the orange line, and I am waiting for the tube to arrive. The platform is empty except for a few punks poking fun at an old man, whiskey-faced and disheveled, standing at the white mark. Safety first, it says. They have looked at me, but I can see, in their eyes, they know— I am not the type of damage they are willing to fight with. Not tonight.

The sound of the train, I hear, and when it arrives, its wind, warm and smelling of burnt rubber, brushes against our faces. I step inside the car, find a seat and look through the window at the platform, still empty. The warning of the door's imminent closing, the train moving.

I have introduced some parts of me to you, for you to see—recognize? My story is missing, the one your brain hasn't flagged, and yet it will make sense. It must.

The next stop.

Forshores

The day was crisp; a day Isabelle could bite into it. A mouthful of it. Autumn, the queen of all seasons.

She walked slowly, ploughing through the wind, seeing them as if for the first time in months. Years—maybe?

They see me, too.

My beautiful girls, she thought, as she walked through the city streets. Alice with the wild air pushing into the curls of her hair, her lips, the heart of all hearts, so red and so plump. Beautiful Alice. And Catherine, her darkness now lifted for all to witness. True stories her eyes could freely tell, dark eyes that had mellowed into the promise of a tranquil future. Catherine, the daughter who fled the sinner in her mother, pushing back against the absurd.

But now, all was behind the three of them.

Back from their city walk, the girls watched her stand at the stove, watched her adjust mindlessly the scarf wrapped around her head, and hiding patches of her scalp where hair had once been, lush and shiny hair forever gone. Lost in thought, Isabelle prepared the meal as she always had, in silence, still but not, still and wanting to be still, her daughters' gaze asking, and wondering. Her disappearance never explained, only guessed at. That's what they had, approximative realities that couldn't tell of anything, or at least, the whole truth.

Two years now, two years since Isabelle had come back from Santo Domingo and Managua. Two years filled with hills climbed, and so many therapy sessions. And tonight, following their meal, the wine flowing, lightness swimming inside their veins, the doorbell ringing.

Isabelle turned her head toward the entrance door, surprised. It's 10:00 P.M., she thought.

Isabelle saw the shape of her appear from the landing, understood, and remembered. The braided blonde hair, the eyes, so blue, so limpid, evaporated sugar etched on her white face, the face of a woman who had surfaced to never go down again.

Isabelle, she said.

Roxane.

The girls shuffled to the back of her, watching, holding their breath. They didn't know why.

Isabelle's mind travelled to that time, to that place Janelle and her had visited twice.

You were there with Claudia, you are the one I saw ... that chair ...

The girl, nervous, eyes of a newfound shyness; a newfound purpose. Mom and Dad are sick. They gave me money. So, I decided to travel again. But this time no cult, she smiled.

Smiling, too, Isabelle took her hand and led her to the living room. Catherine, she said, as she pointed Roxane to the sofa, get a glass and pour her some wine. Take your coat off. You drink don't you, yes?

Roxane sat, removed her coat and took the glass offered.

The girls sat, too, intrigued. Why are you here? rushed Alice.

The woman sipped her wine and played with a strand of her hair, like she had been taught to do back in that place, the question floating in the air with the faint music reaching her. She started to rock, staring at her knees. I've heard them before, you know. She smiled. The Hip. The tragic ones. She stood and walked to the fireplace, and she sat on its hearth and let the heat climb over her. I'm so cold, she whispered, as she gingerly placed her coat back on her shoulders. She stared at each girl, as if wanting her eyes to explain, tell a story that had to be spoken of.

Claudia Balasco and I were institutionalized at the same place. I had already been there for some time when she was first admitted. It was my first time. It was a fluke, her and I. She looked at Isabelle. I am the one Benjamin had targeted in Managua.

Isabelle could say nothing, her eyes saying everything for her.

Without knowing who we were, we became friends. It wasn't the type of friendship easily understood. Claudia's self-mutilation was ... extreme. No one wanted to approach her. But with me, it would stop—the hard-core scratching. And the staff had taken note of it. They trusted me.

She stopped for a moment and sipped her wine. I was in Managua, as you know, at the beginning, in 2004, when I dodged that bullet, when Sandy was killed instead of me.

The guilt was the thing that was killing me then, and she paused, remembering. I came back home eventually, from that place, and lived with my parents. Ten years of odd jobs that numbed my memories. Until that night when I opened the bedroom door and read the newspapers they had kept from me. It had taken me awhile to fully comprehend that very thing—her not me. And forgive myself. Until that day when I came across some paper clips and understood even more. Sandy had never been the target. When I read the description of the other girls who had been murdered, saw their pictures—blonde, slender, blue-eyed women—white women—I knew I had been the so-called chosen one. Roxane's eyes left again, for a moment, a far-away sorrow fading as much as it could. Sandy's appearance just didn't fit the bill. And worse, I read about the investigation that went nowhere. The names. The hypotheses never followed up. Women over there, she continued, dead or alive ... they have no value, you know. Not really.

373

Yes, whispered Isabelle.

Roxane nodded. Understanding much more, I lost it again, fled, she continued, and I was caught and sent back to live clustered within those walls, and yeah, she was still there, the scarred face, the mutilated body, all of it.

Alice swallowed as she heard more of the story. This time, Roxane looked straight at her. Claudia Balasco and I barely spoke. We watched movies. We read magazines. We walked the hospital grounds. The silence was our bond. Then, one day, your mother and Janelle came to visit her. An odd thing as only Aitana had visited Claudia before. Once only, I think. It had ended in screams and yells and Aitana had never returned, not while I was there anyway.

Roxane looked at Isabelle. After your visit, I went to see Claudia. The room was clean but for what appeared to be posters scattered under her bed, of you, I now know, and a Mexican blanket spread on the floor. Claudia hadn't heard me walk into the room. She was standing, facing the window. I went to her, held her hand and followed her gaze, her eyes following the two of you. They are coming back tomorrow, Claudia kept repeating.

She appeared to be in a semi-catatonic state.

Funny thing though, the following day, Claudia had returned to her usual self, even better, I would say. But then, the next day, she left. For one week, she was gone. To see her daughter in Geneva, the staff had told me. I never believed it.

Roxane's eyes focused on Isabelle. Why did you come at all? I never got it.

Alice and Catherine looked at their mother and waited.

Isabelle felt it, the urge to talk, to share, to unburden herself. But she wouldn't tell.

Not to them. Not like this. If ever.

The three of them, their bodies leaning toward her, needing to know.

Roxane turned to the girls. It was your mother's second visit to the ward with Janelle that poked my curiosity, she continued, one week after Claudia's return. From where? I don't know, and I still don't know. Why? Because she never spoke again. Never said a word to anyone. Claudia Balasco became mute. She still is. She lowered her eyes, looked at the ashes now meshing with the fire's flames. She is still there. Delusional parasitosis, they concluded. She thinks insects live under skin. That she needs to dig them out. Sadly, her son Sebastián has been admitted, too. With her. The same room. It seems madness can be inherited in many ways ...

Isabelle stood and circled the room slowly. She leaned toward the bottle of wine and stopped for one second, and stared at it, while listening to Roxane continue.

As Janelle and your mother were in her room, I snuck to the reception and checked the names on the register and wrote them down. She turned again toward Isabelle, her face victorious. Then I went back to my room and waited for you two to leave. I stood looking out my room window, watching both of you walk to the car, watching the car slowly roll from the hospital parking lot.

And so, you know, inside these places, sometimes, insanity simply passes through, it comes, and it goes, it doesn't always stay. And this bright young guy, as schizophrenic as you could imagine, this guy would come out of his shitty state at times. He would come and sit beside me to talk and, you know how it goes? Or maybe you don't. Anyway, one day, I asked him if he could help me find you. Your names on the register were fake. But ... the plate linked to the rental, the rental to your name. Easy.

And here you are, Isabelle said.

And here I am.

Why?

Roxane, biting her lips, looked at her. Long seconds. Memories tumbling. A feeling of shame. Because I had to see you, Isabelle, to be able to move on.

Because you survived, too.

Isabelle looked at her daughter's, knowing they would not understand.

The wind was heard but for a second, shaking the windowpanes, a leaf, red and yellow, stuck to the edge, just there, as if watching, as if reminding them of the fall that was there, at their feet.

One that did not come.

They need to know something, Isabelle thought. Something to keep them from waiting. From wondering.

She left the room, coming back to them, smiling. From the back of her pant pocket, she slid it out—the origami that had started her quest, the piece of paper that had been folded and folded and refolded. The shape of a lamprey's mouth, she had finally decided on. And it was now dead, wasn't it?

There is only one thing I can tell you, Isabelle said, as she placed the origami inside Roxane's hand, bending each of her fingers over the madman's map, a genesis of sorts. Here, she said, and she pulled the woman up, to stand closer to the fire's flames. That is how and why all this came to be. Isabelle looked at Roxane, and this is how it ends, and together they watched the puzzle made of paper disappear, the fire indulging into a feast, fast, and lean.

Roxane took a few steps back and repositioned her coat; it had cascaded to her hips. She waited, knowing she had to, for Isabelle's words to come, some form of luggage that she could keep with her, ringing in her head, within her core, inside the life that was coming back, inside the promise of forgetfulness and lucidity. A common thread of fate, perhaps, that could be shared? She looked at Isabelle, who she could see was struggling to speak her words, and she said, there is never just one thing,

Isabelle, and I see that, now, having been here. She looked at the girls, then she looked back at Isabelle. There is just sometimes fate. Uncorralled. Uncontrollable. Unexplained. And for that—something like that—there can be no answers, and so, we must let go of the questions, too, must we not? Especially, the questions of why.

Isabelle's daughters looked at their mother, where they saw tears in her eyes.

Looking back at the woman—Roxane, they watched her walking away, to what? A future, untold, from a past now understood.

CODA

The smell of coffee woke Isabelle, and she stretched her arms out, her hand feeling the cold space that should have been warm, and she thought, time gone, and now, this time that is time here.

From her bedside table, she picked up the wooden bust Claudia had carved of her, and she looked at this version of herself, and she thought ... the eyes, a window to a wooden soul? No, and she looked at the sun starting to break through the window, and as she tilted her face to the warmth of it, and she closed her eyes, the sound of laughter coming from her home, just past her door, reaching her. She smiled, and she thought of Peter. And again, she thought of time here. Time right now.

And no matter what, so am I, Peter. Here, and still.

Wanting to be.

She placed the wooden bust back onto the side table next to a postcard Janelle had written from somewhere in Puerto Rico: We won, pretty white one, we won!

Wrapping her hands around her teacup, she looked into the milky liquid, staring at its opacity, and she paused, then said to herself, I am so sorry, my dearest Peter, I cannot keep my promise.

But wait for me, still, she whispered. Wait.

Her tears coming, and as they did, she carefully placed the cup back on the side table, understanding of herself, more. She looked to the large tree, its branches scratching at the half-opened window. She closed her eyes, listening to the sound of the branches moving in the wind—a sound reaching her, and one she knew. Understood, too.

A beautiful reminder called forgiveness.

Forgiveness.

Mom, she heard Alice yell from behind the door.

Breakfast is ready.

"Listen to me, I know what I know, and in the night, evil begets evil, and that's the truth of it. It accumulates and has since the beginning of time. And keep in mind, too, it knows no alliance, not even to its own self, especially its own self. Be careful out there, that's all I'm saying."

- *Christian Fennell, The Fiddler in the Night*

Montreal Publishing Company publishes works of poetry, drama, fiction, and non-fiction. We seek writers that dare, and make us think—reconsider.

Relevance without fear.
Montreal Publishing Company
montrealpublishing.com

A Note From the Publisher:

Thank you for reading, *When I Became Never*. Should you wish to include it in your book club, get in touch, and let's see what we can help you with.

info@montrealpublishing.com

If you'd like to leave a review, that would be most appreciated, and you can do that here:

Goodreads
Amazon

If you'd like to keep up with what's going on with Nathalie Guilbeault, she can be found at:

nathalieguilbeault.com

Manufactured by Amazon.ca
Bolton, ON